Diary of a Wayward Widow

CAROLINE FABRE

Copyright © 2023 Caroline Fabre

All rights reserved.

ISBN: 9798857441695

IN LOVING MEMORY OF
ANNE MADELEINE CURRAN

Prologue

I still can't talk about the ending. About that stormy afternoon of the summer solstice; the longest day of the year, the longest day of my life. And yet the question arises again and again. How exactly did it happen, people enquire – without any sense of shame? It is human nature, after all, this insatiable curiosity around a tragedy, a desperate need to know the details. As if by knowing, we can rest in peace in the knowledge it would never happen to us.

Everybody wants to know how the story ends, how a life can be brutally cut short without warning. I wish they would ask about the living years instead, how he and I had met and fallen in love, about his talent for restoring old buildings, his love of speed and surfing, his altruism – even though that would end up having repercussions for all of us.

I would talk about anything rather than that midsummer afternoon when the earth tilted on its axis, and I was to learn the true meaning of the phrase, 'no good deed goes unpunished'.

DIARY OF A WAYWARD WIDOW

CONTENTS

ACKNOWLEDGEMENTS I
JUNE 21ST – THE MORNING OF THE SUMMER SOLSTICE 1

PART ONE _____ 3

JUNE – FOUR DAYS AFTER THE SUMMER SOLSTICE 3
LATE JUNE 7
JUNE 21ST – THE MORNING OF THE SUMMER SOLSTICE 9
LATE JUNE 10
JUNE 21ST – THE MORNING OF THE SUMMER SOLSTICE 15
EARLY JULY 16
JUNE 21ST – THE MORNING OF THE SUMMER SOLSTICE. 18
MID-JULY 19
LATE JULY 25
EARLY AUGUST 28
MID-AUGUST 31
EARLY SEPTEMBER 32
MID-SEPTEMBER – A DARK NIGHT OF THE SOUL 34
EARLY OCTOBER 40
MID OCTOBER 44
EARLY NOVEMBER 48
LATE NOVEMBER 56
DECEMBER 58
MID DECEMBER 65
EARLY JANUARY 80
EARLY FEBRUARY 84
LATE FEBRUARY 89
EARLY MARCH 91
MID-MARCH 96
LATE MARCH 102
APRIL 108
EARLY MAY 118
MID MAY 120
LATE MAY 122
EARLY JUNE 123

PART 2 ... 127

- MID-MARCH ... 127
- 105 DAYS BEFORE THE SUMMER SOLSTICE ... 127
- NINETY DAYS BEFORE THE SUMMER SOLSTICE ... 130
- EIGHTY DAYS BEFORE THE SUMMER SOLSTICE ... 134
- TEN DAYS BEFORE THE SUMMER SOLSTICE ... 140
- THE SUMMER SOLSTICE ... 142
- MID-JUNE – ONE YEAR AFTER THAT DAY OF THE SUMMER SOLSTICE ... 157
- THE WEEKEND OF THE SUMMER SOLSTICE ... 160
- EARLY JULY ... 164
- MID JULY ... 176
- LATE JULY ... 179
- MID-AUGUST ... 183
- EARLY SEPTEMBER ... 186
- MID-SEPTEMBER ... 196

PART 3 ... 198

- LATE SEPTEMBER ... 198
- EARLY OCTOBER ... 202
- MID OCTOBER ... 203
- 8 MONTHS LATER ... 211
- MID JUNE ... 211
- MID-SEPTEMBER – TWO YEARS AND EIGHTY SIX DAYS AFTER THE THAT DAY OF THE SUMMER SOLSTICE ... 214

ABOUT THE AUTHOR ... 220

ACKNOWLEDGEMENTS

My love and heartfelt gratitude go to the following people for their vital help and support:

Simon Saunders dear friend, mentor, brilliant designer and advisor.

Madeleine Cotter who read an excerpt of the first draft and encouraged me to keep going.

Nicky Lovett – who steered the story back in the direction I wanted it to go.

My best friend, and razor-sharp mentor Gina Hingerty – who read every single draft and never lost faith.

Patricia White who had a vision of the ending before I did.

My beloved sister Sue Larsen, who has always believed in me.

And my other beautiful sister, Anne Curran, who left us far too soon.

JUNE 21ST – THE MORNING OF THE SUMMER SOLSTICE

I open my eyes to find M is standing over me, holding a mug of coffee sprinkled with chocolate in one hand, in the other a long-stemmed red rose. On the dresser is a bouquet of flowers – all mauves and purples; lavender and lilacs, verbena, a violet and cream orchid in a froth of Queen Anne's lace.

'Happy birthday, beautiful.' He smiles, leaning over and attempting to kiss me. He is wearing a shirt that matches the azure blue of his eyes.

I put my hand over my mouth. 'I've got morning breath,' I groan. 'Do you think it gets worse when you turn forty?'

'Didn't notice.' He grins, perching on the edge of the bed and handing me two packages loosely wrapped in brown paper. I unwrap the first; a vintage box in the shape of a miniature treasure chest, all black and gold and embossed with Greek figurines.

'It's exquisite,' I breathe.

'It's to store your jewellery or anything you hold precious. There's a handwritten note inside saying that, unlike Pandora's box which contained all the evils of the world, this one is filled with only good things like patience and hope.'

'Are you saying I'm impatient and without hope?' I tease.

He brushes a strand of hair from my face. 'There's always hope.'

Our problems are finally behind us, we're going to be OK, I think to myself.

The other package is a leather-bound notebook with thick vellum pages. 'You talked about writing a diary. I thought you could start with this, or use it as a journal to write about all the interesting people you've interviewed for your column.' He pulls out a third, slimmer package. 'This will help.'

Inside is a silver pen engraved with my initials.

'I'd better write something of note,' I say, smiling up at him.

'I have no doubt about that.' He pulls aside the duvet, his hand circling my breast.

I wriggle away. 'I need to clean my teeth.' I hop out of bed and spend a few moments in the bathroom looking for mouthwash. By the time I return to bed he is talking urgently on the phone. The moment is lost. Just as all those other moments would be lost; making love in the early morning hush, lying tangled together in the sheets afterwards planning the day. I would never again feel his arms around me, his body melded to mine.

I would never hear him singing in the shower, or his deep voice murmuring, 'loving you.'

Afterwards there were only the echoed imaginings of all the things I would never hear him say.

PART ONE

JUNE – FOUR DAYS AFTER THE SUMMER SOLSTICE

SHOCK AND DENIAL

DENIAL: (*noun*) the refusal to believe or accept something as the truth.

Everything has taken on a sense of unreality, as if I too have died, only instead of joining M in some heavenly place, I have gone to purgatory.

I wake up every hour on the hour, stomach curdling, afraid to go back to sleep and forget. Only to wake and remember. I lie there, numb and burning eyed, listening out for the heavy tread of his footsteps on the staircase, his voice issuing from some distant place.

I re-live the moments leading up to midsummer afternoon over and over. I have re-written the story again and again, altering the timing, diverting each happening towards some other conclusion, changing the narrative.

But I can never change the ending.

I drift through the empty spaces of Rosewood Barn like a sleepwalker, watching the rain streaming down the glass fronted elevation like tears. As if the world is weeping too, mourning the loss of a good man. I pace the length and breadth of the barn, my heart lurching at the sight of his oil-stained jeans draped over a chair, his half-packed suitcase on the floor, a moleskin diary filled with his handwritten notes on the bedside table, his reading glasses on top. A chipped mug with the dregs of the last coffee he drank. On the dresser the bouquet of purple flowers already starting to wilt.

Rosewood Barn, which he spent almost two years converting into a family home, is a constant reminder of him. All open plan with vaulted ceilings, heavy oak beams and arched windows, light pools into every nook and cranny. A wide staircase with twisting rosewood bannisters leads to a mezzanine floor above and the bedrooms. The walk-in wardrobe is still filled with his clothes and shoes. His electric shaver and comb are where they have always been on the bathroom shelf, his toothbrush in a mug beside the sink.

Outside, everything remains as he left it as if frozen in time; the paving stones for the courtyard piled up on the lawn, part of the scaffolding still clinging onto the north wall for the extension he would now never build.

He is everywhere and nowhere.

'Give me a sign!' I shout into the silence.

Silence that feels like a punishment.

Grief is a demanding companion that accompanies me wherever I go. It has taken up residence high in my belly which has swollen oddly, while the rest of my body seems to have shrunk. Somewhere around the solar plexus, guilt resides like some loathsome lodger I can never evict. Grief and guilt, living side by side, constantly vying for my attention, taking turns to consume me. Where to turn, I ask myself? The future is too overwhelming to confront, the past too painful to recall, the present intolerable.

I want to be absent and unaware.

A stream of callers trickle through the open spaces of the barn to pay their respects and huddle together, talking in hushed voices. My sister Fern hovers by the door, receiving their offerings – a fish pie still warm from the oven, a basket of homemade scones, a plate of chocolate brownies for the boys. They bring flowers and sympathy cards, which Fern places around the room amidst the flickering candles and family photographs. She tells them I'm asleep, and offers them tea and sandwiches, or a glass of wine, but they don't stay for long. I can't bring myself to greet them; the words simply won't bypass the great lump in my throat. Every sound they make appears amplified, the clash of a teacup against a saucer, a chair being scraped back, the front door closing. It is a cacophony of decibels which echo in my head, lingering long after they've gone.

My best friend Holly brings wine, chocolates and magazines. She barges past Fern, demanding to see me, then launches herself onto the bed, sobbing wildly.

'It's so surreal…tell me it's not true?' Her hazel eyes brim with tears and questions I can't answer.

'…not able to talk about it right now, Holly,' I reply, thickly. I'm not sure I ever will be.

She makes a hiccoughing sound, almost choking on the words. 'Promise you'll call me, day or night?' she begs. It is almost as if her need is even greater than mine.

The boys have locked themselves away, lying side by side on Sam's bed as if shellshocked, Sam silently raging against the fates that have stolen his father, while Liam's grief seems to have mutated into an unspoken accusation, his inky-blue eyes barely meeting mine.

Meals have merged into one another or are skipped altogether, Liam appearing at odd hours to grab a bowl of cereal, or a slice of microwaved pizza. I creep downstairs in the night and stand by the fridge, cramming the remains of the pizza into my mouth, gulping orange juice straight from the carton, trying to stave off a raging hunger that will never be satiated.

I sit on the leather sofa watching rolling news reports of impending doom for the climate, a seasonal flu virus that is threatening the elderly, the death of a celebrity that turns out to be suicide. I take in his haunted face, struck by the irony of it all; how some people will cling to life at any cost, while others are determined to end it. None of it seems real, rather it belongs to the world out there, while I re-live a personal drama. One that can never be aired.

Fern sorts through the piles of sympathy cards and flowers, writing brief thank-you notes on my behalf. Another lavish bouquet has been delivered to the door, all mauves and purples, a violet orchid in the centre, almost a replica of the flowers M had bought me for my birthday. The hairs on the back of my neck are standing up.

'Who are these from?' I demand.

'They came with a blank card,' Fern says, turning it over. 'There's just the name of a website on the back. She reads it out. 'grieveandheal.com.' 'How strange that there's no note.'

For a wild and impossible moment symptomatic of the grieving, it feels like a sign that M is trying to reach me from whatever celestial place he has gone to.

Fern takes in my distraught face.

'Whoever sent them must have called Heavenly Blooms, she says gently, referring to the florist in Highbury M frequented. 'They know your favourite colours. 'I'll find somewhere else to put them.'

My mother calls in most days, striding through the door in a designer suit. A waft of pungent scent follows in her wake. She brings gifts for the boys, a book on astronomy for Liam, pocket money for Sam, some ready-cooked meals from the local deli, which pile up in the freezer.

 My mother was well-known model in the sixties, her perfect bone structure, rosebud lips and eyes the colour of burning embers had graced many a Vogue cover and other glossy magazines. She modelled swimsuits and lingerie and most of the images of long, shapely legs on the packaging of stockings and tights around that time belonged to her. Neither Fern nor I have inherited her vain streak, nor her beauty. We were both affected by watching her pirouette in front of the mirror when we were children, singing 'Mummy's the fairest of them all!'

She's not good at dealing with grief and never talks about her own loss; the tragic death of her only son, my half-brother Timmy. She seldom stays long, claiming she has a lunch invitation, or is on her way to London for one of her 'procedures.' The fact she had never liked M and had done her utmost to stop me from marrying him has created an even greater chasm between us. She hovers by the kitchen counter, keeping a measured distance, as if she doesn't know how to cross it. Instead, she fires instructions across the living area, like a teacher dealing with a traumatised pupil.

'You're going to have to fight this, Willow, pick yourself up and get back to work. I know it's hard, but Max isn't coming back. You can't risk losing your column!'

I want to tell her I'm incapable of writing a shopping list, let alone my column, that words have become meaningless now, like the platitudes that hang in the air from well-meaning friends and acquaintances who come to pay their respects.

I was starting to make a name for myself as a journalist, with a weekly column in Lifestyle and a regular slot in The Weekend. I had been put forward for Columnist of the Year in the spring, but it was unlikely I would be a contender now. Jason, my editor, had sent an email offering his sincere condolences, before suggesting I take some time away.

Susannah Frost will be taking over your column until you're ready to come back, he'd written. Even in my numb and shocked state, it felt like yet another twist of the knife. Susannah, who is eight years my junior, had been vying for her own column for months.

Jason had followed up the email by sending a lavish arrangement of day lilies and vibrant stargazers. I'd asked Fern to get rid of them, sickened by their cloying scent.

LATE JUNE

I stay inside as the summer blazes, yet there is no escape from the outside world; the barrage of calls from sympathisers and hangers-on, some of whom had barely known M.

Frida, my eccentric neighbour who lives alone in the cottage further along the lane, brings cuttings from her garden which I leave to die in their pots, marmalade and chutney from the artisan market which remain unopened, and her signature chocolate torte which none of us can face eating. She sometimes brings old paperbacks or a vintage shawl from the charity shop in Highbury where she volunteers three mornings a week. I seldom invite her in, claiming I'm in the middle of something, or have visitors, or it's just not the right time. But then it never is.

'You know where I am if you need anything at all,' is her inevitable response. I feel a pang of guilt as she turns away and heads back to her cottage and her solitary life. I'm aware that she too is missing M and is desperate to talk about him. I also sense her desire to be part of it all, to read all the sympathy cards, find out which of the neighbours had sent flowers. Mostly she wants to know how the boys and I are holding up.

This morning she has left a plant on the porch with a note reading, *I thought these were rather cheerful. Amaryllis finally in bloom. You need to water them regularly or they won't survive.*

The flagrantly blood-red leaves against the grey flagstones cause a shiver to run down my spine. I don't want to take care of something that might not survive. I carry the amaryllis to the bottom of the garden and throw it into the flower bed, where it lies hidden amongst the weeds.

The mailbox continues to fill up with sympathy cards, leaflets about how to manage your funds after the death of a spouse, a brochure from an insurance company for widows/ers, a letter from the bank stating my account has been frozen pending the receipt of the death certificate, although I have already sent it.

Fern helps me go through it all, often staying until after supper before heading back to her rented flat in Chalmsford near Highbury. She is the head mistress of a prep school and teaches Science and Maths to eight-year-olds.

After she's left, the long evening closes in. I scroll the internet, looking for what? Some kind of cure for the grieving heart, a miracle pill that will dissolve the pain.

I click onto grieveandheal.com, wondering if there was anyone else floating around in this purgatorial place between Heaven and Hell. A blogger named lifeafterdeath has written a post about gratitude being 'a portal through grief'.

It might help to write a list of all the things you are grateful for.
Count your blessings, then name them one by one....

I fire off a sharp response:

What if you're unable to feel grateful and are angry at the fates that have taken your loved one? After all, for those of us left behind to grieve, we feel cheated, bereft and betrayed. We are lost, angry and confused. I don't feel blessed at all. I feel cursed.

I sign off as the waywardwidow.

Willow is such a wayward child; my mother would say when I was growing up.

A response from somebody calling himself blackwidower appears moments later.

Indeed! 'Rage, rage, rage against the dying of the light,' because not everyone goes peacefully into the night!

Dylan Thomas, I think, imagining him to be a university lecturer who has lost his loyal, long-suffering wife after a painful illness.

The following morning, sadeyedlady has responded with *anger and confusion are all part of the grieving process.*

lifeafterdeath comes back with: *confusion stems from brain fog or the inability to process the enormity of loss and the life-altering changes after the death of a partner. Widower brain is actually a well-known condition, described as a fogginess and disconnect after losing a spouse. The fog will lift in time.*

He or she is right about the life altering changes, I think as another long, painful day bleeds into a short summer night. Less than a month ago, we were a complete family. M and I were a couple – Max and Willow Goodhart. Now I am a widow. A nasty, spidery word evoking shrouded women in black, cloaked in sorrow, drifting anonymously through a twilight world, always on the periphery of some brighter place they have left behind. A branch of the tree that was our family has been severed, leaving us like a ship with a broken mast, listing on the high seas. Our close little unit has splintered. We have lost our ballast.

I am unable to comprehend how in the space of a few weeks everything has changed so dramatically; the hectic swirl of family life, the four of us sitting around the breakfast table making plans for the day, packing up the car for a weekend trip to Cornwall, driving up to London to see a show – all ended in the absence of a heartbeat.

JUNE 21ST – THE MORNING OF THE SUMMER SOLSTICE

'How about I take you out for a birthday breakfast? It's a beautiful morning. We could take the bike,' M is saying.

'I'll have helmet hair,' I groan.

'I fell in love with you with helmet hair, remember.' He smiles.

I think back to my rock-climbing days – how I'd thrown vanity to the wind, caught up in the thrill of the climb, being able to look down on the world from a dizzying height. Tethered to the ancient rock face, I had felt safe. But I'd never shared M's thrill of speed.

'Maybe we should take the jeep, what with the weather forecast?'

'The storm is not predicted until late afternoon,' he replies.

'OK, you win,' I say, giving in.

I climb onto the bike feeling the usual twist of anxiety in my gut. Then wind my arms around his waist and bury my face in his worn leather jacket. He smells of leather and the olive soap he uses even to wash his hair.

We are off, the sound of the engine piercing the morning hush, as we weave through lanes overgrown with cow parsley and brambles. The air smells of almonds and cut grass and clouds of midges disperse as we fly past. Some of the neighbours are already out and about in their gardens. Frida is wielding a garden hose, sending silvery jets of water into the air. She is wearing a green vintage dress and tendrils of her long white hair have come loose from the silver combs she uses to anchor it on top of her head. She stands to attention like a Viking woman amidst the tall sunflowers and calls out as we pass. But her words are drowned out by the sound of the engine. I try to relax and lean in as we curve into the bends, but my body instinctively shifts to the opposite side. This is probably the way I'll die, I think, clutching M even tighter, a vision of Sam and Liam's shattered faces....I just pray we don't go together...

LATE JUNE

I am forced out of the barn to stock up on groceries, painkillers for the permanent pounding in my head, light bulbs – four have blown in the last couple of days, a visit to the bank which I keep putting off – the domestic chores that are part of everyday life. I knock on Liam's door asking him to come with me. He is sitting on his beanbag playing on his computer. He looks up briefly. 'Can we go later? Sam and me want to hang out in the treehouse.'

'I'd like to get it over with,' I begin. There was less chance of running into somebody I knew, if we left now.

'Please can I stay home?' he begs.

'Of course,' I say, with a heavy heart.

'Can you buy a different type of cereal, Mum?' he calls after me. 'Not the one with nuts.'

At the supermarket, I am making my way through the frozen food section when I spot Carrie and Jen, standing at the far end of the aisle chatting to one another.

I attempt a swift turnaround, but the trolley jams and veers to one side, clattering into the steel support of the giant freezer. In any case, they have already seen me. I hadn't responded to their phone calls or cards and yet they still rally sweetly. 'Willow,' Jen exclaims. 'We've been thinking about you constantly, and wondering whether to drop in, but we didn't want to intrude.' Her voice trails off. 'How are you doing?'

She looks tanned and glowing, perfect hair and make-up. I am conscious of my grubby t-shirt and tattered skirt, the fact I haven't washed my hair for days.

'Fine…busy, you know how it is.' Busy falling apart and trying to piece myself together again, I think.

She reaches out a cool manicured hand and pats my arm, murmuring, 'You poor thing! I can't imagine what you're going through.'

Well, you clearly don't have any imagination, I want to say. Up comes the bitter retort. 'No, in fact you can't.'

In the awkward silence that follows, Carrie chimes in with, 'Willow, we're here for you always. You know that.'

'Thanks,' I manage to say through the swelling obstruction in my throat. 'I need to get going,' I mumble.

'Of course... er if you wouldn't mind returning my casserole dish,' Jen begins. 'It's just I have a dinner party coming up. You know how it is?' she adds with a nervous little laugh.

I think about the fish pie she had brought over after the funeral, the lingering smell of baked cod in the bin. I had forgotten all about returning her dish.

'Of course,' I back away, and head straight for the checkout with my almost empty trolley, forgetting everything I'd come in for.

The main street is thronged with shoppers; shiny happy couples caught up in their private world of everyday plans. Where to eat lunch, what to buy the mother-in-law, whether to book a late flight to Spain. The little market town of Highbury, on the Wiltshire border, now attracts people from all over the county and beyond.

My heart constricts at the sight of an ancient couple hobbling along hand in hand, pausing by the window of Heavenly Blooms to admire a vibrant display of crimson roses. M and I often went shopping on a Saturday morning, heading towards the hardware shop on East Street, or the Reclamation Centre where we would browse for hours amongst the stone troughs and artefacts, searching for unusual treasures for the barn; a vintage clock, a stone birdbath, or something for the extension we were planning to build in the autumn.

I give up trying to find a parking space and pull into a loading bay. Rules and regulations have become meaningless since losing M and I've accumulated a pile of parking tickets, which I throw into a drawer along with all the unpaid bills.

I make my way along the high street, dazed and untethered as if set adrift in a sea of aliens, pulled along in the slipstream of other lives. It is one of those flawless English summer days, hot and still. Women swish along the pavement in their summer dresses and sandals, a busker sings a tuneless rendition of Bob Dylan's 'The Times They Are A-Changing'. I keep my head down as I pass the thrift shop where Frida volunteers, and see 'mad Mabel' who is rumoured to be a witch and trawls the high street with a supermarket trolley stuffed with bin bags, rusting saucepans, old clothes and bric a brac – all the detritus of other people's lives. Today she's dressed in a green velvet ballgown, and has wound a wreath of everlasting flowers around her matted hair. She is handing out sprigs of dried lavender with the promise it will bring good fortune. M would always stop to chat with her, before handing her some coins and more often a note, while politely turning down her dried offerings. I try to melt into a shop front, but she makes a beeline for me and thrusts a bunch of lavender into my hand. 'Free for you, my darlin',' she murmurs as if she knows my good fortune is behind me. She stares at me with a burning intensity, muttering, 'I'm very sorry for your loss.' The news of M's death has travelled far and wide, it seems, and I find myself being approached by total strangers, whose lives he had touched. I listen to the well-worn phrases all of us fall back on; what an awful thing…a terrible tragedy…so cruel and unfair…a huge loss. Then there is the stricken look and lack of comprehension, comments such as '…but I only saw him the other day.' Worst of all are those who can't deal with suffering and cross the road when they see me coming.

Mabel moves closer, her eyes still trained on me. I catch the acid whiff of unwashed clothes and hear her whisper, 'they say no good deed goes unpunished.'

I wander up and down the aisles of the chemist, still clutching the dried lavender, thinking about that comment. Surely it was a case of one good deed deserved another? M was always trying to fix things for other people. Was his death some kind of punishment? And if so, who was it meant for, him or me?

I grab a few items from the shelves: extra-strength painkillers, a new sleep aid that promises a restful night, concealer for the shadows under my eyes, shampoo, then head out into the busy street. At the corner shop I fill a basket with the items I'd forgotten to buy at the supermarket; boxes of cereal without nuts for Liam, more frozen pizza, crisps and snacks, things I would never have bought in the 'before' life. I skip the hardware store, thinking I could do without replacing the light bulbs, would prefer to stumble around in a half-lit world rather than face the manager who had loved M. I make my way back to where I'd parked the jeep. Miraculously I have no ticket, and am planning a quick get-away when I see Clementine Abbot coming out of Café Bella. Clementine's husband, Charles, used to work with M. The four of us had met up regularly in the early days when M was building up the construction business, but we had drifted apart after their marriage broke up. The last time I'd seen her was at the crematorium, sobbing loudly, as if it was her husband who was being trundled away in an eco-coffin about to be turned to ashes.

I watch her face crumple and brace myself, knowing this was going to be an ordeal.

'Willow…oh my god… I can't stop thinking about you! I tried to call, but kept getting your voicemail.' She frowns. 'You've lost weight, you lucky thing! I've put on a ton since the divorce. It feels like only yesterday the four of us were having dinner at The Old Flame and now M has gone…hard to believe we're both single again.' She gazes at me with a look of tragic despair. 'Nobody invites you to dinner when you're divorced! It's like you're some kind of threat! It's totally different if you're a widow.'

She is blocking the pavement, awash with tears, sobbing for her broken marriage and what seems the whole of humanity. In an ironic twist, I find myself trying to console her.

'It will get better,' I murmur, 'just a question of time.' The old 'father time' cliché everybody throws at me. I back away from the stream of shoppers who are weaving past with curious glances. 'Look, I have to go. I'm not supposed to park here.'

She leans towards me, misty-eyed. 'Promise you'll call me? We could meet at the new wine bar in Market Street and drown our sorrows!'

It strikes me I have enough sorrows of my own without drowning hers on top of them.

A female traffic warden has appeared in front of us, legs astride, notebook open at the ready.

'This is a loading bay,' she emphasises. She points at the sign. 'You've been here for more than fifteen minutes.' She is now flicking her pen threateningly as if it's a time bomb.

I swear under my breath while Clementine blurts, 'She's just lost her husband! We both have! Mine buggered off with my son's biology teacher! Hers died! How about you let her off this time?'

The warden is now reading the registration. I have a sudden urge to grab her notepad and clicking pen and fling them onto the pavement.

'I'm sorry to hear that,' she replies, snapping her notepad shut. To my surprise, she says, 'gave up on men years ago! On your way now, please.'

Clementine shakes her head in wonder. 'Would you believe it?' she breathes. 'Widows get away with murder!'

I climb into the jeep, scrunching it into gear, and slam my foot on the accelerator before pulling out and almost knocking over a cyclist who swerves out of the way, mouthing furiously.

'Sorry,' I shout, shaken.

'Stupid bitch,' he calls back, waving one hand and weaving across the high street and almost into the path of the ancient couple attempting to cross the road.

I drive home, Clementine's words echoing in my head: *widows get away with murder.*

Note to blog:
It may be true that when you laugh, the world laughs with you, but believe me, you don't always have the privilege of being allowed to cry alone. Grief seems to attract other lonely souls, keen to share their story, in what can turn into a maudlin game of one upmanship.

Don't allow others to unload their problems on you or drown you with their sorrows - they will only drag you down, sadeyedlady, has responded.

Over the course of the day, it turns into an ongoing discussion.
Tether yourself to buoyant people who will keep you afloat, lifeafterdeath has

suggested.

Although too much jollity and optimism can be equally annoying, from blackwidower.

A number of followers agree with him, including sadeyedlady who has written, *so-called upbeat folk stay buoyant by thriving on other people's misfortunes.*

Grief has a bitter edge, I conclude. I console myself that I have not sunk to such a low level. At least not yet.

JUNE 21ST – THE MORNING OF THE SUMMER SOLSTICE

It's a relief to reach the A road which cuts through swathes of rape and corn fields towards the city suburbs. My thighs are aching from clenching them for so long; the heat from the cylinder is searing my right calf. The growl and roar of the engine resounds in my head as we pull into the municipal car park at the bottom of the main street.

'So… How did you enjoy the ride?' M wants to know, swivelling around and pulling off his helmet.

'Only way to travel,' I quip with a grin. My face feels burnt from the wind, my lips chapped and dry. I climb off, my legs buckling as if they've been liquified.

'You used to love riding with me in the early days, or were you lying to me then as well?' he teases.

'We didn't have the boys then,' I remind him.

We saunter down the street, hand in hand, towards Café Lucia. A couple in the infancy of middle age, our sons almost grown up, as if we have all the time in the world still ahead of us.

He ruffles my flattened hair, saying, 'We're still in one piece, aren't we?'

EARLY JULY

Jake Frasier, M's business partner, calls to tell me some mail addressed to me has arrived at the office.

'Looks like mainly sympathy cards,' he says. 'Are you passing this way, or would you like me to drop them in on my way home? There are a few other bits and pieces, photos and the like that were on his desk.'

I ask him to drop them in. I can't face seeing M's empty desk, the tan leather chair we'd chosen together.

M had started Goodhart Design&Build soon after he'd turned thirty. Three years later, he had formed a partnership with Jake, who ran a construction company of his own. They had had their ups and downs over the years, but Jake had almost fallen apart at the funeral. He had made an emotional speech, saying it had been an honour working with M who was a 'wonderful human being, with a heart as big as the ocean.'

Jake drops by with the items in the evening, stepping tentatively into the barn, his face contorting with pain and sadness at the sight of M's creation.

'You coping OK?' he asks, raking his fingers through his thinning hair.

I nod, not trusting myself to speak, or blurt, no, I'm not…what the hell do you expect?

'Would you like something to drink?' I enquire, willing him to say no.

He shakes his head. 'I'm meant to be taking the wife and kids out to dinner – it's our wedding anniversary.'

I have a vivid image of the five of them sitting around the table, laughing and joking. 'Happy anniversary,' I manage to say, aware my voice has an edge.

M had hinted at Jake's infidelities over the years, and I had learnt through the grapevine of the long-standing affair he'd had with an ex-client. It seemed he had finally pulled his marriage together again, against the odds.

'M put so much into every project he embarked on,' Jake is saying, 'he didn't deserve this.'

Not many of us deserve to die, I want to retort.

'…Why can't Jake deal with it this time…?' I'd fumed the day of the summer solstice.

Where were you that afternoon, I want to demand now? Out to lunch with your lover? Followed by an afternoon of passionate sex in a hotel room, leaving M to cope with the mess alone?

'Well, I'd best be on my way,' he's saying as if sensing my angry thoughts.

'Thanks for bringing over the mail.'

'No prob – any time.' He pauses on the porch, saying, 'Good thing there won't be an inquest, don't you think?'

My heart accelerates. 'Yes, it's a good thing,' I answer, aware of his gaze on me. I turn away, feeling the heat scald my cheeks.

I brace myself to go through the items. There are four framed photographs; one a portrait of the four of us, taken some years ago, which I'd planned to send out as a Christmas card, but never had. The next is of M and me on our wedding day, standing on the steps of the registry office looking slightly bemused. The last two are of the boys in their school uniforms, taken some years ago. I sift through the sympathy cards from clients and people he had employed over the years.

A true inspiration to work with…

Maximillian Goodhart was a max in a million with a good heart, someone has written.

A talented architect with an eye for beauty, our sincere condolences go to his wife and sons.

…the world has lost a good and honest man.

A visionary and beautiful soul, whose generosity knew no bounds.

…he had time for everyone.

JUNE 21ST – THE MORNING OF THE SUMMER SOLSTICE.

'There's not enough time, M, please leave it until Monday,' I beg.
'It'll only take a couple of hours,' he assures me. 'I'll be back by noon at the latest.'
'Why can't Jake deal with it this time?'
'He's already in enough trouble with his wife for taking time away.'
'If you're late, I'll kill you,' I'd shouted after him.

MID-JULY

I wake up with a jolt. Somebody is rapping loudly on the front door.

I stumble across the landing and peer down onto the porch. M is standing there, sheltering from the slanting rain. He is wearing his green raincoat and holding his umbrella like a walking stick. I half fall down the stairs, the blood pounding in my ears. I open the door, wearing his boxer shorts and sweatshirt, ready to fling myself into his arms. Only of course it's not M, but Will wearing his older brother's raincoat. Hope freefalls into despair as M fades away to wherever he has vanished while Will greets me gruffly, as if not at all sure of his welcome.

Will is the antithesis of M; an opportunist with an addictive personality and a need to possess things: expensive clothes, cars, women. His mantra is: 'Where there's a Will, there's a way'. A sense of entitlement that had caused Holly to nickname him 'Will the Conqueror'.

Unlike M, he has never been able to put his troubled past behind him. Their parents had been killed in a road accident when M was ten and Will eight, and the brothers sent to a care home in London before being fostered out. M seldom talked about that period of their lives, but I'd learnt that Will had been badly abused by a foster parent who had later been charged and imprisoned. That had been the beginning of Will's problems, M had concluded. Whenever I'd tried to delve deeper, a shadow would cross his face and once he'd said, 'We just want to put it behind us.'

Will had run a car dealership in the early days, collecting and selling vintage cars, and motorbikes. After that had folded, he'd opened a wine bar in Bristol but his excessive drinking, the drugs and weekly binges had started to take a toll on his health, and he'd been in and out of rehab for months.

We had never seen eye to eye, Will and I, and things had reached an all-time low in the months before M died when we had stopped talking altogether.

But death, with its many loose ends, has a way of bringing you face to face with those you would rather turn away from.

I hope you'd be there for him if anything ever happens to me, M had said in one of those what if...? conversations we'd had about life and death and the future. M had no relatives to fall back on, both his parents had been only children. The brothers only had each other. I had moved the conversation along with: 'If we happened to die at the same time, I would want Fern to take care of the boys.' …and for Will to have nothing whatsoever to do with them, I'd wanted to add. But M had remained fiercely loyal to his younger brother until the bitter end.

Will's startling good looks have waned considerably over the last few months, the pale-grey eyes have taken on a vacant expression. I recognise that look now, having seen it reflected in the bathroom mirror every morning. It is grief.

'Will the Conqueror' has developed the slightly hunched look of the defeated, I conclude.

'I have something I need to discuss with you,' he says, frowning at my undressed state.

'Come in, make yourself a coffee. I'll be down in a minute.' I head upstairs and pull on some clothes, a feeling of unease settling over me like the dense, grey clouds overhead.

I go back down and find him staring into the empty fireplace with a desolate look as if unable to come to terms with his brother's absence. He has made a pot of coffee, poured himself a mug and left the rest stewing on the Rayburn. I switch off the gas and fill a cup, hoping it will clear the fog in my brain. I notice the kitchen drawer has come off its rollers and the sink is leaking again and wonder despairingly how M had managed to keep on top of everything.

'How have you been?' The question sounds trite even to my own ears, a futile attempt to fill the silence between us.

I notice he's wearing the diving watch the boys and I had given M for Christmas two years ago. It is one of the many things he'd helped himself to after the funeral. He was always 'borrowing' M's clothes or tools and not returning them. In the last year, it had been cash loans which he'd never repaid. He had asked if he could have M's leather biking jacket, but I'd stalled, saying I would need to talk to Sam and Liam first. It strikes me I have now inherited the whole drama of Will, and I don't know how to deal with it.

He puts down his mug saying, 'He and I planned to take the bikes to Brittany in the autumn.'

I take a sip of the bitter coffee. 'We all had plans,' I say.

'Are you going to hang on to this place?' he digresses, taking in the dust and mess.

'Yes, why do you ask?'

'He did a lot around here.'

'I have the boys.'

'How are they doing?'

'They're in bits, which is hardly surprising.' We are all in pieces, broken in heart, body and soul, I think. 'They sleep most of the time, when they're not on their computers.'

'Nothing much going on for them here now,' he states.

'We're actually planning a trip to Cornwall,' I say defensively, although that is not true. The boys have expressed no interest in going anywhere. They want to stay at home, remain close to the essence of their father.

I am wondering what's behind this visit, when he says, 'I left some bits and pieces in the shed. I'll go get them. Where's the key?'

'I'll come down with you and unlock it,' I reply, thinking there was no way I was going to let him help himself to anything more.

I have avoided the shed since that day. Everything is how M left it. The antique jukebox he finally got to work, the Coca-Cola fridge he kept stocked with beers, the beanbag lounger in the far corner where I'd sit and watch him tinkering with his motorbike, waiting for a gap in his attention so we could make a plan for the weekend. It's like looking at the past. I feel a jolt at the sight of the wooden toolbox I'd bought him for his fortieth birthday. Sean Maloney, a close friend, and talented carpenter, had designed it from rosewood and carved the initial M on the lid. On the top shelf his collection of antique tools accumulated over the years; planers, clamps and chisels, a brass spirit leveller, already starting to tarnish.

Will seems to have gone into a trance; his eyes fixed on the Triumph.

'He said if anything happened to him, I could take care of the bike.'

'Take care of it?' I enquire. You're not even capable of taking care of yourself, I think.

'Yeah, well be the custodian if you like.'

'Custodian,' I repeat, my mind racing. 'That wasn't mentioned in his will. He would have wanted the bike to stay in the family. Here, that is.'

He stares at me challengingly. 'I am his family! Sam's only sixteen! It's way beyond him!'

'Sam is seventeen and M was teaching him to ride it.'

'When does the insurance run out?' he cuts in.

'It has already run out.' I have no idea if this is the case. I would have to go through more paperwork and I haven't been able to face it.

'It's a seriously expensive piece of machinery.'

'I don't care how much it's worth,' I emphasise. 'I'll learn to ride it myself, if needs be.'

He lets out a snort. 'You'd never be able to handle it!'

I want to slap his smug face. I hate him for being here, for not being M. I take a deep breath, reminding myself he's the closest link I have left to my husband, while raging against the fates that had spared the wrong brother.

'You never liked M riding it, did you?' he says cuttingly. 'It was a real source of contention.'

I hold his gaze. You were the main source of contention.

'The bike stays here,' I say firmly.

His eyes are boring into me like headlights in the gloom. 'That day,' he begins. 'It's all so fucked up. I still don't get it. M was so methodical. He never took his eye off the job, or let anything distract him.'

My pulse quickens, there seems to be no air in the shed. I hold his gaze, saying, 'I need to get on. I promised Frida I'd drive her into town.'

'Go ahead,' he says dismissively. He is walking towards the far side of the shed now, gazing at the poster of a classic bike propped up against the wall that M had never got to hang.

'That belongs here,' I state.

'I was the one who gave it to him.'

And now you want it back, I think, anger rising.

I watch him unhooking one of the spare helmets, hear him say, 'You won't be needing this.' His eyes are now drifting towards the tools on the shelf.

'Please, leave those where they are,' I say sharply. To my relief, he steps away and turns towards the door.

I watch him walk up the path towards the barn, my heart still thudding. I lock the shed door behind me and make my way to where he is hovering at the entrance. He follows me wordlessly inside. The air feels heavy and charged with all the things lying unspoken between us.

I busy myself washing out the coffee pot and hear him say, 'M would have wanted me to have the Triumph.'

Anger uncoils, the words springing up and out before I can stop them. 'Don't you think you've taken enough from M? You wouldn't even be here if it wasn't for him!'

He is standing stock still, his face a deathly white.

'M and I had an agreement,' he begins. 'The debt went both ways.'

'What are you talking about?' I demand. With Will it was always half-finished sentences, cryptic comments and innuendo.

'Nothing that concerns you,' he mutters, looking away.

'If you've got something you need to tell me, Will, say it, otherwise I think we've covered everything.'

He breathes in sharply and looks away as if battling with some inner demon. I wait with trepidation for him to voice whatever it is, but he's grabbing M's damp umbrella and heading for the door.

'Good luck, Willow,' he says in a voice loaded with cynicism, intimating I was going to need it.

Note to blog:

What if you feel unable to honour your partner's wishes or fulfil a last request? Will it haunt you for the rest of your life, I wonder?

I write a brief synopsis of the morning's events. ...*my brother-in-law and I have never got on,* I begin. I'm reminded of the problem page, Modern Moral

Dilemmas, I'd headed for The Weekend some years ago. Only then I was the one trying to come up with the answers.

A lot of family relationships don't survive a death, sadeyedlady has commented. *He is clearly suffering too*, from lifeafterdeath.

When the ties that bind start to unravel, just walk away rather than try and fix it, blackwidower has suggested. *…then put it behind you.*

Easier said than done, I think. Will and I were bound together by everything that had happened, the ties between us too intricately woven for either of us to just walk away.

I sit in a daze after he's left, wondering about this so-called debt that had existed between the brothers.

Will saved my life, M had said a few times, referring to a surfing accident when his make-shift board, which he'd built from old plywood, had flipped up, striking him on the forehead and knocking him unconscious. It had left a scar on his forehead the shape of a waning moon. Will had ploughed into the waves, dived down and rescued his brother before dragging him back to the shore. But since then, in the balance of life's debits and credits, Will was the one who owed M everything, I'd concluded. Even his life.

I continue sifting through paperwork; all the unfinished business the dead unwittingly leave behind for the living. Cancelling M's subscription to Classic Bike magazine, calling the insurance company and the solicitor to discuss the terms of the will.

I go through M's bank statements and discover he had been paying into a life insurance company called Eagle Life. I recall him talking about taking out a policy years ago, joking, 'just in case I fall off a ladder.' There were many hidden dangers in the construction business, he often reminded me. There are a number of standing orders and payments he'd made to various charities, some of which I'd never heard of. It had become a bone of contention between us; this need of his to save the world, the rainforest, help the disabled, and as if trying to make sense of his and Will's past, kids who had suffered from abuse. He had adopted an orphaned teenager from Kenya, set up a foundation for a boy who had been killed in a hit and run accident, and was sending an annual donation to a Syrian girl who had lost both legs in a bombing raid.

M was a bit like *The Giving Tree*, the book I'd read to the boys when they were small. The apple tree which gave away its fruit, followed by its branches and shade until there was nothing left.

I check his savings account, and am shocked to see he had made a withdrawal of twenty-five thousand pounds some weeks before his death. I trawl through the other outgoings, which are mainly standing orders to the charities. I call the solicitor to ask if he knows anything about it. After an awkward pause, he explains M had requested that, in the event of his death, the sum of money in question was to be held in trust for the numerous donations listed under Kids in Crisis, the charity the brothers had started some fifteen years ago. M had stated that Will was to be the sole director of the charity. I hadn't been involved in the running of it from the beginning, so this part doesn't come as a surprise.

'I'm sure he must have discussed this with you?' the solicitor is saying.

'…yes of course, I just wanted confirmation,' I reply shortly.

I hang up feeling sick. M had given away a large sum of his hard-earned savings to charity – money that had been put away for the boys' university fees and beyond. A true philanthropist in life, he'd made sure his good works would continue after his death.

I once interviewed a billionaire for my column, Interesting Lives, who stated his children were not entitled to a penny of his, would have to make their own way in the world. M didn't have a fortune to give away. He has left me Rosewood Barn, a generous life insurance, some stocks and annuities, and the rest of his savings, but all the same, I am trembling with a kind of suppressed rage. I pace the barn, unable to settle.

'Why?' I demand, addressing the smiling photo of him on the mantelpiece. 'Surely you gave away enough while you were alive! What about the boys…?'

I pour myself a glass of wine, and stand gazing out across the unfinished courtyard. The wine tastes sour in my throat. I throw it in the sink, thinking tomorrow I would call the bank and instruct them to close his other accounts and transfer the balance into my own.

I read through M's latest emails, which are mainly spam – advertisements for bike parts and discounted surfing gear and a reminder to renew the insurance for the motorbike – so it had run out. I haven't cancelled his phone contract, for reasons I can't explain. I have taken to listening to his voice messages regularly. I tell myself there might be somebody out there trying to reach him, someone who doesn't know of his passing. I have dialled his number over and over, and listened to his voice with its slight West Country inflection …*leave a message and I'll get back to you in a heartbeat…cheers.*

I'd left a distraught message on it soon after he died, begging him to come home, promising I would be less demanding from now on, more forgiving. I would put up with the sudden change of plan, the missed dinners and long absences, I'd bargained. We would forget all the petty irritations of the past and begin again. I even sent him a WhatsApp one night, when I could no longer bear the silence. He had ghosted me, in the true sense of the word. I'd sat staring at the screen, willing a second tick to magically appear, some sign he'd read it, knowing all along there wouldn't be one, that he would never get back to me.

LATE JULY

Frida drops by with her signature chocolate torte, and hovers at the front door. She hands me a cinnamon-scented candle and a paperback titled The Last Word – A Memoir. I feel a guilty obligation to invite her in. The celebration of M's life has been cleared away, the flowers and sympathy cards long gone. Those who had come to pay their final respects have moved on with their lives. Jake had sent one of his employees over to take down the scaffolding.

I make a pot of tea, and find a knife to cut the cake, while Frida glances around the messy living area M no longer occupies. 'Have you thought of a new start somewhere else?' she enquires, settling onto the leather sofa, 'although I would hate to see you leave.'

'I can't move from here,' I say, immediately wishing I'd never invited her in.

'I sold our family home after Erik left. I couldn't live with the memories,' she states.

Erik, who is her only child, had gone to live in America after leaving university. I gathered he was the result of a one-night stand with a man she'd met while on holiday in Jamaica. She had brought him up alone, in an isolated cottage on the Devon border. Erik was now a freelance journalist who worked as a correspondent with The New Yorker and other newspapers, she'd told me, with a mixture of pride and disapproval. 'God knows why anybody would choose to write about war and violence when there are so many good things in the world,' she'd stated. I'd searched for Erik Andersson online but nothing had come up. Over the years, mother and son had become estranged it seemed. There were hardly any photos of him in her cottage – it was as if she had erased that chapter of her life. Apart from an elderly mother who was now in a nursing home, she had no other family. Her parents had left Sweden when she was a teenager, she'd told me and moved to the South of England.

It strikes me Frida has suffered a different kind of loss – the pain of abandonment. She's still a handsome woman, tall and upright, with strong Nordic features, and eyes the colour of the gentians she grows in her cottage garden.

'I would prefer to stay here and live with the memories,' I tell her now. 'Have you spoken to Erik recently?' I ask, changing the subject.

Her face hardens. 'The last time was on my birthday.'

I calculate that had been at least six months ago. M and I had bought her a plant pot in the shape of a Greek amphora from the Reclamation Centre and invited her over for a drink.

'He didn't tell me what he's working on. He talks to his grandmother regularly, but he never opens up to me. He'll be back one of these days,' she states resolutely. 'I know he misses England.'

I absorb this, thinking that's what loneliness does. After all, I fantasise M will come striding through the door offering one of his many excuses. He'd gone to do a last-minute job, only he'd fallen, injured himself and lost his memory. There were many dangers in the construction business. It had taken him a while to find his way home, but he was alive.

Frida is staring at the smiling photo of him on the mantelpiece. 'He was not ready to leave you. I know you had your ups and downs, but what married couple doesn't?'

No doubt she'd heard M roar off in the night on his motorbike, after one of our arguments.

I try to swallow the torte, which has turned into a solid ball in my throat.

'He was a good Samaritan who had time for everyone,' she continues.

I remain silent, not wanting to tarnish the glowing memories she had of him, tell her how all those good deeds had left little time for his family. And, in the end, time had run out, I think, the inevitable tears springing to my eyes.

Frida fixes me with her blue gaze. 'Have you considered doing some voluntary work? We've been collecting food and clothes for the homeless down at the village hall. It would help take your mind off things.'

'I've still things to sort out here,' I say quickly, 'what with M's charities. The boys need me around right now.'

There's no way I can face all those dedicated volunteers with their sympathetic smiles.

'How are the boys doing?'

I feel a dart of anxiety, thinking of Sam and Liam upstairs, hunched over their computers; escaping into a virtual world where I can't reach them.

'They've lost their dad,' I state. 'It's the worst thing that could have happened to them. M was a great father even though he was so busy with work deadlines.' I have a sudden vivid memory of him arriving home early one afternoon, with the pick-up truck laden with wood. ...*hey guys, we're going to build the strongest treehouse in the whole world...*

'I have no idea how to fill that gap,' I continue, giving up on the torte.

'Your role is to continue being a good mother to them,' Frida replies, 'and providing them the space they need. I made the mistake of trying to be both father and mother to Erik and he turned against me.' She changes the subject suddenly. 'When I was weeding your borders the other day, I noticed you have an invasion of moles. You might have to smoke them out, or they'll wreak havoc on your lawn.'

I stare at her blankly. I have no idea how to deal with a mole invasion. I shiver at a vision of them struggling to breathe in their smoky tunnels deep in the earth.

'Isn't there some other way?' I ask her.

'There is always another way,' she says. 'Let me deal with it for you,' she adds, getting up to leave. 'I need to pay a visit to the colonel,' she says, referring to the retired army officer who lives at the end of the lane. He had dropped in after M had died, with a bunch of forget-me-nots and offered his condolences before admitting he'd forgotten M's name and limping away down the lane. 'He's gone downhill since he lost his wife. There is no easy time to be alone,' she concludes. 'Stay strong, Willow, dear. You'll get through this.'

She pauses at the front door, saying, 'Do you happen to know a good electrician? My porch light has gone again! Max only changed the bulb at the beginning of June.'

I feel as if a draught of freezing air has entered the barn, followed by a shock wave rippling through my body. 'I'll ask M's friend Sean if he knows anyone,' I manage to reply.

Note to blog:

I've been advised to consider a new start, somewhere else away from all the memories.

There is a stream of comments, including:

Moving away won't help you through the grieving process.

It may give you a new perspective which could help.

Relocating so soon could be an added trauma - besides why would you want to move away from all the memories? blackwidower has written.

The comments continue into the evening.

Why not create a new life in your existing home – for instance take up voluntary work in your town or village.

A friend of mine who lost her husband applied for a job as an aid worker in Africa and came back a different person, from sadeyedlady.

Starting a charity in memory of your loved one can give meaning to their passing - the feeling it wasn't in vain, lifeafterdeath has written.

I would never find meaning around the events of June 21st, I think to myself; no charitable cause could come out of it, nor could taking up voluntary work or moving home ever erase the horror of what happened that mid-summer afternoon.

EARLY AUGUST

Sean Maloney drops in on his way back from work. I hear the sound of his motorbike on the driveway. I still listen out for that final splutter of the engine cutting out, signalling M was home.

Sean had worked with M on that final fateful project – the Huntington Hall extension. When everything started to fall apart, Sean had pulled his team of carpenters off the job. By then nearly everybody had walked away except for M. Sean had since spoken of the guilt and regret he felt for having abandoned M at such a vital time. He had dropped in a few times since the funeral wanting to know if I needed anything – as if trying to fix the unfixable.

Just the sight of him, with his tangle of red gold hair and biker jacket, brings back a host of memories.

'I've brought you something,' he says, handing over a wooden-framed photograph. My heart lurches at the image of M on a biking trip in Ireland looking wild-haired and impossibly young. I am flooded with images of Sean and M drinking beer together in the garden on the long summer evenings when they were working on the barn conversion. Sean staying over for dinner when Siobhan, his girlfriend, was on night duty at the hospital, Sean and M playing football on the lawn with the boys, the five of us lying spreadeagled on the grass, studying the night sky. That had been the beginning of Liam's fascination with the stars.

'I made the frame out of some left-over rosewood from here,' he tells me.

'Thanks,' I say, fighting back tears. I offer him a beer and ask after Siobhan.

'She wants to go back to Ireland,' he tells me. 'Settle down, start a family.'

'And you?'

He lets out a long sigh. 'I would be going back to everything I ran away from, and…what happened,' he says. He gazes at the photo of M on the mantelpiece with a haunted look.

He had told us about his Catholic upbringing, being one of seven, struggling to get his father's attention, fearful of his deeply religious mother who had forced him to go to confession when he had nothing to confess, his parents' unhappy marriage, the fact they weren't allowed to get a divorce.

'You know me, live to ride, ride to live,' he says. 'It's been rough on Siobhan. I haven't been myself since M went. Can't function, haven't been able to work …been hitting it hard in the evenings.'

You're not the only one, I think, glancing at the row of empty wine bottles piling up on the kitchen counter.

'I need to get away. I was thinking of doing that road trip in Europe he and I talked about.'

I recall M mentioning a bike trip through France and Spain they were keen to do. I'd pointed out he would be away for weeks on end, more absent than ever.

I tell Sean about Will's visit. 'He wants to take M's bike – be the custodian as he put it!'

Sean frowns. 'Was there anything in the will about that?'

I shake my head. 'M and I never discussed it.'

'Then you have every right to refuse him.'

'He insinuated M owed him something – there was a debt that went both ways. All I know is M paid his debts and more.'

I push the broken drawer in with a vicious shove.

'There's always unfinished business when somebody dies,' Sean comments. 'A lot of things come out of the woodwork. You need to make sure Will doesn't get his hands on the bike. He'll run it into the ground, then sell it for parts. I can come by and check it over for you, keep it running until you decide what you want to do. Now, how about I fix that drawer? I'll go grab the drill from the shed.'

'Let's do it another time,' I begin. 'It's just I can't stand the noise of drilling.'

Sean frowns. 'It'll only take a minute.'

'I know, sorry, I'm a bit sensitive right now.'

'I'll take a look at the sink then,' he says, crouching down to examine the leaking pipe. 'Looks like the valve needs replacing – I'll have to get a new one from the hardware store. I'll come back when you're out and fix the drawer at the same time. Just send me a text and leave the key under the mat.'

He wanders over to the window and gazes out over the unfinished courtyard.

'What's the plan here?'

'I haven't decided. I wanted to put in a water feature, but M wasn't keen… Anyway, he was so busy he never got around to it.'

'I could put you in touch with a good builder,' Sean suggests.

'Maybe next year.'

Apart from the cost, I can't face dealing with builders, the noise and upheaval, making conversation, making decisions.

'Well let me know what you decide,' he says.

We're both silent, M's absence hanging like an almost tangible presence over us. 'Jesus, I miss him,' Sean mutters. 'I feel so bad I wasn't there for him that last week.'

'We all miss him,' I say, my voice sharper than I intend. I can't deal with

Sean's guilt, on top of my own, his aching sadness for his friend. I've noticed the change in him – his quick wit and quirky humour, the jokes which had made us all double up, his conviction that everything would work out have been replaced with a brooding heaviness.

'I would like to go back to the spot where it happened, if only to make sense of it all.' His olive-green eyes glitter with unshed tears.

'I can't go back there,' I say, sharply. 'Look, I'm sorry, Sean, I'm not able to talk about it now, but thanks for coming over.' I am breaking out in a cold sweat, am suddenly desperate for him to leave.

He frowns. 'Is there anything else that needs fixing?'

Yes, everything, I think, relieved he has moved on.

'Frida mentioned her porch light wasn't working – do you have the number of a local electrician?'

'*...where the fuck is the electrician?* I'd yelled that day as the storm raged around us.

'I'll call a guy I know,' he says. He turns away, adding, 'I'll go check the bike. Make sure it's running properly.'

MID-AUGUST

The boys have spent most of the weekend working on the treehouse. I find them perched like owls on a thick branch, deep in conversation.

'We literally nailed it by putting in that new platform,' Sam is saying to his younger brother.

'Genius!' Liam replies.

I climb the rope ladder and sit in the leafy shade, admiring their handiwork. They have carved a skylight in the timber roof M constructed so Liam could gaze up at the stars. 'Dad would love it,' I enthuse, 'I feel sure he's watching over you and is so proud…' My voice trails off at the closed look on Sam's face.

I move on swiftly. 'I was thinking we could spend next weekend in Cornwall?'

The summer holidays would be over soon, I remind them. We should make the most of the time that was left, get out of the house, live a little.

'We could take the surfboards, have fish and chips on the pier, or just swim and picnic on the beach like the old days. The forecast is good,' I add, aware of the note of desperation in my voice.

There's a silence, then Sam says, 'Liam and me are planning to take the dirt bikes to the track.'

'Surfing wouldn't be the same without Dad,' Liam points out.

I nod, not trusting myself to speak.

I climb down the rope ladder with a heavy heart, thinking I'm the one who needs to get out of the house, live a little.

EARLY SEPTEMBER

On the last night of the school holiday, I suggest we go out for dinner. We decide on The Old Flame, a pub M had loved on the outskirts of Highbury.

It's a dull, overcast evening; there's already a chill of autumn in the air. I had woken heavy with dread at the thought of the new term; facing the mothers in the car park, dealing with more condolences, meeting up with the teachers about Sam's less-than-impressive school report, buying Liam a new uniform in the second-hand school shop. He had shot up over the summer and developed a slight stoop, as if weighted down by the loss of his father. Sam is describing a former teacher who's 'a legend', and will now be Liam's housemaster.

'He teaches Science so you can talk about the universe and all that alien stuff.'

'Perhaps I'll become an astronomer, or maybe an astronaut,' Liam says thoughtfully.

Liam reads books with titles like Imagination of the Impossible and Astrological Phenomena, and is always talking about time travel, and how one day we will be able to access the past.

'I can't see you going on the next space mission! Anyhow, astronomers don't do much except gaze at the stars,' Sam points out.

'Yes they do, they study the random events of the universe, and the evolution of the solar system.'

'That's not going to pay the bills,' Sam argues. He is planning on taking a degree course in economics, and becoming a financial analyst.

I think of my dwindling savings account and wonder if the boys will be plagued with student debts in the years ahead.

They move on to their plan to build a new track for their mud bikes, and it strikes me I have no plan but to take up where I left off, try to reclaim my column, start living again. The routine of the school run will force me out of bed in the autumn mornings, bring some structure back into the days.

On the way home, we get caught in a long tailback of traffic. A misty orange glow hangs over the town and I can see a police car with lights flashing, some way ahead. We crawl along towards the bridge where the trains once ran, past the old wool factory, now derelict. A cyclist flies past, weaving his way along the long line of cars. At last, we are drawing level with the police car which is parked on the verge next to an ambulance, its lights also flashing. A stretcher is being carried towards it by two paramedics. As we inch closer, we see a body lying on the ground covered from head to toe with a blanket.

I hear Sam swear under his breath.

We are through at last, and I pull over so the ambulance can pass, sirens wailing.

Nobody speaks.

'Well, that could be a good sign,' I say, breaking the silence.

'What the fuck is good about it?' Sam snaps.

'The fact that they left the sirens on! Please don't swear, Sam! Maybe they were able to revive the person. I mean, if there was no hope, they wouldn't be in such a hurry and would have turned off the sirens and just driven off,' I am gabbling now.

'God, Mum, don't you get it? Whoever's under that blanket is dead! Gone! They're not coming back.'

His deep-blue eyes, so like M's, are ringed as if with charcoal. His boyish good looks have hardened, his jaw is now set defiantly as if he's ready to challenge the world. 'Why do you keep saying those things, that Dad is still around us?'

'Well, he could be,' Liam puts in, 'anyway, we're all made of the same stardust.'

'Give me a fucking break,' Sam mutters.

I remain silent knowing that I can't reach them through the layers of anger and grief.

'I'm so sorry, boys,' I blurt. 'I wish it hadn't happened, and we could access the past, as Liam says. Then we could just cut that day out of the calendar.' I am sobbing now and have to pull off the road for a second time.

Sam strokes my arm while Liam unclips his seatbelt, moves across and nestles against me. I hold him tight, stroking his silky hair.

'It's OK, Mum, you couldn't have done anything,' I hear Sam say. 'Just don't die, all right? Or we'll kill you,' he adds with a weak smile.

It's not OK, I think bleakly. I could have done something. I could have just stayed home and waited.

MID-SEPTEMBER – A DARK NIGHT OF THE SOUL

Sam announces he's spending the weekend in London with his best friend Tom – they are planning to start a band, with Tom on electric guitar and Sam on drums. Their friend Lennie, who sings in the school choir, is going to be the vocalist.

'That's great,' I say heartened by this news. M had bought Sam a drum kit a year ago, but after an enthusiastic start he had stopped playing altogether. I suggest Liam and I light the barbecue. 'We could make hot dogs. You could cook the sausages. And bring out your telescope so we could do some stargazing?'

Liam shifts in his chair and looks away. 'Can I spend the weekend at Harry's house? It's no fun here without Sam and Harry's got the new *Mission Impossible.*'

'Of course,' I say, with a plunge of heart. Having not wanted to leave the house for most of the summer, now it seemed they both couldn't wait to be away.

The weekend yawns emptily ahead. I drop Liam over to Harry's house, which is only on the other side of Highbury, but all the same feels like a whole county away. I can feel the premature chill of an empty nest looming ahead, a time M and I had talked about buying a camper van and travelling around Europe. I return to the barn, open a bottle of red wine and drink two glasses in quick succession, then sit on the sofa glazed and glassy-eyed, a drunken parody of self-pity. No wonder people jumped off bridges, walked into the sea, or hung themselves, I think headily. They could no longer carry the burden of it all. I gaze up at the cross beams, thinking I was going to need a tall ladder to get up there, an image that causes a shiver to run through me.

I drag myself upstairs with the rest of the bottle and stand in M's walk-in closet, desperate for the smell of him. I wind his blue woollen scarf around my neck, wondering if I have the courage to strangle myself with it, then pull on his leather biking jacket, which I'd hidden away from Will.

…here, take my jacket, he'd said that day in the gorge as I stood trembling in the cold shadows of the rock face.

I had been climbing with a boyfriend who was in my English Literature class at university, and it was my turn to lead the way. It was an easy climb but we had made slow progress, before suddenly becoming unsynchronised, and he'd unclipped his rope before I'd managed to properly anchor mine above. We weren't far up the one hundred metre rock face, but all the same, I felt the terror of free-falling in my gut, the sickening pull of gravity about to take us hurtling down. In a desperate attempt to find a ledge, my flailing feet had struck him on the head, dislodging his helmet, causing him to curse and swear and accuse me of trying to kill him. We had somehow managed to inch our way down the jagged rock face with him shouting furious accusations that I was dangerous, an accident waiting to happen, me yelling back that he was at fault for not waiting for the signal to continue. Back on solid ground, he'd unclipped himself angrily from the rope that had bound us so uncomfortably together and marched away, muttering he needed to cool off. I was to put the gear in the car and meet him in the pub further along the road, he'd instructed, before storming off with the car keys, leaving me with cords, harnesses and yards of thick rope coiled at my feet.

'Idiot!' I'd shouted after him, trembling from nerves and fury. I was standing there, debating what to do next, when I heard the roar of engines echoing through the gorge and saw a stream of motorcyclists racing towards me like a horde of angry wasps. The bike at the front suddenly slowed and veered towards me before skidding to a dramatic halt. The rider pulled up his visor, saying, 'Are you OK?'

I took in azure-blue eyes, and a square jaw shadowed with dark stubble, the slow smile, and felt my stomach turn over.

'Max Goodhart – better known as M,' he'd said.

'Willow Monroe,' I'd replied, trying to breathe through the sudden tightness in my chest. I ran my fingers through my hair, which was plastered to my scalp from the helmet.

'Are you injured?' he enquired with concern.

'No. Although it was a close call. My climbing partner claimed it was my fault, and stormed off. He told me to put the equipment in the car, only he left with the keys! I will never allow myself to be tethered to that idiot again,' I'd fumed, shivering from cold and adrenaline. M had smiled then climbed off his bike in one fluid motion, kicked the stand down with a booted foot and walked towards me.

'Here, take my jacket,' he'd said, shrugging it off his shoulders and draping it over mine.

I stood there enveloped in the heat from his body, breathing in the scent of leather and olive oil soap, my body trembling while my heart seemed to be doing a crazy dance of its own.

Now I fumble around in the pockets of the jacket searching for something, anything, but there are just a couple of business cards, some loose change, and two receipts, one from a company called Access Mobility for the staggering amount of three thousand, four hundred pounds, the other for a pair of binoculars. I stand there trying to work out what he could have possibly needed from a shop that sold mobility scooters and wheelchairs, and why binoculars when I had given him an expensive pair for his last birthday. I think about the withdrawal of twenty-five thousand pounds from his savings account and now this.

I pour myself another glass of wine, concluding it had to be another of his charity donations for Kids in Crisis, then climb into bed, in that heightened state of drunkenness that normally leads to wild sex, dramatic revelations and regret. My only option is sleep which comes instantly; a total blackout, a falling away into nothingness.

I wake up two hours later in a sweat, my head throbbing, my throat parched. My tongue feels swollen and there's a metallic taste in my mouth. I reach for my water, but it's not there, just a wine glass filled with the dregs of Pinot Noir. A wave of nausea rises. I sit up abruptly, swallowing acid, and am suddenly shaking violently, filled with a nameless fear. Sweat prickles on my scalp and I can't catch my breath. My heart accelerates, the sweat on my forehead has turned to ice. I stagger out of bed and look around wildly for a paper bag, having read it's meant to help you breathe through an asthma attack. I can't find one, so grab my swimming cap and sit taking deep, rubbery breaths. This is the first night I've slept alone since I can remember and I don't think I'm going to make it through to the morning. It occurs to me I'm having a heart attack. Isn't this what I wished for earlier, an escape from it all, no more weighty sorrow, no more dark nights of the soul? Only the very thought of being wrenched from this earth is now a terrifying prospect. It strikes me I have a better chance of surviving if I go downstairs to the living room, presumably thus named for the living. I stand by the kitchen door gulping in the cold night air, concluding it's an anxiety attack. I can hear a faint scuffling sound outside. Was this what had woken me earlier, the feeling somebody was prowling around the barn? I peer through the window into the foggy night, bracing myself against an intruder, but everything is eerily still and silent. A badger, I tell myself, checking the back door is bolted and pulling down the blinds. Having searched for an escape through wine and oblivion, it now feels imperative I stay alert and conscious. I consider making some coffee but decide it will only increase my heart rate. My teeth are chattering, so I wrap myself in the soft blanket M had brought back from a biking trip in Ireland. I am desperate to talk to somebody, only it's 3 a.m., too late to call Fern. I catch a glimpse of myself in the antique mirror and reel back. Grief has etched new lines on my face, bracketing my mouth, my eyes are ringed with violet shadows like fading bruises. I sink down onto the sofa thinking there's nothing to be done except live through each moment and all the following moments, through the darkest hours before dawn and the arrival of a new day.

Daylight is creeping in at last, the world turning from black to ashy grey. A shard of weak sun slices through the skylight. I hear the faint sound of birdsong, a dog barking from a nearby house. I am spent from exhaustion, hungover, but alive.

Note to blog:

Last night, I reached rock bottom - drank too much wine and had an anxiety attack. I never want to go through that again. Alcohol and grief are a terrible combination.

Those dark night of the soul are inevitable and are sent to remind us that that there is no way to bypass the grief, no way around it, only through it, blackwidower has written.
This too shall pass, a new follower called notdeadyet has suggested.

I settle down on the sofa, craving sleep, thinking about blackwidower's comment, 'there is no way around it, only through it.'
How do you get through it? I write.
You are already on your way, he responds.

My mother arrives unexpectedly, jolting me out of an unconscious sleep. I bolt upright on the sofa, trying to orient myself. There's a pounding in my head that beats in time to the sound of her footsteps marching across the wooden floor. She trips into the living area in a maroon fur-lined cape and matching high-heeled boots, knocking over an empty wine bottle on her way. I had rashly given her a key to the front door after M died. She stops short at the sight of me wrapped in a blanket, M's blue scarf still wound around my neck. The TV is on, frozen on Netflix, advertising what to watch next.

'Goodness, Willow! Are you sick?'

Yes, heartsick, I want to say.

'Heavens, what is that smell? Is it alcohol?' She stares at me blankly. Her latest cosmetic procedure has given her a marbled expression which is unnerving.

Now she stands at a careful distance, rattling her car keys, waiting for an explanation.

'I fell asleep in front of the TV,' I tell her. 'What are you doing?'

'I was on my way to London and thought I'd better drop in to make sure you were still alive,' she says without irony. 'Fern has been desperately trying to call you. She said you weren't answering your phone. We were worried.'

'The signal here is awful, as I'm always telling you.'

'She folds her arms across the ample expanse of her chest. 'I know it's tough, but you can't just fall to pieces. Those boys need you. Are they still asleep at this hour? They need stability, Willow.'

'There're not here – Sam's in London at Tom's, Liam was invited to a sleepover.'

I'd wanted to remind her of how she'd locked herself away for weeks with depression when Fern and I were growing up, the lack of stability we'd felt when she'd taken too much Valium and couldn't even remember what day it was.

'You can't just come bursting in on me! I might have had company.'

'I'd be delighted if you had,' she states, 'you clearly can't look after yourself. This place is a mess. I'll send my cleaning lady over. You can't continue living like this!'

I stand up, head thumping, and face her full on. 'Don't send anyone over! Thanks for dropping in, but I need to get on. I've an article to write,' I say, rashly.

'You got your column back! Well, that's a start. I'm planning to write my memoir. I went through some very tough times when I was your age, but I always had my hair done, and lipstick on ready for any eventuality.'

'I'm sure you did,' I reply, imagining her dressed to the nines, as one by one her lovers walked out.

'You have a whole new life ahead of you, Willow.'

I want my old life back, and for you to leave now, so I can go back to sleep, I think.

'Thanks for that reminder, Mother. Now, if you'll excuse me, I need to get on, make a hair appointment, be ready for any eventuality, the next catastrophe whatever that might be!'

I attempt a dignified exit, pulling up M's boxer shorts which are creeping down my thighs, aware his scarf is trailing on the floor behind me.

'You're going to have to let him go,' I hear her say in this ominous voice, the same voice she'd used to try and stop me from marrying him.

'Maybe you should get going Mother,' I say, 'I wouldn't want you to miss your appointment!'

She glares at me for a moment with that deadpan expression, then turns around without a word and heads for the front door.

I immediately feel guilty, but then guilt and anger are woven into the very fabric of my relationship with my mother, stretching back through the years for as long as I can remember.

I listen to the sound of her Mercedes purring away, then step out into the garden, in need of some fresh air. The lawn is pockmarked with hundreds of mole hills, neat little piles of earth marking each hole. I recall the scuffling I'd heard in the night, and remember M throwing coffee grounds into the holes to keep them away. I had paid little attention to it at the time – it was just one of the many things he did on the side lines, along with fixing leaking pipes, unblocking the drains, mending drawers, dealing with mice – all the things that, at the time, I had taken for granted.

Liam calls to ask if I can pick him up from Harry's house early.

'Is everything all right?' I enquire with concern.

'Yeah, I just miss Dad.' His voice wobbles as if he's holding back the tears.

I grab my handbag, then take a while searching for the car keys. I find them eventually in the drawer with all the unpaid bills, then set off and arrive to find Liam sitting on the front step. Claudia, Harry's Mum, comes out to greet me.

'Willow, I'm so sorry. I couldn't get him to eat any lunch. I think he just wants to be at home.'

She trips down the steps holding Liam's backpack and telescope, and gives me a hug, murmuring, 'take good care of yourself during this desperately sad time.'

'Thanks,' I reply, thinking she always seemed to hit the right note. 'And for having him to stay.'

Liam barely talks on the drive home, then steps into the barn and looks around wildly, as if perhaps expecting M to appear. His face falls as if I'm the one at fault for not having been able to conjure his father back from the afterlife. He helps himself to a bowl of cereal, sloshes in milk, then disappears to his room.

Without Sam around, he spends the rest of the day lying on the sofa, wrapped in a blanket, flicking through TV channels.

When I ask how he's feeling, he says, 'I don't see the point of it. Human beings are just drifting stardust, sucked through a black hole, meaningless atoms, destined to decay.' He flings the remote down and glares into the middle distance.

'I suppose that's the sum of it,' I say, smiling in spite of everything. 'Maybe you don't feel a purpose now, but you will. You have your whole life ahead of you.' Isn't that what my mother is always telling me? 'I'm not doing very well either, but I promise I'll try to do better if you will. We'll make Dad proud of us. I mean if we're just drifting stardust, we'll surely end up swirling about with him one day, so maybe we'd better be prepared!'

He offers up a ghost of a smile.

I take in the angry spots on his cheeks and feel as if my insides are being wrenched apart.

Moments later he gets up, wanders over to the entrance of the barn and gazes at his reflection in the antique mirror.

'Have you got something I can put on these?' he says, examining the swathe of pimples with a mixture of horror and fascination. 'They look exactly like the Milky Way.'

EARLY OCTOBER

ANGER: *(noun)* also known as wrath, or rage, is an intense emotional state. Described as a 'strong, uncomfortable and hostile response to a perceived provocation'.

I call Jason and tell him that I'm ready to get back to work.

If I'd harboured any hope that he would hand me back my column, I'm in for a shock. 'Interesting Lives' had been doing very well without me, under the young and talented Susannah Frost. I had been reading it online and found her style quirky but overdone. However, readers liked her confessional approach and sharp wit. The magazine was evolving, taking on a racy, more personal slant.

'There must be something I can cover,' I say, trying not to sound desperate, thinking that first my life and now my career was falling apart.

'Look, I do need to work, Jason. I'm on my own now, I have to pay the school fees. I haven't earned anything since June.'

Now that I was paying for everything myself, I was shocked by the cost of living, or in my case of simply existing. There is an ominous silence.

'Well, I do need somebody to do a piece about living to be over a hundred,' he says at last. 'Susannah has a lot on her plate and this means a trip to Wales to interview one of the oldest women in the UK. She's just turned one hundred and ten. She did a sky dive on her ninetieth birthday.'

'I'll do it,' I tell him.

It would be good to get out of the house for the day, lose myself in somebody else's life for a change. Perhaps she could give me some advice on how to fill my days – after all, she'd got through more than forty thousand of them. How to live again.

I set off early, driving over the suspension bridge to the home of one hundred and ten-year-old Ethel Mary Bosley.

I discover she still lives in the same pebble-dashed cottage outside Swansea, where she'd grown up. Only the cottage had been surrounded by fields then. Since then, the city had spread out, claiming that green and pleasant land, filling it with dreary housing estates and busy arterial roads, turning it into a concrete landscape. She leads me into an over-heated living room smelling of cat litter. I learn she has been widowed for fifty years. Instead of concentrating on her great age, her letter from the queen nine and a half years ago, her career as a piano teacher or her sky dive, I find myself asking how she has managed to fill the last half century. Even my forays into other people's lives have become marred with self-interest. Her cat, a spooky-looking tabby, glares at me balefully as I sit on the chair it had occupied, facing the old lady.

What is the secret of living a full and happy life after the death of a loved one, I want to know?

'To be happy in yourself,' she replies immediately. 'Every morning when you wake up, count your blessings, name them one by one.'

'…then you'll know what the good Lord has done?' I fill in.

'Oh, I'm an atheist,' she laughs. 'Sadly the good Lord, if He does exist, can't fill your days.'

'But there must be times when it's a bit of a challenge?'

'Challenges are there to be overcome. Never dwell on what you don't have,' she advises. 'Or waste time thinking about what might have been. Find some hobbies, use your imagination. I taught the piano for forty years. I can't play now because of arthritis, so I listen to classical music and imagine I'm still playing Chopin.'

It strikes me I have no such resources and precious few hobbies, apart from swimming and writing my blog. I hadn't been rock climbing since Liam was born and had abandoned the idea of trying to write a witty novel about modern moral dilemmas years ago.

Ethel Bosley is the proverbial 'merry widow', twinkly eyed, face creased with a map of the years, a living monument to longevity. And what is the secret of longevity, I'm obliged to ask. That's what the readers will want to know.

'Making the choice to be happy,' she answers. She smiles revealing a set of oversized teeth. 'Right here,' she adds, touching her bony chest. 'And a little bit of vanity goes a long way,' she adds meaningfully, her glittery eyes taking in my limp hair.

But does time hang heavily, I want to know? After all, she doesn't appear to have a computer to browse the internet, or fall back on the distraction of YouTube.

She frowns. 'Time is your friend, not your enemy, my dear. It is a gift, to bend to your own will.'

I find myself telling her about M, whose time had been cut short. I don't tell her how and she doesn't ask.

'I thought we were going to grow old together.'

'We always believe we have unlimited years ahead of us,' she says, 'but that was never a given. You will eventually overcome the sadness and find joy again.'

I wonder if that's at all possible after what had happened the day of the solstice.

Lastly, I ask her about the sky dive. 'Weren't you afraid?' I say, imagining those brittle bones splintering into hundreds of pieces.

She shakes her head. 'The only thing to fear is fear itself, some wise politician said.'

'Was it hard, though?' I want to know, 'finding yourself widowed after being married for fifty years?'

'Of course. Jack was everything to me. He was no saint, but he was a good provider, and we muddled through the bad times.'

I am immediately curious. 'You mentioned that he was no saint, and yet he was everything to you? This is off the record of course and I'll be sending you a proof before it goes to print, but how did you…that is, how does one reconcile those two things?'

She shrugs. 'I've reached the age where I have few secrets. He had a dalliance. She was a rather dumpy woman. It all came out after he passed away.'

'How did you find out?'

'I had my suspicions. There were letters. I should have let it be, rather than pursuing it.' She gazes at the tabby cat, adding, 'The truth doesn't always set you free, does it, Tastrophe?'

I christened him Catastrophe when I got him,' she explains, because he was always knocking things over. I've since shortened it to Tastrophe.'

I smile. 'Did you manage to forgive him? Jack, that is?'

'It took me a long time. I wanted to dig him up and throttle him!' She smiles, adding, 'I even put chrysanthemums on his grave. He detested them, said they were deceitful for looking so pretty and smelling so nasty. But in the end, I came to understand that forgiveness is a form of love.'

'So, to conclude, what do you believe is the secret of a long and happy life?'

'Find yourself a lover, have some passionate nights.' She winks. 'Good sex. And if you can't sleep, pour yourself a stiff whisky.'

I smile, thinking I would give that a try.

Note to blog:

The secret of living with grief is to try and be happy in yourself I was told by a formidable lady of hundred and ten years' old '….to overcome the sadness and find joy again.' She recommended finding a new hobby, getting a lover and having some passionate nights. And if you can't sleep to pour yourself a stiff whiskey! Who knows, you may live to be over one hundred!

This produces a number of comments from followers, including

Seize the moment
Indulge in your whims
Live in the now
Write a bucket list
One life, live it your way, blackwidower has written.

The article takes up most of the following morning, and I send it off just before the deadline. Ten minutes later, Jason calls.

'Willow, the Ethel Bosley piece! Is it an article about the old lady or yourself? All this padding about your generation lacking resources, unable to spend time alone! It was meant to be about her if I recall?'

'Well, I thought I made some interesting comparisons,' I say defensively, 'don't worry, I can do some editing.'

I've noticed Susannah always makes comparisons with her life.

'Too late. I've asked one of the juniors to do a re-write. I think you need to take some time out.'

'I've already taken time out, Jason. The last thing I need is more!' I remind him of the paragraph I'd written of how hard it is to fill time. 'I've always submitted everything within the deadline, even today.'

There is a strained silence.

'Are you saying you don't want any more submissions from me?'

'I get the feeling you're angry, Willow, and it's coming through in your prose. Take a break. Find your voice again.'

I am not fucking angry! I want to shout down the phone.

'Get your life back on track and then we'll see what's what.'

To hell with you, Jason, says the voice in my head.

I hang up before my lips will mouth it, then pick up an empty wine bottle from the floor and hurl it into the recycling bin, watching it shatter to pieces.

Note to blog:

I've read that anger is one of the enduring stages of grief. Buddhists believe that anger will inevitably backfire on you.

'Like a man who wants to hit another and picks up a burning ember or excrement in hand and so first burns himself or makes himself stink.'

You will burn yourself over and over, but eventually you'll learn to control the flare-ups, and wonder what it was you were angry about, lifeafterdeath has written.

I'm not angry, I'm fucking furious, a new follower has written. *There is no justice!*
Anger is the second stage of grief, blackwidower has commented, *which means you're moving forward. No point looking for justice in an unjust world.*

MID OCTOBER

It is almost half term. I have spent the last few weeks emailing newspaper and magazine editors, trying to get my career going again, only to receive the standard reply: thank you for your enquiry, but we have enough contributors for now. However, I was welcome to try again in a few months.

I decide to put it to one side and spend the half term break with the boys, cooking their favourite food, watching action movies, maybe take a day trip to the beach, if the weather should hold.

Sam spends the first fifteen hours in bed then comes downstairs and paces the barn like a caged animal. He is moody and monosyllabic, and refuses to discuss his half term report, which is worse than ever. Rather than pursue it, I ask him what he'd like to do over the next few days. He shrugs, saying, 'I just want to chill.'

I'd gathered from Liam that he'd broken up with Mel, his first serious girlfriend, who we had all loved. When I broach the subject later on in the day, he says crossly, 'She keeps saying I need to talk about Dad!'

Liam is deathly silent. I suggest a trip to London to the Royal Observatory but he says, 'We went there last year with Dad, remember?'

I return from Highbury and the supermarket, having planned to make chocolate brownies, to find the barn empty and silent. I make my way down the garden to the treehouse, but there's no sign of the boys. I notice the shed is unlocked and guess they've taken their dirt bikes out into the fields.

I push open the door and see the two bikes are in their usual place in the far corner. I register the empty space in the centre, the large oil stain from M's motorbike on the concrete floor. The Triumph has gone. Will, I think, furiously, and then a thought far worse rears up like a dark spectre, causing my heart to accelerate. The boys have taken the bike out for a ride. I call Sam's phone over and over, but there's no answer. Fear swells like a balloon in my chest. I run down to the bottom of the garden, straining my ears for a sound of the engine. As time passes, I imagine them lying in a ditch somewhere, broken and bleeding, and head off blindly along the narrow lane past the crumbling hay barn and row of thatched cottages that leads to the main road. There is no sight nor sound of them. I return to the barn, not knowing what to do. I can hardly call the police and announce my seventeen-year-old son has taken his thirteen-year-old brother on a joy ride on their dead father's uninsured motorbike. I am overcome by a feeling of helplessness. The light is already starting to leach from the day – a day so unlike the one I had envisaged, with the three of us sitting around the kitchen table eating chocolate brownies.

My phone rings, making me jump. The police, I think, announcing there's been an accident.

It's Frida. 'Willow, my dear, I was wondering if you could drive me into Highbury tomorrow. My car is playing up again and I need to open the shop at nine. We have some lovely vintage dresses – you could come in and have a look.'

'Sorry, I can't talk now, Frida. Sam has gone off on M's motorbike and taken Liam with him.' I can feel hysteria rising.

'They'll be back as soon as they're hungry,' she soothes. 'Erik disappeared for hours on end, but he was always back in time for his supper.'

'I'm going out to look for them. I'll talk to you later,' I say looking around wildly for the keys of the jeep.

I accelerate down the driveway, not knowing whether to turn left towards the reservoir or right which leads to the main road.

I speed along the narrow lane, memories of that midsummer day, when I'd gone in search of M flooding back, the wind tearing through the trees, lightning splitting the sky. But today everything is eerily still, a low fog hangs over the fields, a pall of smoke from a bonfire of autumn leaves rises like a smoky exclamation mark in the air. I reach the dirt track where M had often taken the boys. It is deserted.

I call Sam's phone again, filled with a piercing dread. There is still no answer. I turn back towards the barn, thinking I would check to see if they were back, then drive on down to the reservoir.

As I approach the barn, I hear the snarl of an engine behind me. I glance at my side mirror and to my astonishment and relief see Sam crouched low over the handlebars, Liam clutching his brother around the waist. Sam accelerates and weaves past me, then turns up the driveway, across the lawn scattering earth from the mole hills, before coming to an abrupt halt in front of the shed.

My initial relief is replaced with a full-blown rage. I stop the car halfway down the drive, and march towards them.

'Hey, Mum,' Sam says warily.

'What the hell were you thinking…where did you go?'

'To our secret place,' Liam replies.

'What secret place? Where?' I demand.

'The twisty track through the fields where Dad took us when he was teaching Sam how to ride the bike.'

'You can't just take the bike out for a ride!' I fume. 'It's not insured! I couldn't even call the police!'

Sam looks at me with alarm while Liam mutters, 'Sorry, Mum.'

'Yeah, sorry,' Sam repeats. He rakes his fingers through his mop of dark curls, and kicks the ground miserably.

'I'm getting rid of it,' I fume. 'Will can take it off my hands. He asked if he could be the custodian.'

Both boys stare at me in horror. 'Don't give it to Uncle Will,' Liam cries, 'he's already taken everything. Sam knows how to ride it and he can do a wheelie. Although he didn't do one exactly. What's a custodian?' he adds.

'Someone who takes care of something or is responsible for it, without owning it,' I say.

'What's the point of that?' Liam demands furiously.

'Will has never taken care of anything in his life, including himself,' Sam states. 'He was locked up for stealing cars! He drove his bike into a ditch if you remember! He'll sell it to the first person who comes along! God, Mum!' He turns his back on me and starts pushing the bike into the shed.

'I'll never forgive you if do that,' is his parting comment.

Liam's shoulders are shaking. 'I miss Dad,' he sobs. 'I hate home now.' He follows Sam into the shed, slamming the door behind him.

I feel as if I'm sinking into a bottomless pit. So, this is how it feels to be a single parent. Having to deal with all the fears and worries alone. How will I ever protect them from life's dangers, from broken limbs and broken hearts? In the absence of their father, they have turned to one another searching for that old sense of adventure. I feel a crushing sense of defeat, Liam's comment, 'I hate home now,' like the twist of a knife inside.

I knock on Sam's door later and find him and Liam lost in a game in which a fleet of motorbikes are buzzing around a track. Neither of them look up, reminding me of M and how absorbed he would become in whatever he was doing, his inability to multitask, how oblivious he was to the elements that day when the storm was raging around him.

'Sorry, guys. I promise I won't get rid of the bike or let Will take it. I just got scared, I couldn't cope if anything happened to you!' I take a shaky breath, 'I can't take another loss.'

'It's OK, Mum,' Liam says, dragging his eyes from the screen.

…it's not OK, and never will be again, I think, closing the bedroom door behind me.

Over breakfast Sam says, 'how about we take the dirt bikes to the fields?' As if to make amends from the horror of yesterday, he adds, 'you can come too if you want, Mum.'

I follow on foot, comforted by their laughter as they skid down the muddy tracks. In the afternoon, I find them in the shed, cleaning and polishing their bikes. They have pulled out M's toolbox and left his tools scattered all over the floor. The sight of the rosewood box causes my stomach to lurch.

'Make sure you put them all back once you've finished,' I tell them. 'I'd like that toolbox to be put away.'

The boys look puzzled. 'Dad always let us use them,' Sam says.

'Dad was totally cool about it,' Liam adds.

'Just put it away as soon as you are finished,' I say firmly. Some place where I can't see it and be reminded, I think.

In the evening, we pull out the barbecue, Sam builds a fire and we sit around it eating steaks, and sausages, and Liam's favourite sweetcorn salad. Liam brings out the telescope, announcing he's searching for a special star. Afterwards they set up the movie projector and we watch an old action movie. I find myself gazing at them instead, each of them the two halves of M somehow making the whole, and for a moment it feels as if he's physically with us and the family is complete again.

EARLY NOVEMBER

I have started swimming again, finding a release in the cold chemical water. I plough up and down the twenty-five-metre pool at the leisure centre in Highbury, envisaging I'm swimming in a turquoise sea, purged by the clear salt water. I imagine the splashing of the other swimmers are the waves, the tiled floor of the pool the ocean bed with a coral garden alive with algae and sea grass shifting with the current. I can swim a whole length underwater now, which is something I suppose. I drink less wine on swimming days, which is also good. My body feels lighter afterwards, temporarily eased from the straitjacket of grief.

I return from the pool to find Holly waiting on the porch, leaning against a large metallic suitcase. We had spoken on the phone a few times, and she had suggested coming over to stay the night, but each time I'd come up with an excuse.

Holly and I had been inseparable once, but her marriage problems had started to wear me down. M, who liked her husband Peter, had not wanted to hear about the constant dramas, or witness the breakdown of their marriage. I had come home late one evening to find her sobbing her heart out to M, who was listening patiently, and handing her tissues. I had noticed her flirting with him on a couple of other occasions, but then Holly tended to flirt with every man, was adept at playing the femme fatale. She looks beautiful and tragic, her long fair hair tousled, her eyes smudged with mascara.

'I've been calling and calling. Where have you been, why didn't you answer your phone?'

'I was at the pool. I've started swimming again,' I tell her.

'I didn't know where to go! Peter and I had the worst fight ever. I threw our wedding photo at him. The bastard asked me to leave the house!'

She is following me inside now, dragging her suitcase behind her.

'I wanted to kill him!' she adds, making me flinch.

I pick up an empty wine bottle from the floor, and put it in the sink as the bin is overflowing.

'What happened?'

'It was a culmination of things – he knows his mother hates me, and this morning he announced she's coming to live with us! Apparently I have no say in it. He spends more time with his twenty-one-year-old son than he does with me. I feel like a guest in that house. It's hard trying to be part of a ready-made family.' She leans against the kitchen counter, taking in the mess, the mugs of half-drunk coffee, scraps of paper with scribbled notes to blog, the remains of breakfast still on the table. 'Looks like you've been having a rough time yourself,' she remarks, 'why on earth didn't you call me?'

'I'm not great company right now, to be honest.'

'God it's freezing in here,' she comments, pulling her fur-lined jacket around her. 'How about we light the fire, have a glass of wine and sit on the sofa like the old days?'

'I have to collect Liam from school later, but you have one.' I pour her a glass, while she fills me in on the latest saga, how Peter had found out she'd had an affair, and had asked her to leave.

I notice she's trembling, and feel a pang of sympathy for her, coupled with the weary sense that she has sabotaged yet another relationship. She had made an emotional speech at her wedding calling Peter her 'soul mate', 'confidante' and 'the love of her life', only to announce, less than two years later, it was all over.

She skims over the affair, saying, 'Just somebody who helped when I was at a very low ebb.' She fiddles with a lock of hair and looks away. 'It didn't mean anything. I'm going to fight this,' she says angrily. 'I've got the number of a divorce lawyer in Bath. I was hoping you'd come with me.'

When I don't respond, she says, 'You and I haven't had the best of luck.' She lights a cigarette and gazes at me through the smoke, as if we are now allied in misfortune, equally alone and adrift.

'The difference is, Holly, I didn't have a choice! And do you mind not smoking in here?'

'You haven't had to constantly compete with another family, you have your own sons,' she replies, stabbing her cigarette out in a bowl I use to serve olives.

I listen while she relates the injustices of being the second wife, how in spite of the lavish lifestyle, the exotic holidays and designer clothes, she had felt lonely and misunderstood. 'I was just a trophy,' she concludes. 'He refused point blank to talk about us having a child together. He was probably firing blanks anyway as nothing happened.' She knocks back the rest of her wine and stares away.

…maybe you should stop expecting people to love you the way you want to be loved and understand they can only love you the way they're able to… ' M had said the Christmas before he died.

She pours herself another glass and rummages around in the fridge for something to eat while I attempt to build a fire.

'Do you have any cheese or anything?'

'I was planning to go to the supermarket on the way to pick up Liam,' I begin.

'This will do,' she says, pulling out a piece of dried-up cheddar, and cutting herself a wedge. She flops down on the sofa, kicks off her boots and stretches out luxuriously.

I'm about to enquire how long she intends to stay, but as if reading my mind, she says, 'It's great to finally catch up with you, it's been way too long! We can hang out together like the old days. You must be lonely here all day by yourself.'

You're the lonely one. I think. I'm just tormented and heartbroken.

'I'm keeping busy,' I say shortly, 'what with the school run, and now swimming.'

She looks at me with a frown. 'Tell me what's really going on, Willow?' I can feel her hazel eyes boring into me. Holly and I have been friends for fifteen years and although there had been a cooling off period, we have always been there for one another. Now, I feel weighed down by the friendship. I'm not able to be the caring confidante I used to be, or help her through a messy divorce. I simply don't have the energy. But the real reason is I can't deal with her curiosity around 'that day' as I have come to think of it and the weeks leading up to it when M and I were barely speaking.

'I'm OK, Holly. Look, I have a couple of things I need to pick up from town. Why don't you relax, you must be exhausted?'

She casts me a long look, then gets up and throws a log onto the smouldering remains of the fire. 'Can I use this old magazine?' she asks, grabbing a copy of The Architectural Digest which features an article about M winning Designer of the Year, complete with illustrations of an old barn conversion.

I snatch it from her saying, 'No! I want to keep that.'

She shakes her head, as if bemused then sits down again.

'I'll be back in a couple of hours,' I say, heading out into the wintery afternoon. The temperature has plummeted. A low fog has descended over the fields, like fallen clouds. I can barely make out the junction to the main road through the gloom.

I reach Highbury and pull in close to the delicatessen where I pick up some ready-made salad, gluten-free bread, a wedge of Camembert, and some olives, flinching at the cost as the items are added up on the till, but Holly was a fussy eater. I arrive at the school early and sit in the car park with the heater full on, waiting for Liam to emerge. He saunters out later than usual, saying his English teacher had kept him back for not doing his homework properly.

'Are you not enjoying English?'

He shrugs. 'I prefer Science,' he says shortly.

I explain that Holly is staying the night as she is having a few problems. 'Why doesn't Fern come over?' he demands. 'It's been ages.'

'She's busy with school,' I tell him, conscious that I haven't seen much of my sister lately. Liam loved talking to her about black holes, and the beginning of life on earth. She had dropped in every day after M had died, but since term had started, her life had filled up with the usual heavy workload. I make a vow to call her over the weekend.

We drive home slowly through the swirling fog to find Holly fast asleep on the sofa. Liam suggests we wake her, as he wants to watch something on TV.

I gently nudge her awake. She looks around, startled. 'I must have passed out,' she says thickly.

She declines dinner, saying she wants to go to bed, 'take a sleeping pill and crash.'

'I'll make up the bed in the spare room,' I say, remembering I'd dragged M's half-packed suitcase in there. The room has become a depository of the overspill of his belongings, his surfing gear and hiking boots, some designs he'd left lying around. Holly glances around curiously. 'Gosh, what are you going to do with all his stuff,' she enquires, yawning widely.

'I haven't decided.'

'We can take it to the charity shop. You can start by putting aside the things the boys want to keep,' she begins.

'It's too soon,' I say, snapping the suitcase closed and pulling it onto the floor. She stares at me with a look of concern.

'Was M planning to leave?' she asks. 'Did you have an argument?'

'God, Holly! I can't believe you're delving around in my life when your own is in such turmoil!'

'Why won't you talk about it?' You were always complaining that M kept things from you. Now you're doing the same!'

'There's nothing to talk about! There are some sheets and an extra duvet in the cupboard,' I say, closing the door firmly behind me.

'Why are you shutting me out?' she shouts after me.

I go to bed late and lie awake, feeling scrutinised by this once-close friend with whom I had always confided everything. I drift off at last, and dream I'm trying to call M only I have forgotten his phone number. In the dislocated pattern of dreams, I'm now running down the lawn to the shed in search of him but my legs are so heavy I seem to be running on the spot. The shed is filled with his biker friends who are throwing a party. They ignore my presence as I flit amongst them like a ghost. I'm suddenly dialling random numbers and getting the engaged tone. I can hear the sound of his motorbike accelerating, then fading away. Liam is beside me, sobbing uncontrollably.

'It's all your fault, Mum!'

I wake up with a jolt, reality crashing in like a wave, leaving behind ripples of dread. I lie there motionless, as if pinned to the bed like Gulliver waiting for the tide to engulf me.

I drop Liam off at school, leaving Holly still asleep. The fog still hasn't lifted, creating an eerie stillness. I drive to the pool and swim along the tiled bottom, trying to wash away the remnants of the dream.

As I climb out, I'm approached by the lifeguard, who says, 'Excuse me, but swimming underwater is not permitted.'

I take in bulging pectorals and overdeveloped arms bursting out of a skin-tight t-shirt. A tattoo of a hissing snake curves around one wrist like a bracelet.

'I can't see you from my station.'

'I don't need watching over,' I tell him, pushing a strand of dripping hair out of my eyes. 'I did a course in freediving in the Caribbean.'

I have a sudden urge to share this precious memory in case it fades away. I want to tell him about the coral garden M and I had found, where an octopus had made its den. I want to describe the thrill of being under the sea. 'We descended to around twenty metres and stayed under for almost two minutes.'

My lung capacity has plummeted since then, from lack of exercise and too much wine (I don't intend to disclose this) but all the same, I want him to know I can still hold my breath for longer than most people. I had watched *Le Grand Bleu* over and over and, as a child, had dreamed of being a mermaid.

'Anyway, it's the best place to be when the pool is busy,' I point out, attempting a winning smile.

He is studying me as if I am some kind of alien creature from the deep. I have a fleeting fantasy of straddling him. I realise he's not interested in hearing about my magical moments beneath the waves.

'What I'm trying to explain to you,' he says, folding his arms across the bulk of his chest, 'is you're not visible from where I'm sitting and my job is to make sure everybody stays safe.'

I feel all the joy leaking away, like the water streaming off me, the memory of that dive dissolving as I'm brought back to this public pool with its echoing sounds, chemical smell, its rules and regulations.

'…and what I was trying to explain to you,' I say with equal emphasis, 'is I don't want to be visible!'

I turn away, leaving him staring after me.

I drive home with a heavy heart, concluding there was no escape from the world's watchful eye, from the constant scrutiny of others. I brake sharply before the junction, aware another speed camera has been installed, but it's too late – I see it flash, capturing the number plate as I drive past, only ten mph over the speed limit.

Even Rosewood Barn had ceased to be the haven it once was, I think, wondering how to tell Holly she couldn't stay.

She is up and dressed, and has tidied up and stacked the dishwasher. She's wearing one of M's sports shirts, but before I can comment on this, she says, 'I'm afraid you've got an unwelcome guest!'

Yes…you…

'Holly, the thing is—'

'Or maybe a whole family,' she cuts in. 'I found a load of mouse droppings in the cupboard. I'll go out and buy some traps. I'll help you get things back to the way they were.'

How could they ever be?

'I'd rather you didn't wear M's clothes,' I say, my voice trembling with rage.

She looks contrite. 'I'm sorry. I left the house in such a rush, I only managed to scoop up a few of my clothes. I threw them into your washing machine to get rid of the smell of my horrible husband.' she adds. 'He wears this vile aftershave that smells like mosquito repellent.' She flaps her hand in the air as if swatting him away.

I think of the fading scent of M soon to disappear altogether, replaced by the smell of her expensive perfume.

'What on earth are you going to do with all his things?' she says again, as if this is the most pressing issue of the day. 'We'll decide later,' she adds, seeing my expression. 'I was thinking we could drive into Bath, have lunch at The Hot Spot?' I can't believe she's suggested The Hot Spot '…we could do some shopping. The divorce lawyer can't see me until Friday. Maybe we could spend the weekend in London, go clubbing like the old days? After all, we're both single again. It's a new chapter.'

How can it already be a new chapter when we are both trying to resolve the last one? I think.

'Look, Holly, I'm sorry, but I'm afraid you can't stay.'

I simply can't deal with the tangle of your life, while trying to unravel mine…

She looks stunned. 'Are you seriously throwing me out?' I thought you were my best friend? What the hell's going on with you, Willow? We need to talk about what happened that day. Did you have an argument? I know there's something you're not telling me. We both know M wasn't Mr Perfect. But he left you all this…' she waves her arms around the barn. 'A fabulous home, two lovely sons…a future. I have nothing.'

She gazes across the wintry expanse of the garden with a bitter look.

'Frankly it would have been a lot fucking easier if Peter had died,' she says.

I stand there taking ragged breaths. I want to grab her by her mane of hair and drag her out of the barn.

I hear her say, 'Sorry, I shouldn't have said that about Peter dying, but I wasn't expecting you to act like a total bitch!'

'I just can't deal with all the questions, Holly! I need space, I'm sorry but this is a really bad time.'

Her body seems to contract, as if she's been dealt a heavy blow. 'I can't believe you're kicking me out considering what I'm going through,' she storms. 'It's all about you, you and your loss. You can't even talk about it! I know there's something you're not telling me!

When I don't respond, she says furiously, 'I've lost things too! My home, the life I had.'

'That's because it was never enough for you, was it?'

'You have no idea what I've been through, you never even called me! Don't worry, I'm delighted to leave you to your mouse invasion and fucking self-pity!'

'Good, then go,' I shout, 'and have a happy divorce!'

I retreat to M's study and sit amongst the memorabilia, feeling his absence settle over me like the thick fog outside.

I strain my ears for the sound of Holly's car leaving, but there's a deathly hush. I recall her saying she had thrown her clothes into the washing machine and leap up ready to wrench open the door of the machine mid cycle, break it if I have to and fling her dirty laundry back at her.

'...*take it easy...breathe.*' I hear M's voice issuing from his silent place on the shelf. He was one of the few people who could calm me down. I sit there taking deep slow breaths.

At last, I hear the sound of Holly's 4x4 starting up. She has gone, leaving behind a silence that is all at once blissful and filled with regret.

Note to blog:

In life there are fountains and drains it seems. Some people will shower you with their upbeat energy, others – even close friends can drain the very life forces from you, when you're at your most fragile. I've just had a huge fall-out with my best friend...

Not all friendships will survive a death, sadeyedlady has responded.

My closest friend complained I'd changed after the man I'd been married to for twenty-five years was killed in a car accident; a new follower has written.

Step back, for now and allow the dust to settle, blackwidower has suggested...*true friendship will realign and bloom again.*

I spend the afternoon sifting through old photograph albums, lost in the past.

I glance through files of M's architectural designs, plans frozen in mid-sketch, never to be realised. The foyer of a country hotel, a manor house that needed refurbishing, an old barn almost derelict, the original designs for The Hot Spot. A different contractor had been brought in and had changed the concept. The restaurant is now one of the top places to eat in Bath. I cannot bring myself to go and look at the final result; the proof that life goes on with or without you, projects continue, the story evolves. Even though you never get to know the ending.

M's 'to do' lists were endless. He jotted everything down in a black Moleskine notebook.
The sight of his spidery handwriting causes my throat to ache.

Home plants for boundary wall – alpine, succulents Alyssum and Columbine.
Order more paving stones for courtyard.
Light bulbs! Porch light, and sensors on front elevation.
Finish plans for guest house extension. Check out refectory door at RC – source wood-burning stove.
Call Morris re water feature for W.

My heart constricts. So he was planning to go ahead and put in the fountain after all. We had argued over the cost, him claiming we needed to cut down on spending. And yet he'd given away large sums of money to charity.

I scroll through his desk diary. *12th March service bike, 19th pick up new cylinder, 22nd May Eden Gorge rally.* This was highlighted in red. On 22nd June, two days after the solstice, *hospital scan.* He had never made it. I am desperate to hear his voice suddenly. I reach for my phone, call his number and listen to that recording for the hundredth time. *Hi there, leave a message and I'll get back to you in a heartbeat…cheers!*

I dredge through old texts from him to me, and me to him.
Where are u? Let's have lunch in town, I want to show you the new restaurant we're working on. The Hot Spot, where Holly had suggested we go for lunch.

My reply: *Sorry, deadline for Lifestyle, need to submit before 3!*

I remember the column I was writing that day, a piece about adding spice to your marriage by putting time aside to spend with your partner.

I switch on his phone and re-read those urgent messages that had flashed up on his phone that day.

In the end there was nothing that couldn't have waited until after the weekend. The job would have been finished on time. M knew that, and yet he still decided to drive over there in spite of my begging him not to. But once he was on one of his missions there was no stopping him.

LATE NOVEMBER

DEPRESSION: *(noun)* feelings of severe despondency

The days creep by, there is always a 'tomorrow and another tomorrow and tomorrow' and like Macbeth reacting to the news of his wife's death, I too feel as if I have become a walking shadow of my former self.

I spend the mornings online shopping, buying novels I lack the concentration to read, ordering clothes that look stunning on the model, but all wrong on me. I miss the deadline of sending them back so they are now piling up – a guilt-ridden wasteland of unwanted items I can ill afford that bring no comfort whatsoever. I scour the internet looking for Christmas presents for the boys, rather than face the shops. Old friends and companions have drifted away and who can blame them? I have alienated all the ones who tried to help, because I can't begin to explain how I feel and have given up trying.

The afternoons stretch ahead interminably, and then it's time to pick up the boys from school, providing a brief interlude of comfort; the three of us sitting down together for supper and discussing the day, helping Liam with his homework, sipping too much wine, before the long night closes in again.

Note to blog:

Grief can turn you into a recluse. In my case, it's probably a good thing as nobody would want to hang out with me. I'm not even enjoying my own company right now.

Not sharing your grief with others denies them the chance of understanding what you're going through and offering you some comfort, lifeafterdeath has commented.

sadeyedlady has suggested acquiring a pet because animals never let you down.

I wonder if I should get a dog, something M had resisted, reminding me of our plan to travel once the boys had left home.

A new follower has responded with '*making an emotional transfer to an animal is not the answer. Try to surround yourself with sympathetic friends instead.*

Sympathy inevitably runs its course. Those caring friends and acquaintances will grow tired of your woes, and drift away like dust on the wind. Withdrawing for a while is a good thing, blackwidower has suggested.

DECEMBER

Carol singers walk purposefully up the driveway and stand in an arc singing fa la la la la, la la la la. I duck down behind the sofa, reminding myself to pull down the blinds in the future then sneak away upstairs, leaving their songs unheard. They know I'm in. I haven't left the barn for days, the jeep is parked in the driveway and the lights are on, so they carry on singing, to no avail.

I have tried to ignore the run up to Christmas; the frosted shop windows displaying jolly Santa Clauses on sleighs, the ubiquitous seasonal hits piped through supermarket speakers – it all feels as if it's happening from afar, like watching a pantomime performance from the back row of the theatre.

I have been invited to a party by Crispin Le Fanu, the author of the global best seller *The Self* – an exploration of the human condition. Crispin had commissioned M&J to design a bespoke library at The Old Mill House on the outskirts of Highbury and the two of them had struck up a friendship. After the funeral Crispin had sent a beautiful handwritten letter on headed notepaper, saying that M had left 'footprints on the sands of time'.

I decide to decline the invitation, thinking there would be lots of people I know attending when I see he's added a note at the bottom.

Willow, my dear, I do hope you'll come so I can show you the splendid job M did on the library. It is a chef d'oeuvre! A few people from your neck of the woods are coming, so pop in early if you want to avoid the crowd!

Note to blog:

I realise that sooner or later I'm going to have to face the world. I can't stay a recluse forever. It is the season to be jolly after all, or at least a bit more sociable. I've been invited to a Christmas party where there will be people I know. Any advice?

You're going to have to get used to going out alone, lifeafterdeath has countered. *Put on your favourite outfit, and step bravely out into what is now your new life.*

Later rather than sooner as timing is everything, blackwidower has responded. *Otherwise brace yourself for the endless commiserations.*

I find myself vacillating between climbing into bed with a glass of wine and switching the electric blanket on or braving a world which I will eventually have to be a part of. I spend hours debating what to wear. My newly single status has made choosing the right outfit a minefield.

Before, I would inevitably dress for M in a slinky clinging outfit, but that might be construed as a sign I'm back on the market, which is not the case. I end up trying on nearly every garment in my wardrobe, starting with a sheath dress in swirls of greens and browns that M had loved. Depending on the light, the fabric changed colour like a chameleon. I gaze at myself in the mirror remembering the last time I'd worn it, to the opening of The Brass Monkey pub in Chorley. M&J had designed the rustic interior, with tables made from old whiskey casks, and chairs from discarded wooden pallets.

'You look ravishing and I'm going to ravish you,' he'd grinned when we got home. I was a bit tipsy, while he had given up drinking by then and become the designated driver. He had carried me up the stairs, and watched with amusement as I slithered out of the dress like a snake shedding its skin.

'Loving you,' he'd murmured, afterwards.

M saw life in the present continuous. A work in progress, in which time was unlimited, infinite like space. He genuinely believed he had enough of it to give away. I have come to see my life in the past imperfect.

The sheath dress hangs loosely on me, the weight loss I fought so hard for in the old days is a battle easily won since then. I look slightly reptilian, all rough skin and goose bumps in need of a good sloughing after months of neglect. I try on a long tube dress that turns me into an exclamation mark and discard it immediately. Then pour myself a glass of wine, pull on a clinging bright red outfit, jacket and skirt with a slit up the side and pirouette in front of the mirror, reminding myself of my mother. 'The Scarlet Widow,' I conclude. My long purple skirt is more suited to a music festival, the calf length stretchy black number makes me think of a widow in a straitjacket. All I need is the Widow's cap, which strikes me as a fate almost worse than death itself.

Next an old favourite, a maroon silky knee-length outfit, only the hem is unravelling, like my mood. I return to the first option, the chameleon dress and regard myself critically. The shadows and plains of my face have altered in the last few months, my eyes have dulled as if an inner light has been extinguished. I dab on more concealer, realising it's almost nine o'clock – so much for arriving early. I quickly grab my bag and keys and set off in the jeep through the dark country lanes, feeling M's presence beside me in the passenger seat.

'I'm not going to stay long,' I tell him. 'I'll just take a look at the library you designed, then make a quick exit.'

This constructed dialogue between us, in which I put words into his mouth has sustained me, but tonight I can't seem to gauge his response. I am suddenly afraid the memory of his voice is fading. I pull into the side of the lane, fumble in my bag for my phone, dial his number and listen to his deep voice.

Hi there, leave a message and I'll get back to you in a heartbeat…cheers!

My throat swells, I grab a tissue and wipe away the tears plus most of the concealer and consider turning back. I think of lifeafterdeath's comment – *sooner or later you are going to have to face the world* – and pull out onto the main road towards Upper Highbury.

The grounds of The Old Mill House are lit up with coloured lights which have been draped along the topiaried hedges, and around the ornamental pond. A line of cars is parked higgledy-piggledy along one side of the narrow driveway.

I make my way towards the house, pausing on the steps of the over-lit porch. What is it about porches? They seem to symbolise both an entrance and an exit. The party appears to be in full swing – the crowd is shouting and laughing raucously, their joyful reverberations making me flinch. I hesitate, tempted to turn and flee. M would have forged on in a powerhouse of energy and good cheer, greeting people effortlessly, withdrawing as soon as he'd had enough. I take a deep breath, then enter the fray looking around for Crispin but there's no sign of him. A young waiter in a black jacket greets me politely with a glass of chilled wine. I ask him where the library is, and he points through the crowd to a door on the far side of the room. I attempt to squeeze past a cluster of people but am stopped in my tracks by a glamorous-looking couple who introduce themselves to me as Don and Di Lambert. Don announces he is Crispin's literary agent, before launching into a tale about his and Di's recent Greek holiday, all their combined likes and dislikes parrying back and forth. 'We don't really like Greek food do we, darling one? It's the same on every menu, wherever you go.' I edge away in mid description of a rabbit stew that had resembled 'Golgotha and the Valley of Bones'.

A small, stout man I recognise from somewhere edges towards me, announcing he has been recently widowed but has started enjoying himself again. He gazes at my cleavage, muttering 'we've only got one chance in this life, might as well grab it with both hands.' I move away swiftly and forge through the crowd towards the library to where Crispin, in a midnight-blue smoking jacket, is standing in the centre of a group of people.

He pauses, mid-conversation, exclaiming, 'Ah, here she is, the lovely Willow! Max's wife, he adds proudly as if M is still alive. I smile and say hello, taking in M's creation. The entire room is lined with deep, book-lined shelves, interspersed with rich bog oak cabinets, the ancient darker wood against the lighter oak lending a contrast of texture grain and colour. It is breathtaking. My chest swells with pride. M has left his stamp on the world.

A row of Crispin's hardback edition of *The Self* is proudly displayed on the centre shelf.

Everyone seems to be talking at once, in a babble of congratulations: such a talent, extraordinary, what a legacy… I can only nod and smile, hoping that

M could hear their words of praise from some other realm.

Crispin pulls me to one side. 'So brave of you to come, dear girl, only stay as long as you feel.'

'Thanks,' I say, thinking he of all people understands the debilitating effects of grief. I recall he'd lost his wife some years ago and had written about it in *The Self*, something to the effect that grief was 'transformative', giving life meaning and relevance, thereby becoming 'a portal to faith'. I'd re-read the passage recently, thinking in my case it was the opposite. Life seemed to have lost all meaning, and I had lost my faith.

'I'm glad I came,' I reply, gulping back my wine, aware the waiter has filled my glass again.

'Keep the faith, dear girl,' he mutters, astutely.

The wine is soaring to my head. I hadn't eaten anything since breakfast. I recall seeing a table laden with food in the drawing room. I thank Crispin for inviting me, then head back into melee, fortified by the wine and kind words.

I am cramming an oversized piece of sushi into my mouth when I see Jessica McFarlane, whose son is in the same class as Liam at school, on the other side of the room. I have never liked Jessica; a fawning, invasive woman with an insatiable need for gossip, so swiftly turn away, only to collide with her husband, Nigel. 'Willow, good to see you again. Life goes on, eh?' He leans towards me, his eyes glinting behind thick glasses. 'If you ever need some financial advice, please call my office.' Nigel works for an investment company and is always looking for people with cash to spare. 'Have you thought about how you're going to manage your affairs from now on?'

'I'll be fine,' I answer shortly, although I will probably be bankrupt by the age of sixty having squandered the remains of my life insurance on online shopping and red wine. But I don't want to talk about it with Nigel McFarlane.

'Here,' he says, thrusting his card at me. He leans forward, murmuring, 'Call me on my private line any time.'

'I'm fine,' I repeat. 'M took out life insurance for me and the boys.' I force a smile on my face and am about to edge away when Jessica, in an ice-blue caftan, suddenly swoops down like a giant bird of prey. Her expression is one of abject pity, her gushing tones drowning out the chatter around us.

'Willow! You poor darling! This time of the year must be so hard, coping all alone!'

Just when I had managed to put aside my grief for the time being, was trying to be the proverbial 'merry widow', it seems I must assume a melancholic expression to match the direction of the conversation. It strikes me being 'all alone' would be far more preferable right now. Jessica's pitying face causes something to rise inside me.

'I'm doing fine,' I say shortly, 'what have you been up to?' I add, attempting to deflect the conversation back to her.

'Must be hard to fill your time, now you don't have your column anymore,' she continues, ignoring me. 'You should join us on the committee. We're trying to raise funds for the NSPCC this year.'

'I'm already busy with M's charities,' I lie.

'Of course, Kids in Crisis. I liaised with your husband at the beginning of the year about holding a joint fund-raising event, but… Well, he was a bit elusive. Anyway, it was not to be.' She shakes her head sadly. 'M was a true philanthropist who made the rest of us feel horribly unworthy,' she simpers with a look that seems to be directed at me.

We are interrupted by a woman wearing a headband, sporting plastic reindeer horns which sway with the movement of her head. I recognise her as Susie Devine and recall there is nothing divine about her. To my horror, she blurts, 'Willow, poor love, so tragic… How did it happen? What was the actual cause of Max's death?'

My skin is prickling beneath the chameleon dress, the wine has turned to acid in my throat. I feel exposed, caught in the headlamps of these ghoulish women and the group gathering around them, all of whom wait silently for my response.

'Not the time or place,' I mumble and my voice has taken on a haunted, echoey pitch as if it has risen from the grave. 'Excuse me,' I hear the death voice say. I spin around, knocking into a woman in black chiffon who spills her wine over a man who is busy trying to chat her up.

Nigel immediately places his hand on my waist, muttering, 'Steady.'

I push him away and attempt to make a dash for it, but Susie Devine grabs my arm and jerks me backwards, her horns swaying madly.

A murderous rage swells in my chest. I have acquired an excess of Dutch courage with or without alcohol since losing M.

'For god's sake, what else would you like to know?' I hiss. 'How much money did he leave me, although Nigel has already covered that! Were we arguing when it happened? What were his last words…voyeurs, both of you, desperate to know the details so you can gossip about it over coffee.' I take a shaky breath, adding, 'You could have asked about the projects he was working on. The Manor Hotel refurbishment, the Lighthouse conversion, Time and Tythe, which is now a gastro pub. Have you even taken a look at the library?' I storm, waving my hand in the air, and almost hitting Susie in the face. 'M actually won Designer of the Year award for the Huntington Hall extension before he— You could have asked about the living years!'

This comes out with a loud sob.

There's an appalled silence. Everyone seems to be holding their breath. Susie Devine lets out a low whistle. She speaks with terrible emphasis. 'What I was actually going to tell you, Willow, is that your zip is undone!'

There is a sound of throat clearing while I make a clumsy attempt to reach behind my back.

For an awful moment, it seems Nigel is about to do the honours. I feel his hands hovering near the small of my back, but Jessica is shooting him a killer look. Does she really think I'm interested in her ghastly husband?

I push through the crowd, slamming my almost empty wine glass onto a wooden table, knocking over a framed photograph of Crispin's deceased wife. I hear someone mutter, 'Lost her husband…very odd circumstances.'

I dive towards the front door, and stumble across the porch.

…*in the end a porch signals a departure.*

I am hurling myself into the darkness towards the jeep which is jammed in between two cars. I fumble in my bag for the keys, then back out rapidly, slamming into the car behind me, before scraping the one in front with my bumper.

I am heading towards the main road, Susie Devine's voice echoing in my head. *What was the actual cause of Max's death?*

He stopped breathing, I should have replied cuttingly, before making a dignified exit.

Note to blog:

I should never have ventured out – it was too soon. I can deal with anything except the dreaded pity, which leaves you feeling even more isolated and wretched.

Pity weeps crocodile tears, blackwidower has commented. *…empathy flows from the heart.'*

In the morning I receive a curt email from Jessica.

'We regret you feel so misunderstood, Willow. Everybody is trying to do their best under the circumstances.'

Circumstances? Is that what losing M is to them? A circumstance?

'Unfortunately, two cars were damaged last night. One was parked in front of you, the other which was behind you belongs to me and Nigel. I have attached the details of our insurance company, and hope that you will have the goodwill and dignity to sort it out. I have given your email details to Don and Di Lambert whose car was parked in front of yours. By the way, I thought you should know, Susie lost her husband too last year.

Regards, Jessica

PS You missed the raffle, so perhaps you would be good enough to send your donation directly to the NSPCC.'

I ignore Jessica's email for the whole morning, fuming at her choice of words. Goodwill and dignity. Of course I'm guilty. Guilt is my constant companion, living side by side with grief and now shame. It is a large black crow sitting on my shoulder. I console myself with the thought that I would never have asked Susie how her husband had died, had I known.

I send back a brief note.

'I regret any damage or inconvenience I've caused and have attached my insurance details. If you could forward it to Don, I would be grateful. I hope you now have all the information you need. I add, somewhat cryptically.

Regards, Willow.'

I ignore her request for a donation, concluding M had donated enough to last a lifetime.

Note to blog:

If you do decide to go out, choose the right event, for example an evening with a small group of loving friends who want the very best for you.

I follow this up with a short description of the evening, keeping the location anonymous – although Jessica and her entourage were unlikely to read my blog.

I can't resist writing: *avoid loud, tactless women wearing reindeer horns at all costs!*

There is a string of responses from other posters, agreeing to only venture out with close, loving friends in the near future.

blackwidower comes back with ...*at least it gave them something to talk about! Sounds like you grabbed the bull by its horns, waywardwidow*, he's added with a smiling emoji.

MID DECEMBER

I set off for Highbury to buy a Christmas tree, trying hard not to dwell on this time last year, when M and I had one of our worst arguments. He had been busy all week, sometimes not getting home until eleven o'clock at night. He was home early that wintry evening, only to announce he wanted to spend the weekend in Cornwall, 'catching some waves'. I sensed immediately he wanted to go alone.

'I'll be surfing or hiking both days, so it won't be that exciting for you,' he said. He often surfed in the winter months, even though there were no lifeguards on the beaches, which made me uneasy, especially in the light of the accident he'd had as a teenager, when he'd almost drowned. But he claimed there was always somebody watching out for him. He'd returned late that Sunday evening. It was the shortest day of the year, the winter solstice, and felt like the middle of the night when he finally walked in. He planted an absent-minded kiss on my forehead, before dropping his overnight bag on the floor and heading straight for the shed. I followed him down and found him tinkering with his bike. I shouted over the roar of the engine that we needed to talk, but he was so absorbed he didn't even glance up. I waited with my hands clamped over my ears and at last he held up a grease-stained palm intimating he would be with me in five minutes. I paced the barn, my chest heavy with the thing I needed to get off it – the fact that when he was finally home, he was more absent than ever. After waiting another twenty minutes, I returned to the shed and found him talking on the phone. I heard him mutter, 'See you shortly.'

A friend of his had broken down close to Winford Gap, he'd explained. 'I'll take the pick-up. Shouldn't take long. I'll call you.' He was heading for the door, already mentally on his mission.

He didn't call and after numerous attempts to reach him I'd given up and gone to bed. He returned after midnight, claiming it had taken much longer than he thought. There was no phone signal where he was, he'd added.

I'd accused him of always rushing to the aid of some random person, putting their needs first, leaving no time for me and the boys. I demanded to know why hadn't he suggested we all go to Cornwall? Surely he wanted to spend his precious free time with his family? He'd argued that he'd needed time to clear his head. There was a lot going on at the office.

M seldom lost his temper, rather he would withdraw, saying we would talk once I'd calmed down. This time he snapped, 'Can't deal with the inquisition. I'll sleep in the spare room.'

In the morning I found him in his study, where he often retreated when things became heightened. He was poring over the plans for the barn extension. He wanted it to be all open plan, a place where Sam could practise his drums and he and Liam could bring their friends, whereas I'd suggested turning it into a guest wing with a view to renting it out. We had yet to find a compromise.

'Can we talk?' I'd enquired, trying to keep my voice level.

It was the fact he didn't even turn around that pushed me over the edge. That and a sleepless night, coupled with the fear something was brewing, like the storm that would arrive on a different solstice. I told him he was becoming emotionally and physically unavailable along with a lot of other things, my voice growing more strident when he still didn't respond.

He remained as still and silent as a rock, his eyes fixed on the screen, as if lost in the complexity of his creation.

I lurched for the plug where his two computer screens had been carefully hooked up to different outlets and pulled both of them from their sockets. In my anger, I knocked over an antique lamp we'd bought together, which crashed onto the flagstone floor, the bulb splintering.

On the main screen, the draft he'd been working on flickered and vanished.

He turned towards me at last, his face a mask of fury and disbelief, then stood up and slammed his fist into the wall. 'Have you quite finished destroying my office and sabotaging my plans?'

'I'm sorry,' I said, shocked by his response, the blank screen and shattered lamp. 'What about our plans?' I'd asked, my voice trembling. M may have been a brilliant designer and architect, but this was my home too.

'Scuppered,' he stated, clutching his bruised hand and there was something chillingly final in the choice of word. He stood up then and pushed past me, heading for the door. I heard the roar of the bike starting up and cursed myself for having lost my temper, while still fuming over the way he'd ignored me, and then disappeared yet again. I was suddenly afraid we were in trouble.

Please come back, so we can talk about it, I texted. *Loving you.*

Will sleep at the office tonight, was his short reply.

He didn't return until noon the following day, then headed straight into the shower. I made a pot of coffee and brought him up a mug, then perched on the edge of the bed, waiting. He stayed in the bathroom for ages before stepping back into the room, a towel wrapped tightly around his waist as if sealing himself off from me.

I was desperate to ask where he'd been, but said, instead, 'Did you manage to retrieve your designs?' I handed him the mug of coffee, but he placed it on the bedside table and left it there untouched.

'Most of them,' he answered, in a flat voice.

'I'm sorry about the lamp, and for over-reacting.'

'I was going to show you the plans, once I'd worked out the layout of the kitchen,' he said, moving towards the wardrobe.

'I thought it was going to be open plan? I didn't realise you were going to put in a kitchen?'

'You wanted a guest wing. I was working on that,' he stated, disarming me.

'You never said anything.'

'You never asked.'

He pulled on a clean pair of jeans and a sweatshirt, then grabbed his blue scarf, saying, 'I need to get back to the office – I've a pile of work to do.'

We managed to talk it through later. I highlighted how difficult it was to get his attention. He reminded me of his inability to multitask, reiterating he was always there for me and the boys.

'It doesn't feel like it at times.'

'That has got more to do with your feelings than mine,' was his response. 'Maybe you should stop expecting people to love you the way you want to be loved and understand they can only love you the way they're able to,' he'd said then.

We had kissed and made up, and I'd spent weeks trawling the antique markets looking for a lamp to replace the one I'd broken. I never found one.

He had loved me the only way he was able, I concluded. While I had been searching for some other kind of textbook affirmation of love.

A memory of our final argument comes unbidden to mind.

If only we knew what tripped so thoughtlessly off our tongue would be the last words ever heard, how differently might we have phrased them, I wonder?

Note to blog:

It's hard not to dwell on the inevitable arguments and bitter wrangling that are part of married life ...or regret the things you did or didn't say. To accept that you can never put it right then learn to live with that regret.

Regret is often related to a perceived opportunity, blackwidower has commented. *But if the opportunity never presented itself, there is nothing to regret.*

I am still thinking about this hours later, only to conclude that the opportunity to take a different course had presented itself, but I had chosen not to take it.

I choose the tallest tree on offer, thinking I would make this first Christmas without M the best it could possibly be, then stop off at the delicatessen and buy a small hamper which I fill with pate, cheeses and a bottle of wine for Frida. I plan to drop in on her on the way home and check if Sean's electrician has fixed her porch light, but her cottage is in darkness. I guess she has gone to visit her mother in Devon and decided to stay up there for a few days, so leave it on the front step with a note saying, *Happy Christmas from Willow and*— I'm about to add *M,* but write instead *..and the boys.*

I pull up the driveway, wondering how on earth I'm going to get the tree out of the pick-up truck. I should have bought a smaller one, or even a fake one, but this thought evaporates into the pine-scented air once I've managed to drag it inside, leaving a trail of needles in its wake. It's a small triumph, a sign I will not be defeated, felled like the unfortunate spruce itself. I light the cinnamon-scented candle Frida had given me, then pour myself a glass of red wine and sit on the floor feeling oddly at peace. A luminous, wintry light streams through the skylight. It feels like a kind of transfusion, pouring into an aching wound and, for a moment, the pain of losing M eases, dissolving into the fragrant air.

On Christmas morning I busy myself making our traditional breakfast of pancakes. Sam squeezes fresh oranges, Liam sets the table and the mood is light, almost normal again. After breakfast I suggest a game of charades which the boys had loved when they were younger and we make a valiant attempt at enacting a couple of film titles. It strikes me we are already acting out a charade, a game of pretence at normality. The boys grow tired of it, after I fail to guess *'The Sons of Anarchy,'* even though they are pointing frantically at themselves and making angry faces. They head upstairs, Sam to FaceTime his new girlfriend Caz, giving Liam strict instructions not to come into his room.

If only I could fast forward this day, I think, wake up and find it was all over, or better still re-wind to a past Christmas, and somehow change the direction of all the Christmases to come.

My mother arrives at noon wearing a low-cut crimson dress which shows off her famous cleavage, a new man trailing in her wake. This one is at least ten years younger than her, with a shock of peppery hair and a thick grey beard. He introduces himself as Jeff Darlington, originally from Tennessee, but now working in Bristol, before handing over a magnum of champagne. I gather he's in the music business and a friend of my Aunt Camilla, mother's sister, who lives in New York. She had insisted he look up Mother while he was in England. He was currently working on a talent show, featuring songwriters competing against one another to see who could come up with the most 'catchy' lyrics. I can barely concentrate on this, as I'm too busy trying to adjust to my mother's face. I recall her talking about undergoing some kind of thread lift, and if this is what she's done it has erased nearly all her lines and most of her expression. It also has the curious effect of making her cat-like eyes look smaller while stretching her lips into a kind of grimace.

'Are we too early? she asks, her feline gaze taking in my grubby shirt and leggings.

'I'm still preparing dinner,' I answer. 'I'll go up and change in a while.' I feel weary already at the thought of the long afternoon and evening stretching ahead. 'Come in.'

The fire is lit, the tree is twinkling with coloured lights and, on the surface, everything is normal. Only M's absence hangs like a miasma over Rosewood Barn.

'Goodness what a big tree,' she comments, 'I should have brought you some decent decorations to put on it.'

I ignore this dig at the motley collection of baubles and bedraggled tinsel I'd draped over the tree. Jeff is now gazing up at the ceiling with its giant A frame crisscrossed with beams which are peppered with LED lights, half of which have gone out, like extinguished stars.

'This is impressive,' he breathes. 'Did you undertake the conversion?'

'Yes well, M, my husband, mainly,' I reply.

I cannot bring myself to say 'deceased.' 'Late' seems even more inappropriate. M was always late in any case. Late in this world only to arrive early in the next.

'I'm very sorry for your loss,' Jeff says quietly. He squeezes my hand. 'It's a lonely ole road to travel.'

I smile and nod, thinking it sounded like a line from a country song.

My mother stands there rigidly, glancing at the trail of pine needles on the floor, the dust and cobwebs accumulating around the fireplace.

'You must let me send my cleaner over,' she begins. 'Are you short of money, because if that's the case…'

'No! I'm fine,' I cut in, 'how about we have a drink?'

'Any news from your editor?' she wants to know, as I hand her a glass brimming with champagne.

'I hope to hear something in the new year,' I reply evasively.

This is not true. There has been no word from Jason. 'Interesting Lives' now belongs to Susannah Frost, who according to one review has 'a punchy delivery and a wittily acerbic view of life'. Whereas mine has become skewed. Susannah is a rising star in the journalistic world, while I appear to have written myself off with writer's block.

To my relief, Fern arrives laden with gifts and we leave Mother and Jeff beside the fire and retreat to the kitchen area to prepare dinner. In an attempt to keep things the same, I'd decided on the traditional roast turkey, but nothing is the same and the effort of trying to pretend is almost tipping me over the edge. The only way I can get through it is to get numbingly drunk, I think, filling my glass to the brim with champagne.

Fern and I make a toast. 'To the silly season being over,' she says. My sister has come to dread Christmas, saying it's a time for families and that she's given up hope of ever having one of her own. She has just turned forty-four and has also given up online dating.

'It's only at this time of year I wish I had someone to go to parties with,' she says, 'then I remind myself a man is for life, not just for Christmas!' We laugh and drink more champagne before moving on to Mother and the hirsute Jeff, taking bets on how long the relationship would last.

'She'll tire of him in six months,' Fern predicts.

'She's determined to turn the clock back,' I say. 'I can't gauge her mood anymore.'

'The price of beauty!' Fern sighs. 'I could have bought a three-bedroomed house with a garden with what she's spent on cosmetic procedures.' Fern rents the ground floor of a terraced house close to the school. It has a small back yard, which she has filled with pot plants and has strung up hanging baskets over the entrance.

'I wish we could,' I say, 'that is, turn the clock back.'

'Once this first Christmas is over, it'll get easier,' she says gently.

'I hope you're right,' I sigh, a vision of all the birthdays and anniversaries looming up year after year, each one a painful reminder of past celebrations.

We sit down to dinner at last, after Mother having reminded me to 'run upstairs and change into something more fitting.'

Sam makes a brave attempt to carve the turkey, which is dry and unappetising. In fact, the meal is far from impressive, but the conversation flows, helped by the champagne and wine and I start to warm to Jeff, who entertains the boys with stories of his biking days when he owned a Harley-Davidson. 'Rode that Fat Boy all the way east,' he tells them. 'Best time of my whole goddam life.' My mother is glaring at him, but it's difficult to work out if she's interested or appalled by this remark.

Appalled, as it turns out. 'Beastly things,' she says, 'I would like to see them banned.'

Jeff winks at the boys, who want to know about the best years of his life riding the Harley.

'I hope you boys won't attempt to ride your father's motorbike. You need to sell that dangerous machine, Willow, before they get any silly ideas.'

The boys send me alarmed looks.

'It's fine, Mother, nobody is planning to ride it.' I re-fill her glass, while Jeff thankfully moves the conversation on with, 'So who can come up with the best Christmas lyrics?'

'Christmas songs are so cheesy,' Sam wails. He tells Jeff he is now the drummer with his own band, and about the song he and Lennie are writing.

'It's called "Out of the Shadows."'

'I'd be very keen to hear that,' Jeff grins.

Outside, a light snow starts to fall. I shiver in the green silk dress I had put on to please my mother, and fill my glass with Prosecco since we have finished the champagne. We unwrap predictable presents; scarves and hats for the boys, a smart SMEG toaster for me from Mother, while Fern and I have bought each other similar tops from a boutique we both love on the high street. I hold up the sheer biscuit-coloured cardigan that appears to be woven together by silken threads.

'It's beautiful,' I exclaim, hugging her.

'It looks like a cobweb,' Liam comments.

'Spun by a black widow?' I giggle, giddy from the champagne.

My mother attempts a frown. 'What a dreadful thought,' she says.

I had bought the boys leather biker's jackets, which I could ill afford, but was determined not to stint on this first Christmas without M. I hesitate before handing them over in front of my mother, but she doesn't make the association. 'Very nice, but I can't see them keeping you dry,' she comments.

After dinner, the boys and I retreat to M's study and sit amongst the memorabilia; photos of him on the bike, or surfing, the two of us on our wedding anniversary arm in arm against a background of glittering turquoise sea.

I gaze upwards to the shelf where the earthenware urn is flanked by two thick candles. We tell ourselves we will let go of the ashes when the time is right. M wanted to give his body to science, but he never got around to filling in the forms, so I chose the second option which was cremation. But the thought of driving to some chilly Atlantic beach and scattering them in a grey ocean is a bleak prospect. We light the candles and sit holding hands.

'We have a new bike rally game, Dad,' Liam says. 'I'll show it to you, as soon as I'm in your world.' He turns to his older brother for approval, but Sam snaps, 'whatever.'

We emerge, emotions spent, into the parallel world of my mother who has drunk too much and is now lecturing Fern on her single status. 'You've always been far too fussy. I'll never forget that lovely man, Tom. Wasn't he in property? Then there was the Frenchman, who was very charming. You'll end up a spinster if you don't act soon! Who'd have thought I'd have a widow and a spinster for daughters,' she says, as if both were terrible afflictions. Fern takes it in her stride. 'Tom turned out to be gay, and Yves was already married and wanted a mistress! I'm not going to settle for somebody just for the sake of it!'

Unable to rile her older daughter, my mother now looks squiffily at me, taking in my tear-stained face and ruined eye make-up.

'As for you, Willow, you have got to stop wallowing!'

WALLOW: *(verb)* chiefly of large mammals; to roll about or lie in mud or water to keep cool, or avoid 'biting insects'.

Or pestiferous mothers, I think angrily.

Something rises inside me as it always does when I'm around her. I have never been like Fern; able to shrug off what trips so loosely off my mother's tongue.

'It's only been six months! One hundred and eighty-seven days! M and I were together for almost nineteen years, but you wouldn't be able to relate to that!'

'What a wicked thing to say,' she flares.

Jeff gets up swiftly, 'how 'bout we take a rain-check. It's been a big 'ole day. Give the family some space.'

My mother glares at him, her face a frozen mask. 'Sit down, Jeffrey! This is my family, and I will say my piece for what it's worth. What I was trying to say, Willow, is that you need to move on with your life; especially for the sake of the boys.'

'Move on?' I reiterate, 'in other words write off the last twenty years!'

Sam and Liam are now nudging one another, planning an escape. 'Let's go play Mission Impossible,' Sam mutters.

'Oh, for goodness sake, I didn't mean it like that,' she flares, waving away her words with a flip of her hand, her bracelets jangling.

It's too late. I have lost the run of myself. 'You never liked him, Mother . . you never even tried to get to know him. M was a good person through and through, and there aren't many people I can say that about! Everyone wrote amazing things about him.'

Fern moves over and puts her arms around me.

'I'm sorry, Willow, I am very sad for you,' Mother is saying. 'I tried hard to engage with Max, but he always made me feel as if I was interfering . . a bit of a nuisance,' she adds with a wounded look.

'He knew you didn't approve of him. What did you expect?'

'I didn't expect you to run off and get married to a man you knew nothing about,' she states angrily.

'And yet our marriage stood the test of time …unlike…'

'Leave it, Willow,' Fern hisses.

But it's too late, the unspoken has been spoken. '…any of your relationships.'

Mother sits bolt upright, her impressive chest heaving, her face so taut I'm afraid the thread or whatever it is, is about to snap.

'I too have loved and lost in case you've forgotten,' she announces dramatically. 'Timmy never even had a chance to grow up and have a family of his own!'

We are all silent. Nobody has mentioned Timmy, for some time. Timmy was the only child from her first marriage to a wealthy fashion designer. He died at the age of fifteen after being catapulted from the back of a motorbike, his head slamming into a low concrete wall. He hadn't been wearing a helmet. I was only five at the time but have a vivid memory of an adventurous boy with laughing brown eyes and a shock of muddy blonde hair. I remember the aftermath of the accident, Mother taking to her bed for weeks leaving Fern and me in the care of a nanny. Her third husband - my father, had died of heart failure by then. It was the nanny who had explained to us in her clumsy way that Timmy would not be coming home, that he'd gone to a better place. For a long time, I wished Fern and I could go to this better place wherever it was, away from our mother's grief, her erratic behaviour and mercurial moods, her often violent temper. She didn't talk about Timmy much over the years, but both Fern and I knew she had never managed to get over his death and that neither of us could fill the gap he'd left behind. It was only when Sam was born that I understood how devastating it must have been for her to lose a beloved son.

It had been a cause of great angst to her that M owned a motorbike. But she took comfort in the fact I seldom rode with him after the boys were born.

'He would have turned forty-five this year,' she sobs, fumbling for her handkerchief.

Two years older than M.

I can think of nothing to say in response. It is all too much suddenly, grief on grief, layer upon layer. I don't know how to comfort her. Fern moves forward and tries to take her hand, but she shakes her off, saying 'time to leave, Jeffrey. I think I've heard quite enough.'

Jeff is already fetching her coat and finding her car keys. She attempts to snatch them from him, but he says, 'take it easy, Michelle, let me drive.'

Liam comes back into the room, followed by Sam, who is trying to restrain him. 'You don't have to go, Gran,' he says anxiously. 'You can stay.'

Mother has a soft spot for him, mainly because he reminds her of Timmy. Liam has the same vivid imagination and curiosity about life, she'd said once. She is always hugging him and buying him little gifts. She then gives the equivalent in money to Sam saying, 'I know you like to buy things for yourself young man.' This seems to be a pattern. Fern would always be at the receiving end of the gifts. I was given money – although that had ended abruptly after I married M.

'I'll come back and see you another time, darling boy,' she says, patting his arm, her lower lip quivering.

I stand by the front door, knowing there's nothing I can say or do to salvage the evening. Jeff grabs my hand in both of his and squeezes it gently.

'Sometimes you gotta let it out,' he murmurs. He raises my hand in an old-fashioned gesture and brushes it with his thick beard, adding, 'then you hav'ta let it go.'

They make their way towards the car, Jeff guiding Mother along the slippery paving stones using the torch on his phone to light the way. I still haven't replaced the outside lights and the path has become overgrown with weeds so it's a mission to get to the car.

Liam glares at me. 'Why did you have to say that, Mum? Everyone leaves because of you!'

I stand there, feeling the weight of failure settle like a leaden cloak around me, Liam's accusing voice echoing in my head… *everyone leaves because of you.*

I am a killjoy, a useless single mother, a bad daughter.

I am Willow the wicked widow.

Note to blog:

Christmas is a testing time for families in general but a major ordeal for the grieving. The forced jollity, putting on a good face and trying to do everything that's expected of you has pushed me over the edge. I just can't wait for it to be over!

blackwidower is back with, *Christmas or no Christmas, forget about living up to other people's expectations and allow yourself to howl at the moon if you need to, get blind drunk or just sit with your memories and allow the grief to wash over you.*

Wallow I think, smiling to myself.

The boys disappear upstairs, and Fern and I open another bottle of prosecco and flop onto the sofa.

'I feel awful! I shouldn't have spoken to her like that. I should have just let it go.'

'You can't allow her to get to you every time,' Fern says. 'Come here, you wallowing widow,' she adds, hugging me. 'At least you're not a spinster destined to spin out the years at the wheel, without hope of ever finding love!'

'You'll meet somebody, I know it.' I have said this so often, it has started to lose meaning. Now it strikes me it might be better to go through life alone rather than find that elusive love, only to lose it again.

We talk about Timmy and the effect his death had on us. Of our unconventional childhood brought up by a solipsistic mother who believed the sun, moon and stars shone only for her, while Fern and I circled in her orbit. About our very different fathers; Fern's a struggling actor, who had left our mother for a younger model - in both senses of the word - soon after Fern was born. I was the result of a passionate love affair with the famous photographer Tony Monroe. That marriage had lasted less than a year. While Timmy's father had been the love of Mother's life, only to die tragically in a helicopter accident. He had left her a manor house in Charlton Haven plus a substantial fortune, more than enough to last her a lifetime. We discuss the nannies and au pairs, the constant changing of schools. The many lovers who had come and gone. Then there was what Fern and I called the 'angry years', when our mother's beauty was fading and she had railed against living in the country, hating the weather, her life in general. Restless and needy, always yearning for pastures new, forgetting to pick us up from school, to buy our school uniform, our doctor's appointments. She hired a cook and a chauffeur to drive us to school so we seldom saw her, and Fern took on the role of helping me with my homework every evening. Once I started university, I saw even less of my mother, although she would come up to London from time to time to shop and take me out for lunch. She never asked about my course, or if I was seeing anyone. She didn't want to know about my new passion of rock climbing – why on earth would you want to do something so dangerous and unnecessary? Rather she would regale me with her latest drama; a lover who had walked out on her, the loneliness of living in the country, inevitably ending on an angry note as to why I hadn't been back to see her for weeks.

M was like a soothing breath of healing air, coming into my life and paying me all the attention I lacked – at least at first.

'I know it's hard, Willow,' Fern is saying, 'but she does have a point. Sooner or later you're going to have to find a way to move on.'

Note to blog:

Family and friends will keep telling you it's time to move on. The very word feels like abandonment, or worse betrayal. .

Maybe they are the ones that need to move on, when giving advice, blackwidower has suggested. *While you will eventually move forward.*

I lie on top of the bed too weary to undress, then reach for M's phone and switch it on, wondering if there are any messages from somebody out there who has not learned of his passing. The screen is cracked and opaque along the outer edge. He'd refused to upgrade it insisting it was still working perfectly. I am startled to see he has fifteen missed calls, each one reading *Caller ID Unknown*. M received a lot of spam as well as calls from clients who withheld their numbers. There are no new messages since the incoherent one I'd left some months ago begging him to come home. I'm about to switch off the phone then leap up realising its vibrating with an incoming call.

'Hello,' I say, my heart thumping.

I hear a slow intake of breath, followed by a humming silence. In the background, a faint hiss like the sound of a wave being sucked back into the ocean.

'Who's this?' I demand, sitting bolt upright. I can make out some more background noise now, a garbled conversation, and then a prolonged mmmmm that makes my blood run cold. Followed by 'eeee', turning into the word 'meeeeee' before the line goes dead.

I have this eerie feeling M is trying to reach me, just as I had the day the bouquet of purple flowers had arrived with the unsigned card. I lie back trembling all over, still holding the phone, wondering if it would ring again. I drift in and out of sleep for the rest of the night, and dream I'm trying to call him. I can make out his voice through the crackling airwaves, only our wires are crossed and he's deep in conversation with somebody else. I hear him say, *I'll be with you in a heartbeat.*

I call my mother around midday to apologise. 'Yes, what is it?' she demands coldly.

I decide to keep it brief. 'I'm sorry I lost my temper. I didn't mean what I said. Please apologise to Jeff. Thank you for the great toaster.'

There's a silence, then she says, 'do you know, when Timmy's father died, I wanted to give up too.'

But you did give up, Mother, I want to say.

'You must do better than I did,' she says to my surprise. 'You have those lovely sons. How I wish I had boys. Timmy was such a joy. I wish you had known him better.'

'Well, you have Fern and me,' I remind her.

'Yes, I know and you must buck up!' She is off again. 'You know, a bit of lipstick and some highlights can go a long way towards making you look and feel better. You're too young to mope around.'

'Wallow?' I suggest.

'Yes, well, I didn't mean that exactly. It's just you still have lots of good years ahead of you. You can't afford to waste them. You're a talented journalist. What about your idea of trying to write a book based on your column about modern dilemmas?'

One of many ideas I'd had but had never pursued.

'I'll be talking to some editors in the new year,' I say, vaguely.

I am close to tears suddenly, have not been able to stop thinking about M's phone ringing in the night, that haunting disjointed voice. When I'd told Fern about it, she'd said, 'no doubt a crank caller. You need to cancel his phone contract. You've got to stop torturing yourself, Willow.'

I'd remained silent, not knowing how to explain the feeling that M had left behind something unresolved. Now, as if echoing Fern, Mother says, 'it's almost a new year now, a perfect opportunity for a new start. It's time.'

I'll add it to my new year's resolutions, I want to snap. Give Up Grieving – Move On, Make A New Start, like one of those magazine headers, prescribing how to step out of the old persona, reinvent yourself, become a brand-new you.

Note to blog:

Surely grief doesn't have a timescale? Do you wake up one morning to find your time is up and you're expected to feel normal again?

Grief needs to run its course, sadeyedlady has commented.

Your time is never up – there is no cut-off date. You will carry it with you always. It will become a vital part of you, blackwidower has written.

It is the last day of the year. Tomorrow there will be a different number on the calendar, charting a period in time M will not be a part of. The start of a new year heralds a new beginning according to Caesar.

I push aside memories of past new year's eves; M and I dancing the night away, at a party or sipping champagne on a beach in Cornwall. Last year we'd invited some friends over for dinner and M had disappeared into the garden and set off a dazzling firework display. We had hugged and kissed as the clock struck twelve and he had made a toast to 'a long life, health and laughter and happy ever after.'

I plan to go to bed early and miss the celebrations.

Sam asks if Tom can stay the night, so they can practice for the band. 'We want to stay up and see the new year in. I can't wait for this shit year to be over and gone forever,' he adds, with a stricken look.

'I know,' I say, hugging him, feeling the pain of his loss like a stab wound in my heart.

I plan to make a family favourite of sticky chicken wings, ribs, and loaded potato skins, for dessert a white chocolate mousse.

'Why don't you invite Harry for a sleepover,' I suggest to Liam.

He shakes his head. 'They've gone to Spain for Christmas. Anyway, I want to hang out with Sam and Tom.' He glances at his older brother hopefully.

'Tom and me need to drive into Bristol and pick up some stuff,' Sam announces.

'Like what?' I ask.

'Just things for the band,' Sam replies evasively.

Tom's mother, Ella, drops her son off in the early afternoon. 'it's very good of you to do this, Willow, what with everything you're going through.'

'I'm happy to have him,' I answer, thinking it would be nice to have four of us sitting around the table again.

I watch Sam and Tom set off for Bristol with a sense of unease, which increases as the short wintry afternoon closes in. I'd told Sam to check his headlights were working before leaving and to be back in plenty of time for dinner. He'd responded with, 'Yes, Mother,' making me flinch as that's how I address my mother.

By six thirty there's still no sign of them. I call Sam's phone twice, but he doesn't pick up.

Liam sits poised and alert in front of the TV with the sound down, listening out for their return. He finally gives up and heads out into the garden with his telescope, muttering that he's searching for a particular star.

I turn the oven off, cover the ribs and chicken in foil, then pace the barn. 'For god's sake, Sam, call me…' I say out loud.

The phone finally rings. It's him. 'Sorry, Mum, we ran out of diesel, but we found a fuel station only we don't have enough money, so the guy said, if you could give him your credit card number, um, so we can get home.'

I breathe out with a mixture of relief and anger. 'OK, I'll get my card.'

I speak to a gruff-voiced man who says, wearily, 'Fire ahead with the number.' I wait, knowing what he's going to say before he says it. 'Card hasn't gone through.'

'I'll give you another one,' I say, searching for the credit card I used for work before, remembering that account was empty.

It strikes me I am going to have to drive into the city centre to sort it out.

'Could you put my son back on the phone,' I say, trying to remain calm.

'Hey, Mum?'

'Where are you?' I demand.

'Not far from Hartcliff.'

'What the hell are you doing on that side of the city?'

'Just looking for some things…' There's a silence, I hear Tom's voice in the background. 'Don't worry, Mum, Tom's managed to get hold of his dad. He's going to pay for it.'

'OK, then just drive straight home,' I snap.

It's almost ten o'clock by the time I hear Sam's car pull up on the driveway. I stand at the front door like a drill sergeant, waiting for them to get out of the car.

They appear at last, carrying two bulky brown paper bags.

Sam hands his bag to Tom, muttering, 'Take them down to the shed.'

'What's in those bags?' I demand as soon as we're inside. Every horror goes through my mind – from stolen goods to drugs and illegal firearms.

'It was meant to be a surprise,' Sam replies. His cheeks are bright red and I realise he's on the verge of tears.

He sinks into an armchair, overcome with sobs. 'Sorry I messed up, Mum. I couldn't stop thinking about this time last year and Dad's firework display and how he couldn't get that rocket to light. He wipes away the tears, with the back of his hand. 'We drove to this warehouse near Easton where Dad went to buy them.'

Tom appears through the back door. He pauses at the sight of Sam's distressed face.

'I hope we haven't ruined everything,' he begins.

'No, you haven't,' I say, hugging Sam. 'I'm just glad you're both safely home.'

Liam comes over and pulls his brother to his feet. 'Come out and see what I've found. Mum, you and Tom can come too.'

We troop out to where Liam has set up the telescope beside the pile of paving stones. 'It's just left of the Plough and The Stars. There's a cluster of four. It's the brightest one of all. I've named it "Maximillian the Second".

We take it in turns to look through the telescope into the clear night sky but I can barely see anything through a film of tears.

We finally sit down for dinner, the boys claiming it's the best meal they've ever had, then Sam insists we fill the last hour of the year with a game of charades. 'Try to pick a movie we know this time, Mum.' He grins.

As the clock is about to strike midnight, we gather outside and Sam and Tom disappear down the garden path. I watch the light from their torches slicing through the darkness and, moments later, there's a sound of crackling and fizzing followed by the explosion of gunpowder and the sky lights up with a giant palm tree, dripping golden leaves.

Sam runs back to where we're standing. 'It was to remind you of your anniversary with Dad in the Caribbean,' he says breathlessly.

I hug him, my throat aching. 'You are full of surprises.'

He dashes off again, shouting 'fingers crossed' and, moments later, a rocket whizzes into the sky leaving behind a starry trail.

'It's headed straight for Dad's star,' Liam breathes.

Note to blog:

I have resolved not to make any New Year's resolutions this year except to try to feel better if that's at all possible.

And you will in time, WW, believe me, lifeafterdeath has responded.

Don't keep trying to feel better, get better at feeling what you need to feel, blackwidower has come back with.

Are you a counsellor, by any chance? I write back. *As you seem to have the answers!*

Ha! Not sure I even understand the questions, he has replied.

EARLY JANUARY

The boys have gone back to school. I still hear the echo of their voices in the silence that hangs like smoke from a funeral pall over the empty spaces of Rosewood Barn.

There is maintenance to be done. One of the skylights is leaking, and I noticed a damp patch spreading along the bathroom ceiling. This morning the heating has gone off and there's no hot water. I realise with a plunge of heart that the boiler must have broken down. M always dealt with issues like the Rayburn and boiler, while I exchanged pleasantries with the rather dour man who arrived in his overalls, bearing a large tool box. I pull on a pair of M's woollen socks, light the gas fire, and settle down to wait.

He calls back informing me he's booked up until the end of January. I explain it's an emergency and that I'm here alone. It strikes me he would have dropped everything for M.

'I don't know what to advise,' he begins, 'there is a lad who's just starting out, I could give him a call for you. I'm sorry about your husband,' he adds. 'He was a proper gentleman, he was. I thought he was going to put in underfloor heating?'

'He never got around to it.' In the end M had decided it was too expensive, and a wood-burning stove would be a better option. We had ended up with neither.

I receive a call an hour later, telling me a Ron Diamond would stop by this afternoon.

I call Sam and ask if he could stay on and pick up Liam from school then climb into bed, wearing a fleece and a pair of M's boxer shorts. I doze off and wake up to the sound of somebody knocking on the door. I jump out of bed looking around for my dressing gown only to remember it is in the wash. I pull on a silk kimono but can't find the belt so give up and head downstairs clutching the slippery fabric together with one hand.

'Hi there, Ron Diamond at your service,' he greets me. 'Heard your boiler needs attending to.' He raises one eyebrow as if there is clearly some other reason why I've summoned him over on a freezing January afternoon.

'This way,' I say, coolly.

I lead him into the utility room and hover while he checks the thermostat, humming tunelessly to himself.

'Bloody freezing out there,' he comments, his eyes running up and down the length of my body. 'Any chance of a cup of tea?'

I nod and withdraw to the kitchen, uneasy suddenly.

I pull on a jacket of M's that reaches my knees, wrap his woollen scarf around my neck and switch on the kettle.

Ron reappears silently, startling me. 'Nothing wrong with your boiler,' he announces. 'My guess is you've run out of oil. I'll go check the tank.' He heads outside in the direction of the oil tank, whistling loudly, and moments later stomps back inside declaring, 'Empty as I suspected!'

'I'll order some oil tomorrow.' I say, thinking I should have checked it myself. Now there would be a large call-out fee on top of everything. I've been trying not to dwell on my dwindling savings, telling myself I will find work soon, even if I have to go back to editing.

He is pulling off his boots and making his way towards me. He perches himself on a stool and studies me curiously as if trying to read a meter.

'Look, it's too late to make tea now,' I begin.

He ignores me. 'Sorry about your husband, I heard he passed.'

I think about the word 'passed'. Passed a test, passed out, passed on…passed into the past.

'Heard he did a lot for charity. Bad things happen to good people,' he states with a look that sends alarm bells clanging.

'I need to get on,' I say, 'finish an article I'm writing, just send me your invoice.'

'You know, you're still a good-looking woman,' he says, consideringly. 'This place must have cost a few bob!'

I have now become a good proposition. The wealthy widow of Rosewood Barn.

I'm starting to feel afraid. I guess he's in his late twenties and believes the notion that women in my situation are desperate for sex, widows being particularly easy targets.

I notice his fingers are thick and calloused and feel my stomach turn over.

'Must be hard being here all on you own,' he says, a smile playing around his lips.

'I'm not on my own, my sons will be back from school any minute.'

What is the protocol in this kind of situation? To scream and shout, threaten to call the police, or try to negotiate my way out of it, announce I have a sexually transmittable disease? Or make a dash for the stairs, but there are no locks on any of the bedroom doors. I move towards the knife rack looking around wildly for my phone. I consider fleeing through the back door, but I'd then have to run around the outside of the barn to get to the jeep, and the keys are in my handbag which is upstairs. I have a vision of leaping onto M's bike, and making a quick getaway. I have somehow mastered riding a motorbike in this fantasy.

I am starting to shake with nerves and fear.

'Cold getting to you,' he leers. 'How about you let me warm you up?'
'You need to leave now,' I state, inching towards the back door.
'Chill out, woman, have a drink, it's still early.'

The sense of entitlement, the assumption I'm game, a woman who needs to 'chill out, have a drink' causes something to rise, hot and all-consuming surging through my bloodstream like lava. My uncontrollable temper – only this time it's fuelled by grief and fury against the world in general. I grab the breadknife and brandish it in the air, like a deranged thing. I approach him, swearing foully. I am beside myself, my other self, the one that's capable of plunging a knife deep into his chest and watching him keel over. After all, widows get away with murder, don't they?

He backs away with a look of bewilderment and, to my satisfaction, alarm.

'Now get out,' I say, my voice low and curdled, 'before I call the police.'

'Yeah right, and how about I tell them you opened the door in some skimpy dressing gown. Aren't you some kind of journalist who writes about spicing up your sex life? Don't worry, I'm on my way,' he adds, grabbing his tool box. He's on the porch now, his face yellow in the light from the lamp above.

I watch him disappear down the path before sinking in front of the gas fire, with a sob.

I can't do this, I think, glancing up at the smiling photo of M above the fireplace. 'Please come back,' I beg. 'I'm just not equipped to deal with mice, or boilers or predatory men!'

I pour myself another glass of wine, then drag myself upstairs and pile on three layers of clothes. I want M back so badly it hurts. I check his phone. There have been no new calls or messages since the night of Christmas. I have turned it on and off so many times the power button is broken so now it's permanently on. I'd put it away in a drawer, afraid of those ghostly vibrations in the night.

The screen has since turned black, the phone appears to have died. I plug it into the charger and wait, afraid that tenuous connection with M, which was no more than an illusion, has been severed. I hold the power button down for thirty seconds, and the phone finally lights up. There are five more calls, stating Caller ID unknown, but no messages.

Note to blog:

Attention widows – all sorts of unlikely men will hit on you wanting to wanting to service your boiler. Don't let them in!

I'm tempted to describe the encounter but, instead, write tipsily, *after all, women are self-sufficient. We can do it all – hold down high-powered jobs while bringing up our kids. We are perfectly capable of everything, even having our own orgasms.*

Too right! notyetdead has responded.

I wonder what blackwidower will make of this, but there is no comment. Half an hour later, he responds with: *Sounds as if you're keeping on top of it WW!*

EARLY FEBRUARY

The temperature has plummeted further, the garden is covered in a glittering blanket of frost. I worry about the families of moles, trapped beneath the frozen earth, dying from suffocation.

I'd seldom noticed the cold when M and the boys were around. Now it seems to lie in wait for me, seeping into the house through my clothes and into my bones. I had ordered a full tank of oil, then nearly passed out at the cost, so have taken to turning the heating off once I'm up and dressed and leaving it off until early evening. I walk around the barn wearing an old ski jacket over three layers of clothing, M's scarf permanently around my neck.

The mice have moved in again, to escape the bitter cold. I watch one streak across the floor, like the clockwork mouse I used to play with as a child and feel a tingling in the soles of my feet. I had put down some humane traps after Holly had stormed out, but it appears a new family has taken up residence behind the dresser.

This morning the toaster is jammed. As I attempt to push a slice of bread into the slot, I feel a solid resistance. I peer into the glowing elements and see something grey and furry shifting amongst the burnt crusts.

I freeze as two jewelled eyes look up at me and lurch for the plug, wrenching it from its socket but it's too late. There's a strangled squeak as the little creature is caught in the fiery inferno.

I stand there trembling, then take the toaster outside and turn it upside down, but the mouse is wedged deep inside and I don't have the wits, or the tools to dismantle the toaster. I sit there shivering in the icy wind, then pick up my mother's expensive Christmas present with its cremated contents and hurl it into the recycling bin.

Back inside I'm overcome with shame. I didn't know I could sink this far. I take in the mess and squalor, thinking tomorrow I would clean up and get my life back in order.

I'm up early, filled with a new resolve to tackle the kitchen, when I hear the sound of wheels scrunching on the gravel outside. I glance through the window and see a mobility scooter parked on the driveway.

Mad Mabel, who trawls the high street dressed in a velvet ball gown, is walking towards the front door. Today, she's wearing a pair of voluminous beige trousers and a retro leather jacket, and is holding my mother's discarded toaster under one arm, whilst brandishing a bunch of dried herbs.

'Can I help you?' I enquire tentatively.

'Found this in the recycling bin, and wondered if you threw it out by mistake?'

She holds up the toaster like a trophy. A drop of water hangs perilously from her nose.

'There's a dead mouse in there,' I explain. 'I managed to cremate the poor thing.'

'I have something for you,' she says, thrusting the dried herbs into my hand. 'Sage,' she announces, 'to help release the spirit of the departed. You lost your husband on the summer solstice and you can't let him go.'

This gives me a start, although it's fairly evident by the state of the house, my unbrushed hair and M's sweatshirt, which now smells of my unwashed body. I see myself through her eyes as a once-attractive blonde, gone to seed, dried up like one of her bunches of herbs.

'He was a decent man,' she states, 'unlike his brother.'

She must have read about Will's antics in the local papers – the arrests for drunken driving, an assault on a night club owner, the drug-dealing offences, driving his bike into a ditch high on cocaine and tequila.

'How about you make me a cuppa, an' I'll give you some advice for what it's worth.' She jabs me in the shoulder, grinning toothily. 'In this case it'll cost you nothing, if you're happy to give me the toaster!'

I'm about to make an excuse, but curiosity gets the better of me. Perhaps I can interview her for 'Interesting Lives', write an article about modern-day witches that will convince Jason to give me back my column.

I reach for the loose-leaf tea, then switch to a tea bag, thinking I'd rather she didn't predict some awful fate awaiting me in the leaves. But she's telling me all about herself, which is a journalist's dream come true.

'I was married once,' she begins. 'To an artist. Randolf Vale was his name. I wore a green velvet ballgown on my wedding day, and a wreath of everlasting flowers in my hair.' I think back to that day she'd approached me in the high street in the green velvet gown, and it strikes me she hasn't been able to move on either.

'...but nothing lasts forever, as we all know,' she states, with an air of fatality. She's now telling me an extraordinary story of moving from place to place, giving birth in a field and squatting with her twin boys in a warehouse, one of them dying in her arms. How she'd moved into a caravan and lived in a field on the Isle of Sheppey. Of the numerous affairs Randolf Vale had had, and how she'd had a premonition he would be taken from her.

'When he died it was a "vale" of tears.' She smiles at the analogy. 'I thought about ending it all, and then I woke up one morning and knew I had to find a new path. I do readings now, if you'd like to know what your future holds, my darlin'?'

'That's OK,' I say swiftly, thinking I would rather not know if any more horrors lay ahead. 'How long did it take?' I venture, 'for you to find a new path?'

'It took as long as it took,' she answers evasively.

She has now digressed to her market stall and how she drives around on her mobility scooter, collecting items from recycling bins. 'You'd be amazed by what people throw out.' I tune out for a moment, then hear her say, 'It's early days for you, but the fog will lift and you'll see the way forward. You may not want to move on, but life will take you along with it. Believe you me.'

She is reaching for her leather jacket. 'I'll be on my way then. Anything else you need gettin' rid of, my darlin'?'

I shake my head, thinking there were a number of things, but I couldn't let go of any of them.

She looks at me directly. 'Your husband was a good man. I knew the Goodhart brothers from way back when they lived with that cursed family in Kent. I recognised Max straightaway, although I only met him a few times back then.

…never saw such blue eyes on a man. The mark on his forehead was fresh then – word had it that Anthony Jessop went for him with a broken bottle.'

I stare at her. M had told me it was from the surfing accident.

'That monster should never have been allowed to take on those brothers after turning on his young son like that – and that poor boy already damaged from birth. My aunt lived a few doors down from them. Said she could hear that boy crying out like a banshee on a bad night.'

I recall M's description of that bleak estate on the outskirts of Ramsgate, where he and Will had lived with 'the foster family from hell', as he called them. The Jessops had a son of their own called Toby, who was autistic. When the abuse had started, M had managed to get Will away from the family and had later convinced social services to intervene and have Toby taken into care.

I think about that lisping voice on Christmas night, the unlisted calls.

'What happened to Toby? Do you know where he is? Only, I think he might have been trying to get in touch with my husband.'

She shakes her head, 'I wouldn't know where he's to,' she says, using West Country jargon.

'Would your aunt know, do you think?'

'She moved away from there years ago – couldn't stay in that blighted neighbourhood, what with that and the boy who was run over and left to die on the side of the road.' I absorb this, thinking how M and Will had set up a foundation in his name.

'It's all in the past now,' I hear her say, 'it's the future we need to focus on. I've a reading to do now, my darlin',' she adds. 'If you change your mind,

I'll do you one for free in exchange for the toaster. In the meantime, watch out for the signpost, the one that will lead you onto the right path.'

'Wait, please, I want to ask you a couple of questions…' But she's heading for the door.

I follow her out to where her scooter is parked. A large metal contraption is hanging on the front, crammed to the brim with things she's picked up along the lane; old newspapers, magazines, a rusting saucepan, a kettle and now an expensive toaster.

'What about Toby's mother? She must know where he is?'

'She went off with a man from Wales I believe. Can't stop now,' she adds, revving the engine. She is gone in a spurt of noise, leaving me staring after her.

I go back inside, my thoughts tumbling over one another, thinking how little I knew about that period of the brothers' lives. Why would M have lied about the scar?

Will bore the brunt of the abuse, he'd told me, once. *I was out working on building sites most of the time.*

He'd told me how they had managed to escape one night, describing it as the worst moment of his life, having to leave Toby behind. He had never said anything about being lashed out at with a broken bottle.

I call Will over and over, but he doesn't pick up. I'd tried to reach him a few times but had got his answering service. I send him a text saying. *Please call me – I need to ask you something. It's important.*

When there's no reply, I send him an email. *I think Toby Jessop has been trying to get in touch with M. Do you know how I can contact him? We owe it to both of them.*

Will's response finally pops up the following afternoon. *Don't go there. It would do more harm than good.*

I search the internet, trawling through old newspaper reports from the early nineties, when the brothers were living in Kent.

There is a short piece, in the Kentish Gazette.

Anthony Jessop, 43, of Bunkershill Crescent, has been found guilty of violence and abuse against minors. He has been sentenced to fifteen years at HM Standford Hill.

Underneath is a blurry photo of a sandy-haired man with a thin moustache and goatee. I take in the dull brown eyes, the cold stare and wonder queasily what unspeakable things he had done to his own son and to the brothers, that neither of them could bring themselves to talk about.

There is a late addition to the story reporting that Anthony Jessop of

Ramsgate, Kent, who had been serving a prison sentence for crimes against minors had been found dead in his cell. The verdict was suicide.

I could only hope this would bring some comfort to Toby and Will and all the other kids he had abused, even if it was too late for M.

I switch on M's phone, checking for any new calls. This time the screen lights up with *Phone not Activated*.

I turn it on and off again, but the same message comes up. The phone appears to have been cut off. I am reminded of the recurring dream in which I'm trying to get in touch but can't reach him. I call his phone provider from the landline and am informed that his contract had been cancelled yesterday morning. 'Who by,' I ask? She asks me to hold the line while she looks into it. After a long wait she tells me the authorisation was made by a person who was next of kin.

Will, I think, my thoughts reeling. He clearly didn't want me to make contact with Toby for some reason.

I feel an aching sense of having been cut adrift from everything that once was, from M's past as well as the life we'd shared together. I call his phone again, while knowing I would never again hear his deep voice, or hear him say, *I'll get back to you in a heartbeat...*

I listen to the silence – silence that seems to stretch to infinity.

LATE FEBRUARY

I have taken to driving into Highbury in the mornings wanting to escape the empty barn and bleak view of the garden which is frozen in the interminable grip of winter. I scour the high street searching for Mad Mabel, thinking I would ask her for a reading then use my interviewing skills to find out more about Toby Jessop, but she is nowhere to be found. I recall how M would always stop and greet her, and hand her a note. I visit the places M frequented, the hardware store, the antique shop, and the reclamation centre where I wander through cluttered aisles, as if searching for answers in the rusting vintage mirrors and antique furniture, piles of old journals charting the past. The stone fountain with the gaping fish is still in the far corner with a ticket marked SOLD on it. I think of how M had planned to buy it, only time had run out and somebody else must have claimed it. Morris, the lugubrious owner is making his way towards me with a sombre look on his face.

'Willow, there are no words,' he begins. He is wearing a pair of open-toed sandals and socks. I remember M describing him as a crusader, a man who lived and dwelt amongst relics of the past, wanting to preserve it at all costs. 'Max asked me to put this aside for you,' he is saying, pointing at the fountain.

My throat swells.

'You can pick it up anytime.'

He stares at me from faded brown eyes. 'He understood the beauty of what was and knew how to preserve it.' He clears his throat and looks away. 'I shall leave you alone to browse.'

My eyes are suddenly drawn to a vintage poster of an orange Cadillac propped against the wall. I had commented on it to M, saying it reminded me of the car in that photo of him and Will when they lived in Ramsgate. It was one of the few photos I'd seen of the brothers during that time. In this one he and Will were leaning against an old car. Beside them, a small, fair-haired boy who must have been Toby Jessop was gazing up at M adoringly.

M had been searching for posters of classic motor bikes to hang on the walls of the shed, and we had found one in this very spot. As he glanced at the poster of the Cadillac, I noticed his face drain of colour. He suddenly turned and headed towards the outside area where the garden ornaments were stored.

I followed him out and found him standing by a stone effigy of a griffin.

'Are you ok? You're acting a bit weird.'

'I'm fine,' he answered. 'I just realised I need to get back to the office. I need to deal with this lunatic woman who wants to take us to court – I never wanted to sign a contract with her but Jake overruled me. Now we're going to have to go to arbitration.' He rubbed the scar on his forehead, a nervous habit of old.

'What do you think?' he digressed, pointing at the griffin. 'For the garden?'

'It doesn't look very friendly,' I replied, taking in the cruel eagle face and talons, the powerful neck tapering down to the body of a lion.

'They're the super heroes of mythological creatures,' he'd said. 'Nobody messes around with griffins.'

Now I remain rooted to the spot, staring at the poster of the Cadillac, grappling with something half formed, a missing piece of the puzzle I was sure had to do with the time the brothers had lived in Ramsgate. Something Will didn't want me to know about.

EARLY MARCH

Fern calls to say she has something important to tell me. 'Meet me at Café Bella,' she says.

I sit by the window writing notes for my blog while waiting for her.

Steve, the young barista, swirls a perfect heart on my coffee and asks if I'm writing a bestseller. I tell him it's a blog about grief and how to cope after the death of a partner.

'My grandad should read that,' he comments, 'my gran died last year, and he's useless without her. He's made a list of all the places she loved to go, so he can go back and remember her there.'

I consider this. M loved going to Cornwall to surf, he loved riding his bike through the Wiltshire countryside, or trawling antique markets and reclamation centres. Or just pottering in the shed, fixing things.

I don't need to go anywhere to remember him, he will always have permanent residence inside me. Only now the memories have become scrambled, like looking into a triptych and seeing multiple Ms. The M I'd known and loved was in the forefront, striding into the barn in his leathers with a bouquet of purple flowers, pulling me into a bear hug and murmuring 'loving you.' The other Ms, the child and teenager, were blurred around the edges, like looking into an antique mirror oxidised with time.

Note to blog:

I wonder, does it help to revisit the special places you and your loved one frequented to keep the past and the memories alive?

According to L.P. Hartley, how we understand the past and how we come to terms with our own memories is an unpaid debt that all humans share, blackwidower has written.

I sit thinking about this, trying to understand the meaning behind the words. I would never be able to come to terms with the memories of that day. It would remain an unpaid debt – one I would never be able to share.

I watch life swirling around me; a group of mothers trying to calm their hyper-active children. The mothers pick at pastries, the toddlers fidget and squirm in their high chairs. It's noisy and hectic and I miss that era. I miss my old life and the person I used to be.

I listen to the drift of their conversation. Some of them are clearly new mothers. I think about them setting off on their solitary journey of motherhood, protecting their little ones, unaware for now at least, that they would not be able to safeguard them from life's cruel twists and turns, from tragedy and loss.

Fern arrives looking particularly lovely; her skin glowing, her thick honey hair smooth and shiny. She is the better-looking of the two of us now, I think dispassionately. I recall hearing Mother say, 'when the good looks were given out, Fern was in the other room.' Fern had heard it too. She had been an awkward, angular child, with her father's sharp nose. But today she looks beautiful and radiates happiness, which is the part I do envy.

'You look great,' I comment.

'And you look a lot better,' she replies, giving me a hug.

I have put on one of the dresses I bought online low cut and fitted, the best of a bad lot. I've washed and blow-dried my hair and am wearing eye make-up for once. My tears have dried up a bit lately so I've risked a non-waterproof mascara.

'Trying to shrug off the widow's cloak,' I smile. 'No more wallowing. So, what's your news?'

She takes a deep breath, her face lighting up.

'I've met somebody. His name's David Archer. He's the new art teacher. He walked into the staffroom and it was a coup de foudre!'

I feel a jolt at her choice of words, 'struck by lightning, a thunderbolt.'

'I think he's The One, Willow! Just when I'd given up hope of it ever happening. He looks a bit like M,' she adds gently. 'Tall, dark-blue eyes. He has the same generous spirit. He's incredibly talented. He wanted me to see his new painting, which is why I'm late.'

My face seems to have frozen mid-smile.

'This is what he wanted to show me.' A flush suffuses her cheeks. The photo shows a painting of her sitting on a rumpled bed, semi-naked, a sheet draped over one shoulder. 'We're already making plans.'

'Gosh, that's fast, I mean, isn't it a bit soon? Have you met his family? Does he have any kids? Do you know anything about his background?' I'm interviewing her rather than leaping up and down with joy, celebrating this wonderful news.

'He might have a dark past,' I add, my voice trailing off.

I take a gulp of my coffee which has gone cold.

Fern frowns. 'You know when it's right,' she says crossly, 'and, yes, David has an eleven-year-old daughter, Charlotte, from a previous marriage. I have met her and we hit it off straight away. He lives in a thatched cottage in Tidworth with a beautiful garden with Charlotte and their two cats. I don't *think* he has any dark secrets.'

'Don't pay any attention to me,' I say hastily. 'I've been going down a few dark avenues myself, wondering about M's past,' I add.

'Why do you want to go there?'

'That phone call at Christmas triggered it,' I begin. 'But let's not talk about that now. Have you got any photos of David?'

'I was going to show you his Facebook photo, but maybe another time when he and I are a bit further along the road!'

'I'm sorry,' I say, mortified. 'I am happy for you, I really am.'

'It doesn't mean I won't have all the time in the world to spend with you,' she says astutely.

'I know, please show me his photo.'

She brings it up on her phone immediately.

My heart skips a beat. He bears an uncanny resemblance to M. Vivid-blue eyes, only his jaw is less defined, his hair thinner. But David Archer is older than M would have been, had he lived. My heart seems to be breaking all over again. I blink back the traitorous tears.

You're the one I intend to grow old with, M had said six months after our first meeting. I recall the early days when my stomach was permanently in a knot, waking up late on Sunday mornings in his Harbourside home, giddy with the knowledge I had met the love of my life. I didn't need to know about his past then. All I could think about was our future.

I think of my older sister setting off on her journey, while mine seems to have ended.

It's the green-eyed monster all right, unable to see its own verdant future.

Note to blog:

Grief can turn you mean-spirited, unable to celebrate other people's happiness. It's hard to accept that life goes on for those around you, while yours has stalled. Friends and family will fall in love and get married. New chapters will begin for your loved ones - while you have to find a way to rise above your own despair and celebrate with them. Easier said than done, I'm finding!

There are a number of comments from this, including one from lifeafterdeath who's written: *it is possible to feel a number of different emotions at the same time – but if you truly love somebody, you will be happy for them.*

Grin and bear it, then go home and punch the wall, blackwidower has suggested, making me smile.

That night I cry myself to sleep, leaving streaks of non-waterproof mascara all over the Egyptian cotton pillow case.

Fern has invited me over to dinner to meet David.

'He wants to cook dinner for us – says he can't wait to meet you,' she adds excitedly. She has sent me his address and added: 'wait till you see his garden!'

I brace myself for the evening, dressing casually in jeans and a caramel-coloured jumper, determined to cast aside any feelings of lack and envy, ashamed of my earlier reaction.

David Archer is less like M in the flesh, although there is an uncanny resemblance. He has the same easy manner. He greets me warmly, saying, 'I'm so sorry to hear about M. I gather he was an exceptional man.'

'Yes, he was,' I reply, 'my better half in every way!'

Maximillian Goodhart: even his name conjured up the good and the great. A man who wanted to put right what was wrong in the world, fix the unfixable, put aside the horrors of the past.

The evening is strangely lopsided. It was always Fern who had been the odd one out, graciously partaking at our dining table, engaging with the boys, listening to their latest adventures. Now it's me who sits there, mute and rudderless, unable to keep up a lively banter although I have drunk more than both of them put together. Charlotte, David's daughter, had appeared briefly at the start of the evening before announcing she was meeting up with a friend who lived along the lane. She had hugged Fern, then wound her arms around me, saying, 'I wish I had a sister. You don't look very alike.'

'We're half-sisters,' Fern had explained, 'but we think of ourselves as whole sisters.' She'd laughed.

Now, as David heads into the kitchen to fetch the dessert, Fern turns to me saying, 'So what do you think?' Her eyes are shining with happiness.

'I think he's wonderful,' I tell her, hoping my voice conveys this. 'Handsome, a great cook,' – he had prepared and cooked his specialty dish of baked chicken in lemon and olives – 'he's also a brilliant artist and he obviously adores you.'

He is all that and more.

He is also a painful reminder of what I have lost.

I pour the dregs of the Pinot Noir I had brought into my glass and tell Fern about the visit from mad Mabel. 'Her sister knew the Jessops – the foster family from hell as M called them – anyway, she mentioned their son, Toby, who was taken into care. I believe he's been trying to get in touch with M and it was him who called on Christmas night. I emailed Will about it, and he told me not to get involved, then immediately cancelled M's phone contract. He clearly doesn't want me to make contact with him.'

Fern frowns.

'Toby doesn't know M has died,' I continue. 'I need to find him and tell him.'

'Short of calling every care home in the country, I can't see how you can trace him,' my sister points out.

David emerges from the kitchen with a bowl of fruit salad and the conversation moves on.

After dinner, Fern leads me out into the garden. We stand amongst the hyacinths and dwarf daffodils and she shows me the patch where she plans to plant purple sprouting broccoli and runner beans.

'I know it's upsetting about Toby, but I can't see what you can do,' she says intuitively. 'Sometimes it's best to leave the past alone.'

I sigh. 'I still don't know what really happened during that time. M told me Will was abused, but he never went into the details. Mabel intimated the scar on his forehead was from a broken bottle after Anthony Jessop lashed out at him. M told me it was from a surfing accident. Why would he lie about something like that?'

Fern shrugs. 'Maybe it was all too painful and he didn't want to take you down that road. Who knows? M was such a private person; he rarely talked about himself.'

I nod. 'He spent his life protecting Will,' I continue. 'They kept a lot of things between them.'

'You and I have kept things between us,' Fern says. 'Isn't that what siblings do? Protect each other?'

It was an accident, Willow, she'd repeated over and over that day at the hospital.

Now she hugs me, saying, 'hold on to the memories of the happy times you had together and remember the M you knew and loved.'

'I'm starting to wonder how well I actually did know him,' I say at last.

Note to blog:

I've read that grappling with unresolved issues is common after a death, that a search for answers can be all-consuming. It strikes me as normal to want to piece together a life that has ended if only to know more about who you are grieving for.

Many people take their secrets to the grave with them, sadeyedlady has written. *Maybe they should be allowed to rest in peace.*

The things that happened in the past are of no use to you now. Time has reshaped them, turned them into mere whispers in the wind, blackwidower has written.

MID-MARCH

There's a thaw in the air at last, patches of yellow and white crocus have sprung up on the lawn. In Highbury the trees are heavy with cherry blossom. The time has come to clear out a few things, de-clutter, or so everybody keeps telling me. I decide to start in the shed by throwing out all the empty cans of oil, old brushes stiff with paint, rusty nails and bits of rotting wood.

I sit on the bean bag lounger, looking around, thinking I would ask Sean to fix the door which looks as if it's about to fall off its hinges. M's Triumph, all gleaming black and red chrome looks crouched and oddly forlorn, as if its glory days are over. That inanimate but curiously alive beast of a machine I had competed with for his time.

I have an urge for a drink, but have finished the last bottle of wine. I peer into M's Coca-Cola fridge. There are four beers in there still, icy cold. I drink two in quick succession, then switch on the antique juke box, wondering what was the last song M had listened to. He loved listening to Motorhead on biking trips. Meatloaf comes up. I have a vivid image of him sitting on the bike, his visor raised, a smile spreading on his face. 'Climb on… I'll give you the ride of your life.'

I move towards the bike, as if in a trance, and swing my leg over the cool leather seat, imagining I am winding my arms around his waist. I can almost smell the scent of him – olive oil soap mixed with the tarry smell of leather. I'd watched him start the bike numerous times, pulling out the kick starter, pumping it for ages, flinging his head back and forth in a hectic ritual, as if in the throes of some primeval dance to coax it to life.

I pump the starter experimentally. The engine emits a half-hearted growl, before spluttering out with a sigh. I climb off, grab a third beer and listen to a live version of Bat out of Hell, then make my way back to the barn and sit on the sofa researching: 'how to start a motorbike'. The boys would be impressed by my knowledge and prowess, I think headily. They were both away for the night; Liam had been invited to a birthday sleepover, Sam was staying with Tom's dad and new wife in London. I find a help forum and am suddenly engaging with a man named Mike the Bike. I call myself Confused Chris, deciding the name is fairly ambiguous and the next moment his reply pops up. *Hey there, Confused Chris, I suggest you check your petcock.*

I'm not in the mood for vulgar idiots on bike forums, and am about to write back 'tosser!', then decide to look up 'petcock' just in case. It turns out to be the fuel line. I exit the forum, then listen to a long tutorial on how to drain a petcock.

Energised now, I pour myself a gin and tonic and grab a packet of crisps, deciding I might as well make a night of it. Hold my own party in the shed.

It's all quite straightforward after all, I think, remembering Will's derisive remark that I'd never be able to handle it.

I grit my teeth and follow the instructions, finding the funnel I'd seen M use to drain the fuel, carefully unscrewing the gas line from the tank, letting it drip into a plastic receptacle I'd found on the shelf.

'Petcock drained,' I announce. I go through the motions I'd gone through earlier, switching on the ignition, pulling out the choke, setting the Kill Switch to Run, then pumping the kick start. The beast suddenly roars to life, causing me to leap up from the seat in fright. It is a boiling cauldron of noise and chaos. I can feel it straining and vibrating beneath me, as if ready to bolt. I settle back on the seat grinning wildly, thinking it's the only throbbing thing I've had between my legs for months, then grasp the throttle and rev the engine, listening to the different pitches: a low tongue-curling growl, followed by a familiar deafening roar. I stagger forwards tipsily, easing the bike off its stand, but in my struggle to keep it upright, I squeeze the throttle causing the bike to shoot forwards like a startled horse. We are off, charging headlong towards the narrow gap of the open shed door. I desperately try to orient it as we burst out onto the lawn. I manage to squeeze the brake which stops the bike in its tracks, almost pitching me over the handlebars, then hit the Kill Switch. To my relief, the engine cuts out. I sit there stunned and breathless, aware of a pulsing throb in my right ankle. I push down the stand lever with my other foot, but the bike immediately keels over onto the soft lawn. Swearing, I glance down, groaning at the sight of blood seeping over the top of my boot. I must have grazed it on the shed door, which is now swinging open on its remaining hinge. I sink down onto the grass, pull off my boot and survey the damage. I've removed a whole layer of skin which is bubbling up with blood. I peel off my jeans, hobble back into the shed and look around for something to staunch the flow, but apart from a few oily rags there's nothing, so I pull off M's sweatshirt and wrap it around my ankle then limp back to the bike in my underwear. I have no idea how I'm going to explain this to the boys, nor what to do with the bike since it's now pouring with rain. I attempt to heave it upright, only to wrench the seat upward, revealing a small storage area beneath. A few coins spill out plus a pair of worn leather gloves. I notice something wedged in the space below, and realise it's a photograph creased with time. I examine it curiously. Two small boys are standing in front of a semi-detached house clutching the handlebars of their scooters. One has fair hair, the other a frizz of orange curls. I turn it over and read *Toby and Archie O'Neill, Bunkershill Crescent*.

M and Will had started a foundation for Archie O'Neill. The thing that had been eluding me, that had lain dormant in my subconscious, suddenly springs to life in one of those illuminating moments. I recall reading an article about the hit and run some years ago, stating the driver of the car could not be named for legal reasons. I think of how Will had been arrested for hot wiring and stealing cars. He had got in with a bad lot from the other end of the estate, M had told me once, and had been sent to a juvenile detention centre for over a year – a particularly harsh sentence, I'd thought. I'd suspected there was more to it. I now wonder if Will could have been involved in the accident that had killed Archie, which would explain why he'd cancelled M's phone contract. He didn't want me to contact Toby, the one link with his past who knew what had happened.

I manage to limp back to the barn, still holding the photo, then flop onto the sofa debating whether to call Sean, explain I've somehow managed to drive into the shed door and have left the bike lying on its side in the rain.

My ankle is throbbing and pulsing so badly, even though the wound is superficial. I can no longer think straight so swallow two painkillers, drag myself upstairs, and fall into bed exhausted. I slip the photo of the two boys into M's bedside drawer, then lie back on the bed, my mind racing, visions of Archie O'Neill with his orange curls lying on the side of the road.

This morning it's still sore, but I can just about walk. I send a text to Sean, explaining the shed door has fallen off its hinges and ask if he could come over. He replies he's in Spain on a biking trip and won't be back until next week. He promises to call Declan, his brother, and ask him to drop by and sort it out.

Sean rings half an hour later. 'Dec will be over in the next hour or so.' 'What happened? Did Will try to break in?'

'No, in fact it was my fault,' I say after a pause. 'I'd had a few drinks – I drove into it. The bike just took off.'

'Jesus, woman! Are you OK?'

'I'm fine, apart from taking a layer of skin off my foot! And feeling foolish!'

'You're not the first person who's done that,' he laughs. 'Glad you're OK.'

'Thanks,' I answer, gratefully. I tell him the story of the petcock, and how I'd almost called Mike the Bike a tosser and hear him chuckle.

My mother has organised a get-together at her house so she can meet David and welcome him into the family. I dread her gatherings, which always turn out to be an ordeal. Besides, she's bound to ask why I'm limping. I didn't tell Fern about the incident with the bike, knowing she's already worried about my state of mind.

I arrive late to find everyone gathered in the living room. Mother has hired caterers and waiters wearing black ties are serving champagne and canapes.

There are lavish arrangements of flowers everywhere. She has invited her wealthy neighbours and some of her Bridge-playing friends, who are spilling out into the conservatory. The setting is more fitting for an engagement party than a family get-together. Fern had been horrified when she'd learned of the plan, reminding her that David disliked large social gatherings, but Mother had waved away her protests, saying, 'it's about time we celebrated some good news in this family.'

Everyone is standing around expectantly as if waiting for an announcement. I make my way over to where Fern, David and Jeff are huddled together by the entrance of the conservatory, David looking awkward in a green corduroy jacket, camouflaged behind a giant Ficus.

Mother, resplendent in white and gold Chanel, hurries over, her bracelets jangling, a fixed and terrible smile on her face. 'I was wondering if you were going to grace us with your presence, Willow?' Her marmalade eyes dart to my bandaged foot. 'What on earth happened?'

I'd rehearsed this on the way over, deciding to stick as close to the truth as possible, but leaving the Triumph out of the story.

'I had a collision with the shed door. I was trying to put Sam's dirt bike inside and the door came away. It was partly off its hinges anyway. It's only a graze.'

She attempts to raise her eyebrows. 'We need to find you a handyman – or just a man! You can't cope with that sort of thing on your own.'

'I'm managing fine,' I begin.

She breathes out impatiently. 'Willow always was a wayward child,' she announces to the group, causing me to hurtle back through time, to past drawing room parties; when I would sneak into the kitchen and help myself to the canapes, then have a picnic in the garden, hiding away until the last guest had left.

'...very temperamental and determined, weren't you, darling?'

'We know who she gets that from!' Jeff comments with a smile. He turns to me. 'I've really enjoyed reading your column. Michelle has kept every article you wrote. I'm looking forward to reading more.'

'It might not be for a while,' I say, keeping my voice low.

'I thought you were taking back your column?' my mother says immediately. 'I see Susannah Frost is still heading it. Don't tell me they're keeping her on?'

'I'm not sure, but I've been talking to a couple of editors,' I improvise.

'You need to get your career back on track, Willow! Readers have short memories.'

Fortunately, Jeff distracts everyone with a story of his reality show and the low standard of lyrics that had been demonstrated so far, which were now on everyone's lips, creating great publicity and the conversation moves on. 'Maybe you could come up with some good lines?' he says, turning to me.

Mother is looking at me encouragingly.

I shrug, thinking people must be fed up with songs about broken hearts.

Fern skilfully diverts the conversation, complimenting Mother on her outfit.

I try to slip away early, but my mother catches up with me in the hallway.

'You're not leaving already? You've hardly got here!'

'I have somebody coming to fix the shed door,' I tell her, although Declan has already fixed it and put the bike away, covering it with a tarpaulin.

'Really?'

'Yes, I managed to find a couple of handy men,' I joke, but she doesn't attempt a smile.

'Well can't they get on with it without you?'

'I really need to be there.'

She breathes out impatiently before launching into delaying tactics. 'David seems solid enough, although he's not very sociable…she needs to sort out his wardrobe! I assume they intend to marry! It's a bit late for her to produce a child, but all the same I hope he doesn't dilly-dally. We could do with a family celebration especially after the horrors of last year.'

'They haven't been together that long,' I point out.

She is no doubt dreaming of a lavish wedding with all the trimmings, the kind of celebration I had denied her. 'We shouldn't put them under any pressure,' I begin.

'I wasn't aware I *was* putting them under pressure!'

'It's just this whole get together! The champagne. I think everyone was expecting an announcement.'

'Oh, for goodness sake! I thought it would be nice for David to meet a few of my friends. It's been a dreary old winter. I can't seem to do anything right…?'

'All I'm saying is…'

'I know what you're saying Willow,' she cuts in, 'but time's marching on! None of us are getting any younger.'

I wonder where she's going with this.

'I'd like to see you both settled, and happy. It's been how long now? At least eight months.'

I feel the inevitable rise.

'Two hundred and sixty-two days,' I say, shivering in the blustery March wind.

She was right, time was marching on, but I had stayed static, frozen in this afterlife, with no real purpose but to get through each and every day.

'These years won't come round again,' she continues. 'Life goes by so fast and can end without any warning. You of all people should know that.'

'Thanks for that reminder! And for the party. I'll call you soon.'

She stares at me as if there's something else.

'I'd better get going,' I say. I can't listen to any more reminders of how life can end without warning.

'Off you go then,' she says briskly.

As I make my way towards the jeep, trying not to limp, I notice she's still standing on the porch. 'I'd like to drop over and see Liam, and dear Sam of course as soon as they're home,' she calls after me.

'Of course. Give me a call first.'

Just in case I'm making passionate love with a handyman on the sofa, I want to add.

But she's heading back inside, raising one hand in a dismissive little wave.

LATE MARCH

I return from the leisure centre to find the landline ringing. I'm always uneasy when I hear its insistent tone, fearing some unforeseen disaster. It's Mother.

'Where on earth were you?' she demands.

'At the pool, doing some lengths.'

'Goodness? On such a filthy wet day!' My mother hates even getting her hair wet, will go to any lengths to avoid going out in the rain. 'I need you to drive me into Bristol this Thursday. I don't want to ask Jeffrey. In any case, he's planning to return to New York to see his family now the reality show is over and Fern is in such a joyful state with David! I'd rather not bother her.'

I swallow my irritation. Don't bother the happy lovestruck daughter, ask the other one whose life is already in tatters. Why on earth can't she drive herself to Bristol?

'I'm actually booked in for a rather invasive procedure.'

'You don't need to do this,' I tell her. 'You're fine as you are! You look amazing. Jeff clearly loves you and he could have easily attracted a… Well, a younger woman.' I pause, aware this is not hitting the right note.

'You don't know a thing about it,' she snaps.

I forge on. 'Anyway, you were always telling Fern that beauty comes from within.'

'Not that kind of procedure, Willow! They've found a lump in my breast. It has turned out to be malignant, according to one doctor. I told him to whip it out, do a lumpectomy or whatever ghastly word they use, but they want to take off the whole breast! I intend to fight this.'

For a moment I can't speak. I recall the conversation after the party about time passing. She had clearly been trying to tell me then.

'I wish you'd said something.'

'You have enough problems.'

I am suddenly panicked by this news. My mother has hardly had a day's illness in her life. Apart from periods of depression, she's never spent a day in bed.

'I'll come over,' I begin.

'I'm having my hair done at three,' she cuts in, 'and this evening is Bridge night.'

'Well let me know the time of your appointment, and I'll drive you there.'

I hang up, shaken, thinking about the inexorable march of time and how little heed I had paid to its swift passage.

I tell Sam and Liam over supper that Gran has to have an operation. 'She's going to be fine, so try not to worry,' I say.

'What sort of operation?' Sam frowns.

Liam stares at me worriedly.

'They found a lump in her breast. They're going to take it out – just to be safe.'

Sam is silent while Liam says, 'You'd better not fight with her, Mum. She might die, then you'll be sorry.'

'She's not going to die,' I say, reeling from his remark.

Liam's words are still echoing in my head, as I toss and turn in bed throughout the night. *She might die, then you'll be sorry.*

Note to blog:

One thing that death has taught me is to not 'let the sun go down on your wrath' if you can help it.

sadeyedlady is the first to respond with: *reconciliation is not always possible, especially if you've been estranged for years.*

Forgive and forget while you still have time, lifeafterdeath has written.

The sun will rise again to another day, blackwidower has commented.

I set off for Charlton Haven early, to pick my mother up and drive her to the hospital for a meeting with the surgeon. I get held up behind a farm tractor and arrive ten minutes late. She flings open the door, cursing that now she's going to miss her appointment. I point out we're only slightly behind schedule. She ignores this and climbs into the jeep, complaining there's something sticky on the seat and her cashmere jacket is now ruined. I am driving too fast, too erratically, there's a nasty draft coming from the air vent.

She's in the middle of telling me her neighbour Gloria is going off on some 'ghastly lonely-hearts cruise', then suddenly yells, 'Watch out for that truck!'

I brake sharply.

I try to stay calm, but when she shouts, 'Slow down, Willow! The lights are turning red,' I snap: 'If you're going to back seat drive the whole way, I can't do this.'

'*You* can't do this,' she fumes. 'I'm the one dying of cancer! I should have called Fern.'

I slow to a crawl, causing the driver behind us to swerve past, mouthing some obscenity.

'Has the doctor actually said that?' I demand, 'did he tell you it's spread?'

I feel sick now, can envisage the regret and remorse that lie ahead, the sense of failure, for not having tried harder, for not having been a better daughter.

'No, but he wants to remove my whole breast.' Her face is a blank canvas of unexpressed misery. 'Which is why I didn't want Jeffrey involved.' I need to have reconstruction work done first.'

'I'm sure he would want to be here for you—'

'I don't want him involved,' she snaps, 'so don't you dare mention it to my sister, if she calls. She'll only turn it into a drama. For all we know it could have spread everywhere,' she adds.

'We mustn't think the worst,' I begin.

'Terrible things happen, Willow. You of all people should know that!'

I have no answer to this. I take my hand off the steering wheel, and place it over hers. It feels cold and remains unresponsive.

She is fumbling in the depths of her large handbag for her phone now. I hear her say, 'Fern, could you meet us at the clinic? Yes, Southmead. The hospital, darling. I have a doctor's appointment. I'm here with Willow. I need you here too. No, I'm not OK. I have cancer!'

As we pull into the hospital car park, she says, 'I don't think I can go through with this.'

'The doctors can do amazing reconstructive work these days,' I point out. She should know all about that, after all the lifting and draining, the tummy tucks. But nothing I can say can lift her from her dark mood. I sense her glaring at me through her sunglasses.

'I feel I would lose a whole piece of who I am,' she says dully.

I can relate to that. Only no surgeon can reconstruct me, turn me back into the person I once was.

We are shown into the doctor's consulting room, and introduced to the handsome Indian surgeon who is direct and to the point. The tumour is large, but contained. He is confident they can remove it, but it would mean a mastectomy. He introduces the possibility of reconstructive surgery at a later date.

Fern arrives just when Mother is saying, 'At a later date? And what am I meant to do in the meantime? No, I will not have you removing my breast. You will have to find another solution.'

The doctor reiterates it would be too big a risk not to, that it could cost her her life.

'And what sort of a life will it be once you've mutilated me?' she demands.

All the same, I sense some of the fight has gone out of her.

The operation is booked for the following Monday and Fern and I spend the weekend trying to convince Mother all will be well. She is angry with us for even bringing up the subject, angry at the world in general, insisting she needs a second opinion. She lets slip she had consulted another doctor in Harley Street, who has given her the same prognosis. Only he had wanted to take off both breasts as a precaution.

I'm beginning to worry she is going to refuse treatment altogether and lock herself away like she had in the past when things got tough.

But she complies, and I am up at dawn on Monday ready to drive her to the hospital.

Fern and I watch our mother being wheeled away and I am struck by how shrunken she looks in her hospital gown. I tell myself all will be well, that she's still young, and sprightly. A woman who will fight illness and aging at any cost. I feel a pang thinking how fiercely proud she is of her magnificent cleavage.

We are told to call in the late afternoon to find out how the operation has gone. We are both in shock, unable to absorb the sudden turn of events, the fact that we could lose this indomitable force that is our mother, who, for better or worse, has always been at the forefront of our lives. Fern's eyes are wet with tears, while I cry openly.

'I told her she was interfering when it could have been her last Christmas,' I sob.

'It'll be all right,' Fern soothes.

'We don't know that. There's no guarantee.'

Since losing M, I worry about everything; envisaging the worst scenarios. In this case Mother's cancer has spread to every part of her body and she only has months to live. I think about losing her and how it would affect us all in different ways. The boys would be devastated, Liam heartbroken, while for Fern and me, there would be the added guilt for the years we had fought with her, when we wished we could have swapped her for a different kind of mother. Regret for not having been more understanding, forgiving. It would be a whole new other loss.

'She'll get through this,' Fern is saying.

'How can you be so sure?'

'She has a wedding to plan, remember,' my sister says with a faint smile. 'She's determined to see one of us walk down the aisle. In the meantime, we're going to have to take care of her.'

After an agonising wait, we're told Mother's operation has gone well.

Dr Samjee explains the tumour was removed, but she'd had a severe reaction to the anaesthetic which meant it was unlikely they would be able to carry out reconstructive surgery in the future.

I think of how she'd said, 'What sort of life will it be, once you've mutilated me?'

'She'll need full-time care for the next couple of weeks,' he is saying. 'As

I mentioned when we first spoke, a nurse will have to come in for the first few days to change her dressings. You need to decide where is the best place for your mother.'

Fern and I exchange glances. 'She can stay with me,' I say after a pause. After all, I have the space and the time and no such luxury as a new lover. I feel a kind of trapped panic, thinking I wouldn't be able to spend hours at the pool, or binge on wine in the evenings. She'd never be able to cope with my terrible housekeeping, the dust and disorder, the lack of proper meals.

Life will continue and take you along with it whether you like it or not. Mabel Vale had said that cold February day.

'We'll take it in turns,' Fern is saying, reading my mind.

'It's very important she has her family around her at this time,' Dr Samjee emphasises. 'You can go in and see her now. She's been sedated, so don't stay long.'

Mother appears to be fast asleep as we enter the room, but she suddenly flicks open her eyes, reminding me of one of those old-fashioned dolls with eyeballs that roll back into their sockets. She looks pale and waxen in the bed, her chest bulked up with dressings. I feel my stomach contract at the sight of the thin cannula feeding into a needle buried in her bandaged wrist, the lily-white hand naked without her rings. I drag myself back from the memory of another hospital, another ward.

'Did either of you bring me a dressing gown?' she says in a slurred voice. 'I'm not wearing this dreadful gown a moment longer. It's not even decent.'

'We'll bring one on our next visit,' Fern promises.

'I had the strangest dream about Timmy,' she murmurs, 'but I'm ready to go home now.'

'You're going to have to rest a bit first,' I begin. I'm about to explain that we'd spoken to the doctor and had discussed her coming to stay with me, but her eyelids are closing again and she's drifting off to sleep.

I spend the day sorting out the barn, cleaning the kitchen and living area, then brace myself to tackle the spare room. I'd crammed M's half-packed suitcase into the cupboard when Holly had stayed, now I pull it out along with his rucksack and surfing gear to make space for my mother's clothes. I drag his suitcase downstairs to the utility room, along with the rest of his things. The thought of moving M out so my mother can move in feels like a bitter pill, but perhaps it's my just deserts, I think, and I have no choice but to swallow it.

I fill the fridge with ready-made soups and quiches from the deli, buy organic fruit and vegetables from the market, a red velvet cake and a selection of her favourite teas. I push aside memories of the empty fridge when Fern and I were growing up, how on the cook's day off we would go across the road to The Melting Pot, and eat giant scones with butter and jam to fill our hollow stomachs.

I drive to the hardware store for lightbulbs so that my mother can read at night, and buy the latest Vogue, Town and Country and Style magazines for her.

I arrive at the hospital at visiting hours to find Mother sitting up in bed reading an old copy of Harper's Bazaar. 'Ah, here you are,' she exclaims, as if she'd given up hope of me ever arriving.

'How are you feeling?'

'Wretched,' she replies.

'It's probably the after-effects of the anaesthetic,' I begin. 'I was wondering if you'd like to come and stay with me until you feel stronger? It's up to you, of course,' I add, trying to decipher her expression.

'How do you feel about it?' she asks, her amber gaze burning into me.

'I think it's a good idea. Of course I want you to come and stay,' I add. I'm back in childhood mode, trying to please her.

Her whole body seems to relax, and a flicker of something akin to pleasure passes over her face.

'I'll do my best not to be in the way.'

APRIL

I bring my mother home on a breezy afternoon and settle her into the spare room. I've put an electric blanket on the bed even though the weather is warmer at last and placed a vase of spring flowers on the dressing table.

She insists she's not hungry, will sleep for a bit and come downstairs later. 'I don't want you waiting on me,' she states, sinking onto the bed and closing her eyes.

I wonder if her passive behaviour is due to depression. On the way back from the hospital she'd made no comment about my driving, had barely spoken. As we'd approached Rosewood Barn, she'd said, 'When will I be able to read your column again?'

'They're keeping Susannah on. I haven't actually got any work for now,' I'd confessed.

'Well, everything in its own good time,' she'd answered.

I had never heard her use that expression before. She was always reminding me how time was running out. As we pulled up on the driveway, she'd said, 'Susannah Frost is not an engaging writer.'

Now, as she settles down for a nap, I ask if she would like me to bring up some tea and cake later.

'I'm not an invalid,' she states. 'I'll be down as soon as I've had a little rest.'

It strikes me she's fearful of losing her independence and is putting on a brave face. I withdraw, feeling oddly redundant. I would have liked to have sat with her and got an insight into how she's feeling.

I go downstairs, glance through the window and see Frida standing in the middle of the lawn wearing a long flowery dress and a pair of gardening boots. I step outside and watch as she pushes a silver tube into one of the molehills.

'It's a sonic spike,' she tells me. 'The little creatures hate the noise. It sends a pulse deep into the earth. They'll be gone before you know it.' She sees my face and says, 'It's not going to kill them, love, just send them packing.'

I let out a sob. 'It's my mother. I just brought her back from the hospital. She's had a mastectomy. They found a lump in her breast. It was malignant…she's being so brave – it's so not like her…. I mean she is brave but not about things like this…'

Frida pulls me into her arms and holds me against her angular frame. She smells of laundry powder and the outdoors. 'Try not to fret, the doctors are excellent these days. She's a strong woman, from what you've told me.'

'It could have spread, she might die...' *the doctors weren't able to save M.*

'Listen to me, Willow,' Frida says. 'She's going to be all right. 'Mama was diagnosed with breast cancer ten years ago but she decided it wasn't her time and now she's ninety-eight years old! She just fought it with the power of her will. Let us not assume the worst, or make a mountain out of a molehill,' she smiles, plunging the tube viciously into another hole. 'At least until we know more.'

The boys return from school wanting to know how their grandmother is. I notice the ease with which they embrace her and her joy around them. Sam asks when Jeff is coming back as he wants to discuss the song he and Lennie have written. 'It's called 'Out of the Shadows', he tells her.

'Maybe you could make a recording and we could send it to him?' Mother suggests, smiling at him fondly.

They pull out the giant jigsaw M had had made, a kind of 3D construction of Rosewood Barn and the three of them set about putting it together, heads bent over the task while I prepare supper. I feel oddly superfluous, adrift. As if I have somehow lost my bearings.

A young Spanish nurse arrives in the late afternoons. I hear her and Mother chatting and my mother's infectious laugh. She is definitely not her old self. Rather, she seems to have become a completely different self. The nurse assures me she will heal quickly, that she's 'a strong and determined lady'. 'And very beautiful,' she adds.

I nod and say, yes, she is all those things. Strong, determined, beautiful.

I think of how she'd said, 'I feel as if I'm losing a whole piece of who I am,' and pray she can get through this, find a way to come to terms with the missing piece.

I knock on the door in the early evening and when there's no response, push it open and find my mother and the nurse standing in front of the long mirror. Only instead of pirouetting in her latest outfit (Mummy's the prettiest) she's naked from the waist up, and is frowning at her reflection. The vivid gash running across the flat plain of her chest gives me a jolt.

'I'm sorry, I didn't realise you hadn't finished,' I say to the nurse. 'I'll come back later.'

'You don't have to rush off, unless you've things to do?' Mother says, our eyes meeting in the mirror.

'I don't. I could bring you up a cup of tea?'

She shakes her head. 'I've had enough tea to last a lifetime. How about a glass of white wine? I'll come down and join you.'

She comes downstairs half an hour later in a cream satin dressing gown, and matching slip-on mules. I hand her a glass of wine and hear her say, 'No matter what I wear, I'm going to look lopsided. I've lost my sense of balance.'

I feel a pang. I wonder if the doctor had told her reconstructive surgery was not an option. She places her hand just below where her breast had been. 'This is where I stored it all these years.'

'Stored what?'

'My sorrow. My grief after losing Timmy. In the end it turned cancerous.'

I think about the ache that resides permanently beneath my breast bone.

'You can't allow these things to fester, you know,' she says.

We have developed a ritual, which begins around 6 o'clock with Mother settling herself on the sofa to watch a quiz show on television, while I prepare supper. She doesn't comment on my lack of cooking skills, the messy kitchen or even my six o'clock wine habit. Instead, she says, 'Pour me one too,' then takes delicate little sips, making her glass last the whole evening, while I finish the bottle. She calls her sister in New York from time to time and I hear her say, 'No, Camilla, I haven't told Jeffrey about the operation and don't you dare mention it to him. Have you spoken to him by any chance?'

The boys appear and we eat supper together, my mother wanting to know all about their day at school, then they head back upstairs to do their homework, leaving us alone. She teaches me her favourite card game Spite and Malice and when I win for the second time, she laughs and says, 'I'm clearly not as spiteful as you thought!'

'I never thought you were,' I reply.

'I know I failed you and Fern when you were growing up,' she begins, 'but Timmy's death turned my whole world upside down.'

'I can only imagine how devastating it must have been.'

'I had this vivid dream about him. He was wearing his blue baseball cap and an orange t-shirt that was almost threadbare. He was standing at the end of my bed making a silly face as if he was about to tell me one of his jokes. It was so real. I can't remember much of what we spoke about, all I know is he didn't blame me for what happened. We had this argument, you see. I was angry with him that day. It seems so trivial now. He wanted extra pocket money so he could buy a new bike and I refused. I often think how I could have just given it to him. She fiddles with one of her rings, adding, 'He left the house in an angry mood and went over to his friend Jerry's house. Jerry's older brother persuaded him to get on the back of the bike. Timmy didn't have his helmet with him. I have been consumed with guilt all these years.'

> GUILT (*noun*) the fact of having committed a specified or implied offence or crime.

'You never mentioned this before,' I say after a pause.

'I couldn't bring myself to talk about it, which was a mistake. Now I feel as if a burden has lifted.'

'Guilt seems to be an inevitable part of the grieving process,' I say, at last.

Over breakfast one morning she says, 'What happened to the toaster I gave you for Christmas?'

Several answers flash through my mind.

'I had to get rid of it. There was a mouse trapped inside it,' I tell her, my cheeks burning. 'I can make us toast under the grill,' I add.

'You threw it out?' she repeats incredulously.

'I'm sorry, it was an amazing gift and it must have cost a lot.'

'I wish you'd confided in me.'

'You hate mice,' I remind her. 'Remember you booked a room at the Chelwood Inn once, because there was one in our kitchen!'

'That was a rat, Willow! What I meant was I wish you'd confided in me as to what you were going through instead of shutting me out. I know I wasn't supportive of your marriage. It happened so fast and you were so young and naïve. I couldn't just sit by and watch you make the same mistakes I'd made.'

'So you think marrying M was a mistake?' I say heatedly.

'I just felt you didn't know anything about him. You were so open and innocent, while he was a closed book.'

I had known enough to know he was The One, I think, my mind travelling back to the day I'd told her he'd asked me to marry him. He had hidden an antique engagement ring of rose gold with a solitary diamond in the sleeves of a first edition of *Wuthering Heights*.

It had taken me weeks to introduce him to Mother. She kept making excuses claiming she was busy, but she had already made up her mind he was unsuitable. I had foolishly let slip that he rode a motorbike.

'I hope you're not riding around on it,' she'd warned. 'Those things are death traps.'

'Not if you know how to ride them properly,' I'd argued fatally.

Her face had turned livid, her mouth a taut line.

'How can you say that after what happened to your step-brother!' For a moment I thought she was about to hit me. She had lashed out a few times when we were children, her anger spilling over – no doubt that's where I get my short temper from. This time she'd simply turned on her heels and marched out of the room, slamming the door behind her. By the time she met M she had already decided he was the wrong man for me. She'd invited us over for 'a light lunch' and my heart had sunk as she'd set about interviewing him. I watched him withdraw into himself, shifting in his chair, rubbing his scar, as she empathised over the tragic death of his parents, enquired about the care home in London's East End, followed by an inquisition on the foster families. Afterwards, she'd gazed at M as if he was damaged goods. 'It must have been very difficult for you and your brother growing up in those circumstances.'

M had shrugged it off and forged on, describing the happy times he and Will had spent in Whitsand Bay with the Clarks, how Jenny and Owen Clark had been wonderful foster parents, teaching them how to swim and surf, only Owen had had a stroke and the couple had had to give up caring for them.

'How very destabilising,' Mother had commented, 'being moved from one family to another.'

'We came through it just fine,' he'd replied shortly.

When I'd announced that M and I were getting married, she'd flared, 'you've only just graduated from university. What are you planning to live on?'

I'd just landed a job working as a copy editor for an independent publishing house and although I was making very little money, it was a start.

'He's not right for you, Willow, there's no reference point.'

'He's starting his own design and construction business,' I'd told her. 'He put himself through college by working on building sites every summer, he's going to be a famous architect one day.'

'That's very commendable,' she'd replied, 'but, all the same, you barely know the man.'

'I know enough! I've never felt like this about anyone.'

She'd let out a furious breath. 'I had such high hopes for you! I've met men like him in the past, the dark and mysterious type. You have a passionate fling with them, but you don't marry them! He didn't have a normal upbringing. I noticed he was very cagey about his brother. His past can rear up anytime – manifest itself through violent behaviour, anything.'

'What are you talking about, Mother? M is the most loving, caring person I've ever met!' I wanted to point out that mine and Fern's upbringing had been far from normal either. 'He wants to make a difference – renovate old buildings, keep the past alive, make the world a better place,' I'd finished dramatically.

My impassioned speech had been lost on her. 'We all want to make a difference, but that doesn't pay the bills! I simply won't sit by and watch you throw your life away,' she'd finished in an ominous voice.

'You can't stop me, Mother,' I'd reiterated, my voice equally threatening, 'so don't even try.' With that I'd stormed off and caught the bus to M's flat in Harbourside, announcing there had been a change of plan. Instead of the traditional wedding I'd always dreamed of, which ironically was also Mother's vision, I wanted us to get married on a white beach under a palm tree far away from here, just him and me. M had calmed me down, suggesting we give her time to come around.

'I don't want her to come around or ever come anywhere near me again,' I'd raged.

In the end, I reluctantly agreed to postpone the wedding, but my mother refused to even discuss it.

M and I were married at the end of September in a registry office in Bristol. Mother claimed I'd chosen that particular date to get married as a 'wilful act of revenge', knowing she always went away at that time of the year to New York to visit her sister. Over the following years we developed an uneasy truce, and she would talk wistfully about the wonderful wedding plans she'd had for me, if only I hadn't rushed into marriage with the first man who'd come along.

Now she says, 'I'm sorry, Willow. I know you loved M very much. It's a terrible loss for you and the boys, but you'll meet somebody else, and fall in love again – when you're ready, that is.'

'Nobody could ever replace him,' I say defensively, 'nor would I want them to.'

'You would love whoever it was differently,' she states.

'No I wouldn't. He was "the one".'

'We'll see. In the meantime, you have to start living again, get your career back on track, land another column.'

I tell her about my blog, about blackwidower and his wisdom, the bitter sadeyedlady, and philosophical lifeafterdeath, the angry notdeadyet.

'I'm the waywardwidow,' I add daringly, wondering what she will make of that.

A faint smile plays around her full lips. 'Maybe you could turn it into a book about grief, and how you overcame it?' she suggests.

'The Wallowing Widow?' I suggest, archly, thinking I was a long way from overcoming it.

'The Wayward Widow describes you much better,' she concludes.

The week passes by in a flash. My mother has remained unaccountably upbeat. It's hard to believe she has gone through a major operation. Even during her follow-up appointments and waiting for the doctor to give her the all-clear, she has kept her good humour. She sits on the sofa, sipping a glass of wine and reading back copies of weekend supplements containing articles I'd written in what I now think of as 'the before life.'

'Have you tried submitting anything recently?' she wants to know.

I tell her about the interview with the old lady and how Jason had rejected it, claiming I sounded angry.

'Well, anger is all part of grief. You lost your husband, and it's tough! I lost two in the space of four years! It would help if you could talk about it.'

'There's not much to talk about,' I answer, thinking anything I said would only add fuel to the already burning issues she'd had about M. I wanted her to focus on the good parts.

We sit up late one evening after the boys have gone to bed and she talks about her many love affairs, including her brief marriage to my father, the photographer Tony Monroe.

'He was a notorious philanderer, but so charming,' she smiles. 'He was constantly tempted by young models knocking on his door. I had dreadful post-natal depression; my career was over. I was doing the odd leg shot for stockings. I would come back from a dreary shoot, while he'd been away in some sunny location, doing a cover shot for Vogue. He was taking LSD and dabbling in heroin at the time. He died of an overdose when you were still a baby.'

'You told me it was a heart attack?' I say with confusion.

'It was, brought on by a drug overdose. I didn't mention it because I wanted you to think of him as the talented photographer he was, rather than a drug addict. We're all the sum of our parts,' she concludes. 'I prefer to remember the good parts. I still have fond thoughts about him, but maybe it's easier to forgive the dead than the living.'

I think about M and his good deeds; rushing off to assist somebody while the boys and I waited for him to come home. Roaring away on the bike that day in spite of my begging him not to. How, in the end, he had put Will's life ahead of me and the boys.

'About Jeff?' I begin tentatively. 'I feel he should be with you while you're going through this?'

She sighs. 'He wanted to spend time with his daughter and grandson in New York, but the real reason is I told him I didn't want him around.'

'Why?'

'I'm hardly a pretty sight now, let's face it!' she replies, shuffling the cards with concentration.

'I reckon he would have wanted to be around. Anyway, you're still beautiful. And, as you pointed out, we're all the sum of our parts!'

She laughs throatily. 'Well, I'm not very good at following my own advice, love. You should know that by now.'

I smile, thinking about my blog, which had gathered thousands of followers, how my comments had recently taken on an advisory note, with tips on how to move forwards, while my own life had remained on pause.

'I do. I also know where I get it from!'

As we are making our way upstairs to bed, I say, 'Mum (I have started calling her that more often recently), I think you should call Jeff and tell him about your operation. He would want to be with you right now.'

She glares at me for a moment then her face softens. 'You're probably right. He's not getting any younger. He's been having problems with his prostate! And he hums in his sleep! He's come up with a few dreadful lyrics himself, I can tell you!' She smiles, adding, 'but he has a wonderful singing voice. I suggested he put himself forward for his own show!'

It strikes me she is deeply smitten with this man.

'Give him a call,' I urge, thinking it must be the first time ever I have given my mother any advice. It's still early in New York.'

'I'll think about it,' she answers primly.

Fern and David return from the Lake District, dropping in on their way home. I feel a stab of envy as my sister prances into the room showing off a beautiful engagement ring with three bands of different shades of gold, studded with miniature diamonds. Fern seems to be floating on air, reminding me of that weightless feeling of joy when it seemed that love was a given and would last forever. They have brought a bottle of champagne and I go in search of some glasses. I glance across the room to where she and David are sitting on the sofa next to Mother in a bubble of happiness, light pooling around them. Once again, I feel that sense of separation and hesitate for a moment, afraid to enter lest I burst it.

Mother is full of ideas for the wedding and is already planning the venue and what she's going to wear. Fern reiterates that they want a modest ceremony, adding that her dream is to be married in a garden centre. 'Maybe next autumn,' she adds.

'A garden centre?' Mother repeats, 'how very quaint!'

I listen to them making plans and witness Fern's face suffused with happiness, David beside her; proud and smiling, Mother basking in the light of it all. My eyes fill with happy tears as I move over to join them.

David wanders out into the garden, leaving the three of us to talk and Mother says, 'I do hope it's going to be a traditional wedding all the same, as we didn't get to celebrate Willow's.' She notices my expression and adds, 'But of course, that was a different situation.'

'David and I don't want a big wedding,' Fern repeats. 'And it definitely won't be until next year. We want to do some trips away, get to know each other better.'

'Well, don't dilly-dally for goodness sake! I might not be around! I'm still waiting for the all clear,' Mother says with a strained little laugh. 'I'm determined to see one of you settled at least.'

Fern and I exchange glances.

'You will,' I say. Although it strikes me this too is not a given. But for now, I savour the joy of my sister's news, thinking it's a sign of better times to come.

A few days later, my mother floats into the room in a cream skirt, yellow silk blouse and impossibly high heels. Even with the loose blouse, her missing breast is painfully absent. Without the support of a bra – she's still not able to wear one, the solitary breast hangs at half-mast as if mourning the loss of its lifelong companion.

Her face breaks into a photographic smile as she announces the doctor has called to say her tests were clear. Relief washes over me. I want to hug her, but am afraid she might recoil from me. In any case, she's never been one for hugs, or any display of affection, at least not from me. 'Run along to bed now, Willow,' she would say, when, as a child, I had attempted to kiss her smooth cheek.

'It's the best news ever,' I say, smiling at her. We have time…a chance to forge a better relationship, I think.

'Yes, it is, but now I need to think about going home. I can't play the invalid any more. It's been lovely, but I need to get on with my life. And so do you,' she adds meaningfully.

'You don't have to rush off. You could stay over the weekend?' I suggest, surprising myself. Her visit had given me a sense of purpose. Now I was going to have to reclaim my life, move forward.

She shakes her head. 'The time has come. Besides, I took your advice and called Jeffrey. He's coming back from New York. He wants us to give it a go. He reckons I might be less of a handful now! Well, there is less of me,' she smiles.

'That's great, Mum.'

'Everybody needs somebody to accompany them on this bumpy road of life,' she says, using one of Jeff's sayings. 'Now, how about I take you to the Pump Rooms for lunch to thank you for putting up with me?'

'You don't have to do that.'

'I'd like to,' she insists.

Note to blog:

Life is filled with unexpected moments. Relationships can shift and evolve, loss can bring you closer. Bridges can be mended after all. It's the proverbial silver lining shining through the dark times.

There are only a couple of responses to this. It's clearly too optimistic for sadeyedlady, but blackwidower has written: *loss is part of the human condition, universal and unifying – teaching us how to live and love again.*

At the Pump Rooms, Mother insists we stop to 'take the waters'. 'It's meant to cure a host of ailments,' she says. I take a sip, trying not to gag at the malodorous taste. We gaze down at the steaming bottle-green water below. 'They were a vain lot, those Romans,' she comments. 'Did you know they used kohl in those days and malachite as eyeshadow? How about we go to Jolly's after lunch and buy you some new lipstick?'

'I don't need any for now, but if you want to get a new shade,' I begin.

'Willow, it's not always a case of needing,' she says firmly.

Over lunch, she orders a bottle of champagne and as the classical string trio plays a poignant piece by Bach, she raises her glass 'to a new chapter'.

'To your amazing recovery!' I toast, 'I can't believe how brave you've been – it's a tough thing to go through.'

'In life there are small losses and great losses.' She pauses, then adds, 'Maybe it's time you started talking about yours?'

'There's nothing to talk about,' I say, gulping back champagne. 'M's gone, and I'm trying to move on as you keep telling me.'

'And you must! Otherwise, you'll be left behind.'

'Turn into "the old widow of Rosewood Barn?"' I suggest.

She shudders. 'Heaven forbid!'

Our attention is taken by two overdressed women who have just sat down at a table at the far end of the room. 'There's that dreadful Lady Priscilla,' Mother says.

I follow her gaze and freeze at the sight of Lady Priscilla Huntington, the owner of Huntington Hall.

'Ghastly outfit, looks like a copy of a Jaeger. So outdated.'

'M and I were arguing that day,' I blurt, the words bubbling up like the champagne.

There's a silence and then my mother does an extraordinary thing. Instead of encouraging me to talk about it, she waves it away, saying, 'Arguing is all part of married life. You mustn't dwell on it, or blame yourself. He was very fortunate to have you. You gave him two wonderful sons. Now, where is that wretched waiter to refill our glasses?'

I drive my mother back to Charlton Haven and carry her suitcase into the house. As I'm about to leave, she hands me an envelope full of crisp notes. It's the first time she has given me money for years, and although I could use it right now, I feel uncomfortable. Earlier, she had insisted on buying me four different shades of lipsticks from nude to a blood red, and some magic stick that promised to erase the shadows beneath my eyes.

'What's this for?' I say holding up the envelope. 'I don't want anything for having you to stay. I'm going to be earning again soon.' I feel immediately affronted and wonder if we've made any real progress after all.

'It's not for you,' she says bluntly. 'I want you to buy me some underwear. Designer mastectomy bras if you can find such a thing. I simply can't face that side of it. They fitted me for a bra at the hospital, but it was too ghastly for words. I took down the measurements. 36D cup and don't expect me to settle for any less.'

I smile. 'You never do, Mum!'

We kiss each other on the cheek and I make a promise to drop in next week.

'More importantly, Willow, start writing again. I've been reading your blog. Maybe it's time you started acting on your own advice.'

EARLY MAY

Fern and I head into the city centre to shop and look at wedding dresses. We spend hours sifting through rails of frothy gowns, which she dismisses as too fussy. She tries on a couple of dresses, but complains they make her look like an old bride. 'Maybe we should just book a registry office like you did,' she says despondently.

'You're getting married in a garden centre, remember? Come on, we're going to find you the perfect dress.'

I had filled her in on the week with Mother, marvelling at how well it had gone.

'I haven't seen her so relaxed for years. She opened up for the first time ever, told me she'd been feeling guilty for years over Timmy's death. She had an argument with him the morning before he died and has never forgiven herself. He asked for some extra pocket money so he could buy a new bike and she refused to give it to him. Now I understand why she was always giving me money and buying you gifts you didn't even want. Anyway, she dreamed about him while she was under the anaesthetic and knew he'd forgiven her. She regrets not having been able to talk about it until now. It's as if she's unburdened herself. Perhaps there's a lesson in there,' I add after a pause.

Fern looks at me directly. 'Some things are better left unspoken,' she says firmly.

We buy a selection of bras for Mother, which the sales assistant says can be worn with either foam or silicone fillers. Fern wanders off towards the designer rails. It occurs to me I could do with some new underwear and pull out a beautiful matching lacy set, the colour of ivory. I think of how the passion had started seeping out of our marriage in the final months when the deadline to finish the Huntington Hall extension drew closer. Or perhaps it had begun earlier, when M had made that fateful decision to risk his life for his brother. A decision which had created a bitter feud between us. It was then that he'd started to withdraw from me. I am brought out of my reverie by the sales assistant, who asks if I'd like to try on the items. I nod and head towards the changing room.

I pull aside the curtain, and find Fern trying on a silky peach combination. It was a tradition that we crammed ourselves into the same cubicle no matter how small. She grimaces at her reflection, patting her midriff which has increased since meeting David. Whereas I had lost too much weight – my breasts had shrunk, my hip bones were starting to show. I should have picked up a smaller size, I think.

'You walk into the changing room with so much hope, only to come out in despair,' Fern groans.

'What do you think of these?' I say, holding up the ivory lace ensemble.

My sister frowns. 'For you?'

'Well hardly for Mother!'

'Gorgeous, but let's just hope it's not to no avail!'

'Are you trying to say I'll never have sex again?'

A voluptuous-looking woman glances curiously through the gap in the curtain with raised eyebrows.

Fern looks embarrassed. 'It's just that I didn't think you were getting close to dating again?'

I fling aside the curtain and flounce away towards the cashier with my items, too upset to try them on. To no avail? What did she mean? That I'll be wearing M's boxer shorts to bed for the rest of my life?

Fern has awakened something in me, brought me face to face with that other loss; a physical ache I can't satisfy myself. My body is screaming to be touched, held, stroked, made love to. I'd thought it had shut down, never to be re-awakened. Now I fantasise about strangers on trains; faceless, nameless men who will seduce me then disappear into thin air. I consider my options. Dating sites seem a long shot, hanging around bars not appealing. I feel too old to go clubbing and Fern is too 'loved up' to go with me. Besides, if I should meet somebody, where would we go? I could hardly bring anyone back to the barn, with the boys around. It would have to be a hotel, turning it into an illicit, clandestine thing which leaves me feeling cold.

Note to blog:

How do you deal with the lack of physical contact after losing your loved one? It is likely that you have shut down and are no longer giving out a signal that you are available. The flame of passion has died along with him or her, but your body still yearns for what it has lost.

You are going to have to ignite the fire again, lifeafterdeath has commented.

Suggest that you carry a condom with you at all times, blackwidower writes. *P.S you mentioned in an earlier blog that women can take care of it all, even their own orgasms!*

I smile, intrigued, thinking perhaps he's not a fusty old university professor after all.

MID MAY

I set off for the swimming pool with my stopwatch and the vague idea of testing out my lung capacity. The handsome lifeguard is sitting in his high chair, reigning over the far end of the pool. The other lifeguard, a young blonde girl, is walking up and down coltishly, flicking her mane of hair. I swim up and down a few times to warm up, then take a deep breath and dive down at the point where the pool descends sharply into the deep end. I set my stopwatch, planning to break my last record of a minute and forty seconds. It is strangely intoxicating beneath the water. Wallowing in the true sense of the word with that feeling of weightlessness, free from all earthly bondage. My thoughts become fragmented, my lungs are close to bursting, but I'm determined to hold out for a few more seconds when the water suddenly explodes around me. I feel a tug as I'm grabbed beneath one armpit and hoisted to the surface. I take in rippling abdominals and a snake tattoo curving around a veiny wrist. It's all very dramatic, as I'm scooped up in a rush of water and deposited on the tiled edge of the pool like a landed fish. Instead of attempting mouth-to-mouth resuscitation, my rescuer is shouting out to the blonde lifeguard. 'Can you check this one out for me. Breathing appears normal…it's the invisible woman,' he mutters, 'thinks she's a fucking mermaid!'

'Can you hear me?' the girl shouts, her breath hot in my ear. She grabs my wrist and searches clumsily for a pulse. Swimmers have paused in their lanes to watch, so I'm far from invisible.

'I was just trying to see how long I could stay underwater,' I gasp.

His tone is far from friendly. 'I told you last time underwater swimming is not permitted.'

'You can hardly stop people swimming under the water!'

'We can by barring them from using the pool,' is his sharp response.

'I won't be coming back, in any case,' I announce, suddenly repelled by the chemical smell and echoing sound of splashing, the stale air of spent energy. The rules and regulations. I take in his bulging arms with their tributaries of thick blue veins and turn away, attempting a dignified exit only to slip and fall on a wet tile.

What on earth was that all about, I wonder as I stand bruised and shivering under the tepid shower? A subliminal desire to be rescued from the depths of despair? I drive home, heavy-hearted, with the sense there is no escape, no place to hide from the rest of the world.

LATE MAY

I sit listening to M's favourite soul music. It is only now that I can bear to listen to it. I think of how he had found his sanctuary by withdrawing to the shed to tinker with his bike, or setting off for an evening ride to Winford Gap, Deer Leap, or Eden Gorge.

I long for a similar escape – to discover a passion I can lose myself in, find some place where peace and contentment lie – if there is such a place.

M had appeared to fill his days effortlessly; rushing off to work in the early mornings, claiming he was late, yet still stopping on his way to check on Frida or chat with one of the other neighbours, making long to-do lists of tasks which often remained undone, choosing instead to head to Cornwall to 'catch some waves'.

I have failed to be happy without M in my world. I couldn't continue living this diluted half-life for the rest of my days. Maybe I should try to live in his.

I make my own list:

Ask Sean to call builder about finishing the courtyard and discuss installing water feature.

Find a gardener and cleaner, or just a cleaner – better still, buy one of this robot cleaners that won't talk or be horrified by the mess!

I finish the list with: *get life in order!*

That night I sleep on M's side of the bed. The sheets are cold and uninviting without an electric blanket and I keep reaching across the expanse to where I usually lie for my glass of water. I flick through an old copy of Classic Bike, which falls open on a page on which the corner has been turned down with a full-page article headed, 'The fearless falcon is ready to re-launch herself again'. There is an image of a female rider crouched over the handlebars, bike and rider frozen in mid-air.

I had stopped climbing soon after Liam had been born. I recall the thrill I'd felt of reaching the highest point of the gorge and wonder if I have the courage and strength to launch myself again.

EARLY JUNE

Almost a year has passed, and yet there are days when I believe M is still around, his physical form insubstantial, ethereal yet heart-achingly familiar: lounging in front of the TV with his long legs stretched out in front of him, sitting at his desk lost in a design, standing in front of the bathroom mirror shaving the stubble that would cast a new shadow across his jaw before the day was done. Once I even thought I heard him singing in the shower. Today, as I return from Highbury, I hear the sound of his motorbike idling in the shed. I make my way down the path and pull open the door filled with that ridiculous expectation he is back in the flesh.

Sean Maloney is crouched on the floor polishing the already gleaming chrome of the Triumph to the gurgle and tick of the engine.

'Thought I'd better check if there was any damage after your encounter with the door!' He grins and stands up, pushing a lock of coppery hair out of his eyes.

I notice he too has lost weight, which has made his face look sharper, edgy, his features more defined.

'Thanks,' I answer, summoning a smile. 'How was your trip?' He had sent a few photos of his road trip, as he'd made his way along the Spanish coastline.

'Bittersweet. How are you doing?'

'Some days are better than others.'

'It's hard to accept, even on the better days,' he says, cutting the engine. 'I've been thinking if you're going to keep this beauty, you should learn how to handle it. I could show you a few tricks, so you could take it out for a spin yourself, keep it ticking over.'

'You must be joking! The last time I got onto it, I crashed into the shed door, and ended up hobbling around for days,' I remind him. 'I've never felt safe on a motorbike. My mother drummed it into me how dangerous they are.'

'All the more reason to conquer it,' he replies. 'Imagine how impressed the boys would be!'

'I wouldn't be able to handle it,' I say, quoting Will.

Sean reaches for the spare helmet, saying, 'You'll never know unless you try! Let's see how well this fits you?'

He's runs through every feature of the bike, glancing at me every so often to see if I'm following. 'The throttle is a portal,' he explains. 'With the twist of the wrist, unlimited power is in your hands. Here, hop on behind me and we'll take it for a blast.'

I climb on reluctantly winding my arms around his waist, the bike roars to life and we're off heading down the driveway, turning left towards the reservoir. We drive along the back lanes through a tunnel of trees, past fields and farm holdings and out into the sunlit afternoon. The wind whips strands of his hair into my face and I bury my face in his leather jacket, imagining he is M and we are one again. We circle the reservoir where fishermen are casting their lines into the silvery water. I start to relax, settling into the rhythm – the pitch and thrum of the engine. At last, we're turning away from the sharp rays of the sun towards home. As we reach the lane that leads to the barn, he slows to a halt, plants a booted foot on the ground and swings around. 'Right, your turn.'

'There's nothing to fear but fear itself,' the old lady had said.

I am conscious of his hands around my waist, his voice in my ear urging me to lean in. I take the corner too wide, only to weave across the road, ending up braking sharply.

'Too much front brake and you'll be ejected, too much rear and you're going to skid,' he warns as we turn into the driveway and slow to a shaky halt. 'Nothing that can't be improved with a bit of practice. You need to relax into the bends and trust yourself. How about we give it another go tomorrow?'

We ride out in the late afternoons, cutting across the fields to the track where M had taken the boys with their dirt bikes. Sean stands propped up against his bike, shouting out instructions to accelerate, lean in, take the bend wider, and, as I become more confident, to slow down. And for a moment I feel as if I have entered M's world, and am living the life that had been stolen from him.

One evening we sit in the half-finished courtyard sipping a beer. Sean tells me how he and M had planned a trip to Dartmoor, only M had picked up a young hitchhiker on the way and driven thirty miles in the opposite direction so the boy didn't miss his first job interview. They had never made it to Dartmoor.

'He spent his whole life picking up waifs and strays,' I sigh. I tell Sean about the day M had stopped to help a woman who had broken down on the side of the road while we were on our way to London and how we'd ended up missing The Lion King. 'The AA were on their way, but he still insisted on staying with her. It was hard to live with at times, watching him rushing around after people we'd never meet again, helping lost causes like Will. All that time we'll never get back.'

'He lived his life the way he wanted,' Sean states, 'something not all of us get to do.'

Had I tried to stop him living his life the way he wanted, I wondered? I thought not. Had I nagged him about spending more time with his family? Without a doubt.

I listen to Sean's descriptions of the road trips they'd done, the places they'd visited, and the people they'd met along the way. I ask him about the more recent times, when M was spending less and less time at home.

'The last trip we did was in the October. After that he was always too busy with work, or the bikers' club. He went to Cornwall a few times to visit some relative of his.'

'M didn't have any relatives,' I say, frowning. 'I wonder who that could have been?'

Sean looks uncomfortable. 'I don't know – somebody he grew up with maybe? He seldom talked about his past.'

I tell him about Toby Jessop and how I believed he'd been trying to get in touch with M, before moving on to how Will had cancelled M's phone contract. 'I have a feeling Will may have been involved in a hit and run accident that happened around the time they lived in Ramsgate. I read about it online. Apparently, the driver couldn't be named for legal reasons.'

Sean frowns. 'M would have told you if something that bad had happened.'

There were a lot of things M didn't tell me, I think.

Sean stays over for dinner, I open a bottle of wine, and we sit up late talking. He tells me how he'd set up an online company, bringing together teams of carpenters, joiners and roofers to undertake large building contracts.

'After what happened at the Hall, I needed to change direction,' he says.

The conversation inevitably moves to the Huntington Hall project that he and M had been working on. I drink more wine and describe how I'd tried to dissuade M from signing the contract, believing there was a curse on the place.

I have opened the floodgates, knowing I'm about to drown us both, but the words are pouring out in a rush, like a tidal wave, unstoppable.

'…M thought it would put M&J on the map. It almost became a personal mission, but he tended to become emotionally invested in a project. Once he was engaged there was no getting through to him. He'd go into another zone. The boys found it so frustrating. We all did…he wouldn't listen.' Tears are snaking down my cheeks, like the rain that had streamed down the arched windows the day of the summer solstice.

Sean is staring at me with a haunted look. 'Why did he go over there?' he says at last. 'It makes no fucking sense. It was chucking it down. Why didn't he wait until Monday?'

There's a ringing in my ears like the persistent tone of an alarm bell that grows louder. I'm back there, with the storm raging around us.

'He was trying to fix the mess everyone left behind after walking out on him,' I blurt. 'You all deserted him. He wanted everything to be in perfect order for the wedding, and it backfired on him.'

No good deed goes unpunished, I think.

Sean reels back as if he has been struck. Then stands up and walks like a sleepwalker towards the fireplace, leaning against the rough stone for support.

'I still can't work out how...'

'It was an accident,' I state, the blood pounding in my ears.

There are lots of hidden dangers in the construction business.

My voice sounds echoey as if there's a time lapse between what I'm saying and hearing.

'But how?'

'It's all a blur,' I hear the disjointed voice echo.

He leans back further, dislodging the smiling photo of M in its rosewood frame which crashes to the floor, the glass splintering. 'Fuck,' he breathes, crouching down and attempting to gather up the shards.

'Sorry,' he mutters.

'Leave it,' I say. 'I'll sort it out.'

I go in search of a dustpan and brush, trying to gather myself.

'Let me do it,' he says, taking the brush from me.

I watch him sweeping up the shattered glass, my head swirling. 'I need to go and lie down,' I mutter faintly.

'I'll clean this up, and be on my way.'

Not long afterwards, I hear the sound of his bike starting up, the roar of the engine becoming fainter before fading away into the night.

I lie there for a long time, sleep for ever out of reach, then creep downstairs to my desk beneath the eaves. I pull out the leather-bound book M had given me on the day of my fortieth birthday. Then find the pen he'd had engraved with my name, and begin to write.

PART 2

MID-MARCH

105 DAYS BEFORE THE SUMMER SOLSTICE

'Will got the results from some tests back from the doctor,' M announces as we are about to sit down to a late dinner. It was the third time that week he'd arrived home at ten o'clock. The lasagne I'd made hours ago had dried up. I was about to vent my anger, but was alerted by something in his voice. 'It's not good. He has stage four kidney disease. He's on the waiting list for a donor to come forward.'

'I'm so sorry,' I answer, shocked by this news. Will had always seemed to bounce back from the binge-drinking up until then. He'd even managed to retain his good looks as if somehow immune to the ravages of alcohol. But mentally it was taking a toll. M had mentioned Will had been feeling unwell, had been suffering from depression, was plagued by thoughts of suicide again. He had been going through a particularly bad patch after his recent business venture had failed, and his latest girlfriend had walked out after discovering he was seeing somebody else. The drinking was spiralling out of control, but all the same, I hadn't realised quite how bad it was. 'This is a wake-up call for him,' I'd concluded. 'He's going to have to drastically change his lifestyle.'

'It's more than that,' M replied, and I heard the fear in his voice, 'if he has to wait for a donor to come forward, it could be fatal.' He looked exhausted suddenly. M&J Design and Build was going through a difficult patch; he was worrying about the mounting debts, and now there was Will. The strain was beginning to show.

My heart ached for him, but I had little sympathy for Will. I was tired of his dramas and of M's attempts to bail him out each time. I'd never understood his unwavering loyalty towards his dysfunctional wreck of a brother.

I tried to offer some words of comfort, reminding him Will was a survivor, that he always fell on his feet, thanks to M. I felt sure a donor would come forward in time. Later that evening I heard him talking to his brother on the phone, saying, 'It's going to be all right, Bro. It's the only solution. We're bound to be compatible. Yeah, I know there are risks, but I'm good with it. Thick and thin, eh? To infinity and beyond!'

A wave of dread washed over me, a presentiment of what was to come perhaps.

'Please don't do it,' I begged, when M announced he'd made his decision to donate a kidney to his brother. 'What if something happened to you?'

'People live perfectly normal lives with one kidney. It's a much bigger risk for Will. He'll have to be on medication and special drugs for the rest of his life to stop his body from rejecting it.'

He's taken drugs nearly all his life, I wanted to point out. Only weeks before, Will had been hospitalised after swallowing a lethal concoction of ecstasy and alcohol.

'Look at it this way, I'll be able to drive you home when you've had one too many,' M grinned.

'He'll start drinking again,' I warned.

'He knows he won't be able to.'

There was nothing I could say or do to dissuade him from going ahead, it seemed. That night I woke up at two a.m. and found his side of the bed empty. I'd spent the evening researching the risks and possible side effects of donating a kidney; high blood pressure, proteinuria, reduced kidney function…. and what if the remaining kidney should fail? Statistically it was unlikely, but anything was possible. I knew I wouldn't be able to get back to sleep, so made my way downstairs, determined to persuade him not to go ahead. He was on his computer.

'Please don't put yourself through this,' I begged. 'There are risks involved. It's a big operation.'

He turned to face me, squinting in the dim light. He hadn't bothered to replace the antique lamp I'd broken before Christmas, even though he'd been struggling with his eyesight recently and needed new glasses. He had missed his last appointment with the optician claiming he was too busy with work deadlines. Yet he was not too busy to go through an operation for his brother, it seemed.

'They use a laparoscope, which is not invasive. He's my brother, Willow, imagine how you would feel if it was Fern?'

'Fern's not an alcoholic,' and a lost cause, I wanted to add, 'and if she was, she would never allow me to donate an organ without thinking it through.'

'I have thought it through. Will and I have been through a lot together. He rubbed the scar on his forehead, adding, 'He saved my life. I owe him one.'

'What if something goes wrong?' I reiterated.

'It won't! Time's running out, nobody else compatible has come forward. He's in a bad way!'

He turned back to his computer, bringing the screen to life. I glanced over his shoulder and saw he'd been drafting a living will. It stated that in the event of anything happening to him, he was not to be kept alive on any form of life support.

'Just a formality,' he said, when I questioned him as to why he was writing a will after claiming the operation was straightforward. 'I was planning to write one anyway.' He met my gaze, saying, 'I need to do this. I'm asking for your support.'

'If anything goes wrong, I'll never forgive you,' I said.

He made a face. 'Willow's wrath! That would be a fate worse than death!'

WRATH: *(noun)* strong vengeful anger or indignation.

I pause, thinking about the vocabulary we fall back on in our everyday lives, often not considering the true meaning of the words.

M must have decided to put his affairs in order that week, calling the life insurance company, setting up a meeting with the bank and the solicitor, and creating the trust for Kids in Crisis, knowing deep down that there was a risk. But he'd made his mind up by then, and there was no going back.

NINETY DAYS BEFORE THE SUMMER SOLSTICE

The operation went well, and M was discharged from the hospital four days later with strict instructions not to lift anything heavy or engage in contact sports. He was told he could go back to a normal existence. Will was kept in under observation while they monitored him for signs of the transplanted kidney being rejected. He was sent home a week later. The donated organ was functioning properly, he was told, and he too could resume a normal life. He was warned not to touch a drop of alcohol for the rest of his life.

M was delighted. Will was home and dry in both senses of the word. He had been given a new lease of life. I heard him and Will making plans to take the bikes to Brittany in the summer.

Life is rosy for the benevolent, a gift of that magnitude a source of great joy for the benefactor. I heard M singing in the shower, as if all his problems were behind him.

'I told you all would be well that ends well,' he said, giving me one of his bear hugs.

I couldn't shake off the feeling that it hadn't yet ended.

Five days later M came down with a violent strain of flu that lingered for days. When he complained of a persistent pain in his lower back, I persuaded him to go to the doctor. He ended up seeing a locum who was standing in for his usual doctor. She diagnosed a kidney infection and prescribed antibiotics.

'Nothing serious,' he tried to reassure me. 'I just have to drink lots of water to flush it out.'

'Well, it is serious considering you only have one kidney! Think carefully before giving away any more of your organs,' I warned.

I had read on one of the medical sites that a single remaining kidney can increase in size to compensate for the loss of the missing one. All the same, the worry persisted. I would wake at odd hours and reach out to find M's side of the bed empty. He wasn't sleeping either. It was as if we both sensed the storm was heading straight towards us, and there was nothing we could do to avert it.

It wasn't long after the operation that things started to come crashing down. M was moody and withdrawn that spring. I wondered if he blamed me for not having supported him over the donation, or whether it was something to do with the psychological effects of losing an organ, that it had somehow taken away his zest for life, altered him in some subtle way. I now know that the veil of illusion was finally falling away, the scales were being lifted from his eyes. Will had started drinking again and M couldn't bring himself to tell me. I was to find out from Holly, who had met Will at a party in Clifton. It was one of those wild evenings, fuelled with alcohol and cocaine, to which Will always gravitated.

'I thought Will wasn't supposed to be drinking,' Holly said, as we chatted on the phone the day after the party. 'He was way over the limit! I ended up putting him into an Uber.'

I was shaking with rage. I set off for a walk in the rain trying to calm my thoughts. I debated calling M at work, then decided I would wait and discuss it with him over dinner. I walked all the way to the reservoir, the rain stopped and the sun came up. Steam rose from the wet tarmac and I walked on, thinking of how Will destroyed everything he touched. My anger curved back onto M. I was fed up with him playing the hero, his futile attempts to fix the unfixable.

He didn't get home until after midnight, by which time I was in a heightened state, unable to sleep. I took in the haunted look on his face and listened to his explanation with shock and disbelief.

'I was at the hospital. Will went on a binge, but he's all right now. They had to pump his stomach, it was a close call.'

He waited for me to rant and rave, say, 'I told you so.' Instead, I said coldly, 'no comment,' which was worse, but words were beyond me. And just when M needed me to show some solidarity (he genuinely believed that even though I didn't support his decision, I understood he had acted for the greater good) I turned my back on him. 'If you're going to continue to try and save Will from destroying himself and you in the process, please don't involve me. I don't want to hear about it from now on.'

How deeply damaging words can be and how badly I had misunderstood the bond that existed between the brothers. M started to withdraw more and more, heading off on his bike in the lighter evenings, without saying where he was going, or when he would be back. His face had taken on that shuttered, wary look he had around my mother. Only now it was me he was desperate to escape from.

I distracted myself with a series I was writing for The Weekend about modern moral dilemmas, inviting readers to comment. I went as far as writing an emotive piece headed, 'would you donate an organ to a sibling even if you suspected it was a lost cause?' The responses had been an overwhelming 'no' although some readers believed it could prove to be a catalyst and the sibling would dramatically change his or her ways. Jason seemed to welcome my angry voice then. But if I'd hoped to get through to M with the power of words, I was mistaken. When I asked what he thought of the article, his expression had hardened. 'I only read the title. I didn't need to read the rest. You've already expressed your views, loud and clear,' he'd added coldly, before turning away.

One evening I found him and Will in the shed, deep in conversation. Will was avoiding me altogether by bypassing the barn and heading straight down to the shed to wait for M. They were sitting on the bean bag lounger in the semi-darkness. I heard Will mutter, 'Better change the subject.' As my eyes adjusted to the gloom, I saw they were drinking cans of some branded beer.

Something rose inside me. 'I knew this would happen,' I fumed, 'but you just wouldn't listen.'

M looked up with a mixture of bewilderment and anger. 'You wanted to stay out of this, so I suggest you do just that,' he stated icily.

I withdrew, slamming the shed door so hard the top part came off its hinges.

'Unhinged,' M had said, when I described how my mother had lashed out one terrible night, raining blows on my head with her ringed fingers, until I was spinning around with the stars.

When M finally returned to the barn, having said goodbye to Will on the driveway, he announced they had been discussing Will's plan which was to admit himself into the Hope and Faith Rehabilitation Centre on the outskirts of Bath. 'For your information,' he added, 'that beer we were drinking is a non-alcoholic lager, which Will brought over himself.'

He'd turned away then, muttering he was going out and I wasn't to wait up. He didn't return until around three in the morning and then went straight to the spare room. In the days and weeks that followed, he would suddenly announce he was off to Cornwall 'to catch some waves', even if the weather was bad. Once he left without taking his surfboard and when I questioned him about it, he said he'd checked the weather forecast beforehand and had decided to go for a hike instead.

The rift between us was widening, the boys were starting to notice. Liam became increasingly anxious and asked why I was always complaining about Dad. Sam demanded to know what was going on. 'Ask your father!' I'd snapped. M insisted I wasn't to tell the boys Will was drinking again. He didn't want them to think badly of their uncle, or question him (M) as to why he had gone to such lengths to save his brother's life. M would end up paying for Will's rehabilitation, digging into our savings to cover the costs.

I buried myself further into my work. I went up to London to interview a rock star who was writing a musical and stayed over the weekend. Jason called to say I'd been nominated for Columnist of the Year. I called M, to tell him the good news, but he didn't pick up. He had been visiting Will in the rehab centre where they didn't allow mobile phones, he told me afterwards.

Another time he was with a client until late and couldn't talk. But the most common excuse was he'd been out riding his bike and hadn't heard his phone ringing. Twice I'd walked into the living area and heard him say, 'Going to have to call you back.'

Holly and I decided to go up to London to shop and see a show. She listened to me ranting about Will, how it had caused a rift between M and me and urged me to accept that what was done was done.

'It was his decision to donate his kidney to Will,' she emphasised, 'now he has to live with it. And so do you, I'm afraid.'

She was right. I didn't own M body and soul. I was going to have to live with it. I was also going to have to live with the fall-out.

I returned from London planning to tell him I was sorry about the way I'd behaved. I'd decided to open a bottle of champagne to celebrate the Columnist of the Year nomination, but the barn was in darkness and there was no sign of M or the bike. I called his mobile several times. Again, he didn't pick up. That was one of the first of many nights he stayed away. When I demanded to know where he'd been, he said he'd been in Winford helping out a friend re-build his bike. It had got late and had started to rain, so he'd decided to spend the night there. He'd left his phone charger in the office.

The tension was building. I was barely sleeping and feeling anxious all the time, prone to sparks of childish anger which M had always been good at diffusing. Only now he was the one who was igniting them.

EIGHTY DAYS BEFORE THE SUMMER SOLSTICE

Jason called and asked me to interview Miranda Huntington for Interesting Lives. The story of Miranda's accident had touched the nation. The twenty-six-year-old society girl had been thrown off her horse in the grounds of Huntington Hall ten months earlier and was now confined to a wheelchair. The accident had happened in almost the exact spot where her father had dropped down dead from a heart attack, four weeks earlier. The tabloids talked about 'the curse of Huntington Hall'. At the time, Miranda had been engaged to Jonathan Dubarry, heir to the Dubarry hotel chain, but their relationship had fallen apart after the accident. She insisted it had been a mutual decision to cancel the wedding, but the tabloids were not convinced.

'There's clearly an interesting twist to that tragic tale,' Jason stated. 'She's now announced she's getting married to her first boyfriend, who she met at university. He has no money or title. Her ladyship must be up in arms! The Mail claims it's a rebound thing. Find out if it really was a mutual parting of the ways between her and Dubarry, or whether he threw in the towel when he found out she'd never walk again.'

I said we should stay true to the column and focus on Miranda's interesting life, rather than her broken engagement. Jason argued that the breakup was interesting and the column needed spicing up. To which I replied, 'spicing up, or dumbing down?' Looking back, he and I were starting to clash by then. He'd barely commented on my nomination, except to say, 'no doubt you'll move on to bigger and better things if you win the award?'

Now he barked, 'Just write the piece.'

I drove to Huntington Hall the following week, lighter of heart after M and I had spent the weekend lazing in bed and talking for the first time in ages. He understood my frustration over the donation, and the fact that Will had been binge drinking again. He even confided in me his anger and disappointment over his weak-willed brother, adding, 'I'm sorry if I took it out on you. But I could never walk away from him, not after everything he's been through.'

When I'd asked if he was referring to the abuse, his face had darkened, and he'd muttered, 'he took the rap for everything. I should have got him away from that bastard sooner.' After that the shutters had come down.

Was this the debt that went both ways, that Will had spoken about, I wonder now? M felt guilty for not having rescued his brother from the evil clutches of a child molester while Will, with characteristic flawed logic, held his brother accountable.

As I turned up the driveway of Huntington Hall that spring morning through a tunnel of giant oaks, I thought about the curse that lay over the ancestral home, and wondered if it was true, or had the family simply brought ill-luck on themselves.

I was shown into the drawing room by an elderly housekeeper. Lady Priscilla appeared moments later, a brittle, angular woman with hair like spun silk, scraped back from her forehead in a widow's peak. She greeted me coldly, her thin arms folded across her chest, as if defending herself from an attack. 'You must be the journalist!'

'Yes, Willow Monroe, thank you for letting me interview Miranda.'

'I had nothing to do with it,' she snapped. 'She told your editor she wanted to go ahead. I hate journalists. You people lie through your teeth.'

'We have an obligation to write the truth,' I'd replied coolly. I was about to point out that Interesting Lives was not exploitative, rather it highlighted the defining moments of people's lives, the new paths they forged, the challenges they overcame. Fortunately, Miranda wheeled herself into the room and the conversation moved on.

I took in a petite girl with silky blonde hair falling to her shoulders and grey-blue eyes. 'It's OK, Mummy, this is my interview. Could you ask Bethie to make us some coffee. Or maybe you'd prefer tea?' she enquired.

'Coffee would be great, thank you.'

'Well, I'll leave you to it,' Lady Priscilla said, casting me a daggered look before marching out of the room.

'I hope she didn't give you a lecture on the evils of the press,' Miranda began. She's had an awful time, what with losing my father and then dealing with my accident. She wasn't cut out to be a widow.'

'It must be tough,' I replied. Little did I know how tough.

I explained to Miranda I wasn't here to disclose her private life and that she would have a copy of the proof before it went to print.

She immediately relaxed into the interview, telling me how she hoped to be able to ride her horse again and eventually open a riding school for the disabled. The accident had given her the chance to re-evaluate her life, she said. I was touched by her courage and determination. She went on to disclose she was getting married in June to her first love – a boy she'd met at university. Her father had disapproved of the liaison and had stopped them from seeing one another, but Lord Huntington was no longer alive, and her mother had come to accept that Miranda would marry him with or without her blessing. Lady Priscilla was now planning the wedding of the year, which was to be held here at Huntington Hall.

I was reminded of my mother and how she'd wanted the perfect wedding for me, only she had decided M was the wrong man.

'She's planning to build an extension onto the north face of the house. The idea is to hire it out as a venue for future weddings and events. She's interviewed five different architects, but hasn't liked any of the plans they've submitted so far. She keeps changing her mind. She wanted to build a replica of a tithe barn, now she's talking about an oak and timber-framed construction using reclaimed materials.'

'My husband undertakes projects like that,' I told her.

And here is the part of the story I wish I could re-write.

'He converted our barn into a two-storey home.' I pulled up some photos of Rosewood Barn on my phone and showed them to her. 'He won an award for a lighthouse conversion last year.'

'It's stunning!' she'd exclaimed. 'I'll tell Mummy. What's the name of his company?'

'M&J Design and Build,' I answered. 'They do mainly conversions. I'm not sure he would be able to undertake a project like this,' I'd added, back-pedalling. M was used to working with difficult clients, but there was something about the angry, grieving Lady Priscilla, who kept changing her mind, that alerted me.

Later, when I told M of Lady Priscilla's plans to build an extension onto Huntington Hall and how I'd mentioned him, he'd dismissed it, saying, 'I imagine she'll opt for one of the bigger firms.'

'You wouldn't want to work with her, anyway,' I'd stated. 'She's the proverbial "wicked widow of Westward Ho". The rudest person I've ever met. I read that she cracked a horsewhip over her son's head after she found out he was gay! Poor Miranda! I thought I had a difficult mother, but Lady P is in a league of her own.'

I was surprised and uneasy, when, two days later, M announced he'd been asked to submit some drawings for the Huntington Hall extension. I too had imagined Lady Priscilla would go for one of the big firms.

'She's a nightmare,' I reiterated.

M was silent for a moment. He rubbed his scar distractedly, saying, 'It could put us on the map, pay off some debts. It's a big contract.'

He had just paid a substantial bill for Will's ninety-day stay in rehab.

'There's a deadline,' I warned. 'The wedding's in June.'

'We put together a similar building last year in eight weeks with only six carpenters working flat out. This is more bespoke, but it can be done. I could bring in Sean's team for the finer work. I've dealt with a few difficult clients....and I like the concept.' He was already drafting plans in his head.

'It'll end in tears,' I'd warned. 'You've read about the curse of Huntington Hall!'

'Sounds more like a dysfunctional family behaving badly,' he'd responded.

He had been particularly affected by the article I'd written about Miranda. 'Poor girl confined to a wheelchair so young. Tragic.' He couldn't fix

Miranda, but he would make sure the venue was perfect and ready in time for her wedding day.

Lady Priscilla rejected his first two drafts, insisting the accessible toilets needed to be moved to the far side of the building, where they would be 'more discreet'. It was clear she was in denial over the fact her daughter would never walk again. She then decided she wanted to add a raised area at the front of the building with an altar where couples could exchange their vows. M pointed out that would escalate the cost, and not be wheelchair friendly, to which she replied, 'put in some kind of ramp then, as long as it's invisible.'

And so it went on.

'Back to the drawing board again,' M said.

She didn't like the refectory-style doors he'd suggested, the arched windows were too narrow.

He submitted a third plan, creating a gentle slope to access the raised area for the altar. It was the kind of job he loved under normal circumstances. Huntington Hall was not listed, so there would be no complications or interference from local planning authorities. He was used to dealing with difficult clients, and was confident he could work with the demanding Lady Priscilla.

His plans were finally accepted. I concluded that the other firms who had been bidding for the project had just walked away.

By late April, the scaffolding was in place and the massive A frame structure had been slung up with a giant crane. M had employed a top structural engineer from London to work with partnering the timber with the steel work. He and Sean spent hundreds of hours drafting and redrafting the plans, using a special computer programme to make sure everything was in place.

I drove over to Huntington Hall one rainy afternoon to see how it was going, and saw Lady Priscilla walking around the site, a thin figure etched against the skeletal steel frames, her expression as black as the thunderous clouds above her.

By the middle of May, the project was behind schedule but M was still confident he could finish in time. He was working longer and longer hours, sometimes not getting home until midnight, and returning to the site at dawn the following day. And then Lady P announced she wanted to make a major change. She called an emergency meeting stating she didn't like the oak flooring. It was too dark. When M pointed out they would not be able to change it within the timescale, she suggested he bring in another team of carpenters, adding the work had to be completed by mid-June, and it was not negotiable. She subsequently fought with the project manager which meant

M had to bring in a new one, creating a further delay.

She swore at one of Sean's team of young carpenters, saying the site was a mess, and somebody was going to break their necks and then sue her. She later threatened Declan, Sean's brother, accusing him of stealing materials from the site. M pointed out he had given Declan permission to take some offcuts of wood, but she refused to concede, claiming it was daylight robbery.

'Grief has unhinged her,' M said, pacing the floor. 'Sean and his guys are tearing their hair out. Sean wants out! None of the team can take much more of this. I should have listened to you.'

'I just want it to be over,' I'd said, worriedly, never dreaming of the horror that lay ahead.

As the summer blazed, I would wake up early and find M's side of the bed was empty. I wasn't seeing much of him, so didn't register the physical changes at first. It was Sam who pointed it out first, saying, 'Dad's lost weight. He doesn't look well.'

'He's been working way too hard,' I replied. I registered it then, the odd pallor and sallow hue of his skin. M had always had a healthy appetite, now he left half his food on the plate, or skipped meals altogether, claiming he'd eaten a sandwich with the builders. Never a man of many words, he spoke even fewer and less often. It had been months since I'd heard him singing in the shower.

I watched him one morning through half-closed eyes as he headed downstairs in his boxer shorts to make coffee; his long muscular legs strangely altered; his calves, once so defined, now swollen.

I urged him to make an appointment with the consultant surgeon who had operated on him to remove his kidney, but he kept putting it off, claiming he couldn't take time off, what with the deadline to finish the build in time for the wedding. I went ahead and made the appointment, and insisted on driving him there, as Jake was using the pick-up. Frida flagged us down on the lane, asking if M could take a look at her car as it was making an odd noise. He was about to leap out, but I'd cut in saying, 'Sorry, Frida, we have a doctor's appointment. We'll stop in on the way back.'

'Nothing serious, I hope?', she'd enquired, with concern, her blue gaze trained on M.

'No, just a check-up, but we can't stop now,' I'd answered, accelerating.

'It would only have taken a few minutes,' M had said, irritated.

The doctor informed M his blood pressure was high, adding that he wanted to do some more tests, including a scan. He prescribed medication and scheduled the scan for the following week. I had read that high blood pressure could lead to kidney damage and according to one website possible failure. I was beginning to feel horribly afraid.

I called the doctor to discuss my fear. Doctor Ramsey assured me that any damage could be reversed as long as M took his medication. 'We will know more after the scan,' he said. 'In the meantime, it's vitally important he manages his stress levels.'

'He's working for a really difficult client,' I told him. 'He's been under a lot of pressure.'

'Your husband is clearly good at managing difficult people,' he commented.

'Well, he managed to stay married to me!' I'd said wryly.

Dr Ramsey laughed. 'He's an exceptional man.'

'Too good for his own good,' I replied.

M tried to wave away my worries, promising that once the extension was finished, he would take some time off. We would fly to the Caribbean for a fortnight, go free diving and drink rum at the local beach bar in the evenings.

'I shall hold you to that,' I'd answered. I had held onto that tantalising image like a lifeline.

M never went for the scan, even though I reminded him over and over, left a message on his phone and put a post-it sticker on his computer and another one on the fridge. I was in London that day interviewing a mountaineer who had been one of the few climbers to get to the summit of Everest without oxygen. He was now writing a book about his experience.

I returned late (having listened to a gruelling story of frost-bitten limbs followed by amputation) eager to know how M's scan had gone. Again, he hadn't answered his phone. I found out he'd spent the whole day at Huntington Hall briefing the new carpenters he'd hired to replace Sean's team, and had genuinely forgotten all about the appointment.

The scan was re-scheduled for June 24th, three days after my birthday. He went as far as pencilling 'hospital scan' in his desk diary. But it wasn't to be. By then our lives had turned upside down, changing everything.

TEN DAYS BEFORE THE SUMMER SOLSTICE

The extension was almost completed. M, in his inimitable way, had convinced Lady P to leave the oak floor as it was, reminding her she'd agreed on the materials and he was under contract to finish the job following the original plans. She was distracted with the wedding and apart from insisting the porch was completed, and he put in a mounted wall light, snapped, 'Just get on with it.'

Meanwhile my mother was organising a get-together to celebrate my fortieth.

'…we need to celebrate your birthday properly this year Willow! After all, life begins at forty, although I don't know who came up with that! I remember it as the slow slide into anonymity and a futile fight against wrinkles! Let's celebrate while you're still thirty-nine. I thought about a midsummer night's party at Rosewood Barn, but what with the courtyard still in such a ghastly mess, that's out of the question. Such a shame Max never managed to finish it, but there we are – he's always so busy with other people's projects. I thought I'd book Ashlington House, and we could have dinner in the log room with a few chosen friends. Then you and me, Fern and the boys, and Max of course could stay overnight. We could spend the following day at the spa having some treatments, the boys can swim in the pool. They do a marvellous facial so I've heard.'

I tried to wriggle out of it. Apart from the cost, I couldn't see how a small gathering would work. Who would be the chosen few? Holly and Peter were arguing bitterly, Jen and Carrie were close friends, but I didn't particularly like either of their husbands. Clementine and Mike were on the verge of divorcing. I would have liked to invite Sean and Siobhan, but they were not part of that group. M would go along with it, but that was not the point. He'd talked about us going to Cornwall for the weekend. He was feeling guilty about the thwarted party plan due to the unfinished courtyard.

'We were actually thinking about going to Cornwall with the boys,' I told my mother.

There was a long silence. 'You know, Willow, I've tried so hard to be a part of your life and see a bit more of my grandsons. It wasn't easy for me when you shot off and got married without including the rest of us, but now you have a chance to make up for that! However, if that's what you've decided!'

'OK, I'll have a word with M,' I'd conceded, the old guilt kicking in.

M had long since concluded the best way to deal with my mother was to let her have her way, then slip away from whatever event she had foisted upon us. The Huntington Hall extension was almost finished and he had started to relax. He was looking better, making me wonder if his weight loss had been due to stress. The building was magnificent with its bespoke timber frame, gleaming oak floor and arched windows. Lady Priscilla had already begun furnishing the interior with long refectory tables and chairs, in preparation for what was expected to be the wedding of the year.

'We can go to Cornwall any time,' M said equitably. 'If your mother wants to put on a birthday celebration for you, why not let her go ahead?'

'All right,' I'd agreed reluctantly. 'At least we get to spend a night in a country house hotel, and I'll have the whole day with you for a change!'

I was determined to put aside the frustrations of the last few months, remind him how much I loved him.

And so the die was cast. It was just as well I wasn't holding a mid-summer night party at Rosewood Barn, I concluded as my birthday drew closer. The weather forecast was predicting a massive storm that was brewing out on the Atlantic, bringing torrential rain and flash flooding. I would have had to hire a marquee, and the rain would have turned the courtyard into a quagmire.

THE SUMMER SOLSTICE

Note to blog:

The events leading to that moment, that nanosecond when the heart that has beaten for you ceases, will remain indelibly stamped on your mind. You will remember everything that happened before or afterwards, each moment taking on an added poignancy; the colour of the sky, the first drops of rain, what you ate for breakfast, the things you said and the things you didn't say, every loving word, every slight....relive it if you can, in all its stark and painful truth.

And then allow yourself to let it go, blackwidower has responded.

I open my eyes to find M is standing over me holding a mug of coffee sprinkled with chocolate in one hand, in the other a long-stemmed red rose. On the dresser is a bouquet of flowers – all mauves and purples; lilac and lavender, a violet orchid in a froth of Queen Anne's lace.

'Happy birthday, beautiful.' He smiles, leaning over and attempting to kiss me. He is wearing a shirt that matches the azure blue of his eyes.

I put my hand over my mouth. 'I've got morning breath,' I groan. 'Do you think it gets worse when you turn forty?'

'Didn't notice.' He grins, perching on the edge of the bed and handing me two packages. I unwrap the first, a vintage box in the shape of a miniature treasure chest, all black and gold, embossed with Greek figurines.

'It's beautiful!' I exclaim.

'It's to store your memories or anything you hold precious. There's a handwritten note inside saying that, unlike Pandora's box which contained all the evils of the world, this one is filled with only good things like patience and hope.'

'Are you saying I'm impatient and without hope?' I tease.

He brushes a strand of hair from my face. 'There is always hope.'

Our problems are finally behind us - we're going to be OK, I think to myself.

The other package is a leather-bound notebook with thick cream pages.

'Maybe you could use it as a diary, to write your darkest secrets,' he suggests with a grin. He pulls out a third slim package. 'This should help.'

Inside is a silver pen, engraved with my initials.

'I'd better write something of note,' I say, smiling up at him.

'I have no doubt about that,' he says, pulling aside the duvet, his hand circling my breast.

I wriggle away, murmuring, 'I need to clean my teeth.' I hop out of bed and spend a few moments in the bathroom looking for mouthwash. By the time I return to bed he's talking urgently on the phone.

I know immediately it's her, Lady Priscilla.

I hear him say: 'I'll drive over later this morning and sort it out. Yes of course it'll be finished in time, we're almost there. Oh I see, the rehearsal is today, but you can use the other entrance. Don't worry, I'll get onto it.'

'Lady Poisonous?' I say, making a face.

'She's worried about the porch entrance. The floorboards are uneven – the new carpenter needs to clamp them down before somebody breaks their neck.'

'The wedding isn't for another ten days,' I point out.

'I know, but the snag list is growing longer by the day. She says the LED lights keep fusing, and she has a rehearsal planned for later.'

'Can't you send over the electrician? How many rehearsals do they need for God's sake? Poor Miranda!'

'I'll go over later and take a look. I don't want this to encroach on the weekend. Now, how about I take you out for a birthday breakfast? It's a beautiful morning. We could take the bike?'

'I'll have helmet hair,' I groan.

'I fell in love with you with helmet hair, remember!'

'Maybe we should take the jeep, what with the weather forecast?'

'The storm is not predicted to hit here until late afternoon,' he replies.

'OK, you win.' I give in.

This is probably the way I'll die, I think, winding my arms around him and holding him tight.

I just hope we don't go together…

At Café Lucia, chairs and tables have been set out on the pavement and in the cobbled courtyard around the side of the building. We sit outside overlooking an ivy-clad wall. The details of that birthday breakfast are so vivid I can still taste the food. The hot peppery Bloody Mary for me, Virgin for him, the Eggs Benedict with smoked salmon in the buttery lemon sauce, the caffe latte strong and frothy.

'This is a perfect day,' I say. 'It's almost worth turning forty! Can we do it again next year when I'm forty-one?'

'We shall do it when you're eighty-one,' he promises, distracted by a motion at the entrance to the courtyard, where a girl in a wheelchair is trying to manoeuvre her way through the narrow space between the tables. Behind her, an intense young man with dark hair is saying, 'Steer a bit to the left, babe.'

'Miranda,' I exclaim, smiling over at her. M immediately stands up and moves the chair that is obstructing her. 'Max!' she grins. Lady P insisted on calling him Maximillian, but he was Max on site.

'Hello, Max,' the young man says, beaming at M. He turns towards me. 'Martin Hope, I don't think we've met?'

'Nice to meet you,' I say, understanding immediately why this young man with the apt surname of Hope who couldn't keep his eyes off Miranda was 'the one'.

'How's it going at the Hall?' M asks.

'The usual roller coaster. You know Mother!' Miranda sighs. 'The building is spectacular! The editor of Architectural Digest came to have a look at it yesterday. He wants to put you forward for Designer of the Year!'

'That's wonderful news,' I breathe. I think of how I'd tried to dissuade M from taking on the project and now here he was, about to win a prestigious award. 'I'm so proud of you,' I begin.

I wonder now if he heard me as the waitress interrupts with, 'I have one caffe latte and one espresso.'

'We have a rehearsal later,' Miranda is saying, making a face. 'I gather Mother has spoken to you about the lights?'

M nods. 'I'll try to get in touch with the electrician, but his wife is about to give birth any moment. I also need to contact the new carpenter about the porch. I'll stop by later this morning to see what needs doing. We're celebrating Willow's birthday today,' he explains, smiling at me.

'Happy birthday!' they chorus.

'I'll try to persuade Mother to do the rehearsal tomorrow, so you don't have to come over,' Miranda suggests.

'In any case, there's some bad weather forecasted,' Martin puts in, 'so she might have to postpone it.'

'I'd still like to get the lights sorted before the weekend. I'll see what I can do.'

As we finish our coffee, I say, 'Why don't you put it off until Monday? The electrician won't want to come over if his wife is about to give birth.'

'You're probably right.' He kisses me on the cheek. 'You very often are, when it comes to this kind of thing.'

As we approach the car park where we'd left the bike, his phone starts vibrating.

'It's her.' He frowns. 'Her ladyship!'

'Don't answer it,' I beg.

He zips his phone back into his jacket, but, two minutes later, it buzzes again.

Back home, he listens to the four frantic messages she's left on his answering machine. Something about no water in the washrooms which meant nobody could use them during rehearsals. These were typical teething problems when it came to a new build, but for Lady P they were an international disaster.

'I'll have to go over,' he says, 'otherwise it'll hang over me all weekend.'

I glance at my watch. It's still early. 'Remember my mother wants us to be at Ashlington House by six.' It was typical of him to try to fit a whole day's work into half a day.

'It should only take about an hour,' he says, revving the engine.

'You're not going on the bike, are you? It's going to pour with rain!' I glance up at the sky which is still an innocent shade of blue. 'There's a storm coming.'

'It's not expected until much later,' he replies. 'I've already packed my bag for the weekend. Put my swimming gear and diving watch in if you can find it. I'll join you in the pool, test out my lung capacity. We need to practice for the holiday!'

'OK, but take the pick-up,' I insist.

'It will be a lot quicker on the bike. I can weave through the traffic faster.'

'If you're late back, I'll kill you,' I warned.

Had I really said that…?

I listen to the sound of the bike fading away, my heart sinking, that sudden plunge in mood that often descends as the sun goes down after a perfect day. Only it was still mid-morning. An hour later, the wind had got up and a mass of black clouds had appeared literally out of the blue, turning the sky a livid shade of purple. By four in the afternoon, it felt like dusk and M still hadn't come home.

I called and called his phone but kept getting his answering machine. *Hi there, leave a message and I'll get back to you in a heartbeat …cheers.*

As time passed, my irritation turned to fury. It was so selfish, today of all days. Miranda's wedding was still more than a week away. My birthday was today. Even if he'd got caught up with Lady P and her endless demands, he knew I didn't want to go through the evening without him.

Fat drops of rain are battering against the skylights like hailstones. I feel a sudden tightness in my stomach, a sick unease. I pace the barn, unable to stay still. The phone rings at last, as I'm halfway through packing M's weekend bag. It's Mother.

'The weather is simply ghastly!' she begins. 'We only just made it here! The back roads are completely flooded. This is a midsummer nightmare! I'm going to ask them to light the fire in the log room. I suggest you set off soon. Fern's already on her way.'

'M's not back from work yet,' I tell her, trying to keep the fear out of my voice, when I want to blurt out that he'd left on the bike and I had a bad feeling. 'He had to go over to Huntington Hall to meet the electrician. As soon as he's back, we'll set off.'

'Today of all days!' Mother exclaims. 'That man never stops! It really is too bad. Tell him to meet us here,' she adds, 'don't be late, Willow! It would not be right, after all the trouble and expense I've gone to get this birthday organised.'

Whether I wanted it or not...

'I'll be there,' I say swiftly, before she can start listing the various occasions on which I'd let her down.

By four thirty I am beside myself. I pull on a waterproof jacket and step out into the stinging rain, then make a dash over the wet paving stones to where the jeep is parked.

FEAR: *(noun)* **an unpleasant emotion caused by the threat of danger, pain or harm.**

My fear is tinged with a mounting dread which increases like the gathering drumroll of thunder in the near distance.

I scour the ditches, my hands clenched on the steering wheel, imagining M lying trapped under his bike, his body twisted and bleeding. I turn up the driveway of Huntington Hall as a zigzag of lightning splits the sky in two, illuminating the main house which was formerly cloaked in darkness. I think about the curse of Huntington Hall, Lady Priscilla's pinched and haunted face. I pull to a halt, where the driveway is partially blocked by the massive trunk of a fallen oak which must have toppled over from the storm. I manage to drive up onto the verge bypassing the tree, churning up the perfectly manicured lawn which has turned to marsh, hearing the scrunch of branches caught in the rear wheels. Then follow the winding driveway past the house, towards the extension, taking in M's creation; the timber-framed roof darkened by the rain, which is streaming down its glassy façade in rivulets. There is no sign of the bike nor M.

Another fork of lightning and then I see him. He is on the porch, standing on top of a tall ladder, shining a torch along the central beam, seemingly oblivious to the elements. On the floor beside the ladder, his toolbox with his initial carved on the top is open, the tools strewn all over the floor. I beep the horn and he glances around briefly, then continues examining the beam. I drive right up to the entrance, roll down the window and shout, 'I've been calling and calling! Why the hell didn't you answer your phone?'

All the stress and worry as to why he hadn't called rises like an incoming tide; my growing fears for his health, the recklessness of him having given away his kidney, the endless hours he spent trying to mend things. For putting Miranda's wedding first, for all the disappearing acts and no shows, for helping the whole of humanity while the boys and I waited for him to come home.

'For God's sake, M, we're meant to be at Ashlington House in less than an hour!' A clap of thunder crashes overhead as if to echo my fury. I think of my mother's wrath, the flooded roads, while trying to calculate how long it would take to drive home and change, blow dry my hair. I remember his half-packed weekend bag, which I'd left open on the bed. 'We need to get going now!'

He still doesn't respond.

'Did you hear me?' I yell, knowing after all these years that he is so absorbed with the task in hand, everything else has fallen away, his one and only mission is to make sure everything is in order for Miranda's big day. I leap out of the car and run through the sheets of rain towards the shelter of the porch.

He is now examining a loose wire hanging out of the wall, where the porch light is meant to be. He climbs down the ladder. 'Can't believe the new carpenter didn't finish the job,' he says, kicking the raised floor with his steel-capped boot. 'Just give me a couple of minutes.' He is heading inside now, his face set, oblivious to my frantic state.

I charge in after him and see him striding through the gloom, past the long refectory tables towards the far end of the building, before disappearing into a recessed area at the back. I stand there helplessly and, moments later, the whole interior is flooded with light, the LEDs lighting up like hundreds of stars. I almost forget my anger at the sight of the magnificent, vaulted ceiling the reclaimed wooden beams, the rich dark hue of the oak floor.

'Must be the transformer,' he's saying. He is now rummaging around in a large cardboard box full of light fittings and bulbs.

A sudden crack of thunder overhead causes me to jump.

'Where the fuck is the electrician?' I demand.

'His wife must have gone into labour,' M answers, still rooting in the box. He disappears around the corner to the fuse box again, extinguishing all the lights. M had qualified as an electrician years ago, but claimed his skills were rusty; his knowledge outdated.

'It's fine, I'll just change the transformer, and then we'll be out of here,' he shouts out.

'I'm going to have to call Mother and break it to her we're not going to make it in time,' I shout back, delving in my pocket for my phone.

But I don't call her. Instead, I pace the room taking deep breaths, telling myself to stay calm, while trying to dispel a vision of Mother's rage. He has sorted out the lights now, leaving them on and is in the accessible bathroom, while time gallops on like a freight train hurtling towards some unforeseen disaster.

'How much longer?' I shout.

'Don't know...just need to finish this.'

Something snaps inside me. 'I can't wait around for you any longer, M! I'll assume you won't make it to my birthday dinner! Even if you do drag yourself away there's bound to be somebody broken down on the side of the road you need to rescue! Go save the rest of the world, M! That's where your priorities lie!'

He emerges from the bathroom and faces my fury head on. 'If you could stop bloody ranting, woman, and give me a few more minutes to sort this out! This has been the most stressful project I've ever worked on, but we finished on time, against the odds, with a whole lot of casualties along the way. Your mother doesn't give a damn if I arrive late, or if I get there at all! She won't even notice! All I want is to get this job finished, get that poisonous woman off my back, so I can take some time off.' He rubs his scar viciously. 'You're becoming more and more like your mother!'

This gives me a jolt.

He storms off towards the porch, drags the ladder over the uneven floorboards, places it beneath the loose wire and grabs the cordless drill. Then climbs the ladder as if mounting a stairwell to some higher place, away from me and my anger.

The noise of the drill has entered my head; a relentless, tortuous high-pitched whine, eroding all rational thought. I have become one with the storm, part of the discharge of lightning that's flashing across the sky, while he is in another atmospheric bubble, lost in the task at hand. I am at the end of my tether, no longer tethered, unearthed.

I glance around looking for a way of getting his attention, to get him to switch off the drill. I think of how I had unplugged his computer that day, sending the antique lamp skittering to the floor. But the drill is cordless, there is no way I can stop it from source. I glance at the open toolbox and see the brass spirit level gleaming on the top. Beside it, his weatherproof LED flashlight, the torch that can throw a powerful beam from a distance of seven hundred metres. I have a mental image of shining it on him, putting him in the spotlight so to speak…forcing him to look down at me, switch off the drill, listen…

I make a lunge for it, gasping as my foot catches on the loose floorboard, causing me to trip over the open toolbox, before hurling me like a missile towards the base of the ladder. I grab a rung with an outstretched hand and feel the ladder lurch to one side, M above trying to steady himself on the beam, his hand making contact with the loose wire hanging out of the wall. I watch in horror as the shock causes him to lose his footing. It appears to happen in slow motion, although it's all over in the blink of an eye. M, momentarily suspended between two elements, positive and negative, pulled towards the very thing that was repelling him. Plunging earthwards like in one of those falling dreams, towards me. I almost feel the shock entering my own chest, the thud of a thousand volts echoing in my heart. The memory of his face is forever imprinted on my mind, his eyes unfocused as his body turned in the air. The earth turning on its axis.

He landed heavily on his side, onto the hard wooden decking below, his forehead glancing off the edge of the chisel. I heard a grunt and then a deathly silence. Beneath his half-turned face, something inky and dark red was blooming, spreading its tentacles onto the uneven floorboards.

In the end, a porch represents an exit…

And here lies the terrible truth. M received around one hundred milliamps of current from the exposed wire. He fell off a high ladder onto the ground. He suffered a contusion, or in common terms a bruise to his remaining kidney, caused by a blunt trauma. This led to internal bleeding. And yet he lived.

At least he existed for three and a half more days.

I don't remember much about the hours that followed, blurting out the news to Fern, incoherent with shock, as the ambulance carved its way through the congested traffic to the Bristol Royal Infirmary, sirens flashing. She had been calling frantically to find out where we were as the guests gathered and Mother flew into a rage. I remember Fern arriving with the boys at the hospital, Liam sobbing wildly, Sam swearing and demanding something was done to save his father. I remember pulling Fern aside and spilling out my garbled story, repeating how it was my fault, her desperately trying to calm me, shaking me, her voice a command, as she repeated, 'Listen to me, Willow, it was an accident, you have to think about the boys.'

ACCIDENT: *(noun)* an unfortunate incident that happens unexpectedly and unintentionally, typically resulting in damage or injury.

There is little clarity about that first night and the following day when I drifted numbly from M's bedside to the vending machine to get a coffee which I couldn't drink, a sandwich from the cafeteria that made me heave. M was still unconscious and hooked up to a number of machines while they tried to stabilise him.

I talked to him constantly, telling him how much I loved him, how desperately sorry I was, while my heart felt as if it was disintegrating in my chest. Fern took the boys back to Rosewood Barn in the evenings and stayed with them there, while I sat on the reclining chair beside M, numb with shock. I would drift off for a few minutes, only to wake with a jolt willing him to open his eyes.

The doctor took me aside and explained that if he pulled through, he would have to be on dialysis for the foreseeable future and would eventually require a kidney transplant.

No life support… M had written in his living will.

I asked Fern to stay with the boys, as I needed to go home and pick up a few things for when M woke up; his iPad, his washbag and shaving kit. Fern nodded, her eyes brimming with tears. She was trying hard to stay positive for me and the boys, but I knew she too feared the worst.

I left the hospital that sultry June morning, climbed into the jeep and drove to the outskirts of Bath to The Hope and Faith Rehabilitation Centre.

Will looked up with alarm as I walked into the garden to where he was lying on a chaise longue, a mug of half-drunk tea beside him. He had grown a beard, which made him look a decade older. On the table beside him was a pile of Classic Bike magazines that M must have brought in the previous week.

'Your brother is in Intensive Care,' I blurted out, 'it's critical. You need to come with me now!'

He got to his feet, his eyes wild. 'What the fuck? What happened?'

'We don't have time to discuss it. Let's go.'

A registrar in a white coat called out to us as we headed for the door. 'Excuse me, he's not allowed to discharge himself without permission from his doctor.'

'It's an emergency,' I stated, ushering Will through the swing doors. He climbed into the jeep, his face ashen.

'What happened?' he kept repeating.

'He fell off a ladder after getting an electric shock. He's damaged his remaining kidney.'

'An electric shock from what, for fuck's sake?'

'There was a loose wire sticking out from the wall where the porch light was meant to be,' I said, my voice dangerously calm.

You have to re-frame it, Fern had insisted.

I could see Will struggling to make sense of this. 'Now what?' he said, his voice cracking.

'You are going to give him his kidney back,' I replied.

And in a fictitious world, or a movie, it could have all worked out. The audience would have breathed a collective sigh of relief as the bad brother redeemed himself by returning the gift of life to his dying sibling. An eye for an eye, an organ for an organ.

I drove like a maniac back to the hospital, revving the jeep at the lights, cursing the traffic, wishing for once I was on the motorbike. I was recorded speeding by three cameras, but I didn't care. There was no space in the hospital car park, so I abandoned the jeep on the grass and raced towards the entrance of the hospital dragging Will behind me. Fern and the boys were sitting in the waiting room. The doctor was attending to M.

Fern stood up immediately, muttering, 'No change.' She glanced from me to Will, her face a question mark.

'Will and I need to speak to the doctor,' I said with a calmness I didn't feel.

I paced the corridor, waiting for Dr Reynolds to emerge from the ICU. Will hovered behind me. At last the doctor came out, holding a clipboard. 'We need to talk to you in private,' I said.

We were ushered along the corridor and into a windowless office. He listened as I explained that M had donated his kidney to Will five months ago, but now it needed to be returned. Will remained silent. The doctor looked from one of us to the other.

'You are talking about organ restitution?' he stated at last, his eyes trained on Will. 'I am obliged to point out that you, as the recipient of an organ donated to you by your brother or any other donor for that matter, means that a contract now exists between the two of you. It's what we call a 'designated donation'. Both parties need to be in agreement that the organ is to be returned to the original donor. You would have to undergo a series of tests beforehand to ensure the kidney is still viable.'

I tried to process this. Will had been in rehab for almost three months. I'd read that a kidney was able to regenerate but only up to a certain point. What I was still unsure of was whether he was prepared to go through with another operation. He had been silent the whole way in the car. I had explained the urgency of the situation, stressing there was no time to lose, that he was M's only hope. But his face had remained shuttered as if closed off to any discussion.

'We have to move quickly,' I tell the doctor, 'time is running out.'

Dr Reynolds was now addressing me. 'I would like to have a private word with Mr Goodhart.'

I turned to Will, my heart hammering in my chest. 'You are going to give your consent, aren't you?' It came out as a statement not a question.

Will glared at me. 'Who the fuck do you take me for?' he flared.

'Is that a yes or no?' I persisted, but the doctor was ushering me out of the room. 'Mrs Goodhart, could you give us a moment please?'

When I reported the conversation back to Fern in the corridor, not wanting the boys to hear, she breathed, 'Is it possible?'

'Yes,' I answered firmly. 'I've researched hundreds of sites. Even though Will was a binge drinker, kidneys can regenerate. He hasn't been able to touch a drop since March. It's our only hope,' I say desperately.

There is always hope, M had said only forty-eight hours ago in what now seemed another lifetime.

Fern hugged me fiercely. 'You need to eat something. The boys have had a sandwich. You have to stay strong.'

I shook my head. 'I can't swallow a thing.' My jaw ached from clenching it. I couldn't stop shivering. I felt permanently nauseous.

The doctor returned in the early evening, by which time Fern had driven Sam and Liam home. He informed me that Will had agreed to undergo a series of tests. However, M would not be able to have the operation unless he regained consciousness and his condition stabilised. He promised to let us know the results of Will's tests as soon as he had them. 'Try to get some rest,' he added, gently, patting me on the shoulder.

I sat beside M all through the second and third night, telling him again how much I loved him, how sorry I was for losing my temper, that everything was going to be all right. He finally regained consciousness in the early hours of the morning. I heard him mutter something, then his vivid-blue eyes focused on me. My heart lurched.

'What happened?' he murmured.

'I tripped…the floorboard was sticking up… I didn't see the toolbox. I grabbed the ladder to stop myself from falling. It was my fault you got a shock… I'm so sorry, but it's going to be all right. We have a plan.'

At that moment the nurse came in, then immediately left the room to report that M had woken up. I was ushered out and by the time they allowed me back in, M had fallen into a deep sleep.

Will and I took it in turns to sit beside him.

In the middle of the night, M woke up and murmured, 'Tell Will not to do this.'

Will must have spoken to him about the planned donation while I was out of the room, without having had confirmation from the doctor. I recalled Dr Reynolds saying, 'Both parties would need to be in agreement.'

'Don't worry, we have it all worked out,' I repeated.

You will let me take charge of this. It's the only chance I have of absolving myself.

The following morning the doctor called Will and me into his office and delivered his verdict. They had done all the relevant tests. There was a mild decrease in the 'glomerular filtration rate' and a higher-than-normal level of creatinine in the blood, which was attributable to Will's dependency on pain killers and from the effects of the immune suppressants. But both kidneys were functioning normally, he concluded.

'So, it can be done?' I said, desperately looking at the doctor for confirmation. 'How soon? He's conscious now.'

I thought of how M had said, Tell Will not to do this… Surely he wasn't still protecting his brother at this critical hour? Or worse. Did he believe he wasn't going to recover? The thought was too awful to consider.

'We need to wait until your husband's red cell count has normalised,' Dr Reynolds was saying. 'I would like to get the opinion of a colleague of mine, who's a top nephrologist in Harley Street. I'll be sending over the x-rays this morning.'

Will stood up abruptly. 'I want to spend some time with my brother alone,' he announced. As soon as he'd left, I turned to this serious young doctor, who seemed to hold M's life in his hands.

'I will never forgive myself if he dies.' I sobbed. 'I was...we had this stupid argument... I lost my temper...'

The doctor was silent for a moment. 'The report states accidental injury,' he says gently. He glances at his file. 'Your husband was due a scan in early June, which he missed. He was prescribed an ACE inhibitor for his blood pressure. Do you know if he was taking his medication?'

'I'm not sure. He was so busy with work. He had a deadline.'

DEADLINE: (*noun*) historically meaning a line drawn around a prison beyond which prisoners were later shot.

'He might have forgotten. He's never been good at taking care of himself.' I continue, 'he's always too busy looking after everyone else.'

'He was also diagnosed with proteinuria, which indicates his remaining kidney was not functioning as it should have been.'

Reduced kidney function. I had read about that on a number of medical sites. I recall M's swollen calves, his lack of appetite and weight loss.

'What I'm saying, Mrs Goodhart, is there were already significant underlying problems. In my opinion, he could have withstood the impact of the fall if he'd had a second functioning kidney.' He hands me a tissue. 'To conclude, there are a number of contributory factors. Try not to blame yourself.'

Contributory factors – how I'd hung on to those two words like a lifeline.

When I return to the ward, Will is sitting beside M, his head bowed, talking earnestly. I hear him say, 'Hang on in there, Bro, everything's under control. You're gonna' be fine. I'm going to be the donor this time. Reminds me of that time you gave me your scooter and I ended up in the ditch. Toby was yelling like a maniac, then that fucking bastard lashed out at him... All that's behind us now, and Toby's safe. I gave that scooter back to you, remember, and you managed to fix it up so it looked like new!'

M's eyes are closed, his chest rising and falling rhythmically. A ghost of a smile flits across his face, as if he's taking in every word. Moments later it's replaced with a frown. I take in the crescent-shaped scar which looks oddly translucent, as if it's fading and notice the almost imperceptible shake of his head.

'The doctor is just waiting for you to stabilise and then they'll go ahead,' I add, reaching for his hand and squeezing it, but there's no response. 'Loving you,' I whisper, my tears splashing like drops of rain onto the sheet.

Will and I sit in silence for what seems like an age, then Will announces he needs some fresh air. 'Back in ten,' he mutters. 'Coffee?'

'No thanks.' I'm unable to swallow the metallic liquid that drips like treacle from the vending machine. I watch M and notice his breathing has changed. I approach the bed suddenly, alerted by the angle of his head. It is tilted towards the window, where the sun is throwing shards of light across the vinyl floor. The earth tilting towards the sun.

I am about to pull down the blind, then hesitate, frozen with the knowledge that M is preparing to depart. I grab the bell, which hangs on a long, thin cord over his bed and press my thumb down on it, shouting out frantically for the doctor to come. To stop M from leaving.

By the time the doctor and nurse arrived, and Will had rushed back into the room, M had begun his departure.

Will and I watched in shock and horror, as the beam of sunlight flooded his face and the breath left his body for the last time. He was terrifyingly still.

STILL: *(adjective)* not moving or making a sound, motionless.

I shouted at him to open his eyes, to look at me, the old rage and frustration at not being able to get his attention surging through me. I wanted to shake him alive again. I couldn't comprehend that he would never turn his aqueous eyes on me again, never utter ....loving you.

He had passed on. He was in the past. And suddenly there was no future.

The medical report stated: Cause of death ESKF (end stage kidney failure) following a blunt trauma injury. The patient had only one existing kidney which was presenting Stage One failure, of a high GFR 90 ml/min...

I researched it all, of course. Looking for what? Absolution? A sign that the existing damage to the remaining kidney could have been reversed? I told myself over and over that had he not donated his kidney to his brother he would still be alive.

You can talk circles around the what-ifs, and the if onlys, only to arrive right back at the beginning. If they had removed the defective kidney instead of the healthy one and M had fallen on the side where it no longer was, would he have survived, I wonder?

If I had not driven to Huntington Hall, and lost my temper, none of it would have happened.

Miranda wanted to postpone the wedding. She tried to call several times, but I couldn't bring myself to return her calls. In the end she sent me an email saying how devastated she was to hear the news, and that she and Martin felt it wasn't right to get married at Huntington Hall.

I managed to write back a few lines, urging them to go ahead with the wedding, adding it was what M would have wanted. I told myself then that all the hours he had put in, the stress and worry, would not have been in vain.

I also received a handwritten letter from Lady Priscilla, saying how sorry she was about what she called 'a regrettable and unforeseen tragedy'. She added that she would do her utmost to keep the accident out of the press.

I'm sure you wouldn't want that either, she'd written.

How right she was about that.

M received an award posthumously for the design and build of the Huntington Hall extension.

POSTHUMOUSLY: *(adjective)* arising, occurring or continuing after one's death.

The boys and I went up to London to receive the award, but I couldn't stay on for the speeches. I had rushed us all out of Alexandra Palace and into a taxi, which had deposited us at Paddington Station where we'd caught the train home.

What exactly was the cause of death? Susie Devine had wanted to know at Crispin's Christmas party.

A number of 'contributory factors': an electric shock, a fall from a ladder, an organ donation that had left him with a compromised kidney? Or was it simply a case of Willow's wrath?'

…now that would be a fate worse than death, M had said.

I KILLED HIM screamed a voice in my head, while the voice of reason said it was accident. Meanwhile, guilt and blame took up residence inside, both arguing their cases and winning. But they agreed on one thing. I was culpable.

CULPABLE: *(adjective)* someone who deserves blame for a crime or a wrongdoing.

When Will had demanded to know how M had managed to fall off a ladder, I'd said 'the ladder wasn't stable – the floorboards were uneven,' which was partly true. 'He was under a lot of pressure to finish the job,' I'd added.

'Pressure from you, more like it?' Will had said icily.

'He was constantly worrying about you, as a matter of fact,' I'd retorted. 'You were his biggest problem!'

His eyes had narrowed and he was about to respond, when Sam and Liam appeared on either side of me like bodyguards as if they sensed a terrible war of attrition was being waged.

We had both contributed towards it, I'd concluded.

I gave the boys a censored version of that day. Most of their anger was directed at Will for 'robbing their father of his kidney', Sam remarking with irony that Will had no 'willpower' 'and would always be a hopeless addict'; Liam adding 'human beings wouldn't have been born with two kidneys if they didn't need both of them'.

As I kissed Liam goodnight, he'd turned his tear-stained face towards me, demanding, 'Were you and Dad fighting that day?'

I'd hesitated before saying, 'I was cross with him. We were late for Gran's birthday treat. She wanted us to be there before all the guests arrived. Dad decided to fit in a last-minute job, and then he didn't answer his phone.'

How difficult it is to explain the petty frustrations of married life, especially to your children. And how trivial they sound, once aired.

'I thought he'd had an accident and was lying injured on the side of the road. So yes, we did argue, but before he died, I told him I was sorry and that I loved him.'

I turned away, not wanting him to see the tears coursing down my face.

As I got up to leave, he said, 'It was impossible to get Dad's attention sometimes. It was like he was in a parallel world.'

Sam too had partly absolved me, saying, 'It was so fucking stupid of him to give away his kidney! I would never do that, even for Liam.'

'You might have,' I replied. 'In any case, you know how he was - like the Giving Tree in that book I used to read to you.'

'Yes, he was probably a saint in a former life,' Liam stated.

'He could get quite stressy if you interrupted him when he was in the middle of something,' Sam pointed out. 'He was useless at multi-tasking.'

He and M had had their clashes over that in the past.

The boys didn't seem to blame me for what happened.

But I blamed myself.

MID-JUNE –
ONE YEAR AFTER THAT DAY OF
THE SUMMER SOLSTICE

The first anniversary is looming, like the clouds that had gathered in the sky that fateful June day.

Fern suggests we hold a ceremony to scatter the ashes. 'Some place that was special to him,' she says.

'Cornwall,' I say immediately. I think of how M had described those early years in Whitsand Bay as 'idyllic'. 'There's a beach he loved, close to Perranporth where he taught the boys to surf. We could spend the weekend there – you and David, Mum and Jeff and the boys. I'll try to get hold of Will and tell him the plan.'

'You'd better discuss it with Mother. She wants to organise a birthday celebration for you on the 22nd. I'll let her explain.'

'I don't want any more birthday celebrations, ever again,' I say firmly.

'I understand,' Fern says after a pause, 'but you talked about moving forward?'

Easier said than done. There are some things you can't find your way around. They become woven into your life, an indelible mark on the calendar of your days that can never be erased.

Note to blog:

What do you do if you lose your loved one on your birthday? Decide not to celebrate that day again for the rest of your life?

M had died three days after my birthday, but I had lost him on the anniversary of the day I'd been born, I'd concluded, and in many ways, because of it.

There are no responses from this – even blackwidower appears to be stumped.

But at midnight, his comment pops up.

Birth and death are simply an arrival and a departure. As T.S Eliot wrote: '...and the end of all our exploring will be to arrive where we started ...and know the place for the first time.'

I'm looking up the verses of T.S. Eliot when my mother calls. 'About your birthday, Willow, I have something I need to talk to you about. Can you pop over for lunch on Friday? Jeffrey will be at the studio all day, so it'll just be you and me.'

'OK, but there is to be no birthday plan, Mother, and that's final. Never again,' I emphasise. Not after what you put me through last year.

'We'll talk about it over lunch tomorrow,' she answers, before hanging up.

I arrive at her house on time, and she opens the door dressed in a watered silk printed dress, over which she has slung a soft pashmina. A string of pearls illuminates her porcelain skin. I attempt to give her a hug, but she somehow slips through my grasp, just as she had when I was a child. The warmth and ease between us have gone now that she's restored to her former health. She thrusts a glass of chilled wine into my hand, saying, 'It's too damp to eat in the garden. We'll have lunch in the conservatory.' She has set out bowls of olives, on a low table, a cheese board and a shop-bought quiche, which she's sliced into neat little squares.

'I'd like you to hear me out,' she begins. 'It's about your date of birth.'

'I told you I'm not celebrating my birthday this year and maybe never again,' I inform her. I take a deep breath. It feels stuffy and damp in the conservatory, as if the towering pot plants have sucked up all the oxygen.

'Nonsense! What I wanted to tell you is that the date on your birth certificate is incorrect.'

I stare at her in confusion.

'I didn't think it mattered until now. But you weren't actually born on midsummer day. The cord was wrapped around your neck!' She shudders at the memory. 'It was the longest and most ghastly day of my life!'

'Sorry to have put you through such a terrible ordeal,' I say. I recall her telling me about this years ago, joking that I was 'an accident and an emergency'.

'It was an ordeal for the midwife too,' Mother says ignoring my comment. 'She was exhausted, poor girl – she wrote down your date of birth as the twenty first of June, but you arrived in the early hours of the twenty second. I let it be. I'd recently gone to see A Midsummer Night's Dream and was very taken by it. I kept imagining all the midsummer birthday parties we could hold, but I suppose you won't want to do that now.'

'No! In any case, I'm not sure what your point is?'

'Max's accident didn't happen on the day of your birthday,' she states, as if this makes everything all right again. 'We will celebrate your arrival into the world on the twenty second from now on. I was thinking we could all fly to New York after the anniversary and stay at Jeffrey's apartment which is just off Central Park. It would be my treat. We could get Camilla to take us to her favourite boutiques and update your wardrobe. She tells me there's an excellent hairdresser on Fifth Avenue.'

'Thanks, Mother, but I want to spend the anniversary weekend in

Cornwall and scatter M's ashes. I'd like you and Jeffrey to be there!' I hold her cat-like gaze, thinking: If you come up with an excuse this time, I'll never speak to you again.

'If it's Cornwall then so be it,' she says at last. 'I'll book us into the Cliffside Spa Hotel. Let's just call it my birthday treat.'

Note to blog:

Scattering the ashes is a symbolic way of letting go, but what if you don't feel ready to let go?

You could always put some aside as a keepsake. You could keep them safe in a special memory box, or in a locket, until you're ready to release them, notdeadyet, has responded.

This has released a flurry of comments, including *…or bury them in the roots of a sapling and watch the tree grow*

…turn the ashes into a diamond ring

…send them up into the night sky in a firework

…mix them up with clay and create a piece of pottery

…have a vinyl record made from them and listen to 'soul music'.

This makes me smile.

blackwidower has written: *ashes can help the marine environment and become part of the coral reef and the eternal rhythm of the ocean.*

The night before we leave for Cornwall, I creep downstairs to M's study. I light the candles, then take down the earthenware urn and open the lid. I gaze at the gritty contents, then carefully scoop out a third and pour it into the vintage box M had given me the day I turned forty. Although it turns out I was born the day after.

I think of how he'd told me it was a reproduction of Pandora's box, filled with good things, like patience and resilience and, of course, hope.

I pour the rest of the contents into a biodegradable urn I had ordered on Amazon. Ideal for water burials, the manufacturer claimed. I'd also ordered a new mask and snorkel, a pair of flippers and a red bikini.

THE WEEKEND OF THE SUMMER SOLSTICE

The weather forecast predicts intervals of showery rain, for the longest day of the year. This time last year the sky had been a vivid azure blue; it had started out as a perfect day, I think.

We set off in convoy, Fern and David, Mum and Jeff in one car, the boys and me and the remains of M in the jeep. I had tried to call Will, only to receive an automated message stating the number was no longer in service. He hadn't responded to my email either. I think of how M had said, I know you'd never turn your back on Will. It was Will who had turned his back on me, it seemed.

I'd wrapped the biodegradable urn carefully in a thick woollen sweater and wedged it between the weekend bags. Sam straps the surfboards onto the roof rack, and we are off on M's final journey.

We encounter the usual holiday traffic as we crawl along for what seems like an eternity in a long tailback. By the time we reach the border of North Cornwall, the sky has turned dark and rain lashes against the windscreen. I push aside memories of the darkening sky as the storm gathered, the mounting fear as I waited for M to come home.

Mother insists we eat a buffet lunch at the hotel and we all file into the almost empty dining room, but I can barely swallow the baked salmon and thick potato salad I'd heaped mindlessly onto my plate. Through the windows the sea looks grey and hostile. Jeff announces conditions are set to improve in the afternoon and suggests we congregate at four, before heading down to the beach. Mother brightens immediately. 'How about us girls book ourselves a treatment at the spa?' she suggests.

'I'm going for a swim in the pool,' I reply, wondering at her ability to grab at any opportunity to be pampered. 'But thanks anyway,' I add, ashamed of my lack of gratitude. The boys decide to go beachcombing and head off into the damp afternoon.

I swim up and down the short length of the hotel pool before sinking to the bottom, where I sit crossed legged like Buddha, thinking of M soon to be out there, drifting in the vast expanse of the ocean.

"You are not a drop in the ocean, you are the entire ocean in a drop," Rumi had written.

In the afternoon we set off in two cars to the beach where M had taught Sam and Liam to surf. The beach is unrecognisable since the last time we'd been there. A recent storm has flung up piles of driftwood, day-trippers have left their litter strewn along the sand, and there are charred remains of recent campfires. The air smells of iodine and fish. I gaze out across the Atlantic Ocean where a container ship is sliding away into the horizon and feel an ache in my chest, the hollow pain of separation. I can't release the ashes here, I think. The sea is the wrong colour. It's too windy. Liam would have to wade far out into the swell and then M's ashes, would come straight back onto the beach to lie amongst the driftwood and litter. This is not the everlasting memory I want of his final journey.

Mother, wearing a long white cape – black is too funereal, she'd said firmly, and wedge-heel sandals, her eyes hidden behind a pair of enormous designer sunglasses is looking at me expectantly. But I'm frozen to the spot, clutching the biodegradable urn to my chest.

We have come all this way with our mementoes; poems to read and tributes to be made. Jeff has bought a bouquet of wild flowers, all lilac and mauves to throw into the sea, the boys have set up a speaker so we can play M's favourite soul music. Liam, shivering in his wetsuit, is propping up M's orange surfboard, ready to paddle into the waves with his father's ashes.

'We could go over by those rocks,' Fern suggests. She points to where the edge of the cliff meets the ocean. 'It looks a bit calmer and there might be a windbreak.'

We troop towards the rocks, sliding over ribbons of seaweed and bladderwrack, the wind tugging at our clothes. I notice an oil slick on the wet sand and, moments later, there is a gasp and the inevitable happens. Mother has slipped on her wedge-heels and fallen flat on her back. Jeff hoists her to her feet, while the boys marvel at the black stain on her back. 'Wow, Gran, it's huge,' Liam exclaims, 'it looks like the shape of Africa!'

You ended up in black after all, with a stain as large as a continent on your back! What do you expect in those ridiculous shoes? I want to say.

'Never mind that,' she says crossly, 'let's get on with this business.'

'I don't want to get on with "this business" as you put it,' I snap, hanging onto the flapping sheet of paper, on which the verses of T.S. Eliot are typed. I had printed it out after reading blackwidower's quote.

We shall not cease from exploration. And the end of all our exploring, will be to arrive. And know the place for the first time.

M knew and loved this place, but now it feels unfamiliar; contaminated by the squalid remains of the living. Jeff is trying to steady Mother while holding onto the bouquet of flowers at the same time. The boys are silent, Liam's knuckles white from where he's clutching the surfboard.

'We need to find a better place,' Sam announces.

'Darling, you are going to have to let your father go at some stage,' my mother says firmly.

'Sam's right,' I say turning my back on the restless waves. 'This is not the right place, let's go back to the hotel.' I turn away and head up the beach, leaving the others trailing behind me. Once back at the hotel, we gather at the bar.

'I know what you're all thinking,' I say, 'that I can't let him go.'

My mother raises her eyebrows. Her face is more mobile again, which is disconcerting and a relief at the same time.

'You'll know when the time is right,' Fern says.

On the day after the summer solstice, the sun is shining again, the wind has dropped and the sea is a defiant, glittering blue. The boys, who have been primed about the change of my birth date, leap on me with hugs and kisses, bearing a package wrapped in brown paper. I unwrap a framed photo of M and me standing in the stippled shade of a palm tree, against a backdrop of turquoise sea.

'Where did you find this?' I ask, blinking back the tears.

'In one of the photo albums,' Liam tells me. 'Sam had it reproduced and digitally enhanced.'

I'm back there, reliving those hot blue days; swimming around the point to a hidden beach, finding a coral garden where an octopus had made its den deep in the rocks, drinking rum cocktails in a local beach bar.

After a full English breakfast, the boys pull on their wetsuits and head for the beach with their surfboards. I watch them go, struck by how much Liam has grown, how thin and awkward he appears in his adolescent body, the long spindly legs and rounded shoulders. While Sam seems to have filled out, gained muscle and tone, developing into a young man. M would be proud of them, I think, my chest constricting.

Fern and David, Mum and Jeff announce they want to drive to Falmouth for a pub lunch. 'It will give you some time to decide what exactly you want to do,' is mother's parting remark.

'I'm sorry for not having come up with the perfect plan,' I snap.

Fern squeezes my arm, murmuring, 'Take your time.'

I watch the boys paddling out to where the waves are building and hover, waiting for the right one to carry them to the shore. I stand there for a while then set off along a narrow coastal path towards a small cove which is only accessible when the tide is low. Herring gulls wheel above it, and gorse and campion grow along the edge of the cliffs. I had brought the boys here when they were small, to shrimp in the rock pools. I stand watching the sea eddying and flowing in an eternal rhythm as blackwidower had described. Ahead the Atlantic stretches out like a sheet of silver foil, glinting in the afternoon light. We had come to this very place so many times over the years, but now I feel I know it, as if for the first time.

Later, I stand wedged between the boys, watching the sun sink down into the ocean. Fern and David, Mum and Jeff stand behind us creating a windbreak. We watch M's orange surfboard bobbing along with its cargo of flowers and ashes as it heads out like a little vessel on a ribbon of sunlight.

Note to blog:

Letting go of the ashes feels like an acknowledgment that a chapter of your life has ended too.

   An ending of one chapter, the beginning of a new one, blackwidower has suggested.

   As they say in French, ce'n'est qu'un au revoir – until you meet again, lifeafterdeath has commented.

Back at Rosewood Barn, I lie on the bed numb and dry-eyed, feeling that in the 'letting go', the desire to hold onto the memories had become even greater. I study the framed photo of M and me, setting out on our journey together. I'm wearing sunglasses, but there is no mistaking the happiness exuding from me. M is gazing into the far distance, as if he's miles away in place and time.

  Over breakfast, I announce to the boys that I want to return to the island and scatter the rest of the ashes. 'I'd like to go soon,' I tell them. 'The only problem is Liam will be in the middle of exams and, Sam, you have your work experience.' Sam had landed a summer placement at an accountancy firm in Bristol.

They reply at the same time, Sam a beat ahead. 'I think you should go alone, Mum. It would be good for you.'

'Yeah, Mum, we'll be fine – Harry's Mum said I could go camping with them. I'm going to need a new sleeping bag.'

'We'll get you one,' I promise.

The boys were starting to move forwards. It was time I did the same.

EARLY JULY

Fern and David have agreed to stay at the barn until I return. The flight is booked, as is the accommodation. I couldn't find the pink villa M and I had stayed in all those years ago, but had found a small cottage through a rental agency further along the beach. I had paid for it all with the last of my savings and was now going to have to dip into the remains of M's for the school fees.

I search the forum wondering if anybody has advice about taking ashes to another country and find a post from a few months ago.

If you're planning to scatter the ashes overseas, suggest you carry them with you,' lifafterdeath has written. *I decided to take my gran back to Poland, but my suitcase got lost! I never saw it or her again.*

Pray that some officious person doesn't ask you to open it, notdeadyet had responded.

Make sure you travel with the death certificate and a letter from the crematorium, is blackwidower's sound advice.

'It's just symbolic,' Fern says, watching me repack my carry-on bag for the third time, wrapping yet another layer of clothing around the vintage box containing the ashes. 'We don't know what happens at those crematoriums! You could be swept up with an axe-murderer or, worse, Miss Hampshire, who made our science lessons a living hell!'

I laugh, thinking that would be a fate worse than death.

I spend the day leading up to the trip packing and sorting out the travel arrangements, booking a taxi at the other end. I feel a mounting anxiety as the time of departure draws closer. 'Make sure you drive carefully, Sam, and don't forget to check you have enough fuel…and don't leave your dirty clothes all over the floor. Liam, I don't want Fern cleaning up after you.'

'I won't,' Liam assures me.

'You be careful, Mum,' Sam adds. 'We don't want to end up as orphans like Dad did.'

'That is never going to happen,' I say, holding him tight.

The airport is heaving with travellers in holiday mode. I reach the check-in desk at last and a woman with eyebrows like caterpillars enquires if I'm travelling alone.

'Yes, in a manner of speaking. My husband is with me in spirit. He died a year ago.' What's wrong with me, blurting this out to a complete stranger? Nerves, I conclude. 'But yes, I am travelling alone.'

'Has anybody interfered with your suitcase?' she asks, frowning.

'No, nobody,' I assure her, heaving my case onto the weighing scales. I watch it trundle away, pushing aside a memory of M being borne away in the eco-coffin, the velvet curtains closing.

'Have a lovely holiday,' she says, handing me my boarding card. 'I'm sorry about your husband. My fiancé died in a car accident two days before our wedding. It was six years ago, but I still talk to him every day.'

I tell her how sorry I am, while wondering if l will still be talking to M years down the road. Loss affects nearly each and every one of us, I think. We pack it up and carry it around with us on our journey through life. All the plans we make that never come to anything. I wonder how different this woman's life might have been, the sons and daughters she might have had, all their combined hopes and dreams turned to ashes. I glance back at the long tail of travellers queuing up, waiting to be borne away, wondering how many of them are grieving the loss of a loved one.

On the plane, I make my way down the aisle clutching the carry-on bag to my chest. I find my seat by the window and wait patiently for the lanky teenage boy with whom I'm destined to share the next eight hours settle into his. I step back in alarm as he swings his rucksack off his back, almost knocking into my precious cargo.

'Want a hand with that?' he asks, gesturing towards my carry-on.

'It's OK thanks, I'll keep it beside me.'

He stands aside while I settle into the window seat.

A stewardess is hovering over me. 'Excuse me, madam, but all carry-on bags have to go in the overhead locker.'

'I have something fragile inside,' I begin.

'You can't leave it there, I'm afraid. Let me give you a hand.'

'I'll keep it on my lap,' I reply.

'It needs to be stowed away,' she says firmly.

I hand it over reluctantly, my stomach churning as she jams it into the overhead locker along with all the other bags and duty-free purchases, then sit back with a heavy heart thinking I should have left M rest in peace in a place he knew and loved along with the rest of the ashes.

When all this is done, we'll take a week off and fly to the Caribbean, he'd promised. How I'd clung onto that vision of diving into a turquoise sea, away from all the stress and deadlines, just him and me.

Well, we're on our way, in one form and another, I tell him as the plane lifts into the thick grey clouds.

Before landing, we're handed forms to fill in for immigration. *Reason for travelling* is the first question. *Single, married, other?* is the next. I fiddle with my wedding ring, which I'm now wearing on my right hand. Fern had suggested it was time to take it off altogether. I take a deep breath and write that spidery word *Widow*. It's then that I remember I've left the death certificate and the letter from the crematorium on the kitchen table.

In the customs hall, the man in front of me is being asked to open his suitcase. Sweat prickles on my forehead, and runs down the back of my neck in spite of the air conditioning.

'What's inside the case?' a female official enquires, gesturing towards my carry-on.

'Just clothes, mainly,' I reply, smiling to mask my nerves.

'Open it, please,' she says.

I fumble with the zip and watch in trepidation as she plunges a gloved hand into the centre where the vintage box is carefully wrapped in layers of clothing. She pulls out the tangled bundle, unaware she's clasping my beloved. She's now untying the straps of the red bikini, which I'd wound around it and holding up the vintage box like a trophy.

'What's this?' she wants to know.

'It was a gift from my husband,' I begin. 'He died so I keep a few souvenirs in there. You know, sand from a beach we visited together. And ash from a volcano,' I add. We had visited Mount Etna once and brought back a piece of volcanic rock for Liam.

Her eyes are roving over me like searchlights. I hold her gaze, my heart thumping. After an agonising few seconds, she places the box carefully back into the nest of clothing. 'I'm sorry your husband passed,' she says. 'Enjoy your stay.'

'Thank you,' I say weakly.

We got through that, I tell M, thinking how he would have laughed.

The beach is exactly how I remembered it. The palm tree where we'd had our photo taken is leaning over now, its long leaves sweeping the sand. The pink villa on the far side appears to be boarded up, as if closed for the season. I'm welcomed by the owner of the cottage, a smiling woman called Marcia. She has stocked the fridge with fruit juice, bread, eggs and milk, and there's a bottle of local rum in a make-shift bar. She explains where I can buy groceries and gives me the number of a local taxi driver. I ask about Me Shack's Beach Bar where M and I had spent many a happy evening, drinking rum cocktails and she informs me it's still going strong, then leads me onto the small veranda where there's a dazzling view across the bay. A hammock has been strung up between the posts.

'It's perfect,' I say, feeling the warm breeze on my shoulders. An emerald-green gecko slides through a gap in the shutters, blinks at me warily then darts away. All around is the whistling and chatter of birdsong. Home is another world away, but M feels closer than ever. I have only one thought, which is to dive into that azure-blue sea.

As soon as she's left, I open my carry-on case to grab my bikini, then reel back in horror. Everything is covered in a thick layer of grit. I pull the vintage box free from the tangle of clothes, realising the clasp has sprung open. I spend the next few minutes frantically scrabbling around in the case trying to scoop the ashes back into the box, pausing for a moment to search for the essence of M in the coarse substance, that might have come from the surface of the moon.

We're all just drifting stardust, Liam had said.

I examine the clasp, which doesn't appear to be broken, wondering how it had sprung open in the first place, concluding M was not someone who could be contained for long. I struggle into my bikini, his remains sticking to my damp skin, grab my mask and head down the narrow sandy path towards the beach. A couple sunbathing look up curiously at the sight of a woman covered in ash, clasping a vintage box, rushing headlong into the sea.

I wade out to where the water is a deep indigo then turn on my back and kick out towards the middle of the bay, holding the box on my chest. Then turn onto my front to search the seabed. There it is at last – the coral garden M and I had found all those years ago. It's deeper than I remembered. I take a breath and descend, holding the vintage box out in front of me. I manage to wedge it into a deep crevasse in the rocks, then hover above it to say my final goodbyes. From above it looks like a small treasure chest from a sunken ship. As I make my way to the surface, a formation of silvery particles rises with me like dust motes travelling through a sunbeam.

Memories come and go. M, swerving to a halt on his bike as I stood shivering in the shadow of the rocks. *Here, take my jacket;* M grabbing me in a bear hug, murmuring, *loving you.* M so often absent, lost in his own world, only to arrive home unexpectedly, striding into the barn with an antique clock he'd found at the reclamation centre, a bouquet of purple flowers. M scooping me into his arms, and depositing me on the bed. *You look ravishing and I'm going to ravish you.* M larger than life, rising out of the sea on his orange surfboard only to end up beneath the waves, his ashes drifting with the tide on opposite sides of the ocean.

At least we got to swim together one last time, I tell him.

I mark the spot by counting my strokes all the way back to the shore. There are three hundred and seventy-eight, which strikes me as oddly symbolic, one for each day that he has been gone.

Back at Tamarind Cottage, I pour myself a rum, add orange juice, then sink into the hammock and close my eyes. I wake up at 2 a.m. local time, itching all over. My legs are covered in angry red bites. I retreat inside and climb under the mosquito net, wondering how I was going to navigate this hostile world on my own for the rest of my life.

I'm up at five, too restless and itchy to stay in bed, so sit on the deck watching the sky turn from charcoal to a watery blue. A large schooner has anchored in the bay, close to M's spot. I decide on an early morning dip, thinking I would check the vintage box. I set off counting each stroke until sky and sea seem to merge into a dazzling canvas of aqueous blue. The vintage box is still there, wedged in the crevasse, only there's a thick metal chain lying right across the rock. I attempt to drag the chain to one side, but it falls back onto the same spot, held by the weight of the anchor. I dive down again and again but haven't the strength to move it and, after an exhausting struggle, I have no choice but to give up.

I sit beneath the palm tree, watching a local family splashing around in the sea; the mother wearing a bright-red bathing cap, the father hoisting the younger boy onto his shoulder, while the older boy watched on, sucking on a mango stone as if it was a lollipop. We had been a family of four once, I think, an image of M and the boys racing into the ocean with their surfboards, the four of us sitting on the pier afterwards tucking into fish and chips. Another of M running along the lane behind Liam as he set off on his first wobbly bike ride, Sam and I cheering him on, the four of us driving to the hospital when Sam broke his arm, taking it in turns to sit with Liam when he was covered in chicken pox. M's pride and joy around the boys, how he'd called them his future.

In the evening I head down to Me Shack's Bar. A smiling Rasta, who introduces himself as Manziah, makes me a 'dark and stormy', a potent concoction of local rum and fresh ginger beer, and I sit watching the sun go down behind the peninsula. I glance across the bay which shimmers with flecks of orange. The schooner has swung around on her anchor, the metal chain glinting in the last rays of the evening sun.

In the morning I decide to swim to the point, remembering an isolated beach on the other side of the headland. I set off with my mask and flippers, diving down to follow an eagle ray skimming the ocean floor, before disappearing in a cloud of sand. I reach the headland, beyond which breakers are rolling towards the beach. I recall the ocean bed had suddenly given way to coral, making it almost impossible to access the shore. M had found a gap in the rocks, and we had rested on the beach before swimming back, but the sea had been flat and calm that day.

I tread water, looking around wildly. I'm tiring now, my feet are cramping in the tight flippers. The waves are slapping into my face, the salt sting of the ocean is in my throat. The pull and drag of the ocean is herding me towards the rocks. I glance up, wondering if I can clamber onto the rock shelf but the cliff is too sheer and the sea is swirling and frothing around it. I haven't the strength to swim back to the other beach, am clearly out of my depth.

"…thinks she's a fucking mermaid," the lifeguard's voice echoes in my head.

I force myself to stay calm, at the same time wondering if I'm about to join M in his watery grave when I hear a voice call out as if from the deep. Someone is swimming towards me, blowing plumes of water from a black snorkel. 'Only access to the beach is through those rocks,' a male voice is saying, pointing towards the jagged outcrop ahead. 'Unless you want to get torn to pieces!' He pulls off his mask, and I take in sea-green eyes and an open, smiling face. Tendrils of dark-blonde hair float around his shoulders.

'Follow me,' he instructs, 'we're going to have to wait for a break in the waves.'

I stiffen, bracing myself against being hurled onto the rocks.

'Go when I tell you. Right, now!' he instructs, giving me a shove.

I surrender to the force as it propels me towards the rocks before I'm sucked into a swirl of current and emerge breathlessly in a deep pool on the other side. He appears moments later in a whoosh of spray. 'Tricky place unless you know it,' he gasps. 'I'm Sebastian, by the way.'

'Willow,' I reply, attempting to adjust my bikini top which has been pushed to one side by the force of the waves.

'Saw you from way over there. I was freediving.'

'I've done some freediving myself,' I tell him as we climb out of the pool and onto the hot sand.

'Really? There's a spot over there where if you dive down deep enough, you can hear the sound of whales. Have you ever swum with phosphorescence?'

I shake my head.

'It's a good time, now, while there's no moon. Where're you staying?'

'Just around the peninsula,' I tell him. 'Tamarind Cottage. Is there a way back from here?' I ask, looking towards the wall of thick mangrove framing the beach.

'It's a thorny route without shoes,' he warns.

'I'll have to take my chance,' I say, aware of the burning midday sun on my shoulders.

'I'm going that way,' he says, getting up. 'I'll get my gear.' He heads up the beach to where he's left a string bag, towel and a pair of flipflops.

Then leads the way towards an overgrown path thick with cassie bushes and sharp cones. 'Here, jump on my back,' he suggests, grabbing my mask and flippers and jamming them into the string bag along with his. I attempt a graceful leap only to slide down his back and onto the sand, laughing.

'I have a better idea. Here, hold this,' he says, and the next moment he has scooped me into his arms. I can feel the heat from his chest on my skin and make another futile attempt to adjust my bikini.

'Where do you live?' I enquire, as we duck and weave through the thicket.

'On a boat for most of the year,' he tells me.

I can hear my mother suddenly. 'A sailor? No fixed abode, no reference point, a girl in every harbour.'

'I'm originally from Cornwall, but haven't been home for a few years.'

'I know it well,' I say, imagining a different ocean, M's surfboard floating away on different tide.

The day has taken an extraordinary turn, I think as we reach the other beach. He deposits me on the sand, next to Tamarind cottage.

'You need to put something on those,' he says, pointing to my bitten calves.

He rummages in the string bag, pulls out a diving knife, and disappears around the side of the cottage. He re-appears moments later, brandishing a thick leaf with a sharp point.

'Aloe vera,' he announces. 'Christopher Columbus called it a doctor in a flower pot. Cleopatra bathed in it! It'll sort you out.' I watch as he slices down the length of the plant, removing the outer skin, until all that's left is a piece of semi-transparent gel. Next moment he's kneeling down and smearing the glutinous substance over my calves, circling each ankle slowly.

'Cleopatra clearly didn't have a sense of smell,' I say, grimacing at the acrid scent, but the itching has miraculously stopped. 'Well, thank you,' I smile, 'for rescuing me from the ocean, carrying me through the mangrove and now this!' I glance down at my legs which are covered in a thin green film.

'My pleasure.' He grins. 'How would you like to come night diving with me this evening? I could make you dinner on the boat. A friend of mine caught a five-pound tuna.'

'Where is the boat?' I ask, thinking I'd always wanted to do a night dive.

'Just out there in the bay,' he answers, pointing to the schooner. '*Stargazer*,' the schooner whose anchor was lying across M's grave. 'She's a beauty – like you,' he adds candidly.

'I'm not so sure about that,' I laugh, gesturing towards my bitten calves.

'Will-o'-the-wisp. Wasn't it a sprite in mythology who led travellers astray into the marsh?'

'I believe it's also an elusive or misleading goal, or hope for something.' *...there's always hope*, M had said.

'Ah! Well, unless you decide to be elusive, or are planning to lead me astray, I'll be waiting by the tender at six. Oh, and wear that bikini,' he adds before heading down the path, leaving behind a tantalising view of a smooth, tanned back.

I set off down the beach at six. I had known from the moment I woke up from an afternoon nap that I would accept his invitation to go night diving. There was a warmth and directness about him that had immediately made me feel at ease. I sensed his love of the ocean and wanted to be part of it, to glimpse into a life spent at sea.

He is standing on the shoreline beside a small dinghy which is pulled up on the sand, holding a sprig of bright-red bougainvillea.

'It was to match your bikini,' he says, sounding disappointed. I'd chosen a black one-piece, thinking it was better for a night dive. 'I don't want to scare away the fish.' I laugh. Over the swimsuit I'd thrown a white cotton sundress Fern had lent me. I'd packed a beach bag with a towel, hairbrush, underwear, my mask and snorkel.

We motor out across the bay, the evening darkening around us. The schooner is a sight to behold, with its gleaming wooden deck and varnished cockpit.

'The owner lives in Palma and is shipping her back to the Med next week, so this is my last weekend on board,' he tells me, as he gives me a tour below of the living area and kitchenette.

'Where will you live then?' I ask.

'I'll take a job on another boat,' he replies.

"…a nomad," I hear my mother say. No fixed abode – he'll just sail off into the sunset, then where will you be?

'It must be an interesting life?'

'The ocean can be an unpredictable beast,' he answers as we climb back onto the deck. 'How about we go and see what lies below?'

I glance down into the oily darkness with a sense of nervous anticipation.

'We'll descend to about thirteen metres, then just stay still and wait. Make sure you keep a hold of the anchor chain, or you'll end up underneath the boat – or on the other side of the bay,' he warns as I climb down the ladder after him.

We swim along the length of the schooner towards the bow, then he adjusts his mask, takes a breath and sinks beneath the surface, leaving a stream of bubbles behind him. I recall M telling me to take passive inhalations using my diaphragm before descending. I inch my way slowly down the thick anchor chain that stretches all the way to the coral garden, and to M. I'm aware of Sebastian below, and feel him nudge my foot, intimating to stay still. We hang there as if suspended in space and time, the silence and infinity of the ocean all around us. He directs the light of his torch upwards, and I watch enthralled as a dizzying display of luminescence streams towards the light like a host of shooting stars. Time seems to have ceased as we're caught in the thrall of all those dazzling particles of light. I imagine I'm floating in the midst of them searching for the brightest star, Maximillian the second. I can feel them drawing me into their midst and am all of a sudden overcome by a sense of peace, free from all the grief and sadness. And then everything turns black like the theatre lights going down. I'm vaguely aware of Sebastian beside me, his hair waving around his head like seaweed. He pulls me back, towards the anchor chain, his torchlight slicing through the darkness, and we float back up to the surface together, emerging into the warm night air.

'You were meant to hang onto the chain,' he gasps, 'I thought you'd passed out!'

'I got carried away.' Literally, I think. There is no way I can describe that strange out-of-body experience, the feeling I was floating in space with M. 'I'm sorry if I gave you a fright.'

We climb back onto the boat, and he grabs a towel, saying, 'What the hell was that about? You're not even out of breath! Are you some kind of mermaid?'

I smile. 'I used to dream of being one as a child,' I tell him.

'That was nuts,' he continues. He shakes the water out of his hair, and frowns. 'Do mermaids drink alcohol, because I could do with a beer.' He disappears down the hatch, saying, 'Suggest you get out of your wet gear. Give me a shout when you're dressed.'

I pull off my swimsuit, change back into the sundress and call down to him that he can come up.

'So, what was that about?' he asks again, as we sit in a cushioned area at the front of the boat, sipping icy-cold beers.

'My husband died last year,' I tell him. 'We were married for nineteen years. I brought some of his ashes here to put in the sea. They're in a vintage box just over there in the rocks, only your anchor chain is lying right over it. I tried to move it, but it was too heavy.'

'Were you planning to try and pull it up yourself?' he asks in disbelief.

'No, I just got carried away by that extraordinary sight. It was the most beautiful thing I've ever seen.'

'It was, wasn't it?' He smiles, turning towards me. He pushes a damp strand of hair from my forehead. I take in the sharp curve of his bicep, and feel a stirring deep down, a sense of coming back to life after a long hibernation. 'Right, first things first,' he says, jumping up, and moving towards the prow where he stands like a silhouette staring down into the ocean. 'I'll bring her up.' He makes his way back to the stern and, moments later, I hear the sound of the engine starting up, followed by the slow grind of the anchor being dragged along the ocean floor.

'I'm sorry about your husband,' he says as we motor out into the bay. 'I lost my brother three years ago. You never really get away from it, no matter how many oceans you cross. But you can't allow it to become a life sentence.'

'Were you close?' I venture, thinking how devastating it must have been to lose a sibling.

'We fought a lot like brothers do, but yeah, we were close,' he replies.

He re-anchors the boat further out, then goes below, returning sometime later with a platter of tuna sashimi, a loaf of crusty bread and a bottle of chilled white wine. We eat dinner on the front deck, and he talks about the magical dives he has done, the freedom of being out on the ocean and some of the close calls he'd had along the way.

'So, what brought you to the island?' I ask, curiously.

'Ollie and I embarked on this project to re-build an old Folkboat and sail it across the Atlantic,' he begins, 'only he got sick halfway through. After he died, I was in bad shape. Then one morning I found myself down at the boatyard. I could hear him saying, 'Do it for me, mate, keep the dream alive.'

He smiles suddenly. 'Before he died, he said "seize life by the balls, Seb, before it seizes you!" He had testicular cancer.'

I feel my heart constrict.

'So, I got back to work, finished the overhaul, then waited for a weather window before setting sail.'

'On your own?' I ask, in awe.

'Yeah, mostly. Ollie was with me in a way,' he says.

I listen in fascination as he describes how the boat which he'd named *The Jolly Oliver*, had started to take on water halfway across the Atlantic, how part of the equipment had failed, so he'd had to navigate by the stars. 'I ran into a bad squall off the Windward Islands, and had to hunker down for the night. Drifted off course, then woke up the next morning, and saw the island in the distance. There was a rainbow hanging over it – seemed like a good omen. I headed for harbour and managed to pick up some work on a motor yacht – which was not for me. Moved on to sail boats, and ended up on this beauty.'

'And you haven't been back to Cornwall since?'

He shakes his head. 'My parents split up after Ollie died. No reason to go back. What about you?' he digresses, 'Where's home?'

'Highbury, in Wiltshire,' I reply. I tell him how M had converted an eighteenth-century barn into a home, about the boys, and how our lives had changed dramatically after M had died. I glance away across the expanse of rippling sea. 'We had an argument the day he died. It was an accident, but I've blamed myself since.' The wind has got up, causing waves to slap against the side of the boat. I feel him move away and shiver, my confession hanging in the air. He returns moments later with a windproof jacket.

'Here, put this on,' he says, draping it around my shoulders.

Here, take my jacket...

He hunkers down beside me and pulls me closer. Ollie and I fought like cats and dogs,' he says after a silence. 'I punched him so hard once, he stopped breathing, but fortunately he didn't die that time. Life had something worse in store for him. Guilt is a fucking useless emotion. It will only drag you down. You can't survive in the depths of the ocean. Let it go, Willow.'

I blink back the futile tears. 'You're right,' I say, turning my face towards him. Our eyes lock for a brief second, and then we are kissing urgently. We fall back onto the cushions in a jumble of arms and legs, tugging at each other's clothes.

Don't forget to carry a condom with you at all times, blackwidower had said.

'...haven't got anything,' I breathe.

'I'll take care of it,' he murmurs, slipping away again into the darkness. 'Just promise me you won't swim away,' he adds, making me smile.

It is all at once familiar and unknown, this ritual as old as time and so different in the arms of a new lover. M and I would lie limbs entwined, slowly seeking out all the familiar pleasure points. This feels like an adventure into the unknown; the swell of the ocean below, the star-studded sky above, and then everything comes to a shuddering halt, and I fall back onto the cushions, already mourning for what's passed, yearning for something more, for something lost, now out of reach.

We lie tangled together, listening to the grind and pull of the anchor as if the boat is straining to be free. He would be sailing away tomorrow, he'd told me, to deliver *Stargazer* to the container ship that would transport it across the ocean. It was unlikely we would see each other again. I am struck by the impermanence of all things. There would be no awkward follow up of where and when, or if we should meet again. We might not even swap phone numbers or email addresses, yet instead of regret, I feel a sense of release, possibility, hope almost.

'Wind's getting up,' I hear him murmur. 'I won't be able to take you back to shore until the morning.'

'That's fine with me,' I answer sleepily, thinking I could lose myself for a few more hours out here with him and just the sound of the ocean all around us.

I lie awake in the narrow bunk, listening to the creaking sounds of the boat, aware of him moving around on the deck, checking the anchor. I finally fall into a dreamless sleep and wake up as the sun is pouring through the hatch. I drag a comb through the tangle of my hair and gaze at myself in the porthole mirror. The shadows beneath my eyes have started to fade, my skin is bronzed from the sun. I find some toothpaste in the cupboard below the sink and swill it around my mouth.

I've got morning breath, I'd groaned, that day of the solstice.

I head up onto the deck, eager to seize the day.

This morning the sea is smooth and silky, sparkling with diamond lights. We eat breakfast, watching two pelicans dive-bombing into the sea. Afterwards we swim out to the peninsula and dive down through shafts of reflected sunlight, watching shoals of iridescent fish swimming through the gaps in the coral. The sound is very faint at first, and then I hear it - a low clicking followed by a series of pulses, the muted echoes of whales communicating with one another across the vast depths of the ocean.

'Weather's changing,' Sebastian says as we climb back on board. 'I'm going to have to leave a bit earlier.'

'That's OK,' I tell him. 'It's been wonderful. I'll never forget that dive.'

'I'll never forget you, mermaid girl,' he says, kissing me. 'I'll be looking out for you, next time.'

'Next time?'

'You'll be back,' he predicts, gesturing towards the coral garden. 'He'll be here, part of the rhythm of the ocean, always.'

He takes me to the shore in the dinghy, and I sit in the shade of the palm tree watching *Stargazer*, inching away, the afternoon light catching her sails until she's just a blur on the horizon.

MID JULY

ABSENCE: *(noun)* not being present, the state of being away.

I have returned to Rosewood Barn many times in the past, relaxed in the knowledge that M is working late, or has gone to source materials, or is out riding his bike – although towards the end I'd begun to question his frequent absences. But as I walk into the living area, his absence feels permanent, as if set in the rough stonework around the fireplace he designed. M will not be coming home.

Fern has weeded the borders while I'd been away and planted delphiniums and clumps of purple heather along the hedgerows. She and Frida have filled in all the empty mole hills, and Sam has mowed the lawn.

Fern bustles around in the kitchen, preparing a late lunch. She has organised for David to pick the boys up from school, so we can catch up with each other.

I tell her all about the trip, and about meeting Sebastian, describing that magical night swimming with phosphorescence, and how we'd made love on the deck of *Stargazer*.

'Just what you needed,' she grins. 'Any chance of him sailing this way in the near future?'

I shake my head. 'It was a holiday romance. His life is at sea – mine is here,' I add looking around the familiar home that M and I had created together. 'Sometimes it's best to leave the memory intact.'

'Maybe it will encourage you to start dating again?' Fern suggests.

'I'm not sure.' I think of how Holly had spent her life trawling through dating sites – Fern had done the same. It hadn't worked out for either of them.

'You'll meet somebody one day when you're least expecting it,' Fern is saying.

I smile, thinking of the many times I had said the same to her over the years.

She moves on, telling me how Mother was putting pressure on her to come up with a date for the wedding.

'She's pushing for early spring! Apparently, she's found the perfect venue!' my sister adds, making a face.

'Your dream was to get married in a garden centre next September,' I remind her.

'She clearly has some other idea! No doubt a five-star hotel with topiaried hedges and a marquee. David and I are tempted to book a registry office and repeat our vows on a white beach like you and M did, but I know that would destroy her. In any case, she wants to discuss it with you and me on Friday over lunch. Oh, and by the way, she said you were to call her as soon as you got home.'

'We'll pretend my flight was delayed,' I say, weary at the thought of one of my mother's inquisitions.

The boys come clattering through the front door, David behind them, and fling themselves at me, wanting to know all about the trip.

We hug and kiss then I turn to David, saying, 'I can't thank you enough.'

'We had a great time, didn't we, guys? We have a budding musician on our hands and a talented astronomer here.'

I smile, thinking how he had already become a part of the family.

Liam listens, fascinated, as I tell him about swimming amongst the phosphorescence. I give them a censored version of having been invited onto the schooner, before moving swiftly on. Finally, I describe how I'd left the ashes in the coral garden. They're both silent for a moment.

'Dad would want you to be happy again, Mum,' Sam says at last.

'And we need you to be happy too,' Liam adds, burying his head in my lap.

There are bills to be paid and a pile of mail waiting. I open a couple of letters addressed to Maximillian Goodhart, wondering if they will ever stop coming, those annual reminders to book an eye test, even though I'd asked them to take his name off the register. A letter from HMRC, stating he hadn't filed his tax returns, a couple of leaflets from charities asking for donations. The island and those long hot days already feels another world away.

Note to blog:

Returning home after a holiday is a brutal reminder that you have no choice but to make a new life for yourself now.

As well as an opportunity to create a home for your new life, blackwidower has suggested.

'I was thinking we could go to Cornwall like the old days, Mum,' Liam says over supper. The old days. A time that has gone, gone in the absence of a heartbeat.

'That's a great idea.' I smile. 'How about next weekend?'

I can't sleep because of the time difference, so pull out my laptop and type the heading: Turning The Tide. I finish the article an hour later, a story of a shared dream, followed by a tragedy, and one man's solitary journey across the ocean, through grief. I email it to Jason with a brief footnote. *'Thought you might find this story inspiring. I would like to pitch the idea of a new column, headed, 'Adventurous Lives'.*

An email immediately pings back with an out of office response, stating he's away until the middle of August.

I forward the piece to The Weekend, The Word, and even a couple of local newspapers, including the Highbury Journal. Fern had bought Lifestyle while I'd been away. I'd flicked through it, and there was Susannah Frost, still riding high over what had once been my column. They had replaced her headshot with a full body image and wound the text around her slender frame. She was wearing a pair of cut-off denim shorts, designer wellington boots, and a tank top with ROCK ON emblazoned on it. The column has evolved from dissecting interesting lives, to 'a day in the life of Susannah', it seems. Susannah, behind the scenes at a rock festival, 'glamping', only the article had centered around her choice of outfit, her designer wellies getting 'squelchy with mud' and how she'd had to cross her legs for hours rather than face the 'nightmarish' portable loos. The other column was about the 'untimely death' of her dog Mitch, who had been killed on the road. Is there ever a good time for a dog to be run over? *He may have gone to Heaven, but I have gone to purgatory,* she'd written. I had flung the magazine into the recycling bin.

LATE JULY

I set off to Charlton Haven for the get-together over lunch with Mother to discuss Fern's wedding. I vow to myself I will not rise to my mother. Rather, I would rise to the occasion; remain calm and detached, while making it clear we must support Fern and David with whatever they should decide. It is one of those breathless summer days, hot and still. Early blackberries are appearing in the hedgerows amidst a tangle of whitethorn and cow parsley. I set off in plenty of time, thinking it was the perfect day to be riding M's motorbike. I had taken the Triumph out a few times since Sean had taught me how to handle it. The boys had followed on their dirt bikes, Sam commenting that I needed to relax more in the bends, but all the same he'd been impressed, conceding I looked 'pretty cool' for a beginner.

Mother opens the door, already in wedding mode, in a cream organza dress that flares at the waist and nude high heels.

'Well, you look a lot better,' she says, grazing my cheek with hers. 'I hope you didn't overdo the sunbathing. It can be very ageing. You'll pay the price later.'

'You look great too, Mum,' I say. Her forehead is so tight, pinpoints of light reflect off it, as if she's somehow lit up from within. She's wearing a blood-red lipstick – a sign that she's ready to do battle.

I ask after Jeff, and she tells me he's away working on a new series of Lyrical. 'His show is an overnight sensation,' she adds, puffing up her chest, which appears to be restored to its former glory, thanks to the prosthesis, or 'comfie' as she refers to it.

I'd read a review of Lyrical in The Weekend before throwing the magazine away. The show was a huge success, with even some of the weakest lyrics now on everyone's lips. Fern had showed me a photo of mother and Jeff in 'Who's Who' at a cocktail party at the Savoy with the caption: '1960s model Michelle Monroe with Jeff Darlington, the creator of Lyrical'.

'Now, I want to hear all about your holiday adventures,' she states. 'Tell all.'

'I had a great time, I swam every day,' I begin. 'The sea was so warm. I did an amazing dive one night and saw phosphorescence. It was… Well, therapeutic,' I add, unable to explain that existential moment when I'd felt M was all around me. My voice trails off at her deadpan expression.

'Good, well hopefully you can move on with your life now. Start meeting people, find yourself a suitable partner.' In the silence that follows, she says, 'Thankfully, we have a wedding to plan.'

She leads the way into the garden where she's laid the table with colourful salads from the deli, slices of smoked salmon, a cheese board. A bottle of champagne is chilling in a silver bucket and she's pulled out three of her best crystal glasses. On a side table is a vase of crimson roses in full bloom and a folder labelled WEDDING.

Fern and I exchange glances.

'Open this, would you, Willow?' Mother says, handing me the icy bottle of Mumm, her favourite champagne. 'My wrist has been playing up lately.' Her hands have started to give away her advancing years, but she refuses to admit it's arthritis. I notice her rings are cutting into her swollen fingers. She has all her bracelets on today, which jangle like windchimes on her wrist. She's determined to claw back the years, fill her remaining days with champagne and celebrations, witness her older daughter walk down the aisle in a designer gown, followed by a lavish reception with no expenses spared. While Fern is dreaming of an ivory suit she's seen in a department store in Bristol, she and David exchanging vows in the Secret Garden Centre on Harptree Hill.

I send my sister a look that says, Stand your ground. Tell her you've made your decision, and it's not negotiable.

Fern squares her shoulders and delivers her speech. 'David had a big wedding with all the trimmings when he married Jennifer and they ended up divorced less than two years later. He hates formal occasions. We want a small gathering, just close friends and family.'

Mother's face remains impassive. I can sense her brain whirring madly behind the impenetrable mask of her face.

She listens as Fern reaches the end of her speech. 'I know a big, fancy wedding is your dream, but I'm sorry it's just not ours.'

A faint blush blooms on Mother's cheeks. I don't know whether she's about to burst into a tirade or concede she's lost the battle. 'Well, I hope I can change your mind when I tell you my idea for the venue.'

Fern casts me a helpless look.

Mother takes a delicate sip of champagne, then sits up straight, her eyes on fire.

'I have been in contact with the event organisers and there are a few dates still available for a late spring wedding.'

'Event organisers?' Fern repeats faintly. 'Spring wedding?'

'Yes, I thought Huntington Hall would be the perfect venue. Lady Priscilla has linked up with a top wedding planner. They normally hold celebrity weddings and that kind of thing, but she has followed my career and, after all, I was a celebrity in my day, if there was such a thing! Besides nothing's too good for my older daughter.' She has opened the wedding file now and is pulling out a glossy brochure and some magazine cuttings. She hands Fern the brochure. On the cover is a photo of a smiling bride and groom standing beneath the arched beams of the porch M designed, in a shower of white confetti.

I feel a current of pain going through my chest, as if my heart is thumping with the echo of a thousand volts. Fern seems to absorb some of my shock. She sits back heavily in the garden chair, almost tipping backwards. She manages to right herself, but her glass with the remains of her champagne falls in a perfect arc onto the manicured lawn. Mother leaps up with a little cry, intent on rescuing her precious crystal. 'Thank goodness it hasn't broken!' she exclaims while Fern sends me a shattered look.

I am beyond words, can barely see my mother through the crimson mist where she presides behind the roses. I stand up abruptly, sending my glass toppling. This time it snaps at the stem, causing her to let out another cry.

'Are you serious?' I say, finding my voice at last. 'Haven't you listened to Fern at all? She told you she wants an autumn wedding in The Secret Garden – her passion is gardens – you got that part right by naming her after a plant. I can't believe you would even think of Huntington Hall as a venue after what happened.'

'OK, let's calm down,' Fern states, as if she's dealing with an unruly class.

'I am perfectly calm,' Mother replies. Her forehead is now covered in little dew drops of sweat, her lips moving spasmodically. 'I'm shocked by your reaction, Willow. I thought it would be the perfect tribute to Max. It's as if you feel responsible for what happened to him, which is ridiculous nonsense. It was an accident.'

I curse myself for having confided in her that M and I had been arguing that day.

'If you hadn't insisted on a birthday celebration, which I didn't even want... I was pressuring him to hurry up so we could get there on time, so you didn't throw a fit! You always do that! Organise some over-the-top event, without asking us what we want!'

'Take it easy, Willow,' Fern urges.

'Ah, so it's my fault your husband died,' my mother says, her amber eyes blazing, her fury matching mine. We are made of the same substance I think – guilt and blame. We have the same short fuse.

'No! I never said that! It was my fault! And I'm going to have to live with it for the rest of my life!'

I stand up blinded with tears, and set off across the lawn into the cool interior of the house, gagging from the cloying scent of lilies, all my good intentions ruined like her precious crystal.

Fern catches up with me as I'm about to climb into the jeep. 'You can't drive home in this state,' she says, taking me by the arm. She leads me across the road to the cafe where we had often retreated in the past when Mother's fury echoed through the house like thunder.

We make our way down the narrow street, past the old fabric store, which is now a charity shop, past Fusion Flowers where Fern had worked in the summer holidays tying up exotic bouquets with cellophane, to The Melting Pot. It had changed owners several times. Instead of the giant scones and Victoria sponges, they now served red velvet cupcakes and quinoa and lemon slices. We order lattes and share a salted caramel square.

'I made a pact with myself not to rise to her,' I say, miserably. 'I obviously haven't moved on.'

I stare at my latte, sick at heart.

'You have to learn not to react to her,' Fern is saying. 'It was incredibly thoughtless, but you know Mother, she's always been over the top, desperate to push us into the limelight.' She stares at me directly. 'Willow, it was an accident,' she states, just as she had said that day at the hospital after I'd blurted out my garbled confession. 'M has forgiven you. Now you have to try and forgive yourself.'

FORGIVENESS (*noun*) the act of forgiving or the willingness to forgive.

Note to blog:

I believe grief resides just beneath the solar plexus. It is a tender aching spot of exposed nerve endings which when activated by a thoughtless remark, can become inflamed, climaxing in an outpouring of anger and tears. Be aware of your G spot, in this case where you store your grief – and learn what triggers it.

There are a lot of exclamation marks, and comments to this such as *well put, how true…, love it, WW!*

…eventually it will turn into an understanding that the remark was without thought, and you will no longer be triggered by it, blackwidower has suggested.

MID-AUGUST

Fern and I decide to spend the day in Bristol, shopping and having lunch. Fern is keen to try on the ivory suit and get my opinion. After the drama with Mother, she had gone ahead and booked The Secret Garden for her wedding, and chosen a date in September of next year.

'How very original!' Mother had commented dryly. 'I'm going to have to find something appropriate to wear if I don't want to be outshone by the hydrangeas.'

Fern and I trawl The Mall, dipping in and out of our favourite boutiques, searching for bargains in the summer sales. I spot a stunning tan leather jacket, part designer, part biker. I try it on, then glance at the price tag, my spirits sinking. I was going to have to get a job soon, or else start digging into my life insurance.

Next, we make our way to the department store where she'd spotted the ivory suit.

'It's perfect,' I breathe. 'You look elegant and pure as well as drop-dead gorgeous and sexy at the same time!'

'Are you sure I don't look fat?' she enquires, anxiously. She pinches her waist. 'This has got to go.'

'You look beautiful,' I say. 'David's a lucky man.'

She smiles. 'I still can't believe we found each other. Now we have to find someone for you.'

'A suitable partner?' I grin, quoting Mother.

'You'll get a second chance. There's someone out there for you,' she says assuredly.

He would have to be very different to M, I think, so I would never be forced to make a comparison.

'How about we have a makeover?' Fern suggests as we are strolling through the beauty department.

'Why not?' I smile, caught up in her mood of exhilaration.

We perch on high stools while the sales assistant transforms our faces with blushers and highlighters, bronzers, eyeliners and lipstick.

We leave the department store half an hour later: over-made up, garish in the midday light. I glance at Fern's face. The makeup has had the curious effect of making her look ordinary, no different to the crowd of young women on their lunch breaks, with their matt complexions, heavy eyebrows and outlined lips. The beauty about Fern was her glowing skin, which has now been dulled by too much foundation.

I'd attempted to wipe off the crimson lipstick which reminded me of mother's battle shade, but it had left behind a blood-red stain, which, coupled with the smoky eyeliner, made me look slightly wanton.

We eat lunch in an Italian cafe on a cobbled side street and I'm suddenly assailed by a host of memories – M and I sitting down to brunch at Café Lucia, Miranda and Martin arriving, Miranda saying, 'I'll ask Mother to postpone the rehearsal. M's reply: 'I don't want it hanging over me the whole weekend…'

I'm back in that moment again, re-writing the scene, with M agreeing to leave it until Monday.

'OK, you win, he is saying, kissing me. After all, I can think of a much better way to spend your birthday…

'Are you OK?' Fern is enquiring.

I pull myself back into the present. 'Sorry, I went on a trip down memory lane.'

'That's a good thing,' my sister assures me.

Not if it leads you down a blind alley, I think.

After lunch Fern drives us home, taking a route she knows to avoid the rush-hour traffic. The radio is playing Phil Collins' Just another day in Paradise. An old man is hunkered down by the railings of the bus station, with a cardboard sign reading: HUNGRY AND HOMELESS, PLEASE HELP. Next to him is a younger man with a thatch of matted brown hair. He is wearing a ragged azure blue shirt and looking around with the bewildered air of somebody who has lost their bearings. There is something strikingly familiar about his profile, although the lower part of his face is covered in a thick beard. He suddenly turns his face towards me and our eyes meet briefly. I have time to take in sunken eyes, the palest shade of grey before Fern accelerates.

'Will,' I gasp. 'Stop! I think I saw Will.'

'I can't stop here,' Fern answers, glancing into the mirror. She slows, causing the driver behind to blast his horn and the next moment we are being swept along with the flow of traffic towards the roundabout.

'Are you sure it was Will?'

'I think so…go around again,' I beg her.

I know you'd never turn your back on him… M had said.

'… we haven't spoken since March,' I say, as we inch our way back towards the bus station. 'His phone is no longer in service. He could be living rough on the streets.'

'And if he is, what are you going to do about it?'

'I don't know, try to help,' I say, leaping out of the car. I am running along the line of moving cars towards the entrance of the bus station, dodging through the throngs of people. The old man is still there, but there's no sign of Will.

'Did you see a man in a blue shirt?' I ask him.

He stares at me from rheumy eyes. 'Haven't eaten anything for days, miss. Please,' he mutters.

'His name is Will Goodhart. He has light-grey eyes,' I continue.

He shakes his head.

I make my way back to where Fern has pulled in beside the taxi rank, grab my handbag, and pull a note from my purse.

'Did you find him?' Fern is saying.

'No, this is for the homeless man.'

'So, you didn't see Will and you weren't even sure it was him in the first place? And you just gave twenty pounds to a homeless guy?' Fern says, as I get back into the car.

'I'm not sure…' I begin. All I knew was I had glimpsed into those hollow eyes, and witnessed the abyss of grief and loss.

I drive back the following morning, and circle the bus station, but there's no sign of him. I discover there's a shelter for the homeless nearby, and find their contact number. Nobody seems to have heard of a William Goodhart or have seen a man who fits his description.

'We don't have a record of every homeless person who passes through here,' a grumpy-voiced woman informs me. 'Half of them don't even know their own names.'

I think of how Frida had suggested I volunteer to help the homeless, and how I'd resisted. The desperate plight of those who lived on the streets had seemed remote to me then – yet another cause amongst many. M would have rushed to help, I think. But then M had been homeless himself once, albeit not living rough on the streets. He would be devastated if he knew his brother was out there somewhere. I was going to have to try and find Will.

EARLY SEPTEMBER

A text from Holly pops up on my phone. *I did receive your messages. We need to talk. H*

Great to hear from you, I reply. *How about you come over for lunch? I want to make amends.*

When there's no response, I write, *I'm free any day this week.*

Friday works for me; she replies some hours later. *12:30*

I consider this brief and chilly exchange, wondering what it is she needs to talk about. It seems unlikely she intends to re-kindle our friendship, so I can only conclude she wants to teach me a lesson, remind me of how badly I've treated her.

...some friendships will not survive a death, sadeyedlady had commented.

But I would do everything I could, I decide, as I set off for the delicatessen to buy gluten-free bread, a vegetarian quiche, a flourless cake. At least I would be able to relax in the knowledge I'd tried.

By one fifteen, she still hasn't turned up. It strikes me she must have changed her mind and is enacting some kind of revenge - a dish that has long gone cold, like the quiche I'd put in the oven to warm, and had taken out again. I remind myself Holly was always late, but now it's almost one forty-five. I'm nibbling on a piece of gluten free bread which tastes like cardboard, when I hear her car pull up on the driveway.

'Sorry I'm so late,' she says, handing me a jar of Greek olives and a cardboard box. 'I stopped at the deli.'

'You didn't need to do that,' I begin. 'I was there earlier. But thank you,' I add, wondering if the olives symbolised the proverbial branch.

I take in her beautiful face, noticing the new frown lines etched on her once smooth forehead. We circle each other cautiously, like martial arts performers, waiting to see which one of us will strike first.

She declines a glass of wine with, 'Better not, I have to drive.'

'Whereabouts are you living now?' I ask, tentatively.

'I've rented a flat in Bridgend.'

'I'm so sorry about the way I behaved, Holl,' I begin. 'It was unforgiveable.'

'I wasn't much of a friend to you either, landing on you with all my dramas, then making that tactless remark about wishing Peter was dead! Divorce is an ugly business,' she adds bitterly.

I absorb this, thinking it is yet another kind of loss, the end of a reunion, all those shared plans for the future.

She perches on a stool while I assemble the food, telling me about the end of her marriage, how she'd come out of it with virtually nothing. 'It turned out Peter was up to his eyes in debt, and has been living on credit most of the time. He invested heavily into his son's new business which was a non-starter. Anyway, it's history now. On a positive note, I've just had an interview for a PA job, which is why I was late. The guy has a superyacht and homes all over the world. I seem to spend my life going to interviews these days. It's not easy when you're forty-one and divorced, with no decent qualifications,' she sighs. Maybe I will have a glass of wine.'

I pour us both a glass. 'So, what was it you wanted to talk about?' I feel a momentary dread, fearing she's about to reveal something terrible; she has terminal cancer and only has months to live…

She takes a gulp of wine and twists a lock of hair around her finger. 'It's about the affair,' she says, without meeting my eye.

I frown, remembering how cagey she'd been. *Just somebody who helped, when I was at a very low ebb. It didn't mean anything.*

Why hadn't she gone into the details? We had told each other everything once. But that was in the early days, when neither of us felt we had anything to hide.

'Who was it?'

'It was Will,' she answers, after a pause. 'I couldn't tell you, knowing how you felt about him, how angry you were over the kidney donation.'

I stare at her in astonishment. 'You were the one who christened him Will the Conqueror, and called him a hopeless addict!' I have a vision of the man at the bus station, the haunted look in his grey eyes.

'Will has a different side not many know about. He's actually incredibly charming and kind, like M. He would do anything for you when he's not drinking. He's always felt misunderstood – especially by you – like he's the bad brother. We both kind of fell back on one another. It was during a horrible time in my marriage. Will saw me as someone. Peter never really looked at me.' She hesitates. 'You wouldn't even allow me to mention Will's name after M went ahead with the donation. I was planning to tell you that evening you threw me out, but there was this wall around you.'

'I probably wouldn't have taken it very well,' I admit after a pause.

'Peter's older son, Matt, found out we were seeing one another,' she continues. 'He followed me into Bristol one evening and reported it back to his father.'

I absorb this. 'Where is Will now?' I ask, 'I haven't been able to reach him for months. His phone is not in service. I thought I saw him at the bus station looking destitute.'

'He's been admitted into St Jude's, psychiatric ward.' Holly states. 'They managed to get him there just in time.'

'Oh my god, what happened this time?'

'He tried to commit suicide.'

I stare at her in shock. 'What! When?'

'The day before yesterday. He was found lying unconscious down by the river. He'd taken an overdose of painkillers and drugs, and God knows what else. He has been living rough so you probably did see him at the bus station. Someone called an ambulance and he was taken straight to A&E. I went to visit him yesterday. He looks terrible. He doesn't want you or the boys to know about it. I told him you and I had fallen out, but I felt you needed to know.'

I sit there stunned, struck by the irony. Will had attempted to take his life, after everything M had done to try and save it. This time he had not been able to call on his Good Samaritan of a brother to rush to the rescue.

I remember how our eyes had met briefly. I was sure he'd recognised me through the mask of make-up, while I had gazed at the ravaged features of the handsome brother-in-law I had previously known.

'I need to go and see him,' I say, after a silence.

'I'll go with you.'

'Thanks, Holl, but I should go alone. I owe it to M.'

'I understand,' she says. 'You know, if you ever feel like talking about... Well, anything at all, I'm here.'

She of all people would understand, I think. She has the same rotten temper as I do.

We sit there until the courtyard is in shadow and I pour out my tortured tale in a rush of half-finished sentences. I reach the end, and watch the tears snaking down her cheeks. We are both crying now. It's 'a vale of tears.'

'Let's go inside,' I say, shivering. The warmth of the day has long gone.

We lounge on the sofa eating the passion fruit cheesecake she'd brought. 'It's divine. It doesn't taste gluten free,' I comment.

'Oh, I gave all that up,' she tells me. 'In the end it was just a load of effort for nothing. I'm over the whole diet business, although I might try the Keto plan to get rid of this,' she says, prodding her flat stomach.

'Holly, you're perfect as you are,' I smile.

'I've missed you so much,' she says, hugging me. 'But I should be getting back – it's a long drive.'

'You could stay over?' I suggest. 'We could drink more wine and put the world to rights?'

'Really?' She smiles and settles back on the sofa.

...*true friendship will realign and bloom again,* blackwidower had written.

We sit up most of the night, reminiscing.

'I remember pouring my heart out to M. I asked if he knew the secret of a happy marriage. I was fishing,' she admits, 'trying to find out how things were between you two.'

'God, Holly!'

'I was jealous,' she admits. 'I know M was elusive at times and how hard it was for you to pin him down, but you were so good together. He was so present, that is when he wasn't absent! The way he always said, 'loving you', as if only that moment mattered. Anyway, his answer was, 'being with the right person. He did tell me it wasn't always smooth sailing,' she grins, 'but he said that the key to any relationship was being able to forgive one another. My heart constricts. Can you forgive me now? I silently ask, glancing at his photo on the mantlepiece.

I'd replaced the glass frame soon after Sean had knocked it over that terrible evening, when I'd accused him of deserting M.

We continue talking until our voices are hoarse and Holly's eyes are starting to close, then make our way upstairs. I help Holly make up the spare bed, then fall into mine exhausted.

I dream I'm running through echoing corridors pursued by a tramp wearing a long, ragged coat. I turn around, a silent scream caught in my throat at the sight of Will's emaciated face, two empty sockets where his eyes had once been.

I set off for St Jude's Psychiatric hospital on the north side of the city, remembering that humid June day when I'd driven to the Hope and Faith Rehabilitation Centre to tell Will that M was in intensive care. I remember the fear and desperation, the belief I could somehow fix it – put right a terrible wrong, absolve myself. This time I'm prepared to be turned away, for Will to refuse to see me, in which case I will leave behind the letter I'd written in the early hours of the morning. I have more faith in getting through to him via the written word, than trying to explain verbally.

After a long wait, a nurse appears to say Will has agreed to see me and I'm to wait in the visitor's room. I make my way down the corridor to a large, airy room looking out over a walled courtyard. There are posters pinned on the walls, with reminders to 'find peace in the here and now,' 'live in the moment.' On a white board, somebody has scrawled 'swallow wisdom not substances.'

There is another patient and visitor on the far side of the room, talking to one another in low voices. Will appears at last, and sinks down onto the chair opposite. His right hand is tightly bandaged, his fingers mottled and swollen. I wonder if he'd tried to slash his wrist. I take in the purple shadows under his eyes, and feel his pain so intensely I can barely speak.

'I wasn't sure if you'd see me, so I wrote you a letter,' I begin. 'Holly told me what happened.'

He rubs his forehead in a gesture so reminiscent of M, my throat thickens.

'I never wanted to break up her marriage,' he states.

'I haven't come here to talk about you and Holly,' I say gently. 'I came to tell you that you were right. M and I were arguing that day. I never supported him over the donation and it drove a wedge between us.'

I tell him everything, ending with, 'If it was anyone's fault, it was mine.' I wait in the deafening silence for him to curse me to hell and back. But he's leaning over, his head in his hands as if shielding himself from more revelations. I notice his shoulders are heaving and realise then he's crying. I want to reach out and comfort him, tell him it will get better, only I'm not sure it ever will.

'I should have stopped M,' I hear him say, brokenly. He sits up and stares into the distance, his eyes almost opaque, like a rain-washed sky.

'Stopped him from what?'

'From going ahead with the donation.'

'You couldn't have! Neither of us could have. He'd made up his mind.'

I rummage in my bag for a tissue. 'He said he wouldn't be able to live with himself if anything happened to you.'

Will shakes his head, as if struck by the irony. 'The doctor warned us there was a risk,' he continues.

I can think of no words to console him. I take in his bleak expression, can sense the turmoil raging inside him.

'M never got over the fact that I went down for Archie O'Neill's death,' he states.

I stare at him in confusion The hit and run. 'I read a news report stating it was a young offender who couldn't be named for legal reasons?'

'That was me. Only I never ran over Archie.'

I swallow. 'Why did you confess to it, then?'

'I lied. Told the police I was driving the car.'

'So, who…who was driving?'

The expression on Will's face causes a chill to run through me, the sense that something momentous was about to be divulged and nothing would ever be the same again.

'It was M,' he states.

I feel the room tilt.

'That can't be true. I mean, why would you confess to the police if it wasn't you who was driving?'

'Because M would have been locked away for years. Maybe for life. I was still underage. We figured I'd get a lighter sentence.'

I'm struggling to comprehend this. 'There must have been witnesses? Somebody would have seen if it was M who'd been driving?'

'It was a left-hand drive Cadillac. It was almost dark.'

I recall the photo of M and Will standing in front of the orange Cadillac, the look on M's face when I'd pointed out the vintage poster at the reclamation centre, how he'd suddenly walked away.

'Anthony Jessop suspected it was M and sent him death threats for years, but he was going down for child abuse and the police never took a statement from him. He hung himself in prison in the end.'

'Why did M never tell me this?' I say, my mind reeling.

Will breathes out. 'Think about it, Willow! If it had got out it would have been the end for him. And he didn't want you to think I'd run over the kid. We had no choice, but to keep it between us. M worried constantly that you'd find out, would ask about the foundation we set up for Archie. You're a journalist, you're always asking questions.'

I can barely make sense of this. M had hit a child and driven away, leaving him to die on the side of the road. M, who would stop to let an old lady cross a busy street while the traffic piled up behind him.

Will is talking in staccato sentences. 'Anthony Jessop was always fucking around with me, stroking my hair, talking about some stupid plant called Sweet William. He hated M – they were constantly at each other's throats. He lashed out at him with a broken bottle one night, and ripped his forehead open.'

I breath out. So Mabel had been right.

'He told the doctor M had slipped on the pavement and opened up an old wound from a surfing accident. The guy was a psycho, a pathological liar. Mary Jessop was never around – she was terrified of him. He'd crush up sleeping pills and put them in my hot chocolate. I'd wake up and find him lying beside me – I can still smell his vile breath when I can't sleep,' Will says, in disgust. 'I locked the bedroom door, but that just made him turn violent. He threw Toby down the stairs for shouting at him to leave me alone. The kid was damaged even further after that. M called social services loads of time, but they said they needed evidence before they could file a report against him. The bastard came home hammered one night and tried to break down the bedroom door. M was back from work early and knocked him unconscious. We planned to drive to Whitsand Bay, lie low then go back for Toby.' He takes a shaky breath. 'I hotwired the Cadillac and M drove, but he was swerving all over the place. Toby and Archie came out of nowhere on their scooters. The two of them were like brothers, always hanging out together. Toby was waving and shouting to us to stop and take him with us. He drove his scooter in front of the car. Archie was right behind him and saw what was happening. He pushed him out the way and took the full impact.

I close my eyes in horror at the vision of the little boy with his fuzz of orange curls, tossed into the air after attempting to save his best friend.

I shouted at M to stop, but he was in another zone. He finally pulled in and ran back to check on them.' Will pauses again, trying to gather himself. 'He came back saying Toby was in shock, but not injured, but there was nothing we could do for Archie.' He swallows and stares at the ground. 'Toby refused to leave Archie's side…we could hear the police sirens coming. M was freaking out, saying he was going to go down for this, and we'd never be able to get Toby away from that monster… so I got the idea to say I was driving the car…' he lets out a ragged breath.

My heart constricts at the brothers' desperate mission that was doomed from the start.

'I drove to the first exit on the motorway – we were going to turn back by then, but the cops were right behind us. They pulled us over and I signed a statement saying Archie had run out in front of me and I hadn't been able to stop in time. I got locked up for a year and a half.'

'And M wasn't charged?'

He shakes his head.

Will saved my life, I owe him one' M had said. So that was the debt Will had spoken of that went both ways. While M had lived his life trying to honour it – had ended up paying over and over.

'I convinced the cops not to charge M. I told them he'd begged me to stop but I'd refused.'

'How devastating for you … for both of you,' I say, reeling from the emotional impact of Will's revelations. 'What happened to Toby?'

'He was taken into care. Poor kid was barely able to walk after that bastard had finished with him. We spent years trying to find him. Social services refused to give us any details. We tracked him down a few years later and had him transferred to the Sunshine Home in Cornwall, which is partly funded by Kids in Crisis. It's not far from Whitsand Bay, where we lived with the Clarks.'

I think of the numerous times M had travelled down to Cornwall on the pretence of 'catching some waves'. All the time he must have been visiting Toby.

I sit in a daze, trying to reconcile the two Ms. M the Good Samaritan who wanted to save the world, with the other M who had left a child dying on the side of the road, and allowed his younger brother to take the blame. It was this that had made him withdraw, 'go into the zone'. And yet it was a tragic accident that had caused the death of Archie O'Neill, just as it had been an accident that day of the summer solstice, when I'd launched myself at him in a desperate attempt to get his attention.

Will is leaning forwards again, his head in his hands.

'This has come as a shock,' I begin. I stand up in need of some fresh air, then sit down again, my head spinning.

'You weren't supposed to know about any of it,' he says.

'I wish I had known. Maybe I would have understood things better. I wouldn't have judged you so harshly for a start.'

'Be honest, Willow. If you'd known, you would never have married him,'

Will states.

You don't know a thing about him – his past can surface anytime, Mother had said.

I meet Will's gaze full on. In spite of the sting of his words, I feel a sense of calm, a kind of knowingness – the peace that surpasses all understanding perhaps. I search for a word which describes the antonym of regret, but nothing comes to mind, hence the cliché 'no regrets', perhaps.

'You're wrong about that,' I say at last. 'I would have married him.' I would do it all over again in a heartbeat…

We sit in silence and then I place M's leather jacket on the table between us. 'I know he would have wanted you to have this.'

I get up slowly, hoping my legs will support me, and make my way to the door. When I turn around, Will is holding the jacket to his chest, his shoulders heaving. I hesitate, torn between going back and trying to comfort him, then turn away, knowing now that there are times when you need to be left to weep alone.

The Sunshine Home is half way down the seafront of the little coastal town of Porthaven, wedged between a surfing shop and a cafe. I had called the day before and been put through to a woman named Joanna Evans. I'd told her I was Max Goodhart's wife, 'that is, his widow,' I'd amended, the word falling awkwardly off my tongue, and asked if I could pay a visit to Toby Jessop.

'Firstly, I am so sorry about Max,' she begins. 'You must mean Toby Jamieson,' Mary Jamieson's son,' she adds.

'The Toby who lived in Ramsgate,' I say confused.

'Yes, Toby Jamieson, he lived at Bunkershill Crescent in Ramsgate – he was part of the "Fostergate" scandal.'

So Anthony Jessop was not his real father, I conclude.

'Yes, that's him,' I tell her.

There's a silence, then she says, 'Toby struggled a lot after Max died, but he's been better recently. I'd rather not unsettle him again, so could I get back to you?'

She had called later that afternoon, saying, 'Toby seems fine about you visiting, but he might not be very receptive, so be prepared. He has trouble processing information.'

Now she leads me into a recreation room painted a sunshine yellow, with a large bay window overlooking the ocean. Toby is sitting by the window in a motorised wheelchair, a pair of binoculars around his neck. He swivels the chair around as I walk in, and stares at me blankly. I take in the cropped fair hair and large hazel eyes. I calculate he must be in his early thirties.

'Toby, this is Max's wife,' Joanna is saying. 'You remember Max is not with us anymore, don't you? Willow wanted to pay you a visit. I'll leave you to it,' she whispers to me.

'Hi, Toby, I'm so happy to meet you at last,' I begin, approaching and pulling up a chair.

He regards me suspiciously.

'You must miss M very much. We all do.'

He blinks a few times without responding.

'It must be nice living right next to the beach?' I venture, glancing through the window to where a couple of surfers are ploughing out into the waves.

'I'm going swimming later,' he lisps, the words fusing together, reminding me of that haunting phone call, on Christmas night, the drawing out of each syllable as he'd said, 'It's meeeeeee.'

'I love swimming in the ocean,' I tell him. 'Do you have a mask? We could go and buy you one. I saw a shop next door.'

He fiddles with the strap of his binoculars, but doesn't reply.

'I brought you something,' I say, handing over the black and white photo of him and Archie standing in front of the red-brick house in Ramsgate with their scooters.

He studies it with concentration. 'Max couldn't save Archie,' he says slowly.

'I heard about Archie's accident. I'm so sorry, Toby.'

'I have to go now,' he states.

Sometimes we never get to know the end of the story, I think.

There would always be a doubt in my mind as to whether Will had been telling the whole truth.

'Thanks for letting me come and see you, Toby. Maybe I could visit you again and we could go down to the beach?'

'OK.' He nods.

As I reach the door, he says 'Max wanted to take me with him, but I had to stay with Archie.'

I wait, holding my breath.

He studies the floor with concentration. 'He didn't mean to run over Archie.'

'I know,' I say, swallowing the tears. 'You take care of yourself,' I add thickly.

On the way out, I linger in the reception area, wanting to have a word with Joanna.

She appears from her office, a professional smile on her face. 'How did you get on?'

'I think he's accepted M is no longer around. He talked about going swimming?'

She nods. 'He loves splashing around in the shallows. But he has trouble walking. He sustained severe injuries when he was eight, and has limited movement in his legs, so it's good for him to be in the water. He swims in the pool twice a week.'

'What happened to him?' I ask tentatively. I have to know if only to understand the burden M had been carrying.

She hesitates, no doubt bound by the laws of confidentiality.

'I gathered his best friend was hit by a car?'

'Sadly, Toby was the victim of abuse from a violent stepfather,' she says at last. 'He was thrown down a flight of stairs, among other atrocities. Yes, and his friend was killed by a hit-and-run driver.'

I look away, trying to gather myself.

She is talking about M now, and the generous donations he had made over the years, and how he had personally delivered the motorised wheelchair for Toby. 'We are very grateful for the trust your husband set up for him,' she says.

I think of how angry and betrayed I'd felt when I'd found out about the trust.

'Max visited Toby regularly,' she continues, 'he bought him some binoculars one Christmas. Toby loves to watch the sandpipers and waders on the beach. He would sit by the window for hours watching Max surfing.'

There's always somebody watching out for me, M had said.

I recall the receipts I'd found in his leather jacket, one from Access Mobility, another for binoculars.

'Max was an exceptional man,' she says. 'One in a million.'

'Yes, he was,' I reply.

I walk the length of the beach, M's blue scarf around my neck, bracing myself against the gusts of wind. I think about the early years, when the brothers had lived in the pebble-dash cottage overlooking Whitsand Bay, how they'd learned to swim and surf – an idyllic time that had ended abruptly when Owen Clark had fallen ill, thereby changing the course of their lives.

Circumstances change, bad things happen to good people, good people do bad things, I think. We are all the sum of our parts, neither inherently good throughout, nor rotten to the core.

"Every saint has a past and every sinner has a future," Oscar Wilde had said.

M had tried to act for the greater good, by attempting to drive Will to safety that day. He had planned to return and rescue Toby, only the whole thing had tragically backfired.

I stand on the shoreline feeling the sand being sucked from under my feet, watching the gulls swooping and diving, and it strikes me that it had taken M's death for me to finally understand his life.

MID-SEPTEMBER

I send a text to Sean. *Can we meet up? Wx*

His response flashes up almost immediately: *When and where?*

4 o'clock Huntington Hall, in the car park I type, sending it off before I have a change of heart. I'd contacted Miranda about putting up a plaque dedicated to M, on the front arch of the extension. She'd written back saying she welcomed the idea, suggesting I drive over one afternoon during the week to decide on the exact spot.

I turn up the long drive to Huntington Hall, past the stump of the fallen oak and onto the gravelled sweep. It looks like a different place today beneath a powder-blue sky, the trees still and already tinged with the russet tones of autumn. Sean is waiting in the car park, leaning against his motor bike, smoking a cigarette. He smiles nervously as I approach. 'Good to see you,' he says, giving me a hug.

'You too. You started smoking again?'

'Yeah, bad habit. Siobhan hates it. I promised her I'd kick it for good, but you know how it goes.'

'You and Siobhan are back together, then?'

'We decided to give it a go, head back to Ireland in the spring. There's a place in Cork, near Bantry Bay, that we both love.'

'That's great news,' I say.

'And you?'

'I'm doing better,' I tell him.

'I'm glad.'

We make our way wordlessly towards the entrance, and up the few steps. I take in the carriage-style lamp on the wall, trying to push away a haunting image of the loose wire, then steal a glance at the floor. The deck is flush and gleaming, the oak floorboards painted a rich oak brown.

I stand there, allowing the images to spool through my mind, winding back to that first sight of M standing on top of the ladder, his frame lit up as lightning zig-zagged across a livid June sky.

I start to relate the events of that stormy afternoon: M's insistence on driving over on the bike to fix the lights, how he hadn't answered his phone, how I'd been convinced he'd had an accident.

'When I got here, he was standing on top of the ladder, drilling into that beam…'

I cringe, recalling the relentless high-pitched sound that seemed to be drilling into my brain. I describe how I'd planned to shine the torch up at him to get his attention, only in my heightened state had tripped over a loose floorboard, fallen, and knocked into the ladder, M reaching out blindly, only to connect with the loose wire, before falling like a dead weight to the ground.

Sean's face turns pale as I reach the end. He lights another cigarette and leans against the wooden balustrade, exhaling smoke.

'So now you know why I didn't want to come back here, or talk about it,' I say, my mouth dry. 'It was my fault.'

He takes another long drag. 'Does anybody else know about this?'

'Only Fern. I told her at the hospital, and she insisted we never mention it to anyone. She felt there would be repercussions, possibly an inquest, the boys would be affected and we would never be able to get on with our lives. She reckoned I'd eventually put it into perspective, feel less culpable.' I look away. 'Maybe if I had talked about it, it would have been easier to move forward. But we made the decision to keep it between us.'

Just as M and Will had made that secret pact between them, I think.

Sean is staring at the smooth wooden decking, his face ashen. 'I thought about going to confession and unloading it all on some random priest.'

'Unloading what?'

He meets my gaze. 'When that witch threatened to sue my brother, I lost my rag. Declan and I were working flat out to finish the porch, when she came storming over, ranting like a mad woman, accusing Declan of stealing materials. M had told him he could have some off-cuts of wood that were lying around, so Dec put them in his pick-up. She then complained the place looked like a tip, and that safety rules weren't being observed.' He lets out a breath as if struck by the irony. 'I told M we were pulling out of the job, and forced Dec to down tools. He wanted to clamp down the last floorboard, but I dragged him away.' Sean pauses, before adding, 'I said leave it and let's hope somebody trips over and sues the bitch or, better still, she falls and breaks her fucking neck! Only you were the one to trip…' He closes his eyes briefly as if trying to blank out the image. 'I knew something must have happened. M was so careful.'

I stare at him, trying to absorb this.

There were a number of 'contributory factors' Doctor Ramsey had said at the hospital that day, when I'd blurted out that it was all my fault.

We remain silent for a long time and then I hand over the brass plaque I'd had engraved with the words : IN LOVING MEMORY OF M GOODHART, DESIGNER, ARCHITECT AND PHILANTHOPIST.

'We need to find the right place to put this,' I say at last.

PART 3

LATE SEPTEMBER

An email has arrived in my inbox from the commissioning editor of The Word, who wants to schedule a meeting with me to discuss a collaboration.

We very much enjoyed the material you sent and have considered your idea of a column exploring adventurous lives. However, we are looking for subject matter with a common theme, charting the universal challenges that we are faced with in life. We want to avoid 'parenting' or 'surviving divorce,' which has been overdone. Maybe you have an idea to put forward, with a view to you heading a full-page column with The Word. Let me know what day and time would work for you and we could have lunch near our offices in Chancery Lane. There's an Italian restaurant around the corner, Alberto's, where we could meet?

She has signed off as Ariana Castiano.

I leap out of bed and punch the air. She is talking about a full-page column with a magazine which has a far bigger distribution than Lifestyle or The Weekend. The Word was on everybody's lips, literally and metaphorically, voted the best supplement of the decade. I haven't experienced such a surge of delight for months.

I stand looking out over the garden, racking my brains for subject matter, thinking about the challenges we all face. Nothing comes to mind so I turn my thoughts on what to wear for the meeting instead. It's time to shed the widow's cloak and step out into the world again.

I spend the rest of the morning in a state of excited anticipation, aware I need to come up with an idea soon. I am standing by the window, drinking a second coffee, thinking of the challenges I'd faced over the last fourteen months – not all of which could be described as universal – when Liam walks in, still half asleep. 'Are you all right, Mum?'

'I'm fine – I've had some good news, in fact! I've been contacted by an editor. I'm going up to London tomorrow to meet her. She wants to talk about a new column.'

'Wow! Well done, Mum. 'You do need a purpose, something to give your life some meaning.'

I smile. 'I thought you said there was no purpose or meaning, that we're all drifting stardust!'

'Yes, but eventually order has to prevail. What's the column about?'

'The challenges people have to deal with. I've been asked to come up with an idea, which is a challenge in itself!'

He considers this. 'You could write about losing stuff! Everyone loses things like their keys, then there's bigger things, like the person you love.'

There are small losses and bigger losses, Mother had said after losing her breast.

'Liam, that's brilliant,' I exclaim.

'We can lose stars, and even galaxies in a blink of an eye.'

'That might be a little 'out there,' I grin.

Ariana Castiano is a glamorous brunette, tall and slim with coal-black eyes and Mediterranean skin. I guess she's in her late thirties. She stands up as I enter Alberto's and waves me over to a table in the far corner. 'Thanks for coming up today,' she smiles.

'Thank you for giving me this opportunity,' I reply, thinking I should have dressed up a bit. I'd opted for a short summery dress, ankle boots and a denim jacket, which now feels too casual in comparison with the sharp pencil skirt and silk blouse she's wearing. It's clear I have been out of circulation too long.

'Is sparkling water all right, or would you prefer a glass of wine?' she asks.

'Water would be fine,' I answer, thinking I needed to keep my wits about me.

'I know you were nominated for Columnist of the Year around eighteen months ago? I loved Interesting Lives. It was always the first thing I'd read in Lifestyle, but it doesn't interest me much anymore. What have you been doing in the meantime?'

'Not a lot,' I admit, 'when my husband died, I took some time off – I had writer's block for the first time.'

I think of how words had seemed to lose all meaning, even kind words coming across as platitudes.

'I'm so sorry, it must have been a terrible loss.'

LOSS (*noun*) the fact or process of losing something or someone.

'It was . . well life-altering,' I reply.

'You've clearly found your voice again. Turning the Tide was a brilliant piece. Very evocative. As I said in my email, we all loved the idea of Adventurous Lives as a header, but the truth is the majority of people live fairly unadventurous lives. We want to chart the more commonplace, the ongoing challenges we all have to overcome. I'd like to hear your ideas.'

'I do have something to start with. I've been writing a blog about it since M... Since my husband died and it has gathered a few thousand followers.'

She leans forward with interest.

'Grief,' I state. 'I believe that millions of people carry it around with them in one form or another. Unless you're very fortunate, you're not going to go through a whole lifetime without experiencing loss. I've concluded mine resides right here.' I place my hand on my sternum. 'I wrote about it in one of my blogs, advising everyone to find their G spot! In this case G stands for grief. It caused quite a reaction!'

She smiles. 'Willow's G spot. It does have a certain ring.'

I laugh. 'Anyway, I thought it could lead into all the irrational things you do when you lose somebody you love. Believe me, I've done a few!' An image of driving M's bike through the shed door, passes through my mind.

'I like it very much,' she says.

After lunch, she leads me across the road to the offices of The Word, and introduces me to the deputy editor Guy Adams and the features editor, both of whom look to be in their mid-twenties, plus the marketing and advertising team. I am struck by how relaxed and casual it seems. Everyone is sitting around drinking Nespresso and chatting about where to eat dinner. It's a far cry from Lifestyle, and Jason ruling the airwaves, with his demands and deadlines.

By the time I leave the office it's almost four o'clock. I weave my way through the crowded London streets, desperate to tell somebody this incredible news. Ariana wants the first piece by the end of next week. I remember trying to call M after I'd been nominated for Columnist of the Year, how he hadn't picked up. He had stopped reading my column by then.

I call Fern, but get her answering machine. 'Call me back, I've some amazing news!'

Seconds later, my phone rings. It's Mother.

'Willow, I've found this divine little builder who's re-doing my bathroom for me. I was thinking he could sort out that awful mess in your courtyard.'

'Can we talk about it when I'm home? I'm just about to catch the train.'

'Where are you?'

'In London. I had a meeting with an editor. I've landed a column with The Word,' I say, unable to contain the news a moment longer.

'How marvellous. The Word! My word, what's it about?'

'Life, loss, the chance of finding love again,' I say rashly.

'Well, it's about time, darling. We must have a party to celebrate.'

The week draws to an end on an unexpected note with a call from my old editor, Jason.

'Willow,' he barks, 'I want to congratulate you on your piece, Turning the Tide.'

'So, you did read it?' I keep my tone level, resisting the urge to say, you could have replied sooner. And where were you in my darkest hour?

'I only just opened my emails. My mother died unexpectedly. She was only sixty-four.' He makes an odd sound as if clearing his throat. 'She and I were very close.'

'Oh I'm so sorry, Jason. How awful. Especially as you were so close! My mother can be a living nightmare!'

What on earth am I thinking, bringing it back to myself? Making such a ridiculous comparison. This is far worse than anything anybody has ever said to me.

'Anyway, moving on,' Jason is saying, 'it would be good to have you back on board. The magazine is having a bit of a shake-up. I thought you could seek out and interview the hardy and adventurous souls among us. In other words, I'm happy to give you more leeway.'

'That would be amazing, only when I didn't hear back from you, I sent Turning the Tide to The Word. They're not going with it, but they've commissioned me to write a column about the universal challenges we face and how we come through them, so there shouldn't be any conflict.'

He lets out a low whistle. 'What can I say? You're an excellent writer. The Word is way up there! You'll do a great job. Congratulations.'

'Thanks, Jason. I'm very excited about heading Adventurous Lives. It's something I've wanted to explore for years.' I have already earmarked a young rock climber who was planning to get to the top of the Dawn Wall of El Capitan. Perhaps I would start climbing again, re-live the thrill of it all, the heady feeling of being on top of the world.

'What about Susannah?' I can't resist asking.

'Let's just say, she's moved on,' Jason replies shortly. 'The magazine has been inundated with emails asking when you were returning, as a matter of fact.'

My heart lifts at this news. I feel a surge of gratitude towards my loyal readers out there and just hope I can make a success of both ventures.

'Oh and, Willow, call your mother and tell her you love her, while you still have the chance,' Jason says, gruffly, before hanging up.

EARLY OCTOBER

The Word has published my first column. At the top of the page is a smiley shot of my face. They had sent their inhouse photographer from London to take the photograph. I read the finished article, alarmed by my graphic description of the G spot, which I'd taken straight from one of my posts: *'A tender, aching spot of exposed nerve endings which when activated by a thoughtless remark can become inflamed, climaxing in an outpouring of anger and tears..'*

Fern is the first to call to congratulate me. 'You haven't held back,' she laughs.

'Do you think it's over the top?'

'Yes, and compulsive, funny and true!'

My phone is buzzing with another call.

'It's Mother! I'm sure she has a thing or two to say about it.'

'She'll love it! It'll put her back in the spotlight. She'll be telling all her friends that her younger daughter is a famous journalist, with her own column in The Word!'

'We'll see,' I reply, bracing myself.

'Very racy, Willow,' Mother begins, 'You have a few tongues wagging already. All my friends have been looking for their G spots! I'm glad you've got your career back on track. We must have a little lunch party to celebrate your success. How about this Friday?'

'I'm going to be really busy for the next few weeks,' I say firmly. 'Can I get back to you on that?'

MID OCTOBER

I call Frida's landline, thinking it had been some time since I'd seen or spoken to her. When she still doesn't answer either her mobile or landline, I head over to her cottage and ring the doorbell, but there's no response. I notice her car is still in the garage, so make my way around the side of the cottage but the living room curtains are drawn and there's no sign of life.

I return the following afternoon, and am walking around her garden when a car pulls up and stops in front of the gate. A tall, dark man wearing a black suit and cream shirt is getting out and walking up the paved path. His jacket is looped over his thumb and casually slung over one shoulder. The top button of his shirt is open, and he's yanking his tie loose, as if eager to be free from the stresses of day. There is something strikingly familiar about his features, the high forehead and prominent cheekbones, the generous curve of his mouth. His skin is the colour of caramel, his hair is jet black and braided into neat cornrows. He pauses beside the sunflowers and stares at me, a bronzed and statuesque figure in the afternoon light. I can only stare back.

'Are you looking for someone?' he inquires. His accent is English with a faint American intonation.

'I'm Frida's neighbour, Willow,' I explain, 'I don't normally snoop around her house, but I haven't seen her for a while and was worried . . .'

He flashes me a dazzling smile. 'Hey, Willow, I'm Erik Andersson, her son.' He steps forward and shakes my hand enthusiastically. 'We haven't met in person, but Frida has told me all about you. I dropped her off halfway down the lane to talk to one of the neighbours.'

'It's nice to meet you at last,' I say, dazedly.

'We've been at a funeral. My grandmother died.'

'I'm so sorry, I didn't know.'

'Thank you – it's always a shock, however prepared one is. We left in a bit of a rush, Frida forgot her mobile – ah, here she comes now.'

I turn and see her striding towards us in a black vintage coat, a cloche hat adorned with an array of colourful silken flowers on her head.

'Willow, you've met my son at last,' she greets me, her face breaking into a smile.

'I'm so sorry about your mother, I say, giving her a hug. She smells of the charity shop, of musk and old books.

'Oh dear girl, Mama was ready to go – there is no joy in struggle. How about I put the kettle on and we go inside for some tea. I think there might be some chocolate torte left in the fridge.'

'Unless you have other things to do?' Erik suggests, casting me a sideways look.

'I'd love some tea,' I reply, curious about Frida's elusive son who called his mother by her Christian name and had finally showed up after all this time.

We sit in Frida's chilly sitting room amongst the clutter of old clothes destined for the homeless and stacks of paperbacks for the shop. 'Excuse the mess,' she says, 'I was about to take all this down to the village hall when the nursing home called.'

She withdraws to the kitchen to make tea and Erik turns to me saying, 'I was so sorry to hear about M. I heard he was a remarkable person.'

'He was,' I reply, meeting his gaze directly. A max in a million I think to myself.

'How are your sons doing?'

'They have their bad days, but they're coping. The only way is through it, I've learned. How long are you here for?' I digress.

'I fly out the day after tomorrow. I wasn't able to get more time off. I've taken on a teaching post at a university for a year.'

'What do you teach?'

'English mainly, and Psychology.'

'I'm hoping he's not going to go back to the newspaper,' Frida says, appearing with a tray laden with tea and cake. 'Being sent from one bloody conflict zone to another…putting his life at risk, after the terrible thing that happened …'

'I'm a journalist, that's what I do,' Erik states, getting up and clearing a space on the table for the tray.

I'm immediately curious about the terrible thing that happened.

There's a loaded silence.

I sense the tension between them and notice the way he tries to diffuse it. 'We talked about all this earlier, so let us eat cake! Nobody makes a chocolate torte like my mother,' he adds, sending her a conciliatory look. He busies himself cutting the torte into generous slices, Frida pours the tea and the conversation moves to the funeral service that had been held in the village where her mother had lived for the latter part of her life.

'It was wonderful having Erik with me,' she says, as if he's not in the room. 'I only wish he was here for longer.'

'You could fly back to New York with me as I suggested?' he says, digging into the rich chocolate filling. 'You've never seen New England in the Fall.'

'There's nothing wrong with old England in the autumn,' Frida answers shortly. 'He knows I hate flying,' she adds, 'and who's going to look after the garden and the shop?'

It's as if she's become so accustomed to his absence, she's forgotten how to act in his presence or how to address him.

'We'd be travelling together,' he points out.

'We'll talk about it later,' she says, glancing at her watch. 'I promised I'd bring those clothes down to the village hall if we were back in time. We're opening a new drop-in centre in Highbury,' she informs me.

I have a fleeting image of the homeless man at the bus stop, the day I am now convinced that I'd seen Will.

'Maybe I could bring down some things of M's,' I find myself saying. I take a sip of the strong tea, swallowing the inevitable lump in my throat.

'I think he would be very happy if you did that,' Frida says gently. She reaches over and squeezes my hand. 'I'll leave you two to chat. You have plenty in common.'

'I'll give you a hand,' Erik says, getting to his feet and grabbing a couple of bags. I help him load the car and we watch Frida drive off.

'Thanks for looking out for her,' Erik says, as we head back inside. 'What with everything you've been going through.'

'She's the one who's been looking out for me,' I tell him, describing the many visits, the gifts and flowers and how she'd managed to evict the moles from the lawn. 'I didn't take into account how much she was missing M too,' I confess, making a mental note to blog about grief being a selfish emotion.

He nods. 'Frida and I have had our ups and downs, but she has a good heart. Tell me, what are you writing now?' he digresses.

I explain how my career had stalled after M had died, and how I'd recently landed a column in The Word.

He leans forward with interest. 'What's the subject?'

'It's about loss, and moving forward.' I fiddle with a strand of hair, aware of his dark gaze on me.

'Did you always want to write?'

'Yes, I think so - it seemed like a way of being heard, but not necessarily seen.'

He smiles. 'Where did you graduate?'

'London School of Journalism. And you?'

'Exeter Uni. Favourite authors?' he continues.

I remind myself he's a journalist, always on the quest for answers, digging through the layers, to get to the bottom of the story.

'We need to get that out of the way,' he grins as if guessing my thoughts.

I laugh. 'Probably Emily Bronte, but I read all sorts. Tell me about your work as a war correspondent.'

He hesitates. 'I thought it was my calling. Only to realise it's not easy to remain detached around violence and suffering. I started to become personally affected, and decided to take a year out and go back to teaching.'

I sense his resistance around the subject and notice how he moves the conversation on, asking about good restaurants to eat in the area.

I glance at my watch, and realise we've been talking for over an hour. 'I told Liam I'd be back in ten minutes!' I say, getting up.

He follows me to the front door. 'It's been great to meet you at last, Willow. You are even lovelier than Frida said.'

'It's good to meet you too,' I say, flushing.

The air suddenly feels charged around us. I notice his eyes are the colour of mahogany, with shards of gold spreading out from the cortex.

'Have dinner with me tomorrow night?' he says, the words coming out in a rush.

I feel my chest contract, that giddy sense of anticipation, that I'd thought was long gone.

'I'd like that,' I answer.

'You mentioned a couple of restaurants in Highbury – any preferences? I'd love to go to an old pub. I've heard great things about Time and Tithe in Chorley.'

'We've been contracted to turn an old tithe barn into a gastro pub!' M had announced over dinner – *'it's going to be a great project.'*

'It's stunning,' I say after a pause. 'I haven't been there for a while – but the food used to be very good.'

He arrives at seven, dressed casually in jeans and an apricot shirt. I feel clumsy suddenly, unsure in my skinny jeans and new ankle boots, the silky cobweb cardigan Fern had given me for Christmas. It was just dinner with a neighbour's son, I'd told myself, knowing it was more than that. I'd felt restless and distracted all day, unable to concentrate on my column – a piece about life after loss. I was desperate to know more about him, unravel his story, learn about his adventurous life. I remind myself that whatever the evening might bring, he was leaving on Monday and returning to his life in New York.

As we are driving through the winding country lanes, he tells me he'd managed to persuade Frida to fly back to New York with him for a fortnight. 'I'm going to apply for time off and take her on a trip through New England to see the leaves turning.'

'She'll love that,' I say. It was clear he wanted to mend the rift between them.

'Well, it's a start. I gather Crispin LeFanu lives somewhere around here,' he digresses. 'I've just finished *The Self and Beyond*. I'm a big fan of his work.'

I tell him about the library M had built at The Old Mill House and the ill-fated Christmas party. 'I should never have gone – I was in an emotional state and caused a bit of a drama. But it was amazing to see Crispin's books displayed on the shelf M built...'

I feel his eyes shift towards me but he doesn't respond.

I brace myself as we enter Time and Tithe, taking in the gnarled oak beams, M's signature intermingling of light and darker woods, the gleaming patina of the floor. We sit in a snug at the far end of the room close to a blazing log fire.

'Is this ok?' he frowns, as if sensing my change of mood.

'It's perfect,' I smile. 'I'm glad we came here.'

A young waiter is approaching with menus and the wine list. 'The specials are on the board,' he says gesturing toward a blackboard that has been strung up over the bar. 'I'll be back to take your drinks order.'

'Ok it's my turn to ask the questions,' I say, as we sip a full-bodied merlot. 'Why the long absence?'

He lets out a slow breath. 'Frida and I have always been at odds, as you probably know. She had a tough time, bringing me up on her own. I know I was a bit of a handful, but she tried to be both mother and father instead of just being a laid-back Mum. I never knew my father – he was a Jamaican guy who worked in tourism. It was a holiday romance. I thought about trying to find him a few years ago, but didn't have any leads so decided to leave it be in the end.'

I absorb this thinking Frida had never spoken about Erik's father, except to say she had thrown caution to the wind, one night on a moonlit beach.

'She wasn't happy about me leaving home and going to live in America – and was dead set against me becoming a war correspondent, which is understandable.' He pauses while the waiter brings our food. We had both ordered the beer battered cod with home fries.

'When in England,' he comments, with a grin, 'but I'm glad they've left out the mushy peas! Where were we?'

'You wanting to become a correspondent,' I fill in.

'Yes, I saw myself as a messenger to the world, not really understanding the reality of it all. I met Sandra when we were working at *The Post*. She was a photojournalist and very passionate about her work. We were in Syria together. I brought her home that first Christmas and introduced her to Frida but it didn't go well. My mother was convinced she would take me away from her for good. There was a huge argument, and we left early. We didn't speak for months afterwards. I called it the Cold War,' he adds. He examines his glass with a troubled look.

I think back to the cold front that had lingered between me and my mother after I married M and am struck by the similarities between us.

'Sandra and I were married for a year and a day,' he continues. 'She was injured in a mortar bomb attack not far from the northern town where I was reporting.' He sits back against the high wooden bench. 'She died three days later in hospital. Frida urged me to give up my career, and come back to England. I couldn't handle it …I stopped taking her calls and went back to work, for a short time, which didn't do me any good.'

So this was the terrible thing that had happened.

'I'm so sorry,' I say, my heart constricting. 'It must have been incredibly hard for you.'

'I was angry for a long time,' he says, knotting his fingers together, '...raging against the dying of the light.'

I sit up, the back of my neck tingling, possessed with an overwhelming sense of deja vous. My arms are breaking out in goosebumps as he describes the shock and sense of denial, how he'd found himself bargaining with a higher power to save his wife, the raw anger followed by the painfully slow journey towards acceptance, and finally his hope for the future. It's all falling together; the affinity I'd felt between us, his choice of words and now the reference to Dylan Thomas... *'not everyone goes peacefully into the night...*he'd written.

'I started an online forum after Sandra died,' he is saying. 'The idea was to communicate with people who were going through similar loss...'

'You're blackwidower!' I exclaim, in astonishment.

We have both abandoned our food and are staring at one another as if for the first time.

He opens his mouth then closes it again. 'Oh my God . . I had this feeling about you,' he breathes. 'When you talked about causing a drama at the party it all started falling into place. The tactless woman wearing reindeer horns,' he chuckles 'I've loved reading your blogs - so funny and heartfelt . . . like you,' he adds shaking his head in wonder.

I flush and reach for my wine. I hadn't censored my emotions when writing on the forum. I was used to unravelling people's lives, while hiding my own behind carefully chosen words.

We are both silent, like two people lost in the mystery of chance and coincidence. Only this wasn't a coincidence.

'So it was you who sent the card with the name of the website! And the bouquet of purple flowers?'

He looks awkward. 'When Frida called and told me about M, I wanted to do something, send my condolences. He was so good to her, always fixing things – she adored him. I called the florist in Highbury. They knew about M and suggested putting something together in the colours you like.'

'Why didn't you put your name to the card?'

He shifts on the bench, the reflection of the fire dancing in his eyes. 'I didn't want Frida knowing I'd sent you flowers. She would have brought it back to her loss, and how I'd deserted her. Besides, the idea of a forum is to remain anonymous ...' he pauses, 'perhaps it's the only way we can really express ourselves, 'write from the heart,' as St Exupery famously said.'

'I thought you were an elderly university professor at first,' I say absorbing this.

He grins. 'I am, if you consider forty-five old.'

...are you a counsellor by any chance as you seem to have all the answers? I'd written.

Ha . .. I'm not sure I even understand the questions!

I feel his eyes trained on me. 'I'm glad I sent those flowers,' he says softly.

I sit there lost for words, thinking of how I had waited in anticipation for his responses to flash up on the screen.

The pub is almost empty now – the young waiter is clearing up around us willing us to leave.

'We should make a move?' Erik says, signalling for the bill. I follow him out into the cool autumn night, still in a daze.

We barely speak on the short drive home. He seems miles away suddenly, while I mentally trawl through the blogs, cringing at the memory of some of those confessions. As we pull up on the driveway, he says, 'I'll walk you to the front door then be on my way.'

I climb out of the car with a plunge of heart, coupled with a dull sense of anti-climax. It was over, that virtual exchange, the gems of wisdom and insights, the poetic references and wry comments. blackwidower was gone, had turned into 'a mere whisper in the wind', and Erik Andersson had stepped into his place. Erik, who would be returning to New York tomorrow.

He waits patiently while I fumble in my handbag for the keys of the front door. 'Do you think we could stay in contact?' he says, 'bypass the forum and write to one another directly?'

'I'm not sure,' I say. Everything seems futile suddenly. Liam was right, there was no order or meaning to it all. '…an arrival and a departure, wasn't that how you put it?' I say. 'But no regrets', I add, with a forced smile. 'Regret being 'a perceived opportunity'…that was another of yours. You're going back to your life in New York where you have made a home, three thousand miles away.'

He is silent, as if he no longer has the answers.

I'm still rummaging in the depths of my bag, searching for the keys. Liam was staying away for the night and Sam had texted earlier to say he would be home late. I swear under my breath and empty the contents onto the front step. Then kneel and pluck the keys from the tangle of scrunched up tissues, lipstick, hairbrush, purse and scribbled notes to blog. He leans down to help and we stand up at the same time my head bumping against his chest. I drop the keys on the step and our eyes lock. The kiss is unexpected; almost shocking, like a breathless descent into the ocean, and when I come up for air, I can almost feel the salty sting of it on my lips. He tastes of the sea, of sunshine and hope. He pulls me towards him again, his hands in my hair, and I hear the rush of his voice in my ear, like a murmur which is drowned out by the sound of a car screeching to a halt on the gravel. I hear Sam shouting out, his voice a quaver of anger and fear demanding to know who is there.

It's all confusion from then on: Sam's arrival, Erik's departure, Sam wanting to know why I'm standing on the porch with a stranger, my handbag gaping open at my feet, the contents on the ground.

'I thought somebody was trying to break in,' he is saying, his voice turning into an accusation. Erik calmly introducing himself as Frida's son, the awkward silence followed by the three of us all talking at once. And then Erik is turning away and melting into the night and Sam and I are retreating indoors, Sam's face clouded with suspicion as he says, 'so if he's Frida's son, why the fuck haven't I met him until now?'

I manage to calm Sam down, and explain about the forum and how Erik and I had been communicating online, unbeknownst to one another. 'He flew back from New York for his grandmother's funeral,' I add, but Sam is still edgy and aloof. I head to my room, exhausted, re-living that kiss, followed by the abrupt ending which seemed to represent all the other endings; *Stargazer* sailing away into the horizon, Archie O'Neill lying on the side of the road, Timmy being hurled into the air. M, his face tilting towards the light that streamed through the window, like the earth tilting towards the sun.

8 MONTHS LATER

MID JUNE

The boys and I decide to spend the weekend before the anniversary in Cornwall. We set off for a walk along the winding coastal path to the cove to where M's surfboard had floated away with its cargo of flowers and ashes and stand there watching the herring gulls dipping and diving. In the evening we drive down to the harbour and sit on the pier eating fish and chips and reminiscing about past family trips.

The boys want to know more about the time M lived in Whitsand Bay, so we drive over there the following day and have a picnic in the shelter of the sand dunes, imagining M and Will ploughing into the waves with their surfboards. I think of Toby further along the coast, sitting by the window watching the sandpipers through his binoculars, knowing M will not be returning. One day I may tell the boys about the hit and run accident and M's heroic and tragic attempt to get Will to safety and return for Toby, but for now I watch them riding high on the waves that are carrying them to the shore.

THE SECOND SUMMER SOLSTICE

Note to blog:

The second anniversary will arrive before you know it. With distance, the grief is not so intense, the pain less sharp, or perhaps it's as sharp as ever, but you've learnt to live with it.

Fern and Mother have persuaded me to hold a mid-summer party at Rosewood Barn to celebrate my birthday. The patio is finished at last, the paving stones neatly laid by Mother's 'divine little builder'. He has also installed the water feature of the fish with the gaping mouth.

Mother has invited some of her neighbours over for the early part of the evening. They arrive in their summery dresses, mother in cream and mauve silk like an exotic orchid amongst them. The rest of the guests drift in later bearing birthday gifts; a pair of silver tear-drop earrings from Jen, a framed and enlarged photo of my column 'Willow's G Spot' in The Word from Mother and Jeff, a palette of smoky eyeshadows from Holly, the leather biker's jacket from Fern and David. Sam and Liam have bought me a refresher course with a rock-climbing instructor and a new harness.

Mother trips towards me, swaying in her nude high heels, the beginnings of a frown on her forehead. 'I can't believe you haven't put some flowers in the living area, Willow. It's not too late to call Heavenly Blooms, and ask them to deliver. And some of the glasses I hired are smeary – can you ask the boys to give them a polish?'

'I'll sort it out, Mum,' I say swiftly, heading into the garden on the pretence of looking for Sam and Liam.

I stand by the fountain for a moment, allowing the tinkling sound of water to soothe my frayed nerves. Frida, wearing a green vintage maxi-dress, has wandered away from the guests to inspect the flower beds. She leans down and plucks a stray weed from the border, then straightens up and gazes towards the far end of the garden, her face breaking into a smile. I follow her gaze and see Erik striding up the lawn, holding a bouquet of purple forget-me-nots. I run down to meet him.

'Happy birthday, lovely,' he breathes, pulling me into a fierce embrace. I wind my arms around him, burying my face against his chest and breathing in the heady scent of his skin.

We had been writing to one another since he'd left in October, our emails becoming more intense.

I don't have all the answers, he'd written in one of our recent exchanges, *but I do understand the bigger question, which is where I want to be – and that is with you.*

He had left New York at the end of the summer semester and rented an apartment in Highbury, while we introduced the idea of our living together to the boys. Frida had been ecstatic when she'd heard the news. 'Some things are meant,' she'd said, her eyes misting over.

Sam had slowly started to come around, while Liam's comment had been 'he'd better not think he's my dad!' He had dragged Erik into the garden after dinner one evening and pointed out Maximillian 2 through his telescope. Erik had gone on to name a cluster of neighbouring stars that Liam had never heard of.

'I didn't know you were a budding astronomer as well as a professor and a journalist?' I'd smiled.

He'd grinned. 'I'm not – I've spent the whole week trying to memorise them after downloading the app.'

MID-SEPTEMBER – TWO YEARS AND EIGHTY-SIX DAYS AFTER THE THAT DAY OF THE SUMMER SOLSTICE.

It is one of those golden days, a day 'sent from heaven' M used to say, so perhaps he has sent it. The Secret Garden Centre is bathed in an autumnal light. I sit in the front row with Erik and the boys, Mum and Jeff, listening to Fern and David exchanging their wedding vows. The chairs are adorned with green and white ribbons and have been set up in a shaded clearing, overlooking a lily pond. Fern and David are standing with the registrar under an ivy-clad pergola, Fern resplendent in the ivory suit, her hair in a loose updo adorned with gypsophila and tiny pearls.

'I Fern Rose Morgan do take you David John Archer to be my lifelong companion and soul mate until death becomes a parting, followed by a reunion…'

My heart swells at the words she and David had written together. I remember M and I repeating our vows all those years ago, believing that death would not part us until we were old and grey. Bride and groom are now making their way along the paved path, David's daughter Charlotte walking behind them.

'I don't want you all to think he's leading me up the garden path,' Fern jokes, as she walks through rows of saplings and pots spilling over with fuchsia and verbena. Mother, in a buttercup silk jacket and pleated skirt, as if she's stepped out of a different season is greeting the guests regally and asking everybody to congregate in the marquee which has been set up on the other side of the lily pond.

I hug Fern, whispering, 'it's perfect, as long as we can keep Mother under control!' We glance over to where she's now telling David all about her first wedding to Timmy's father. 'We were married in Salisbury Cathedral and an orchestra played the wedding march,' she tells him. 'He died tragically in a helicopter accident,' she finishes, 'but life has to go on as we all know.'

We had tried to persuade her to keep her speech short and to the point, Fern suggesting Jeff say a few words. 'He doesn't know me well enough to say anything too embarrassing,' she'd pointed out. Now she frowns. 'You know Mother, especially after she's had a few glasses of champagne!'

'I'll remind her again,' I promise, turning to greet Holly, who looks beautiful and waif-like in a rust-coloured dress. She had resigned from the job she landed with the owner of the superyacht, after he tried to set her up in an apartment as his mistress. She's now on the search for another job and had confessed to me over a bottle of wine that she and Will had been seeing one another off and on. Will has been off alcohol and drugs for six months now and is hoping to start up his antique car business again.

After a sumptuous feast of wild mushroom and truffle risotto, followed by grilled lobster (Mother had insisted on booking an award-winning catering firm from London) the wedding cake is brought in and everyone gasps. It's Fern's favourite dessert, a cake made entirely out of profiteroles which are piled on top of one another like a giant anthill.

'Surprise!' Mother announces, flushed with pleasure. I am struck by how thoughtful she can be and wonder if I've somehow got it wrong all these years, have misjudged her. That she had only tried to dissuade me from marrying M, because she genuinely believed he was the wrong man for me.

'Mum, about the speeches,' I begin, 'Fern doesn't want you to say anything... well, too personal.'

'So, I'm not even allowed to talk about my daughter at her wedding,' she says her marmalade eyes blazing.

'I didn't say that …it's just.'

Luckily, Jeff is tapping on his wine glass and standing up, ready to make his speech.

'…this is a fine day y'all, and we have congregated in this beautiful garden to celebrate the special union of Fern and David.'

On the far table, Fern's teacher friends sit up and nudge one another, wanting to know more about the handsome American behind 'Lyrical' who has captured my mother's heart. He is now falling back on his favourite metaphor, that life was a bumpy road, but eventually we learn to drive on it. 'Some of us are lucky enough to meet a special person along the way...' he winks at my mother, before adding, 'Fern is that special gal and we bless this union between her and David and wish them a safe and smooth journey onwards. To Fern and David.'

Everybody claps, and shouts, 'to Fern and David!'

It's Mother's turn next. She stands up and claps loudly although everyone has already stopped talking. She can still hold the attention of the room, this sixties icon whose beauty had once graced the covers of Vogue.

My sister and I exchange nervous glances. Nothing our mother can say or do can shock or embarrass us from now on, is our silent pledge to one another.

'I have been looking forward to this day for a very long time,' she begins, 'and I'm now delighted to welcome David into the family. David is a talented artist, which some of you might not have known. I hope I can persuade him to exhibit his paintings so we can all admire them.' She pauses dramatically.

'Now, we have had our ups and downs in this family.'

I freeze.

'As many of you know, Willow tragically lost her husband Maximillian two years ago. I would like to begin by making a toast to absent friends, and most importantly to M, as he was fondly known.' I sit there mutely, in a swirl of conflicting emotions; sadness and guilt that life had inevitably moved on, an aching regret for M who would never witness the story unfolding, and gratitude for the burgeoning and different kind of love I feel for Erik who sits patiently beside me, looking heart achingly handsome in a cream linen suit. He reaches for my hand and covers it with his.

'To M,' everybody is saying, raising their glasses.

'To Dad,' Liam and Sam echo, their faces flushed with emotion.

'To your dad,' Erik repeats, touching his chest in a gesture of love and respect.

'Willow has turned her life around and is now a columnist for The Word my mother continues.

I shift in my chair, praying she's not going to ask everyone to start searching for their G spot.

'Remember this is Fern and David's day,' I say, trying to keep my voice level, while fighting a rising hysteria.

'Relax,' Erik whispers, 'just enjoy the moment.'

'...this is Gran's speech,' Liam hisses.

'Thank you, Liam,' Mother smiles. 'All I wanted to say Willow, is how proud I am of you. Jeffrey put it more succinctly, 'You have learnt to drive on a very bumpy road.'

'And on a Triumph Bonneville,' Liam announces, causing a wave of laughter.

'Well, you know my feelings about that beastly motorbike,' my mother says. I'm aware everyone appears to be enjoying my mother's speech immensely. I'm the only one squirming in my seat.

'Maybe Erik will drum some sense into you,' she adds gaily.

Erik laughs. 'I'll do my best, Michelle.'

I smile inwardly. Erik had told me about his time in Syria, how he'd lived life on the edge. He was now planning to go into investigative journalism, much to both mine and Frida's relief.

'Frida's son!' Mother had exclaimed after I'd told her I'd met somebody special. 'Well, people do marry the boy next door and end up happy.'

'He hasn't lived next door for years.' I'd told her. 'He's been working as a reporter for the New York Post. He covered the war in Syria.' I had found out Erik wrote under the pseudonym of Jeremy Harper.

'Well, I can't wait to tell Camilla,' Mother had said. 'I must say, he's divinely handsome.'

'Now to my very special daughter, Fern,' she is saying.

She is listing Fern's many attributes; wonderful teacher, patient, caring, and the best daughter a mother could ever hope for.

We drink more champagne. Sam, Tom and Lennie have set up their equipment on the front deck, and we gather around them as Lennie's powerful voice booms out across the garden. Mel looks on proudly, she and Sam exchanging nervous smiles.

Out of the shadows, and into the light,
we won't go down without a fight,
hey babe let me hold you tight,
as we dance out of the shadows and into the light…

Jeff lets out a powerful wolf whistle and claps effusively, then everyone is clapping and spilling onto the deck that has been set up overlooking the scented garden. Sam signals to the band that it's time for the DJ set. He has elected Tom to be DJ, stating he wanted to hang out with Mel. Liam is out on the front lawn trying to point out Maximillian 2 to Charlotte.

Everybody is dancing and swaying to 'The Rhythm is Gonna Get You,' Erik is attempting to teach me the salsa. Mother asks Tom for a special request, and she and Jeff dance a fast rock and roll, coming together in perfect step. He twirls her around causing her buttercup skirt to fan out, exposing her famous and still shapely legs. Everyone clears the dance floor cheering and clapping as they reach the end.

'This really has been the most perfect wedding,' Mother sighs, sashaying towards me. 'Who would have thought it! A garden centre of all places. Clever old Fern.' She smiles at me, her smoothly altered face all at once dear and familiar, then, to my surprise, pulls me into a perfumed embrace. I hug her back, breathing in the silky warmth of her, feeling the soft prosthesis beneath her satin blouse, relishing the unfamiliar feeling of my mother's arms around me.

'Your turn next, darling,' she whispers. 'I do hope I get an invitation this time.'

'What is it with you and weddings?' I smile as we pull apart. 'But if we ever did decide to get married, you'd be first on the list,' I say.

Note to blog:

The loss never goes away. It can be triggered by a family celebration flooding you with memories. It is now a vital part of you, I add, quoting blackwidower, aka Erik. *For better or for worse, a reminder that you loved and lost.*
But the truth is, there is a life after a death for all of us. The life you shared with your partner may have ended, but there is always the chance of a rebirth and a new beginning.

THE END

ABOUT THE AUTHOR

Caroline Fabre grew up in Kenya and was educated at Cheltenham Ladies College in Gloucestershire. She went on to live in Ireland where she worked as a fashion model and freelance columnist. She is the author of Our Father's House and Swan Season, published by Random House, both of which have been translated into German and have sold worldwide. Her other titles are Love on the Run and Love and Loyalty. She has written two children's books, It's Hard to be a Hero, and Henry's Amazing Albatross, and recently produced a cookery book The Magnificent Mango showcasing the island of Antigua where she now lives.
Caroline is a qualified fitness instructor who has run marathons in London, Dublin, Paris, Bordeaux and Kenya and is the mother of two sons.